MISSION OF
FAITH

Dearest my lovely Val!

Have a wonderful read.
Maybe with a beer!

Muchos love n stuff

Ben
X

By
Ben Auker

YA Fiction - Dark Fantasy

The world in which we live is filled with war, pain, suffering, neglect, disease, and discrimination. If you had the chance to purge the world of all evil; to create a peaceful earth where humankind would live happily and healthily in peace and harmony, would you take that chance? One girl has accepted that mission. Let Faith's story begin...

PROLOGUE

<u>Six months ago</u>

'Hello?' Faith calls, nerves causing her voice to tremble as she waves her outstretched arms in the pitch darkness, her hands unseen before her. Hard wooden floorboards creek beneath her feet as she takes a tentative step forward, into the unknown. Gasping, she shields her eyes with the back of her hand as a bright white light explodes before her eyes, a gust of warm wind blowing her long hair into a dark tangled frenzy. As the dazzling light fades, Faith's silver satin nightgown ceases to ripple in the dying breeze. Lowering her hand, she opens her eyes with anticipation. Before her, six kneeling, cloaked figures form a circle around five flaming black candles and a tall iron spike, which appears to be smeared with blood. Faith can hear soft chanting emitting from the circle of hooded figures. Rooted to the spot, the tall girl stands quietly in the darkness that lingers like a thick fog around the scene that unfolds before her. Many of her past dreams have felt real, but none quite so lucid as the one that she currently experiences.

Observing from the gloom, Faith watches as one hooded individual raises a red gemstone encrusted dagger into the air. The figure grasps the weapon tightly around its elaborately carved silver handle of a three-headed hound. Faith's face expresses a mixture of confusion and panic as the dagger begins to glow with an intense red hue, as if it had been suddenly heated to an extreme temperature. As the chanting grows louder, the cloaked figure forcefully stabs the gleaming weapon into what appears to be a pool of blood which coagulates on the floorboards before the tall spike, on which a small dead animal is impaled. A blinding white light blasts from the ground where the glowing dagger strikes, engulfing the bizarre scene and its surroundings within its radiance. Considering the sheer intensity of the light, Faith looks puzzled as to why her eyes don't ache. In fact, the light feels extremely soothing on her gaze. An unexpected feeling of pure blissfulness washes over Faith's tall, slender frame, her fair complexion dewy as the pearly white light drenches her like a waterfall of shimmering photons.

'*Faith*,' a voice suddenly breaks the silence, echoing throughout the luminescent vicinity, grasping the girl's undivided attention. '*Heed these words, my child. Your brethren's bloodline shall be avenged and their great mission must you complete.*'

Faith gazes around, only to be greeted by the soothing white light that surrounds her like a comforting blanket of ecstasy, the speaker seemingly invisible. The authoritative yet kind tone that fills Faith's ears sounds neither male nor female, merely gentle and serene.

'*I am known by many different names throughout religions created by mankind,*' the voice continues, '*yet I am only one.*' Faith drops slowly to her knees, the overwhelming desire to honour the presence of inexplicable power and grandeur taking control of her body. '*The human race has distorted this truth, some abusing their beliefs and wielding them as weapons of destruction against their fellow man. The time has come for this to cease.*'

As a feeling of heaviness suddenly presses into Faith's left hand, she glances down to see the glowing red dagger from the earlier vision within her grasp. She raises her head as the blissful voice continues. *'The name by which you shall recognise me, is God, and I have much to tell you.'*

<u>Current day</u>

'I'm almost ready,' Faith whispers to herself, sitting alone at a table in the back room of a deserted library, a small desk lamp her only light. She stares down at an old musty book, which rests heavily on the creaky table at which she sits. A slight smile crosses her face, the alluring pale blue hue of her eyes glimmering through her small reading glasses with eager anticipation as she closes the red leather-bound book. She carefully places the volume onto the shelf above her before switching off the lamp, casting the room in shadows.

CHAPTER 1

'About time!' Roxanne exclaims with a huge sigh of relief as the school bell rings and the classroom clock strikes 3 p.m. Her dark, south African skin appears silky under the fluorescent classroom lighting as she reaches into her bag, retrieving a shiny emerald green hair bobble and proceeds to tie her black hair into a bun on the top of her head. 'You doing anything tonight?' she asks Heidi, her best friend, as both girls cram school books into their backpacks with vigour.

'Nope,' Heidi replies, swinging her now bulging purple bag over one shoulder, her long blonde hair swaying from side to side as she turns to face her friend. 'But we're still on for the library, right?'

Roxanne and Heidi, both 16, are in the same class at school. Both of average height for their age and slimly built, although they are in complete contrast to one another.

Roxanne wrinkles her nose at the thought of spending the night with her nose stuck in a book. 'Do we have to?' she groans. 'It always smells so musty in there.'

'We have to revise for tomorrow's history test' Heidi replies, waiting patiently for her friend to finish retouching her shimmery green eye shadow and dark red lip gloss. 'And we both know that you'll never study unless I'm supervising you.'

'You know me far too well, Hei,' Roxanne sighs, dropping her make-up kit into her school bag before zipping it up. 'Come on then, let's go get bored.'

Both girls whip their almost identical leather look jackets from the backs of their seats before leaving the classroom, ready for a tiresome night of revision.

The library is sparse of clientele on this blustery autumn afternoon and Faith is making the most out of the temporary lull.

'Miss Bennet,' Mrs. Fletcher, the head librarian, calls from the stock room of the library. 'Would you *please* sort out these books before the end of the afternoon?'

'Okay, I will,' Faith hurriedly answers as she scrawls notes onto a scrap piece of paper in the small occult section of the library.

Faith, 24, works as a librarian in her small home town in the north of England. Her long, shiny dark brown hair hides her elegant features as she huddles over the book that she copies from, the pages reflecting in her delicate reading glasses. Her vibrant blue eyes sparkle through the lenses as she scribbles away, seemingly in a world of her own. Her soft, pale skin glows underneath the strong lights in the library, her complexion complimenting her full crimson lips perfectly.

Faith promptly folds the scrap piece of paper, placing it into her navy blue overall pocket as she notices Roxanne and Heidi stepping through the library doorway.

'Hello, girls,' Faith greets them cheerfully, smiling as the young friends approach.

Heidi bounds into the room with a grin beaming on her pretty, adolescent face. 'Hey, Miss Bennet. We have a history test on Thursday but we're not really sure which books we need.'

Faith glances around the library for any sign of old Mrs. Fletcher. 'I'll meet you over by the history section in a moment and give you a hand. I just need to clear some shelves first.' Heidi smiles as she links arms with Roxanne and they head across the spacious room.

'Heidi,' Faith calls softly after the girls. 'Would you kindly hang this on my peg for me?' she asks, untying her dusty apron and handing it to the young girl.

'Yeah, sure, no problem,' Heidi answers, smiling cheerily as she takes Faith's overall.

'Librarian's pet,' Roxanne sniggers as the friends walk towards a row of hooks which are used for hanging coats, umbrellas, and other items from which the employees and customers wish to be unburdened. Heidi spots Faith's long black jacket on the far-left peg. As she reaches up to drape the apron, something white flutters from the pocket, landing gently on the coarse brown carpet by her feet. Roxanne leans forward and picks up a piece of folded paper.

'What is it, Roxy?' Heidi asks curiously.

'Whoa!' Roxanne exclaims after unfolding the note and scanning the message. Heidi peers over her friend's shoulder to get a look at what is written on the paper. 'This is weird,' Roxanne continues. 'It says that five black alter candles are needed to perform the ritual of Hades. Also required, is the blood of that which flies at night and can see into the darkness by sense alone.' The girls stare at each other with bafflement, not knowing what to make of the strange memo. Another line of writing is underneath; '9 p.m., Tuesday 3rd November, Wiltmore Street.'

Heidi takes the scrap of paper from her friend. 'That's tonight,' she says in a low voice, scanning the scrawling once again. She glances at Roxanne as she refolds the note. 'Do you think that Miss Bennet is going to perform some kind of freaky ritual or whatever it is, tonight?'

CHAPTER 2

Roxanne and Heidi both jump as a voice comes from behind them.

'There really wasn't much clearing needed,' Faith tells the girls as they spin around. 'Old Mrs Fletcher is far too...' she halts mid-sentence, noticing what Heidi grasps nervously in her hand. 'Ha... have you opened it?' Faith asks the girls quietly, signalling towards the folded paper with her eyes. Heidi nods slowly, gingerly handing the note to Faith. 'Well, just pretend that you didn't, okay girls?' she whispers timidly. 'It's nothing.'

'Are you some kind of witch or something?' Roxanne asks bluntly, and not at all quietly. Heidi nudges her outspoken friend with her elbow as Faith places the paper silently into her pleated, black skirt pocket. 'Come on, you've got to tell us now,' Roxanne continues, winking at Faith. 'We won't tell a soul, scout's honour.' Heidi raises one eyebrow as her friend holds up three fingers in jest, pretending to be a member of the scouts, though the scouts is a club for boys and she doesn't even know the correct gesture.

'Fair enough,' Faith sighs hesitantly, realising that the teenagers are unlikely to let the matter drop and also worried that they may inform others about what they've discovered. 'My shift's almost over, come to the park with me and I'll explain everything, and please don't mention this to anyone.' The two friends nod in agreement as Faith grabs her woven jacket from the row of hooks. Roxanne and Heidi quietly pursue Faith as she slips on her coat and leaves the library without so much as a goodbye to her colleagues.

The threesome walks in awkward silence along the street towards the town's main park. Crisp, brown leaves rustle around their feet as a gentle, but chilly, wind blows, cooling Faith's apprehensively burning cheeks. The group walks towards a mossy bench as they enter the deserted park. Faith sighs heavily as she sits on the cold wooden bench, the breeze blowing her dark hair across her face.

Combing her long hair from before her eyes with her fingertips, Faith exchanges awkward glances with the two girls as they also take a seat, maintaining a slight distance from the librarian.

'Okay, listen girls. You come into the library quite often and you know I'm not some crazy person, right?' Heidi slowly nods her head, looking rather confused. 'Well, what I'm about to tell you is true. You're going to think I'm insane, but you have to believe me.' Faith takes a deep breath, tucks her hair behind her ears and begins her tale. 'I've lived in this small town my entire life. I got the job at the library when I was nineteen and I've been there ever since. Around six months ago, I had the strangest, yet most vivid, dream.' Faith relives her lucid dream in detail, as if the memory has become etched in her mind. She informs them of the disturbing ritual and the comforting feeling experienced upon the appearance of the white light, often unable to make eye contact with her young friends from fear of seeing bewildered uncertainty or even notions of lunacy within their gazes. 'That's when I heard it,' she pauses as if she still hardly believes it herself.

'Heard what?' Heidi asks quietly as she and Roxanne listen with intrigued ears.

Faith takes a final deep breath, staring at the young friends. 'The voice of God.'

CHAPTER 3

After a moment of stunned silence, Faith proceeds with her story. 'God explained that all evil on earth, every act of cruelty, all poverty and even illness, exists solely because of the Devil; an immensely powerful and evil force that resides in the very centre of the underworld, known to us as Hell. God also explained that centuries ago, six monks discovered a way to destroy the Devil's very essence. If this task had been accomplished, all evil on earth would have no longer existed. No more hate, an end to wars and to suffering. Humanity would have lived in complete harmony, forever. But the monks failed to complete their mission. God informed me that I continue the bloodline of one of the monks and because of that I had been chosen, chosen to finish what they once begun. God stated that I possess the strength, the courage and the ability to succeed, and that I would know how, and when, to act from instinct alone.'

'...And?' Roxanne presses as Faith falls silent, warming her cold hands with her warm breath.

'And... Then I woke up,' Faith responds. 'I just assumed it was a dream, an extremely vivid dream, but a dream nonetheless. So, I put it to the back of my mind and continued with my normal day to day life. Two days later, I was walking to the shops and I took a different route to my usual one. It was then I passed the little museum on Oakland Avenue. I couldn't even remember the last time I had visited that place. For some reason, I decided to stop and go inside, almost as if I didn't have a choice. Immediately I was drawn to a glass cabinet. Inside were two items, a leather-bound book and a dagger.' Heidi gasps, covering her mouth in surprise as the crazy story begins to piece together in her head. 'A dagger with red stones and a handle comprising of three vicious dog heads. The exact dagger from my dream.' Faith nods as her young friends gasp. 'There was also a passage explaining about a group of monks who went missing back in the seventeenth century. They were never seen again after attempting a dark and powerful ritual that they believed would transport them into Hades, where they would use the blessed dagger to banish the dark force of the Devil.'

Faith rises to her feet and turns to face the astounded schoolgirls who stare up at her, wide eyed. 'From that moment on, I knew it wasn't a dream I experienced that night. It was a vision of what I'm expected to do. Of what I must do. I have the opportunity to change the world.'

Roxanne and Heidi glance at each other in disbelief, not quite being able to accept what Faith has just presented them with.

'Miss Bennet,' Heidi says, clearing her throat. 'Are you saying, for example, that if this were to be true, that things such as the covid pandemic and all the lockdowns, just wouldn't... what... have existed?

Faith nods. "That's what I believe, yes, that and many, many more things. For another example, the horrific Russian war against Ukraine. It just wouldn't happen. Nothing like that would ever happen again.'

Heidi looks thoughtful and somewhat mesmerised. 'Are you going to re-enact this ritual, yourself?'

Faith glances around her to make sure that no one else can hear. 'Tonight, yes, and please, call me Faith.'

'Okay... Faith,' Roxanne pipes up. 'So, you think that by the end of tonight you'll be transported into Hell? Where you will do what, exactly?'

'I've spent months researching and preparing for this night. I also have the dagger that the monks used.' Faith says, looking rather sheepish.

Heidi looks astonished. 'The robbery at the museum a few days ago, that was you?'

Faith gazes shamefully at the ground. 'I had to, it was the only way.' She takes a step closer to the bench. 'The monks who attempted the ritual vanished, never to be seen again. All that was left was the dagger and the book which contained the monks' journal and jumbled incarnations, which were then locked away in the museum.'

A thoughtful expression crosses Heidi's face 'The old abandoned house on Wiltmore Street, that's where it all took place?' Faith nods. 'That's why you're doing it there.'

Faith steps backwards. 'The timings have to be exact. The same date and time that they performed it all those years ago.' She wraps her jacket tightly around her as she backs away. 'Please stay away from that house tonight. It's for your own safety, please promise.'

Roxanne and Heidi watch as Faith turns, placing her hands into her jacket pockets as she walks across the park and out of sight.

'I reckon she's bonkers,' Roxanne says with a nervous chuckle. Heidi remains silent, gazing down at her feet. 'Don't tell me you actually believe her,' Roxanne laughs, nudging her friend jokingly.

'No, of course not,' Heidi answers, looking up with a wry smile. 'To be honest, I don't even believe in Heaven and Hell, or God and the Devil. To me it's as silly as believing in Santa Clause or the Easter bunny or some magical land where unicorns rule the world.' Roxanne sniggers. 'So, no. Even though she was pretty convincing, I don't believe that she will be transported into Hell by the end of tonight. But I do think that she believes she will be.'

CHAPTER 4

The clock in Heidi's living room strikes 8 p.m.

'Mmmm, that was yummy, thank you,' Roxanne smiles, handing her empty plate to Heidi's mum, Ellen, who returns the smile as she stacks the plate on the top of her wooden lap tray, alongside some empty glasses. Using one hand, Ellen turns the wheel on her chair to point herself in the direction of the kitchen. Heidi's mum was diagnosed with multiple sclerosis seven years ago. The disease damaged her spinal nerve fibres which has left her wheelchair bound. Although there is yet to be a cure, she remains positive and likes to be as active and independent as possible.

As her mum disappears into the kitchen, Heidi leans in close to Roxanne so her dad and younger brother, who both sit on the opposite side of the dinner table, are unable to hear her. 'Come on, we have to get ready.'

'Thanks mum,' Heidi yells into the kitchen as she and Roxanne hurriedly leave the table, thundering up the stairs and into Heidi's bedroom.

As Ellen returns to the living room to collect her husband's and son's plates, she notices that her twelve-year-old son, Kyle, has left half of his casserole dinner uneaten. 'Have you finished?' she asks, eyebrows raised.

Kyle looks at his messy plate of leftover food. 'Yeah, sorry mum, I'm full.'

'I don't suppose those chocolate wrappers I found in your bag earlier had anything to do with that?' Kyle shifts awkwardly in his chair, unable to think of an excuse. 'Well in that case you can go and get changed into something clean,' his mum demands, noticing that his once bright red hooded top is now covered in grime, and his fashionably ripped, light blue jeans don't fare any better. 'And I'm certain that you have some homework that needs doing.'

'But, Mum,' Kyle groans, his plan of chilling in front of the TV rapidly dwindling. His mother gives him 'that look' and he realises that he is fighting a losing battle. Kyle solemnly leaves the table and steps quietly up the soft, cream carpeted stairs that lead to the bedrooms and large shared bathroom. His deep brown eyes glint mischievously as he approaches his sister's bedroom. Kyle presses his ear against the door while making a conscious effort not to breathe too loudly.

'I hope you know where this abandoned house on Wiltmore Street is, because I've never come across it,' Kyle can hear Roxanne saying from within the bedroom.

'Of course you know where it is,' Heidi retorts. 'You, me and Kyle were daring each other to go inside last summer, remember?'

'Oh, yeah, I do remember. Kyle almost went inside, but thought he heard a noise and chickened out at the last minute,' Roxanne laughs, her voice becoming louder as she approaches the door.

Kyle quickly dashes into the bathroom as the door to his sister's bedroom flings open and Roxanne strides out, pursued closely by Heidi. Both girls are dressed in similar high-necked jumpers, Heidi's black and Roxanne's white. Navy denim jeans accompany Roxanne's top, while Heidi wears striking red leather-look trousers.

'We're going out,' Heidi yells as the friends dash down the stairs, opening the front door and making a hasty exit before slamming it shut behind them.

Suspicious about the reason the girls are going to the spooky old house, a mischievous expression crosses Kyle's young, but not so innocent, face. He creeps back down the stairs, hoping to avoid his parents. Grasping the handle of the front door, the young boy presses down warily, remembering that the handle has an annoying squeak that really needs a good oiling.

'And just where do you think you're going, mister?' Kyle's mum asks, wheeling herself around the arch that leads into the kitchen as the squeaking of the handle alerts her to his presence.

Kyle jumps at the sound of his mother's interrogating. 'Oh... I'm... just going across to Williams for a bit,' he lies as he leaps from the front step. Ellen speedily rolls herself towards the front door, jamming it with her front wheel before it has the chance to close.

'Just don't be too long, you have homework to do,' she hollers down the dark street as her son disappears into the distance.

CHAPTER 5

'Shush!' Roxanne whispers, her finger pressed firmly across her lips as Heidi stumbles clumsily over a small bush, the sound of rustling leaves and snapping twigs resonating through the chilly November air. The two girls skulk quietly towards the derelict house, which sits in complete darkness and appears to be uninhabited. Roxanne squats, grabbing a large rock with both hands and heaves it from the overgrown garden. She puffs and pants as she waddles across to where Heidi waits uneasily. Roxanne struggles to remain quiet as she places the boulder underneath a large window.

'Well?' Heidi whispers as Roxanne climbs onto the rock, standing on her tiptoes and peering through the grimy window into the dark house.

'She's in there,' Roxanne utters in a low voice, scrambling down from the boulder.

'You mean Faith, right?' Heidi asks with a vacant expression across her face.

'Who do you think I mean?' Roxanne huffs in exasperation. 'Of course I mean Faith. Who else would be alone in this horrible place?'

'I don't know, the Devil maybe?' Heidi retorts sarcastically.

Roxanne raises one eyebrow. 'Don't even joke.'

The two friends begin to edge their way around the crumbling building, towards the front door. They freeze to the spot as a creaking noise emits from the dark doorway ahead. Little do they know that Kyle has been watching them from the bushes that surround the house and the creaking was caused as the boy crept stealthily inside the gloomy building, the intention of scaring his sister and her friend at the forethought of his mischievous mind.

'It's just the wind,' Roxanne whispers as Heidi glances nervously around. 'Stop being such a coward,' Roxanne teases as she drags her tense friend towards the door. They glance at one another with anxious anticipation as they reach the front door, which has been left ajar. Roxanne, usually brave and confident, nimbly switches position with Heidi and pushes her friend gently but forcefully, making her venture into the spooky house first. Heidi gulps and prepares to enter the unnerving dwelling, not knowing what to expect inside.

CHAPTER 6

Subdued, eerie music emits from the living room. The two friends stand in the dark and dusty hallway, unsure of what to do now they are inside the house. They tiptoe slowly alongside the wall, trying their hardest not to make the old floorboards creek under their weight as they move. Gingerly, Heidi pushes open the living room door ever so slightly. She and Roxanne stand each side of the doorway with the aim of keeping out of sight as the door slowly opens.

As the girls peer beyond the doorway, a flickering flame on top of a thick black candle, surrounded by four smaller black candles, appears in view. They watch apprehensively as Faith enters the room from what appears to be the shadowy kitchen doorway. The librarian is dressed in black trousers and a fitted black fleece jacket, zipped to her neck and her hair is tied back in a long ponytail. Her appearance reminds Heidi of a villain from real life crime shows on television. Faith holds a small, black, velvet bag in front of her. Upon reaching the arrangement of candles, she sits cross-legged before them. A lengthy, rusty spike is nailed to the wooden floorboards to the side of the central candle.

The two friends watch in astonishment as Faith reaches inside the bag and retrieves a tiny struggling creature; a bat. The small animal squeaks relentlessly, biting at Faith's fingers as she holds it awkwardly with both hands above the rusty spike. Heidi covers her open mouth with her hand, the realisation of what is about to take place dawning on her. The youngsters watch in dismay as Faith presses the bat onto the spike, sliding the fighting mammal down the rusty implement with great force. Faith's face expresses extreme discomfort as the creature's squealing ceases; she obviously gains no pleasure from performing such horrific actions.

The girls gawp squeamishly as blood trickles down the spike and forms a crimson pool around its base. Faith begins to chant some unrecognisable words as she tugs the deceased bat from the blood-stained spike and holds it above each small candle, dripping blood onto the wick to extinguish each flame in an anticlockwise motion.

Heidi looks as if she's about to be sick as Faith tilts her head backwards, grasping the small bat above her. A drop of blood splashes into her mouth and she swallows with utter disgust. After returning the bat onto the spike, she reaches into a second black bag and retrieves the dagger from the museum. She grips it by its canine-headed silver handle, carefully placing the blade into the flame of the large central candle, chanting continuously as she does so.

'Oh my God, look!' Roxanne exclaims in a whisper, leaning closer towards Heidi. They watch as the dagger begins to glow red, becoming brighter and brighter as if engulfed by a tremendous heat. After a few seconds, Faith tilts her head upwards, raising the glowing weapon into the air. Heidi jumps as Faith stabs the dagger into the pool of bat's blood with vigour.

Roxanne and Heidi hold onto each other in shock as the entire house begins to rumble and shake violently.

Heidi screams, the shuddering building unsteadying her balance, causing her to tumble through the door and into the living room where Faith remains seated, looking shaken and frightened.

Faith jerks her head, staring in horrified comprehension as she witnesses the school girl fall into the room, closely pursued by Roxanne. 'No! You have to leave!' Faith pleads, shouting so that her voice can be heard over the thunderous earthquake. Faith rises unsteadily to her feet, covering her head with both hands as chunks of plaster fall from the ceiling, crashing around her feet.

'Come on,' Roxanne shrieks in panic, grabbing Faith by the arm and yanking her towards the doorway. 'We have to get out of here, now!'

'No!' Faith cries, tugging her arm from Roxanne's grip. 'I have to do this. I have to try.' Realising that Faith is determined not to leave her ancestors work unfinished, Roxanne grasps Heidi by the hand and dashes towards the open door. The two friends halt in their tracks as the door slams shut before them. As Heidi freezes with fear, Roxanne immediately rushes towards the large window. As she approaches the windowpane, an unseen force thrusts her back, preventing escape.

'How do we get out?' Roxanne screams at Faith.

'I don't know, I don't know!' Faith bellows, dodging the once hanging central chandelier as it falls, shattering on the ground. Roxanne rushes back to Heidi who cowers by the closed door. Both girls grab the handle and tug as hard as they possibly can. It's useless. The door won't budge.

The two girls quickly turn their heads as they hear Faith's horrified gasp above the din. The flame of the large black candle is growing, and before anyone can move, it suddenly bursts into a great ball of white light, illuminating the entire room in dazzling brilliance. The petrified screams of the three girls fade as the bright radiance diminishes and the candle snuffs. The room is left completely dark, empty and still, with no trace of the girls.

CHAPTER 7

Hours seem to pass before Heidi reluctantly opens her blurry eyes. An amber rocky wall is the first thing that appears as her vision returns to normal. As she comes round, she realises that a row of brightly burning flames, situated behind her, produce the orange glow.

As comprehension begins to dawn, Heidi sits up, gazing at her new surroundings. She notices Roxanne and Faith slumped against a wall next to her, both motionless. The three girls are located in the centre of a long, murky tunnel. Blackness lingers like velvet curtains at either end. Flaming torches hang along the entire stretch of the tunnel, illuminating several dusty brown skulls and limb bones which scatter the ground like a scene from a horror movie.

Silence suddenly overcomes Heidi's heavy breathing, the humid air causing her to perspire, as she sits in complete bewilderment, not daring to move a muscle. Her head feels like a scattered jigsaw and all the pieces are taking too long to piece back together.

'Roxy?' she finally whispers after what feels like an eternity of sitting in complete silence. A reply does not return from her friend's seemingly lifeless body. Heidi gulps hard as something suddenly moves at one end of the tunnel. 'Something's coming,' she wheezes to herself, the look of terror searing in her eyes.

Heidi suddenly focuses her attention upon a large nearby rock. She scrambles to her feet as a snorting sound accompanies the shuffling within the darkness. Grabbing Roxanne by the arms, Heidi desperately drags her friend towards the rock. 'Sorry,' she apologises in a whisper as she slumps her friend behind the boulder, bashing her head on the hard floor as she releases her grasp in haste. After rushing back to Faith, Heidi becomes flushed in the face as she also drags the librarian behind the rock and out of sight from whoever, or whatever, approaches.

Heidi peers nervously around the edge of the rock, shivering as a chill of terror shoots down her spine. A large silhouette gradually appears at the end of the passageway, looming from the shadows. She withdraws her head behind the boulder, baffled by the sight that she has just witnessed.

A bulky dark shape gradually emerges into the flame lit path. A gigantic lizard, the colour of night, plods heavily along the underground passage, its black forked tongue licking the moist air as its bright red eyes search the tunnel. The lizard's tough, palm sized scales, glint like oil spills in the flickering light of the flaming torches. Droplets of dark blood, from an apparent recent meal, drip from the creature's two overlarge incisors, leaving a crimson trial along the path as the beast advances.

Heidi scrunches her eyes tightly, covering her ears as the beast emits an immense hissing roar, the likes of which she has never heard, or even thought possible for a living creature to produce. The echoing roar stirs Roxanne from her unconscious slumber. Almost immediately, she sits bolt upright, recalling the events that took place in the abandoned house. Heidi reopens her eyes in shock as she feels Roxanne's leg rub against her foot. Roxanne also jumps and turns to see Heidi behind her. Before Roxanne can utter a word, Heidi quickly places a hand over her best friend's mouth.

Both girls sit in silence, quivering with fright as thunderous footsteps pace just beyond the large rock that they hide behind. Heidi quietly gasps, her eyes expressing terror as the footsteps abruptly halt directly behind the boulder. The huge black lizard lowers its hideous head towards the ground, gripping a dirty skull between its bloody jaws. It raises its head fiercely, chomping on the skull with a loud cracking sound, morsels of old bone soaring through the warm air. Roxanne and Heidi cling to each other as chunks of skull rain down on them like a gruesome hailstorm.

The girls remain hushed and unmoving, their hearts hammering in unison as the beast continues its leisurely journey.

'What the Hell is going on?' Roxanne whispers in a panic as the heavy footsteps fade into the distance.

Heidi stares back at her friend with utmost concern flashing in her pale green eyes. 'I think that's just it,' she says shakily, not quite believing the words that are about to come from her own mouth. 'I think we *are* in Hell.'

CHAPTER 8

You mean... Faith's spell thing worked? She's taken us down to Hell?' Roxanne says in bewilderment, her mouth hanging open in shocked horror. She stares at the floor in stunned silence. 'What about my family?' she blurts out as the situation begins to sink in. 'There's loads of things I still want to do. What about finding a boyfriend... or even a girlfriend, I'm still not totally sure, I've never had a real relationship before, or been in love, and now it's too late, it's too late for anything!'

'Roxy, stop it,' Heidi demands, placing both hands firmly on her friend's shoulders. 'We will get out of here. Faith must know a way or why would she even do this to begin with?'

Roxanne glances fiercely down at Faith, who remains unconscious next to them. 'Because she's a mad cow, that's why!' Roxanne yells, punching Faith angrily on the leg, while Heidi rapidly signals for her friend to remain quiet in case the beast returns for a snack.

To the surprise of the schoolgirls, Faith jolts awake as Roxanne lands her aggravated blow. The librarian slouches against the rock, wiping her moist forehead as she gazes around her.

'It worked,' she mutters to herself, eyes adjusting to the dim surroundings. 'It actually worked!'

'Yeah, it did!' Roxanne scolds in exasperation. 'And you brought us with you.'

Faith's attention turns to her young friends. 'I'm so sorry, girls. This wasn't meant to happen. I did warn you not to go to that house.'

Heidi looks over her shoulder to make sure that nothing sinister is lurking in the shadows.

'Some kind of horrible monster thing went past just now,' she informs Faith in a hushed tone. With trembling hands, Heidi prepares to ask the question that she almost doesn't dare to ask, for the fear of the answer that she is likely to receive. 'Do you know how to get out of here, Faith?'

'The only way out is to accomplish what I came here to do,' Faith replies, holding up the dagger she still tightly clutches, the blade now glowing a vibrant red, as if energised. 'We must journey into the Devil's lair, deep in the centre of Hell, and use this dagger to destroy the evil force,' she informs the astounded looking girls as she carefully slips the dagger back into the inside pocket of her fleece jacket before zipping it securely. 'Then, we should be transported back to earth. A much more tranquil and peaceful earth, free from evil and sin.'

If possible, Roxanne's face shines with added fury. 'What do you mean *should?* If we don't get back, I'm going to...' she bites her lip, attempting to compose herself. Heidi calmly places her hand on Roxanne's knee.

'Look,' Heidi says matter-of-factly as she sits and faces the other two. 'Let's not fall apart here. We need to get on with this, the faster the better. Faith, do you know how we get to the centre?'

Faith gazes thoughtfully at the bone scattered ground. 'I know there are meant to be different sections to the underworld. There's a lot of speculation about the levels of

Hell. But after all my research, and from reading what the monks accepted to be true, I believe there to be five or six sections. To get to the devil's lair, we must journey through each level of Hell until we reach the centre.'

'Then what?' Roxanne asks sternly.

Faith caresses the dagger through her jacket. 'Then we use the dagger. Somehow. I will know when the time is right. There will be some kind of sign.'

'Well, as long as you know what you're doing,' Roxanne mumbles sarcastically under her breath.

Heidi climbs to her feet, gawping along the murky tunnel. Both ends appear identical. It's impossible to tell which way to go.

Roxanne jumps to her feet. 'Come on then, we have to get moving, no point waiting around here for that thing that you saw,' looking at Heidi, 'to come back. There's no point sitting around here being terrified when we have a job to do. On the plus side, you said the voice of God told you that you were the chosen one, right?' she asks, directing her question to Faith. Faith nods. 'Then that hopefully means you'll be safe. So, if we stick with you, we should all be okay,' she says, trying to remain positive, although still furious with Faith on the inside.

'Which way should we go?' Heidi asks.

'I would suggest the obvious way,' Faith says as she also stands, dusting chunks of bone from her trousers.

'And which way is that?' Roxanne snaps back, clearly still fuelled by rage.

'The opposite way to the monster you saw, of course.' Faith answers. 'Heidi, which way did it go?' Heidi points in the direction in which the beast vanished. Faith takes the lead and heads in the other direction.

'I guess we follow the master,' Roxanne huffs, rolling her eyes as she and Heidi hurriedly pace after the older girl. The three girls halt as they reach the blackness at the end of the tunnel. The darkness lingers like a blanket, too dense to see what lies beyond. Faith glances nervously at Roxanne and Heidi who stand, one either side of her, in anticipation, staring into the dark.

Faith gently grasps the hands of her young friends, all three inhaling deep breaths as they slowly walk into the unknown, taking their first nerve-racking steps on their long and gruelling journey into the Abyss.

CHAPTER 9

W hoa!' Kyle exclaims, clambering unsteadily to his feet, stepping out from the shadow of a tall, rocky pillar. *What's going on? Am I dreaming?* he wonders in confusion rubbing his sore head, where a definite lump is rising. He leans against one of three stone pillars, which surround the perimeter of a damp, squat cave. As his memories begin to reform, the confused boy watches droplets of water dripping from the rocky ceiling, sizzling as they splash onto the warm, uneven ground. Two giant flaming torches stand either side of the only doorway situated within the cave's walls.

'The kids at school were right! That old house is haunted or something,' Kyle mutters to himself as the fog in his mind begins to clear. He carefully makes his way towards the murky doorway, staring around the small cave uncertainly as he moves. Upon reaching the exit, his eyes open wide, his mouth dropping in astonishment, fear stricken by what lies before him.

He stands in the doorway, staring out across a vast flaming cavern. A long, extremely narrow bridge with no sides, assembled entirely from rock, stretches from the doorway, extending over a pit of steaming lava. At the far end of the bridge, a large wooden door seems to be the only alternative exit. A quorum of pitch-black ravens squawks menacingly as they dart through the moist air, their faces and beaks mangled horribly as if melted.

'Where am I?' whispers the petrified boy, not quite believing that what he sees before him is reality. Shaking in terror, Kyle steps nervously onto the narrow bridge, accepting that he must cross it as his only other option appears to be an empty cave. He carefully edges sideways along the path, watching his feet carefully as he progresses, his arms slightly outstretched by his sides for balance. The bridge seems to stretch miles above the red-hot, bubbling liquid far below. Sparks and blazing flames emit from smouldering rocks that protrude from the lava, causing distracting flashes to Kyle's vision as he continues to move cautiously.

'Bloody Hell!' Kyle exclaims as, like a bullet from a gun, a ball of sizzling lava shoots from the fiery pit below. The trembling boy yells in horror, falling hard onto his knees as the ball of now solidified, steaming lava lands on the bridge, causing it to shake unsteadily. Fortunately, the fiery boulder has come to rest on by the entrance of the cave, to which Kyle defiantly doesn't plan on returning.

After an extremely brief moment of relief, Kyle's eyes express sheer panic as the deadly ball of hardened fire begins to slowly roll along the bridge in his direction. Hastily, yet extremely carefully, the youngster rises to his feet and continues his tentative side stepping along the bridge, silently praying that the rolling ball is too slow to catch up with him. He sighs with relief, his forehead drenched in nervous perspiration as he steps from the bridge and onto the platform before the wooden door. Reaching up he grasps the hooped iron handle, turning it while pushing on the door. The door doesn't budge an inch and is evidently locked. 'No!' He yells, frantically slamming his small fists against the heavy wood in frustration.

Kyle quickly spins around, anticipating the worst. To his surprise, the sizzling ball of lava has come to a standstill in the centre of the bridge. He breathes a heavy sign, wiping his wet brow as he leans against the closed door, his mind

33

racing to discover an alternative escape route. His eyes suddenly open wide with terror as the huge ball of death unexpectedly spins furiously on the spot. He gasps in horror as the ball shoots down the long bridge towards him at a tremendous speed.

Kyle has nowhere to run. Beneath him, a deadly drop into scorching lava, behind him, a sealed door, and in front, a pathway blocked by a rampaging, smouldering boulder. He cowers, knowing his doom is racing towards him, about to splatter him like a scorching steamroller. He closes his eyes, praying that he is trapped in a nightmare and that everything will be okay once he wakes up. Seconds before the fatal impact, the quivering boy soars into the air. Kyle hovers above the bridge as the fireball shoots beneath his feet, crashing through the wooden door.

Beginning to descend back towards the bridge, he glances over his shoulder in bewilderment. He gasps as a faceless figure, dressed in a long grey and maroon cloak, floats directly behind him.

'Let me go!' Kyle bawls, struggling to break free from the clutch of the mysterious being. As his feet regain solid ground, he tears himself away, falling to his knees.

'Do not be afraid my child,' the hooded figure urges in a deep, yet soft, voice, as Kyle shuffles on his knees, turning to face whoever, or whatever, had lifted him to safety.

'Who... who are you? Where am I?' Kyle asks, panic-stricken, staring into the shadowy face of the floating man, only two lifeless yellow eyes looking back. 'Am I dreaming?' The strange figure gradually descends onto the bridge, his long dusty cloak trailing behind him as he lands in front of the boy. 'Don't hurt me,' Kyle weeps, lowering his head towards the ground, expecting the worst.

'You have wandered into the darkness of the Abyss, my son,' the figure informs the young boy. 'You have been transported here by the three girls. They too are nearby.'

Kyle looks up in astonishment. 'The Abyss? I don't understand… three girls? You mean my sister and Roxanne?'

'The Abyss falls under many names,' the figure explains. 'Hell, is the name used by many.'

Kyle stares into the pool of lava beneath him, his eyes expressionless. 'I'm in Hell?' he whispers to himself in utmost disbelief.

'Your sister and two friends performed the ritual of Hades. That is how they arrived here, and how you came to be here also,' the figure informs the boy.

Kyle carefully gets to his feet, thoughtfully rubbing his head. 'I was in the old house with them. I was hiding. I only wanted to scare them. I didn't know what they were doing there.'

'I am here to help you,' the shadowy man says tenderly. 'A long time ago, my brethren and I performed the very same ritual. We came into this pit of despair with the intention of ridding the mortal world of all evil, by destroying the sinister force of the Devil, the almighty peril of the universe.'

Kyle seems intrigued. 'Did it … did it work?' he asks hesitantly.

'We gained great power from performing the ritual,' the monk explains. 'But we were too eager to use that power to triumph over evil. We were hasty and lost our souls to the darkness.'

Kyle looks scared and confused as he once again wipes the sweat from his forehead with the back of his grubby hand. 'What am I supposed to do?' he asks the monk. 'I mean... have I got some kind of superpowers now too?' The monk glides forward and places his cold grey hands on the boy's shoulders.

'You were not meant to be involved in this travesty. Neither were your sister or her friend. The woman is the key. She continues the bloodline, she is the one who performed the ritual and she alone holds the power, the power that we once held, the power to destroy Satan.'

CHAPTER 10

Gripping each other's hands tightly, the three girls creep forward in the darkness. They pace slowly along a pitch-black tunnel, completely ignorant of what they are getting themselves into or where they are heading.

'What's that?' Heidi squeals, a sound of scurrying causing her ears to prick to attention. Rows of tiny red specks of light gleam on the ground as the girls continue onwards. 'Oh no,' Heidi continues, alarmed. 'I think they're rats.'

'Rats!' Faith exclaims, tightening her grip on Heidi's hand. 'I hate rats. Let's get out of here.'

Quickening their steps, the friends stride through the plague of scarlet dots, which dart around the tunnel like tiny laser beams in the dark. Roxanne shakes her leg violently, shrieking as one of the furry rodents crawls onto her foot. The girls storm along the path, their heads lowered in case unexpected collision.

The friends squint in unison as they suddenly emerge from the darkness, stepping into the light of a deep red sun, which looms high in the gloomy, grey sky. The peculiar sun radiates no heat, quite the opposite, as a chill lingers in the damp air.

A widespread field stretches before the friends. The arena is divided in two by a vast, dark river, a hardy wooden bridge draping its sludgy banks. The water lies almost motionless, as if waiting for something. Sorrowful figures wander aimlessly across the overgrown meadow, ushered across the hefty bridge by a giant, iron masked guard. Once across the bridge, the lifeless beings trudge into a dismal forest beyond. A gigantic, seven-walled castle looms menacingly in the distance, shrouding the woodland in a colossal, cold shadow.

Heidi gasps at the unnerving sight that lies ahead of them. She turns, considering retracing her steps into the tunnel. To her horror, the tunnel has sealed, leaving only a rocky cliff and no way back. The only option is to push forward and into the first level of Hell.

'Maybe there's another way across,' Roxanne whispers as the three girls advance with caution towards the bridge, guarded by the fearsome, armoured warrior.

'I think this might be the only way,' Faith responds, halting in her tracks as she realises how to proceed. 'We can't just walk casually over there,' she says, her voice lowering to a whisper. 'We have to act like the rest of them.' She gestures with her eyes at a group of slouching, saddened figures, staggering across the bridge and towards the castle.

'Hey!' The armoured soldier bellows from the bridge in a gruff, accusatory tone, as the girls huddle together, anxiously discussing their plan.

'Get a move on. Don't make me come over there!' he shouts, pointing the sharp, glimmering spear, grasped in his strong leather clad hand, in their direction.

Faith, Heidi and Roxanne turn to face the guard, their faces drooped and miserable as they begin to stumble towards the bridge.

'Move it, whores!' the Hell soldier orders, poking Roxanne in the ribs with his long-handled spear, forcing the girls onto the bridge.

'Ouch!' Roxanne exclaims, holding her side in agony, her face turning red with rage. The Devil's minion or not, she will not take that from anyone.

'Let it go, Roxy,' Heidi whispers, knowing that her friend has very limited patience and a strong temper.

'Did you hear what he called us?' Roxanne asks, disgusted. 'Stupid fat pig,' she grumbles under her breath as she continues along the bridge, her two friends now slightly ahead of her.

Keeping their gaze towards the ground, the girls continue across the bridge, each of them experiencing an overwhelming sense of discomfort as the crimson glow of the sun reflects off the eerily calm river, the aroma of stale dew wafting on the breeze. The friends shudder as they step off the bridge, the icy wind rustling the dead leaves of the forest before them.

The friends stare into the spooky woodland, catching a glimpse of a shadowy, robed figure, who fades into the darkness that surrounds the forest.

'Hey, watch yourself' Roxanne scolds, a frail, old man stumbling into her as he shuffles from the bridge. The girls step aside, observing as a group of lifeless zombies stagger towards the forest. As the sluggish group disappears beyond the trees, the girls turn in surprise as they hear the guard bellowing.

'Halt!' He yells in a raspy voice. 'This is not your realm; you have no place here.'

A scaly green impish creature leaps from the bridge, attempting to swipe Faith with its overgrown, brown fingernails as it darts past. The girls stare in bewilderment as the rampaging being dashes for the camouflage of the trees.

'Whoa!' Heidi exclaims in shock as the ground begins to rumble. The small goblin howls in anguish as the ground suddenly bursts open, swallowing the creature whole. Within seconds, the ground snaps shut like a deadly bear trap, sending a tremor across the land.

'There's no way I'm going through there!' Roxanne informs her friends as she shuffles backwards, returning onto the bridge.

'This bridge is one way only,' the guard barks, noticing Roxanne. Heidi and Faith instantly grab their friend and hurry towards the forest as the brutish guard thunders along the bridge towards them. The girls stop dead as they reach the entrance to the densely-overgrown woodland.

'That doesn't sound good,' Faith remarks uneasily as the ground beneath their feet begins to rumble.

CHAPTER 11

Heidi holds her stomach as she wobbles unsteadily. 'I think I'm going to be sea sick, just the sea,' she chunters, turning pale.

The girls shriek in unison as they are abruptly yanked forward into the dismal forest, as if pulled by an incredibly powerful magnet. They land face down in the dry wispy grass with a thud. Roxanne spits out a mouthful of dirt as she levers herself off the floor using her elbows. Faith quickly turns see a set of razor sharp teeth snap shut in the ground where they had been standing only moments prior. Heidi suddenly screams, covering her head with her arms as the demon guard's spear strikes a tree next to her, sticking into it like an arrow in an archery target. Fortunately for her, he missed his target. Roxanne and Faith promptly drag Heidi to her feet before dashing into the thick of the forest without glancing back.

'Man, it's dark in here,' Roxanne murmurs under her breath as the girls creep, almost blindly, through the dank forest. The bulky foliage conceals most of the of the cold sunlight, the occasional rouge beam crossing the girls' faces as they pass between trees. As they rustle onwards, tiny animals scurry in the gloom, too swift to identify.

'Oh my Gosh,' Faith says, freezing to the spot, grabbing her young friends' arms. 'I've just stepped on something big and squishy.'

The three girls jump backwards, squinting in the shadows at the spot where Faith stood moments earlier.

They gasp in horror as a warm yellow light suddenly shines onto a clump situated on the ground before them.

'That's so gross,' Heidi says, feeling queasy as she stares down at a mossy pile of slimy eyeballs, which sprout from the base of an old tree trunk.

'I think... I think they're watching us,' Faith whispers as the eyeballs twitch and blink in a random fashion.

Roxanne steps bravely forward. 'Not for much longer they aren't,' she says boldly lifting her foot. The eyeballs open wide in shock as she stamps on them with great pleasure. 'Oh great,' she groans as a gooey sludge drips from her, almost new, black boot.

While Roxanne wipes her slimy footwear on the brittle grass, Faith's and Heidi's attention returns to the yellow light. A tall, dark figure looms from the shadows of the trees, the glow emanating from its piercing yellow eyes. Faith grasps Heidi's hand. 'I think we better get moving,' she suggests quietly, stepping backwards.

'You need not worry,' the figure says peacefully. 'I am here to help you with your mission, Faith.' Faith halts in her tracks, the voice alerting Roxanne's attention and she cautiously re-joins her companions.

'I don't think we should trust it,' Roxanne says, her voice lowered and her eyes fixed on the shady stranger. 'This is Hell remember, nothing good can be down here.'

'Faith, no,' Heidi says nervously, attempting to grab her friend's arm as Faith steps towards the intriguing character.

Faith's expression subsides from nervous to calmly inquisitive as she slightly tilts her head to one side to get a better look at the person in front of her. 'You're... you're one of the monks, aren't you?' she asks calmly, noticing the figure's long hooded cloak.

'Indeed, child,' the monk replies warmly. 'You know of the ritual and of we who performed it. You know also of what must be done. This is your reason for existing within this realm. Though the girls and the boy were not intended to be part of this, they will have the courage and the strength to help you succeed with this great mission.'

'What did you say?' Heidi quizzes, taking a step towards the monk. 'You said 'boy', but it's only the three of us.'

'Your brother,' the monk says in a low voice gliding slowly forward, his feet not touching the ground. He rests only inches from Heidi. Heidi seems flustered by the monks words and sudden closeness.

'What's Kyle got to do with this?' she asks in a disoriented tone.

'Your brother was in the house at the time the ritual commenced. He knew not what was taking place. As his presence was not known to you at the time of the ritual and his physical body occupied another room of the building, your brother was transported to an alternative sector of Hell, exactly where, I know not. One of my acquaintances should be with the boy and will help guide him to safety. But don't be fooled. The Abyss is an extremely dangerous and evil place, the odds are greatly against him.'

CHAPTER 12

Roxanne places a sympathetic hand on Heidi's shoulder. 'He'll be okay, we'll find him,' she says reassuringly, glancing at the monk with a doubtful look in her eyes.

'So, what now? I mean... where do we go from here?' Faith asks inquisitively, looking around the dark forest without a clue as to their next move. Faith's gaze follows the monk's arm as he slowly points towards a pair of tall bristly trees.

'Whoa!' Roxanne exclaims as the trees begin to separate, bending at the centre of their thick trunks. The intense sound of splitting timber echoes through the miserable forest, startling a family of decaying ravens from their leafy shelter. Beyond the duo of bowed trees, a gaping black hole, hovering mid-air, is now exposed.

Faith shivers as a chill runs down her spine. 'Is that the way we...?' she pauses, turning back to face the monk. To her surprise, the monk has vanished without a word, leaving no evidence of his presence as only the silent darkness remains.

'Should we go in?' Heidi asks, turning to Faith. 'Or do you think we should...' she quickly spins around, staring into the dull smokiness of the forest, a loud rustling, followed by a low growl, emitting from beyond the trees.

'We go in,' Roxanne announces, hastily grabbing Heidi and tugging her towards the hole. Faith pursues closely, keeping one eye on the forest behind her as she stumbles over the loose debris.

The girls stand between the splintered trees, staring into the cavernous, black hole. Heidi's hair suddenly thrashes behind her head, like paper streamers tied to a blowing fan, as a gust of swirling wind erupts deep from within the pit of darkness.

'Okay, on three,' Faith commands, raising her voice to be heard over the fierce gale.

Heidi stares worriedly into the uncertain darkness. 'I don't know about this,' she whimpers, extremely hesitant about taking the leap.

'We have no choice!' Faith bellows over the gusting wind. 'There's no other way. We have to trust the monk's judgement.' Faith begins to count, grasping Roxanne and Heidi's hands tightly so as not to come separated. 'One… Two…' she gulps as they all take a step closer towards the opening, peering in, preparing to jump.

All three girls scream in unison as a large long-haired creature pounces on them from behind, knocking them into the blackness.

The girls clutch each other's hands tightly as they tumble through the blustery darkness for what seems to be a long while, completely unaware of what awaits them on the other side, or if they'll even survive the fall.

'What's that?' Heidi shrieks, kicking her foot in alarm as the shaggy creature clutches her ankle as it tumbles alongside them through the darkness. 'I can't get it off, I can't get it off!' she screeches, kicking her leg violently, the creature snarling with aggravation.

The girls gasp as a vibrant blue spark flashes across the blackness through which they tumble. The forked lightening crackles, suddenly bursting into a bright blue swirling vortex, almost immediately sucking the terrified friends, and their unwanted hairy companion, within its dazzling sapphire radiance.

'Umph!' Heidi puffs as she and Faith land on the hard stony ground with a soft thud. Roxanne lands on her side, rolling across the floor before crashing into a rocky wall. Heidi scrambles quickly to her feet, crazily kicking to dislodge the beast clinging to her ankle.

'Huh?' she murmurs in surprise, glancing behind her as she straightens up.

Faith also stares around the vicinity for any sign of the beast. 'Where did it go?' she asks Heidi, clambering to her feet and joining her young friend. Heidi doesn't respond, apprehensively checking around for any sign of the furry monster, as if it might appear at any moment.

'Well, at least we made it through,' Roxanne says, rubbing her lower back as she stands up, brushing herself clean. 'I guess we're going to have more than that... that thing, whatever it was, to worry about once we open that door,' she says, pointing to a heavy looking wooden door across the opposite side of the dimly lit cave that they now inhabit.

The girls huddle together, slightly trembling with anticipation as they glance around the cave nervously. The roof looms high above. Thick stalactites hang unnervingly like a magician's bed of spikes that are ready to plunge with theatrical brilliance. Tall burning torches stand evenly placed around the walls, illuminating every detail of the cave in a flickering orange glow.

Faith regards her two young companions, tears in her eyes. 'I should never have performed that ritual,' she chokes, becoming hysterical. 'I had no idea what I was letting myself in for. I didn't entirely believe that it would even work. Now you two, and your brother,' she says looking at Heidi, 'have been dragged into this mess. I don't know what to do and we're all going to die down here!'

'Snap out of it!' Roxanne yells, slapping Faith across the face. 'Sorry, Faith, but you have to get a grip. We are here now and there's nothing we can do about it. We should remain calm and think rationally about what to do and when. We have no clue what's around the corner, and if you continue to freak out then you *will* die here.'

Heidi looks stunned by Roxanne's blunt, but factual outburst. 'She's right,' Heidi says thoughtfully. 'We need to be brave, and we need to think before doing anything rash.'

The girls walk slowly towards the large door, worried about what they will encounter on the other side. They swap uneasy glances as Roxanne leans forward and grabs the massive iron bolt that seals the door. She stands sideways, taking the rusty handle with both hands and attempts to tug it from the lock.

'It's too heavy,' Roxanne pants as she pulls with all her might. 'Damn it.' She releases the handle. 'It's just too heavy to move. I can't shift it.'

The girls stand back, carefully contemplating how to open the door that blocks their path.

'Perhaps if we all grab hold and pull,' Heidi suggests. 'Then maybe we...' she jumps in shock as something touches Roxanne's shoulder, causing her to scream loudly. The girls spin around, expecting to find the hairy beast lurking behind them, ready to maul.

'Oh, don't do that!' Roxanne sighs heavily as the monk once more stands before them. 'I take it you're now going to help us escape from this room, right?' she quizzes the monk who hovers motionless before her.

'Don't be rude,' Faith mutters under her breath, concealing her mouth behind her hand.

Roxanne rolls her eyes before returning her gaze to the monk. 'So, what do we do?' she asks, pointing at the giant lock. 'Either that door is way too heavy, or I'm as weak as a baby,' she states, folding her arms across her chest.

The monk settles onto the ground, his long, dusty brown cloak piling up behind him on the damp, rocky surface.

'Faith,' the monk begins in a soft voice. 'You have much power within you.'

'Power?' Faith asks, confused.

'When you performed the ritual of Hades, you gained a small portion of the power that myself and my brethren once held. The remainder of that power lies here within the Abyss.' The girls exchange perplexed glances as the monk continues. 'My brethren and I now walk the realms of Hell for all eternity. We have been separated and held captive, each inhabiting a separate level of this abomination. You will encounter my brothers as you proceed through each sector of this lower world. They shall guide you along your path to victory. Only then will we be free.'

Heidi scratches her head in a thoughtful manner. 'The rest of the power... where is it? How do we find it?' she asks inquisitively. The monk remains silent, pointing into the far corner of the cave. Roxanne and Heidi gingerly follow Faith who walks in the direction of the monk's outstretched grey finger.

'Wow!' Heidi exclaims as a pile of dusty brown bones comes into focus, concealed within the dark corner of the room. 'I've never seen a real skull in person,' she says excitedly, leaning forward and grabbing a dirty skull from the top of the heap. 'Just think, this is what we all look like under our skin,' she says, tossing the skull into the air and catches it again.

'Heidi, don't,' Faith reprimands, glancing back towards the monk.

'Oh, come on,' Heidi retorts. 'It's not like they're going to mind, I mean... they're dead.'

Roxanne puts her hand on Heidi's shoulder. 'Shush,' she whispers into her friend's ear as she too looks across to the monk, knowing that her best friend's self-awareness can dwindle at times.

'I wonder whose it is anyway,' Heidi continues without taking a blind bit of notice of her friends.

'Mine,' the monk replies solemnly in answer to Heidi's relentless babbling.

Heidi hastily stops playing throw and catch. 'Sorry,' she mumbles sheepishly, placing the skull gently back where she found it.

The monk floats composedly towards the girls, alighting adjacent to the bones. He holds his outstretched hand over the mound of ancient remains, which begin to shimmer with a vibrant blue radiance. Roxanne and Heidi jump backwards as the bright blue swirling light suddenly floods towards them. They watch in bewilderment as Faith becomes surrounded by a beautifully serene aqua aura, the light seemingly absorbing into her body. The school girls remain speechless as Faith begins to levitate, as if possessed by a tremendously powerful flow of energy.

'This is so weird,' Roxanne utters as Faith's feet once again touch the ground and the brilliant light fades to nothing.

'Are you... okay?' Heidi asks Faith, who appears to return to consciousness. Faith says nothing, raising her head, her eyes closed. Roxanne leans forward, cautiously trying to get a better look.

'Whoa!' Heidi exclaims, stumbling backwards in shock as Faith's eyes flash open, gleaming blue sparks shining deep within them.

CHAPTER 13

Faith!' Roxanne shrieks in disbelief. She turns to face the monk. 'What have you done to her?' She turns back to Faith and begins to shake her by the shoulders. 'Faith, can you hear me?'

Heidi slaps Roxanne's arms away. 'I think she's okay,' she says, gazing intriguingly at Faith.

Faith blinks slowly as if waking from a deep sleep. Her eyes return to their normal shade of blue as they open fully.

'Oh my,' she gasps, leaning forward and holding her head in her hands. 'What just happened to me?'

'What did it feel like, Faith?' Heidi asks softly, moving close and placing her hand on Faith's shoulder to prevent her friend from toppling forward. Faith holds onto Heidi's arm as she steadies herself and stands up straight.

'It felt... amazing. A tremendous feeling of warmth and serenity filled me from inside out. I felt at total peace, like nothing could harm me, and at the same time I felt powerful and unstoppable. I can't really explain it any better than that.'

Heidi turns to the monk. 'What *did* happen to her?' she asks, Roxanne moving in closer to eavesdrop on the conversation.

'Mine, and my companions remains are hidden, one on each level of the Abyss, separating us from one another, as we are unable to depart our assigned domain.' The monk turns to face Faith, gliding a few inches towards her. 'You are the key my child. You are the one with the ability to possess great power. But you must earn this power. If you are not prepared when the time comes, then it is you who shall be destroyed.'

Faith stares at the dirty ground thoughtfully before returning her gaze towards the monk. 'Power? I don't understand. How do I earn this power and what will I do with it?'

'You have already earned your first fragment of power, Faith,' the monk informs her as he glides towards the bolted door. 'With each of my brothers' remains, you will gain additional power and become stronger. Now, it is time for you to use the power that you have obtained.'

'Wait!' Faith yells as the monk abruptly floats through the sealed door and vanishes from sight.

Heidi wanders across to the heavily constructed door. 'I have no idea how you use this power,' she looks the door up and down. 'But I'm guessing to open this door would be a good start.'

Faith walks slowly forward, standing directly in front of the door. Heidi and Roxanne watch with silent anticipation as Faith closes her eyes tightly, her fists clenched by her sides.

'Come on, Faith,' Roxanne whispers excitedly, crossing her fingers.

'Shush!' Heidi scolds, whacking her friend on the arm. 'She needs to concentrate.'

All three girls stand silently motionless, Faith focusing her thoughts intently on the tightly sealed door.

'No way!' Roxanne exclaims in a hushed tone, dazzled by what she witnesses. A swirling sapphire mist begins to emit from Faith's clasped fists. The schoolgirls stare in a state of dumbness, not moving a muscle, as they observe the manifestation of Faith's powers. The mist begins to whirl around Faith's hands, expanding like an oncoming storm. Her eyes remain tightly closed as she concentrates.

Heidi shrieks, covering her mouth with her hands as Faith is suddenly propelled backwards with great force, toppling to the ground as a tremendous surge of power emits from her hands. The three friends cover their heads with their arms as splinters of wood scatter the vicinity.

'Bloody Hell, Faith!' Roxanne exclaims in a state of shock. 'Did you really do that?' Faith says nothing as she sits on the hard ground, dumbstruck by what has just taken place. Heidi hoists herself off the cold floor, brushing wood shavings and sawdust from her hair with her fingers. Roxanne joins her best friend as they creep towards the once sealed door, which now looks as if a rocket has been launched directly through its centre.

'That was easy,' Heidi rejoices, stepping through the hole and walking towards a second door, constructed from iron. Roxanne assists Faith to her feet and they pursue Heidi. 'Damn it,' Heidi groans, her face dropping as she tugs on the door, 'it's locked.'

'Hey!' Roxanne exclaims, pointing above the door as she and Faith unite with their friend. A small sign is nailed to the wall above the metal door, the word 'Exit' etched into it.

'I can't get it open,' Heidi pants, yanking again on the door, almost pulling her shoulder out of place. 'Ouch,' she complains as she stops and rubs her shoulder with a defeatist expression on her young face. Her eyebrows rise as a thought suddenly pops into her head. 'Faith...?' she asks sheepishly, turning with an impish grin. Faith looks exhausted. Her eyes are almost shut and her complexion pale. 'I guess not then,' Heidi moans, kicking the door with annoyance and stubbing her toe.

Roxanne wipes Faith's straggly hair away from her friend's eyes. 'Do you feel okay?' she asks as Heidi hobbles back towards them, gawping at Faith enquiringly.

'I feel awful,' Faith answers groggily. 'I think using the power took everything out of me.'

'Yeah, I'd say so,' Roxanne replies. 'It's best that you reserve your strength. We might really need your help.'

'Hey, look guys,' Heidi pipes up as she struts across to a small tile stuck to the wall. The tile is etched with a tiny inscription. She suddenly becomes serious, adopting her 'school head'.

'What's it say, Hei?' Roxanne asks, assisting Faith as they stagger towards their friend.

Heidi squints at the tiny lettering. 'I don't get it,' she says, bemused. 'Nothing makes sense.' Joining Heidi, Roxanne and Faith also squint at the writing. The three girls seem perplexed by the inscription, none the wiser as to what it says.

Heidi's expression changes after a few moments of assessing the plaque. 'Oh, I've got it!' she exclaims with triumph. 'The words are backwards, that's why they make no sense. Am I good or what?'

Roxanne assists Faith to a sitting position on the ground so that she can recuperate while Heidi deciphers the scribbled message. Heidi starts from the last word and begins to read backwards.

'Riap...sed... despair. Despair of... hmmm... pit the to.' Roxanne's eyes bulge in bafflement at Heidi's ramblings.

'Feeling any better?' Roxanne asks, turning her interest back to Faith.

'A little... I think.' Faith replies, the colour slowly beginning to return to her cheeks.

'Ahha, I've got it,' Heidi squeals. She begins to read the sentence aloud as her friends re-join her. 'Through the tomb of sorrow without torment. Up to the mouth of darkness, and down to the pit of despair.'

Heidi shrieks as a round black button, imprinted with the image of a red skull, suddenly morphs on the wall next to the inscription.

'For some reason, I don't like the look of that,' Roxanne says.

'I guess we have to push it, otherwise it would be pointless,' Heidi states.

Faith rubs her tired eyes. 'We have no idea what is, and what isn't, pointless down here. Things may not be as they seem,' she says, leaning forward before hesitantly pressing the button.

An evil moaning sends a shiver down the girls' spines. They gasp as the skull on the button begins to vibrate, flames glowing within its eye sockets. Heidi chokes as thick dark smoke pours from the button, consuming the entire area that they stand in.

'Get back,' Faith commands, shoving her friends away as the button suddenly bursts into a frenzy of flames.

'What now?' Heidi splutters as the smell of burning diminishes and the smoke begins to evaporate.

'Up there,' Faith says pointing above them to the high ceiling. An open hatch has seemingly appeared as if by magic, a bright light shining through the opening. The girls stand back as a mechanical churning sound can be heard from above, becoming louder and louder. A metal object slowly sinks through the trapdoor. Continuing to stare at the opening, the friends witness a grimy escalator, exactly like the ones between the floors of a large supermarket or department store, lowering and coming to rest on the ground in front of them.

The anxious girls step slowly forward, approaching the motionless escalator with caution. Knowing that they must continue their journey if they are ever to escape, Faith leads Roxanne onto the creaky escalator, closely followed by Heidi. The girls stumble backwards as the escalator suddenly jolts into action beneath them.

'You okay, Hei?' Roxanne asks, gripping her friend by the hand to stop her from falling as the moving metal platform begins to transport them upwards.

'Yeah, I'm okay,' Heidi gulps, steading herself with the aid of Roxanne. 'Yeah right,' she whispers to herself, 'who am I kidding?'

Faith swiftly grips the grimy rubber sides of the moving staircase as it once again quivers beneath their feet with a clunking noise. She turns to look at her friends, making sure they are both still with her.

'Well, at least we don't have to walk anymore,' Roxanne says to Heidi, attempting to be optimistic, as the escalator picks up speed and they pass through the hatchway.

'Hold on!' Faith commands as the escalator begins to accelerate at a frighteningly quick pace. Heidi screws her nose at the disgusting stains and dirt that cover the escalators rubber sides as she holds tighter.

Rocky walls surround the girls as they soar upwards, getting faster and faster, with no knowledge as to where they are heading.

'Down!' Faith screams, falling to her knees as a gigantic black dragonfly buzzes over their heads. Returning to her feet, Faith's mouth drops open as she realises that the escalator ends up ahead, an expansive, deep cavern stretching beyond it.

'Do exactly what I do!' Faith commands, reaching behind her, grabbing Roxanne's hand firmly. Roxanne then reaches her arm behind her, expecting Heidi to take hold.

'Heidi!' Roxanne yells, turning to notice her friend staring wide-eyed at the dragonfly, which has come to rest on the arm of the elevator next to her hand.

'Get ready,' Faith instructs as she leans to one side.

Roxanne once again attempts to grab Heidi's hand before it's too late, but Heidi is too slow to react.

'Now!' Faith shouts as the escalator comes to an abrupt end and she leaps to the side, dragging Roxanne with her. The two girls land hard on a narrow walkway, grasping onto the rocky wall to keep themselves from falling. Heidi's terrified shriek sends a chill shooting down Roxanne's spine.

'Heidi!' Roxanne screams, leaning over to witness her best friend plummeting into the dark depths of the deadly cavern.

CHAPTER 14

'W'here are we going?' Kyle pants, pacing quickly to keep up with the monk as they journey along a dank corridor. Warm droplets of condensed air drip from the rocky roof, splattering on Kyle's head as he walks. He stares around the narrow, earthy passage as he continues to pursue the monk, hastily avoiding piles of old bones and oversized hissing cockroaches.

'Where are we going?' he enquires again, his voice raised after receiving no reply the first time he asked and now he is beginning to feel worried. The monk halts abruptly at the sound of Kyle's voice. Kyle, jogging too speedily to be able to stop himself from colliding with the monk, quickly holds his hands outstretched in front of him, ready to brace for impact. To his surprise, he careers straight through his ethereal guide.

'Hmph' he groans, landing hard on the damp ground and becoming winded as he splats into the moist soil. Raising his head and wiping the dirt from his face, Kyle gasps at the sight that lies before him. An extremely high cliff looms ahead. A swarm of disgusting black beetles writhe at the foot, hissing at each other, causing a resonant, skin crawling commotion. Kyle glances upwards as he notices something sprouting halfway up the cliff wall. A gigantic hand, carved entirely from rock, grasps onto something that wriggles between its huge fingers.

'Hei...' Kyle's cry becomes muffled as the monk hastily places his cold, grey hand across his young companion's mouth.

'They cannot know you are here my son,' the monk whispers into Kyle's ear. 'If you make yourself known to them before the time is right, all chaos will break loose on earth.'

Kyle seems confused. 'I don't... I don't get it,' he stutters as the monk removes his deathly cold hand. 'What does them finding me have to do with anything on earth?'

'Well, if you want to be responsible for unleashing Hell on earth and be accountable for billions of people's deaths...' the monk begins.

'No!' Kyle exclaims in a hushed whisper. 'No, I'll stay with you and do what you say until the time is right.'

Kyle's attention suddenly focuses on his sisters petrified scream for help.

'Roxanne, Faith, help!' Heidi shrieks. Kyle's gaze turns to the hoard of beetles that have begun crawling their way up the cliff-side towards his captive sister. He sprightly hoists himself off the ground, racing towards the cliff and the army of attacking insects. The monk's shadowy, hooded face watches as the nimble boy scrambles up onto a narrow cliff ledge that snakes like a path all the way to the top. He gasps as a large rock falls away in his small hand, plummeting through the air and crashing to the ground with an almighty squishing sound as it lands hard in the centre of the beetle clan.

The worried look vanishes from his face as determination takes over. He continues upwards, not looking back. Tugging himself up the final hurdle, he swings his legs onto a wide indentation in the cliff. The gigantic rocky hand that seizes his sister protrudes from the cliff, merely a few feet above where Kyle stands. Grabbing one of many flaming torches from the wall behind him that illuminate the vicinity, Kyle hurriedly strides directly underneath the squeezing fist, making sure to keep himself out of Heidi's eye line. He has to save his sister, but the thought of everyone on earth dying if she sees him, makes him tremble with trepidation. With a vengeful glint in his eyes, the young boy strategically reaches the torch towards the hand, steadying it as the flames lick the base of the palm. Chunks of charred stone crumble from the fist as the flames scorch. A gruff wail emits from the hand and it unclenches, releasing Heidi from its deadly grip.

'Oh no,' Kyle gasps, covering his mouth with his soot stained hand.

'Heidi!' Roxanne's voice can be heard from high above as his sister plummets towards the pit of beetles.

Kyle throws the cindering torch to the ground as he turns, sliding down the cliff's stony embankment. He honestly doesn't know what he can do to save his sister now, but he just he has to try something, anything. He speedily digs his heels into the ground, stopping himself from skidding any further as he gawps at his sister in amazement.

'No way,' he remarks to himself in thankful disbelief. As if by magic Heidi hovers in mid-air, only a few feet above the gang of deadly insects.

CHAPTER 15

Roxanne clenches her small hands tightly with suspended anticipation, staring down at her friend from high on the cliff ledge.

'Come on, come on, come on,' she chants in a hushed tone, so as not to interrupt Faith's concentration. Faith kneels on the brink of the steep cliff-side, her hands placed over her ears, so that no sounds can distract her from the task at hand. She focuses her mind, connecting to Heidi like an invisible fishing line, straining through the humid air.

Heidi squeals, panic stricken, as the beetles leap, chomping their tough jaws as they attempt to gnaw her ankles from where she hovers. She tries her best to remain calm and motionless, not knowing how long Faith's power will hold out.

As Faith focuses concentration onto her young friend, Heidi gradually begins to float to the side and away from the snapping insects. She grabs tightly onto the crumbling, narrow walkway, grasping onto loose stones as she attempts to drag her floating body to safety. She shrieks, a blurry object catching her eye as something dashes into a dark passageway beside her. She didn't get a good enough look and was unable to make out what the dark shape was. Shaking the shadowy figure from her mind, she heaves herself onto the path. She flops flat on her back, her hand pressed on her heaving heart, her heavy breathing filled with terrified relief.

'Heidi,' Roxanne's voice can be heard echoing down through the cavern. 'You okay?'

'F…fine,' Heidi manages to pant, too faintly for her friends to hear her.

'Heidi, answer me,' Roxanne yells commandingly, fearing for the safety of her friend as she peers uneasily over the cliff edge.

'I'm okay,' Heidi shouts back, her voice trembling as she scrambles to her feet. On shaky legs, she makes her way up the narrow cliff path, wiping her sweaty forehead with the sleeve of her jumper. She glances at a smouldering torch which rests by the side of the hand of rock, which appears to have rapidly deteriorated and is now simply a pile of rubble.

'It's just a pile of stone, that's all,' Heidi reassures herself as she treads carefully past the debris. She freezes to the spot as the rocky mound begins to move. She sighs heavily, placing her hand on her heart once again, as a fat black rat scurries from the remains and into a hole in the cliff-side.

Roxanne plods nervously across the mossy cliff top, awaiting the return of her friend. She yelps, struggling to free her leg as something grabs her ankle from below.

'Hold still,' Heidi pants, using Roxanne's leg for support as she drags herself up and onto the top of the cliff. Once Heidi reaches the surface, Roxanne drops to her knees, throwing her arms around her best friend. Heidi smiles, returning the hug, realising how close she came to never seeing Roxanne again.

'Faith,' Heidi says softly, releasing Roxanne and crawling across to where Faith sits. 'I don't know what I can say,' she says tearfully. 'Thank you… thank you so much.' She flings her arms around Faith's neck as she gives her an intense hug. Faith winces. 'Oh, I'm sorry,' Heidi says, releasing her firm grip.

'No, it's nothing,' Faith replies. 'For some reason, I feel incredibly tender all over, like I'm covered in a giant bruise.'

'Using the powers seems to affect you badly afterwards,' Roxanne states, joining her friends.

'It doesn't feel as bad as the last time though,' Faith continues. 'I mean, I don't feel weak or anything. Perhaps I just need time to get accustomed to it.'

From the corner of her eye, Heidi catches a glimpse of the monk who looms in the entrance of a small cave, situated behind them. But in a split second, he has vanished.

'I'm pretty sure I just saw the monk over there. Faith, are you okay to move?' Heidi asks, turning back to her friend. Faith nods and Heidi and Roxanne help her to her feet. Roxanne assists Faith towards the cave as Heidi goes ahead and peeks into the gloominess within.

As she waits for her friends, Heidi glances around for any sign of the monk, hoping he will show them what to do now.

'Oh great,' Roxanne murmurs, peering into the murky opening. A long, muddy staircase spirals steeply upwards and winds out of sight. 'I guess the way is up,' she sighs as the three friends step into the shade.

'Well, it's better than down where I've just been... I hope' Heidi says optimistically as she trudges up the first slippery step.

'Eeewww, these steps are made of clay or something,' Roxanne says, her nose upturned at the thought of getting her brand new, shiny black shoes dirty.

The girls slip and skid up the slimy staircase, one step at a time. They grasp indentations in the wall for support whenever possible.

Heidi screams, as a long black millipede crawls from a hole in the wall and onto her hand. She automatically shakes her hand into the air, flinging the insect in Roxanne's direction. Roxanne screeches, ducking, while Faith quickly flattens herself against the wall as the oversized bug soars past.

'I detest creepy crawlies,' Faith says with a shudder as they continue upwards.

Faith lags behind as Heidi and Roxanne reach the top of the stairwell. 'What's wrong?' she asks worriedly, noticing that her two young friends stand motionless, staring wide eyed and open mouthed.

CHAPTER 16

As Faith reaches her friends at the top of the stairway, her expression mimics theirs. The occasional withered tree can be seen dotted around a field of tall dead grass, stretching as far as the eye can see. A giant rock, in the centre of the field, partially obstructs the view. Castle walls stretch the immeasurably vast perimeter of the area. A deep red sun shines down onto the dismal land.

'We must be inside that scary looking castle we saw before,' Heidi states, glancing around the region below. Roxanne's mouth hangs open as the girls witness hundreds of bodies wandering aimlessly to and fro, as if in a state of eternal limbo. A terrible stench of decay wafts on the slight breeze, making the girls feel nauseous. From time to time, an intense booming siren, much like the sound of a deafening foghorn, drowns out the pitiful resonance of wails and moans.

'This place is just awful,' Faith gulps, covering her nose and mouth with her hand as the breeze ruffles her pony tailed hair. 'It reeks of death,' she whispers to herself, stepping ahead of her young friends.

Clinging together, the three girls clamber from the rock they stand on, crunching patches of crispy dead grass as they step into the bizarre field of mourning. The companions step timidly forwards, pushing aside the long grass that grows almost to head height. They hike in a single line, hand in hand through the grassland, keeping close to the castle's wall. Hundreds, possibly thousands, of people of all ages, shapes and sizes, occupy the enormous field. Some wander sorrowfully, going nowhere. Others slump on the ground, groaning or crying in despair.

'This place is appalling,' Roxanne gasps as the trio treads slowly past an old lady who cradles a young boy in her frail arms. Their skin is pale and sunken. Their most horrifying features are their eyes. They appear to be stitched shut with rusty wire, leaving them not only in Hell, but in agonising darkness, for all eternity. Heidi, who completes the end of the line, reluctantly glances back as they pass the grim pair; a look of horrified sorrow etched deeply on her face before turning away once more.

Nobody on the field appears to pay the slightest bit of attention to the girls, or even notice that they exist. If they do, they don't seem to care. As the friends squeeze squeamishly past a group of saddened individuals, Roxanne stumbles, stepping hard on something with an almighty crunch.

'I'm... I'm... so sorry,' she stammers, looking down to see a teenage girl lying on the ground; her wrist now trampled and broken as Roxanne removes her tough, booted foot. Traumatized by what she has just done, Roxanne stares down at the sallow girl who continues to lie in silence. Her mouth and eyes are open lifelessly. She stares ahead, as if she has lost all hope, and now all that remains is an empty, lifeless shell of her former self.

'Come on,' Faith says softly, placing her arm around Roxanne's shoulder and gently guiding her away from the teenager.

Heidi leans in towards her friend as they continue to walk. 'You okay, Roxy?' she asks.

'No, not really,' Roxanne replies hesitantly. 'But I guess we have to get used to seeing that kind of thing down here.'

'And worse, I'm certain,' Faith chips in, halting in her tracks she reaches the giant rock. Stepping out from behind the large boulder, the friends gain a clear view of the grassland beyond. Both Roxanne and Heidi match Faith's look of alarmed astonishment, their heads tilting slowly backwards, their eyes scanning something humongous. High up on a jagged cliff ledge, some way in front of them, a stone pier protrudes from the castle's wall. Two heavily armoured guards stand on the platform at either side, marshalling groups of solemn bodies towards the brink.

Each guard lifts a coiled brass instrument to their crusty lips, blowing in unison as a group of corpses accumulate at the end of the stone walkway. As the booming alarm resonates through the air, a tremendous thudding shakes the ground. An enormous creature looms from the shadows of a distant cave. On its two huge feet, the monster plods heavily towards the gathered crowd. Its dark green, leathery body, drips with a thick transparent goo. Immense drops of slime flatten patches of parched grass as the beast trudges across the field. Three sizeable black horns project from the monster's grotesque head and two extremely long fangs sprout from its sloppy jaws; its head resembling a terrifyingly evil warthog.

The slimy giant lifts its bulky hand, swiping the bundle of deceased individuals. The sound of weeping and groaning can be heard as the beast turns, plodding a few paces back in the direction in which it came. Standing in the centre of the field is a huge, old fashioned weighing scale, carved from stone. The bodies whimper as the monster separates them into two groups, one group into the hanging dish on the right-hand side and the other group into the dish on the left. Steam emits from the giant's gaping nostrils with a rumbling snort as it concentrates intensely on the task.

'What's he doing?' Heidi whispers in horror as the girls huddle together, observing from a distance. As the scales tilt to the right, the hideous creature swipes three people from the lowered dish on the right, tossing them harshly into the hanging dish on the left. The scales now slant more to the left. The beast snatches one slouching woman, dropping her ungracefully into the right-hand dish. He roars with terrifying glee as the scales now balance, another puff of smoke pouring from its dank nostrils.

The slimy monster snatches the group of living corpses on the left, flinging them to the grassy ground without a care. It then turns, seizing the individuals on the right-hand side of the scales, which has now fully descended. The ground shakes as the beast thunders back towards the cave from where it first appeared. A second cave, larger than that of the monster's, is situated directly above. The creature raises his slimy hand as it arrives at the alcove high in the wall, placing the group of dismal souls onto the small ledge at the entrance of the highest cave.

The girls' mouths drop in shocked disgust as a second grotesque ogre appears in the upper cave. The monstrosity's shabby orange fur wafts in the breeze as it peers from the gloom. Its two beady black eyes scan the group of individuals, its wide mouth slobbering. Its long arms drag across the cave's floor as it approaches the brink. The image of an overgrown, Hellish orangutan floods Heidi's mind.

'Holy crap!' Roxanne blurts in repugnance as the monster reaches the crowd, quickly lowering its frightening head, its mouth wide open and salivating hungrily. A loud crunching sound resonates through the vicinity as the beast clamps its jaws shut around the helpless group.

'Oh no,' Faith manages to mumble, shaken at the horrific sight that lies before her. Splinters of skeleton, accompanied by flesh and gore, drop from the ogre's slobbering mouth as it chews vigorously. The skin crawling sound of teeth and bones grinding together fills the the girl's ears.

The friends stare, speechless, as both gigantic brutes retreat into their dark caves.

'What just happened?' Roxanne asks Faith, keeping her voice low, her heart pounding in her chest.

Faith looks across to the stumbling accumulation of individuals that the huge beast released onto the field.

'I don't know,' she whispers, confused. 'I guess each time new people arrive... die... or whatever, half have to live here forever and half become food for the monsters.'

'Crowd control, maybe?' Heidi suggests, sounding ignorant of the situation.

'Perhaps,' Faith replies thoughtfully. 'Personally, I'd rather be eaten than spend an eternity here. Either way, they all lose.'

From what the girls can see, there are no exits from the field, other than the platform where the armoured guards usher the new arrivals into the land. As Faith glances around the area, the monk once again appears in view. He stands in the entrance to the high cave, the home of the orangutan monster. As Faith watches, the monk slowly raises his arm, gesturing to the inside of the cave. Faith turns to look at her two friends. Their attention appears to be focused on a new army of depressed souls, who have just been cast into Hades.

'Come on guys,' Faith whispers after a few moments of thinking time. Roxanne and Heidi have no time to ask questions. They follow silently as Faith creeps vigilantly through the undergrowth.

'Where's she going?' Heidi whispers to Roxanne as they tiptoe through the long grass.

'Do I look like a mind reader?' Roxanne retorts. 'Let's just trust she knows something that we don't.'

The three girls sneak through the wispy dry grass, avoiding the occasional large thistle and aimlessly wandering corpse. Roxanne and Heidi hold onto each other, gazing around as they try to keep up with Faith. They collide with their friend, who has stopped abruptly, precisely at the foot of a cliff-side. This cliff is slanted, large pieces of rock jut out, creating a climbable route to the platform where the two guards usher a new crowd of despondent folks towards the edge.

'Faith, what are you doing?' Roxanne questions, grabbing Faith by the shoulder, yanking her back down as she attempts to climb the wall.

'Just trust me, okay,' she whispers. 'I think I know what to do.'

Roxanne raises her eyebrows as Faith turns and commences to climb up the cliff-side. 'Oh, she better know what she's doing,' she says to Heidi, unenthusiastically. Heidi sighs, trailing after her friend as Roxanne also begins to climb.

The girls clutch onto the protruding segments of rock, levering themselves upwards. They ascend with care, desperately hoping not to draw any unwanted attention to themselves. Once they reach the summit, Heidi and Roxanne steady themselves on the jagged rocks as they wait behind Faith.

'Okay, on three,' Faith commands in a hushed tone as she carefully peers over the edge. The guards shove and poke the individuals with their glistening spears. Faith watches from her hiding spot until a crowd of victims shield them from the view of the guards, making it possible for them to climb onto the platform, unseen.

'Three!' Faith blurts out as she realises that there isn't enough time to begin counting from one. Roxanne and Heidi follow Faith nervously, heaving themselves over the verge of the cliff. The heavily armoured watchmen are too occupied nudging the hordes of people towards the end of the platform to notice the three new attendees.

'Act sluggish and depressed,' Faith orders as the friends attempt to blend with the shuffling crowd. Heidi winces as she passes a guard, who pokes her in the leg with his spear. The girls shove their way to the front of the corpses, standing directly on the edge of the high platform above the field.

Heidi flinches as the two guards blow their spectacularly deafening horns. The booming sound rings through her ears as if fireworks are setting off in her head.

'Is this such a great idea?' Roxanne whispers, her voice quivering in sheer terror, as the enormous slimy ogre appears from the darkness of its cave. 'Faith, what... what do we do?'

CHAPTER 17

Just make sure it takes all three of us,' Faith whispers from the corner of her mouth, trying to remain inconspicuous. The gigantic beast stomps its way heavily towards the high platform. Heidi's eyes dilate with dread as the troll raises its broad, slimy hand towards them. With a tight grip, the beast squeezes the group of individuals into his dripping palm, the three girls squashed at the front.

'I... I can't breathe,' Heidi wheezes, gasping for air while the monster thuds across towards the scales. Upon reaching them, the monster drops Roxanne and Faith, along with a few other souls, onto the left platform of the scale. The remainder of the group, including Heidi, plummets onto the right, with an uncomfortable thud.

The scales tip to the right, causing Heidi to topple, crashing into a dreary young woman. The ogre hastily snatches two people from the right-hand side, but Heidi misses her chance as she stumbles, falling to her knees. Roxanne jumps backwards as the beast drops the new couple onto their side of the scale. The monster snorts with satisfaction as the huge scales even themselves in perfect balance.

'We have to act fast,' Faith says to Roxanne, panic stricken as the beast lowers its disgusting hand, ready to grab them. The massive ogre stares at Roxanne and Faith with annoyed confusion as they dash forward, leaping from the left-hand side to the right, joining Heidi. The scales fall uneven once again. The brute swiftly knocks all the people from the left side with his gigantic hand, scattering them into the air like bowling pins that have just been blown apart by an intense strike. It glares down menacingly as the right side of the scale crashes to the ground, everyone falling to their knees with a thud. A single puff of smoke rises from the beast's nostrils as it grunts furiously.

Heidi shuts her eyes tightly as the towering monster snatches them, along with the other bodies on their side of the scale. The ground shakes as the beast thunders his way towards the cave situated above his own.

'Faith, what do we do now?' Roxanne shrieks as the cave looms upon them, the hairy orange fiend emerging from the darkness.

'Just follow me when it releases us,' Faith replies, short of breath. 'I'm not sure what to do yet myself.'

Roxanne's eyes bulge in disbelief at Faith's words. 'What?!' she screams in hysteria. 'What the Hell do you mean you don't know?' Faith is being squeezed too firmly to reply.

'Oh no... here we go,' Heidi squeals as the ugly beast lifts them higher, dropping them into the entrance of the cave.

'Faith!' Roxanne screams, Heidi grabbing tightly to her arm. The hairy monster pounces forward, its grotesque, yellow toothed mouth, open and dripping, as if forever starving and ready for its next meal.

'Go!' Faith yells, pushing Roxanne and Heidi to the left. The monster's jagged jaws snap shut around the remainder of the group, barely missing the three girls as they dodge its gruesome attack.

'This way,' Faith commands as she sprints towards a large passage, leading from the rear of the troll's dank cave. Heidi stumbles on the loose stones as they race down the tunnel at top speed.

'A door,' Roxanne pants as the end appears in view. She races ahead, grasping the thick wooden door's handle. She barges the door with her shoulder, expecting it to be heavy and difficult to open. She looks stunned and shaken as she jolts backwards, toppling to the ground.

'You okay, Roxy?' Heidi asks, offering her friend a hand and tugging her back to her feet.

'Yeah, I'm okay,' Roxanne answers, seeming rather dazed. 'But... ouch!' She dusts her jeans as Faith stands next to the door and begins to read from a silver plaque which is attached to the wall next to the door.

'Three switches loom on high. On your judgement, must you rely. All the odds you must defy, for the beast of limbo has the watchful eye.'

The girls spin around as a loud snorting emits from behind them. To their horror, the bedraggled ogre lurks menacingly in the distance, gore from its previous meal drenching its lips.

'Don't move, stand completely still,' Faith whispers as she stares down the long tunnel, unsure if they have yet been spotted. 'Okay... move!' she yelps as the beast suddenly charges along the path towards them. Faith grabs Heidi, dragging her. Roxanne follows as her friends dash down another stretch of corridor to their left.

Half way along the path, Roxanne turns her head to witness the furry giant skidding angrily around the corner, using its long arms like ski poles as it gains ground. A solid brick wall abruptly drops before the fleeing girls, causing them to halt briskly in their tracks, their path of escape now a dead end.

CHAPTER 18

W hat's going to happen to them?' Kyle asks his monk guide, shaky voiced as he gazes down upon the entrance of the hairy ogre's cave. They crouch behind a low cobbled wall on a high pathway that leads around the top of the castle. 'I mean, that... thing has gone after them, right?'

'Your sister and friends are fine,' the monk responds quickly. 'They have escaped the beast and are now safe.'

'Phew,' Kyle sighs, relieved. 'Well, as long as they're okay,' he says, crawling away from the wall. He gazes around while following the monk along the path, consistently distracted by the mass of bumbling bodies in the field below. His attention turns to the monk as they reach a hole in the centre of the path. The monk proceeds to lower himself into the hole.

'Is it safe down there?' Kyle yells into the darkness below. He shrugs when he receives no reply. 'Okay...' he mumbles as he carefully lowers himself through the hole in the ground.

The deafening siren can still be heard as Kyle drops to the ground and then hastily pursues the monk. They tread their way across dirt and loose stones in a narrow gloomy tunnel. The occasional wall mounted flaming torch the only light along the path, creating unnerving shadows that dance and flicker along the uneven, rocky walls.

'How long am I going to be down here?' Kyle asks as the pair trudge along the dreary pathway. 'What's your name anyway? I forgot to ask,' he continues without waiting for an answer to his previous question.

'My name, unimportant as it may be,' the monk begins to reply, 'was Emilio.'

'Was?' Kyle queries, bemused.

'A person has not the need, nor the desire for a name down here,' the monk explains. 'Nobody is special and no one is different. We are all one and the same thing.' Kyle shrugs to himself as they continue along the tunnel, not fully understanding what the monk is talking about.

A light at the end of the clammy corridor appears in view. The monk escorts Kyle into a large room with no windows and no doors, simply a spacious and brightly lit, bare space.

'Emilio, I don't get it,' Kyle says to the monk who stands motionless before him, as if waiting for the boy to react to something. To Kyle's surprise, one of the brick walls begins to fade and then vanishes completely. Another space, equal in size, is now located before him, creating one larger room now that the wall has disappeared. Numbered tiles scatter the floor on the new side of the room. Three shiny, metal levers protrude from one of the walls, although they are far too high to reach. Embedded in the wall, a couple of feet above the three handles, a gigantic, red and black eye stares intimidatingly into the room, seemingly following Kyle's slightest move.

The far wall begins to crack, opening slightly. To Kyle's utmost delight, his sister and her two friends hurriedly squeeze themselves through the divide and step into the room.

'Heidi!' He yells with excited relief, forgetting the monk's words of warning, as he makes a dash for his sister. 'Ouch!' he exclaims, crashing into something hard, causing him to stumble backwards, toppling to the ground. After shaking the confused dizziness from his head, he jumps back to his feet. Walking cautiously towards the three girls, he stretches his arms before him to protect himself from the unseen force that caused him pain a few moments earlier.

'Huh?' he murmurs as his palms flatten onto an invisible wall. 'Heidi, I'm here!' he calls across the room to his sister. 'Hei!' he yells once more when she doesn't react to his cries. 'What's going on?' Kyle quizzes the monk, pushing as hard as he can against the invisible shield in front of him, his face turning puce with the strain.

Kyle can hear the girls talking as he frantically slides his hands across the entire blockage between them. He realises that he stands only a short distance from his sister, but she is unable to see or hear him. Without a way past the invisible wall, must he continue to journey on alone?

CHAPTER 19

'Whoa, that was a bit too close for my liking,' Roxanne pants as the wall behind her seals shut. 'We're so lucky you accidentally stepped on that secret button,' she says, facing Heidi as the furry giant's thunderous footsteps fade into the distance.

The girls begin to take notice of the room they now occupy. Heidi stares inquisitively at the panels on the floor, then at the handles that jut from the wall. 'That eye creeps me out,' she says with a shudder, a chill running down her spine.

'What do you suppose we do?' Roxanne asks her friends, hoping that one of them will have a clever solution.

'That riddle earlier,' Heidi says thoughtfully as she walks past the stone wall, not knowing her younger brother is standing directly behind it and he can see everything that she and her friends are doing. 'It mentioned something about 'the odds.' The floor that the girls stand on is created from large tiles, most of them with numbers scrawled upon, in a grey chalky substance. Faith and Heidi scan the floor with their eyes while Roxanne remains looking dumbfounded.

'Oh, I get it,' Heidi pipes up, noticing that five of the floor tiles have odd numbers, the rest having even.

'Should we?' she asks, glancing nervously at Faith. Faith hesitates for a moment before nodding in agreement. With extreme care, Heidi steps one foot lightly onto a panel with number '7' scribed upon it. She watches anxiously as the square begins to shine with a blue hue.

'Interesting,' she murmurs, removing her foot. As she does so, her thick heel accidentally scrapes the adjacent tile, with the number '36' written on. Heidi freezes, her heel remaining on the tile, as the room ever so slightly shakes. They look upwards, the sound of steel clinking together resonating from above. To their horror, long glistening spikes now dangle from every inch of the ceiling.

'I don't think you should stand on the even numbers,' Roxanne hisses through gritted teeth, not taking her eyes from the cluster of deadly spikes. Extremely slowly, Heidi removes her foot from tile number '36', scrunching her eyes tightly as she takes all pressure off the square. The three girls stand silently motionless, Faith's mouth hanging open with fearful dread. A few moments later and nothing has happened. The room remains quiet and still.

'Phew,' Roxanne finally blurts, wiping her moist forehead with the back of her hand. 'Now, Heidi, don't do that again,' she warns her best friend who still looks rather flustered at the thought of suddenly being impaled. The friends watch as the blue shimmer that surrounds the number '7' square fades away.

'I'm guessing we have to stand on each of the odd numbered squares,' Faith states. 'Although it looks like we need two more people. The odd numbered tiles are spaced too far apart from one another to be able to reach by ourselves.'

Noticing something that she didn't before, Roxanne breaks away from her friends. She dodges the floor tiles as she heads across to a tall rocky statue that blends into one of the far walls. The ornament is slender and shaped like a spear, the sharp head pointing towards the ceiling. Heidi and Faith watch their friend as she gives the statue a slight shove with her shoulder.

'We can move this,' she informs the others, realising that it's light enough to slide across the floor. 'Oh!' she exclaims, staring over Heidi's shoulder, 'that one too.' Another spear statue, the exact double of the one that Roxanne discovered, is situated behind Heidi.

'Well spotted, Roxy,' Heidi praises as she makes her way towards the second statue. 'We can stand these on some of the odd numbers.' She scans the ground. 'Put them on... forty one and... seventy seven. Those numbers are on the edge so we won't have to touch any other squares while we move them.'

Roxanne swiftly begins to heave her statue towards the tiles, shoving as hard as she can with her shoulder. Faith accompanies Heidi as they team up to slide the stone object along the floor.

'Well...' Roxanne pants as she finishes shoving her statue onto the square numbered '41'. 'Mine is done.' Heidi puffs with the strain as she and Faith haul their statue onto tile inscribed with the number '77'. Faith stands back to get a better overview of the ground. The squares beneath the statues glow with a blue hue, exactly like the one Heidi had tested previously.

'Okay,' Faith begins, taking the leadership role. 'We each need to be standing on one of the remaining odd tiles. Heidi, you take number seven, Roxanne, number nineteen and I'll have number fifty three.' The girls begin to take their places on the floor. Heidi carefully steps over tile '36', placing her small feet onto her given square. Faith joins Heidi on square '7', using it as a safe route before taking a giant leap onto her own square. Both squares now shine with a blue shimmer. Roxanne steps slowly backwards, keeping her eyes fixed on the last remaining odd numbered tile. Her friends watch with a terrible preconception as to what will happen if Roxanne touches a wrong square.

'Here goes nothing,' Roxanne gulps before taking a deep breath and dashing towards the floor tiles. She springs with vigour upon reaching the squares on the ground. She lands heavily onto square number '19', the heels on her black shoes almost scraping the adjacent tile.

'Roxy, mind your feet!' Heidi screeches, starting to perspire. Roxanne immediately shuffles away from the edge of the square. She sighs with relief, thankful that Heidi warned her before it was too late.

A sapphire shimmer now surrounds each of the girl's feet. They turn their heads towards the wall where the huge eye looms on high. The flooring directly beneath the eye begins to rise like a platform.

'Do we get on?' Heidi asks. The girls glance apprehensively at each other, the sense of needing to act quickly becoming apparent. They each leap desperately towards the rising tower. Faith and Roxanne puff as they land hard, hauling themselves up and onto the rising platform.

'Help me up!' Heidi squeals as she fails to grab the ledge as her square was further away.

'Roxanne, quick,' Faith commands as she leans over, grasping Heidi by the wrist. Roxanne joins in the tug as she too leans over the side, taking her friend's free arm and pulling with all her might.

'Thanks,' Heidi wheezes, swinging her leg as she scrambles up and onto the moving ledge with her friends.

As the platform suddenly jolts to a stop, the three levers underneath the huge eye come within reach.

'Do we pull them?' Heidi asks, unnerved by the huge unblinking eye that stares down at her.

Faith looks up. 'I guess so,' she replies unreassuringly.

'Okay then, let's do this,' Roxanne says, placing her hand on Heidi's back, guiding her underneath one of the levers. 'When I count to three, we each pull one.'

As Roxanne begins to count, Heidi stands on her toes as each girl reaches and grabs hold of a heavy lever with both hands. The levers creak as the girls struggle to yank them down. As they release the handles, a sound, like that of a kettle boiling, fills the air. They stare down into the room below to see the spearheads of the statues glowing red, as if they burn with an immense heat. A red laser beam suddenly shoots from both spearheads, zapping the huge eye directly in the centre of its oversized pupil.

Faith shields her head with her hands, ducking as the scorching beam misses her by only a few inches. The girls gaze upwards at the sound of a high-pitched wail. Heidi covers her ears as the eye emits a painful scream, its pupil beginning to seep with liquefied gore.

'That's totally gross!' Roxanne squirms as large gooey drops trickle onto her shoulder. She quickly wipes away the cooling, melted gore, smearing her sticky hand onto the stony wall beneath the great eye. 'I hate it when things bleed on you,' she moans.

All of a sudden, the bright laser beam crackles and shorts out. The spear statues return to normal. The girls hold their breath, waiting for something to happen.

'Well?' Roxanne says, breaking the silence, her hands on her hips.

'I don't understand,' Faith states, confused. 'I mean… was that actually meant to do something? Nothing seems to have changed.' Heidi walks slowly past Faith, staring at the eye.

'What is it, Hei?' Roxanne enquires, also looking up but not seeing anything of special interest.

'Give me a leg up,' Heidi commands as she stands directly beneath the eye. Roxanne drops to one knee in front of her friend.

'Okay,' Roxanne says, 'don't take too long. You're too heavy.'

'Oh, stop whining,' Heidi retorts as she straddles Roxanne's neck, perching on her shoulders. Faith assists to steady Heidi as Roxanne rises to her feet with an almighty struggle.

'Oh, my God,' she pants, her face turning puce. 'You've totally put on weight!'

'Hey!' Heidi responds with offence. 'I think it's you who needs to work out more, thank you very much. You're obviously far too feeble for your own good.'

'Oh, be quiet and get on with whatever you're trying to do.' Roxanne answers abruptly.

'All right, hold still,' Heidi instructs her puffing and panting friend, who sways uncontrollably under the pressure.

'Eeewww,' Heidi squirms, slowly reaching her small hand through the centre of the gigantic eye, which has been hollowed by the laser beam.

'Heidi, hurry up,' Roxanne huffs with exhaustion as Heidi thrusts her arm deep into the gaping hole in the centre of the eyeball, reminding her of one of those childhood games where you put you arm into a hold and try to guess the object inside by touch alone.

'Eeewww, I think I touched the retina,' she says in disgust, looking down at Faith who returns a squeamish glance.

The girls scream as a large ceiling tile unexpectedly drops, smashing into hundreds of pieces upon impact with the floor. Heidi topples to the hard platform as Roxanne stumbles in shock.

'I pressed a button,' Heidi says, flicking her hand free from eye goo as she sits upright.

'Hey, look,' Faith says, pointing towards the space in the roof where the tile had been positioned moments before. An old tatty rope begins to lower through the hole. Large knots have been tied strategically along its entire length.

'I guess this means we go up,' Roxanne says matter-of-factly as the platform they stand on begins to descend.

Roxanne and Heidi follow Faith's lead as the older girl steps from the platform and walks towards the grimy brown rope.

'Yes,' she sighs heavily, as they all stare up into the duskiness above. 'And probably up to something much worse.'

CHAPTER 20

Why do they keep staring at me?' Kyle whispers, closely following the monk who leads him down a shadowy hallway. A few swinging chandeliers ablaze with green flames cast the only light along the corridor. The occasional dreary individual slouches against the walls, groaning miserably as Kyle hurries past them.

'Heidi... she's... going to be okay... right?' Kyle asks as he trots beside the gliding monk, attempting to keep up. 'I just know they're going to find me,' he pants. 'I know you said they can't know I'm here yet, but when the time is right, they will find me. That is right, isn't it?'

'That is correct, my son,' the monk reluctantly replies in answer to Kyle's relentless questioning.

A round, metal door greets the duo as they reach the end of the corridor. A small oval is carved into the center of the door, a foreign sentence engraved around it. 'El señor oscuro gana fuerza del thee que abre esta entrada y es puro de alma.'

'What does that say?' Kyle asks curiously, tilting his head as his eyes follow the lettering.

'It speaks of the one who is pure of soul, the one who will triumph over evil,' the monk answers. 'The path that lies ahead may be tough, but you must face the darkness head on if you are to survive and reunite with your sister.' The monk reaches out, taking Kyle's small hand, placing it palm down into the oval indentation.

Kyle flinches as the door begins to shudder, the panel around his hand glowing red. The monk slowly turns, gliding a few feet away as the door rolls to the side, exposing a swirling portal within the space beyond.

'Where are you going?' Kyle calls, spinning around to see the monk drifting away from him back along the passage.

'This you must do alone, my son,' the monk informs the young boy. 'We shall meet again, if you have courage.'

'Wait...' Kyle yells as the monk begins to fade. But it's too late. His companion vanishes completely from sight. 'Well, that's just great,' he sighs, turning back to face the vortex.

Crimson sparks and shimmers whirl within the blackness of the uninviting portal. Kyle walks hesitantly towards the opening, his arm outstretched as he gingerly advances. A crackling emits as he cautiously sinks his hand into the black hole.

'Guess I go in,' he says unenthusiastically. He closes his eyes tightly as he reluctantly ventures into the crackling darkness.

A cold, tickly feeling passes over Kyle's entire body as he continues through the otherworldly doorway. Almost immediately, he steps out the opposite side. The entire operation seems to take only a couple of seconds. Opening his eyes, Kyle's mouth drops open as he witnesses the unbelievable sight that stretches before him.

He stands on a petite wooden pier, a raging ocean extending endlessly before him. The dark and stormy waves exude a salty aroma which stings his eyes. Storm clouds fill the murky, turbulent sky. Following each flash of silver lightening, the crashing of thunder echoes across the restless waves. Miniature tornadoes spread across the water's surface, swirling viciously as they move across the deep ocean. Thousands of bodies tumble uncontrollably in the spiraling, ocean winds, the wailing chorus that they create muffled by the storm.

'Why did Emilio have to leave me now?' Kyle moans to himself, panicking even more than before as he stares across the overwhelming open water. His attention wanders to the left of where he stands, something large catching his eye.

'A boat,' he whispers to himself with curious surprise. A lengthy Viking style ship emerges from below the violent waves, merely a few hundred feet away from the small pier on which Kyle stands. 'I wonder if they're friendly,' the young boy speculates as the ghostly looking ship begins to sail in his direction.

CHAPTER 21

S hould we take it?' Heidi asks Faith as the three girls stand over a large raised plaque that protrudes from the floor. The hole in the ground through which they entered by climbing the rope has now sealed, leaving no exit from the room that they now occupy. This room is small and minimalist, comparable to an attic alcove. Red bricks construct the walls that surround the perimeter of the tiny space. A single blazing torch, nailed to a chunky wooden beam, runs up the side of the back wall.

'I guess we have to do something or other,' Faith replies thoughtfully, crouching beside the plaque. She runs her fingers across a square, copper relic that fits securely within the centre of the stone slab. The design of a sadistic mouth, filled with sharp fangs, is imprinted on the remnant. Suddenly, the copper relic depresses as Faith's fingertips caress the lips. Heidi winces, grabbing Roxanne's arm with the anticipation that something horrible is once again about to occur.

'Oh,' Heidi says in surprise, the room remaining eerily silent. 'I thought something was…' She screams as the entire stone slab abruptly bursts into a fury of flames.

'Faith!' Roxanne shrieks as Faith tumbles to the ground in shock, the sleeve of her black fleece singeing with fire. She hurriedly kneels beside Faith, hastily joining the attempt to beat out the smouldering flames with her hands.

'Watch out,' Faith commands as she hurriedly unzips her top. Roxanne tugs the fleece off Faith's shoulders before throwing it to the ground and stamping out the dying flames.

'Be careful,' Faith yelps, leaning over and grabbing her ruined garment from the floor.

'Hey, chill,' Roxanne retorts, taken aback. 'You can easily get yourself another one. Well, if we get home I mean.' Faith rapidly searches the inside of her fleece, unzipping one of the inner pockets. She sighs with relief as she retrieves the dagger, which still glimmers with a lustrous red tint.

'Oh, I totally forgot about that thing,' Heidi pipes up. 'Good job it's not broken.'

Faith inspects her top, making sure the flames have ceased before slipping it back on. She places the dagger safely back into the inside pocket and zips it securely.

'I look like a homeless person now,' she grumbles, fiddling with the scorched hole in her sleeve. 'But I guess looking your best isn't of the utmost importance down here.'

'Yeah,' Heidi replies. 'I think vanity is the least of our worries,' she says, glancing towards where the plaque had been. 'Plus, at least you'll blend in better, looking like damaged goods, I mean.'

'Looks like we go down,' Roxanne says, noticing that a large square hole is now in place of the stone slab.

'But that's a good thing,' Heidi remarks enthusiastically. 'Remember that riddle thingy we saw ages ago?' she pauses for a moment, awaiting anyone's comment. She rolls her eyes at the sight of her friends' expressionless faces. 'It said that we have to make it to the top, in order to get to the bottom and get out, or something along those lines.'

Faith begins to walk wearily towards the spacious opening, darkness the only thing to greet her. She halts in her tracks as a distant sound rattles from below.

'Something's coming,' Roxanne whispers anxiously as she and Heidi stand either side of Faith, grasping their older friend by the arms before pacing backwards and away from the opening in the ground.

The girls back against the wall of the small room, overcome with nerves as chugging and scraping noises from below grow louder with each passing second.

Faith glances edgily at her young friends, their grips becoming tighter. 'Something's coming. Something big.'

CHAPTER 22

We have to hide,' Heidi whispers fretfully, frantically kneading Faith's arm with her fingertips.

'There *is* nowhere to hide,' Faith replies through gritted teeth, her arm numbing from Heidi's continuous, terrified pummelling.

The three girls slouch against the back wall as the noise from below grows closer and more intense with every passing second. Heidi closes her eyes tightly as something looms from the darkness of the hole.

'Jeeze,' Roxanne sighs, placing her hand across her heaving chest. 'I can't believe how terrified I was just then, and all for... that?'

Heidi reluctantly opens one eye. A round metal platform now fills the cavity where the plaque had once been.

'Oh, I get it,' Faith breathes with a sigh of relief. 'It's a lift, and it's going to transport us down, hopefully to the exit.'

Heidi is suddenly overwhelmed with excitement. 'You mean, this nightmare is almost over? We'll be going home soon?' she asks spiritedly, clapping her small, childlike hands together, full of hope. Solemn expressions appear on both Faith and Roxanne's faces.

'I don't think it's going to be as easy as that,' Faith says, attempting not to dishearten her young friend. 'You see,' she continues, 'this is the first level of Hell. We must journey to the core to achieve what I came here for. Then we can all return home. You understand?'

Heidi rolls her eyes, making a tutting noise. 'Aaawww, I was getting all excited then,' she whimpers.

'Come on, we better make a move,' Faith says, smiling sympathetically, rubbing Heidi on the shoulder.

'Wait a minute!' Heidi abruptly exclaims, looking thoughtfully at the ground. 'Kyle... We haven't found Kyle!'

'Oh, my God,' Roxanne blurts as she moves next to her best friend. 'I almost forgot that he's down here too.'

'We have to find him,' Heidi tells Roxanne, looking her straight in the eyes, seizing both of her hands in hers.

Faith places a comforting arm around Heidi's shoulder. 'We will do, Heidi,' she promises.

'But he's all alone and scared. Maybe even dead,' Heidi replies tearfully as the thoughts of her astray sibling fill her head.

'Kyle's okay, Hei,' Roxanne says, caressing the back of her friend's hands with her thumbs. 'One of the monks is with him, remember? and anyway, your brother can be a right little monkey. I'm sure he can take care of himself until we find him and take him home,' she says as convincingly as she can.

Both Roxanne and Faith guide Heidi towards the lift. The circular platform barely manages to squeeze through the square hole in the ground. An iron pole protrudes from the centre, a silver skull fixed to the top.

'Hurry, squeeze on,' Faith instructs, stepping onto the platform and grasping the iron pole with both hands.

'I don't think this is meant for three people,' Roxanne complains as she squashes herself between her friends.

Heidi gasps as the lift jerks and begins to descend through the ground. 'This piece of junk better hold out!' she moans.

'Is everyone okay?' Faith enquires as the hole, now above them, seals up, leaving them in complete darkness. They grip the iron pole tightly, not knowing what might be lurking in the surrounding blackness.

As they progress, they notice a distant, orange shimmer beneath them.

'Is anyone else getting warm?' Roxanne asks, sweating as a sudden heat wave overcomes her.

'Uh oh, this can't be good,' Faith murmurs, the cause of the glow becoming apparent.

'Is that what I think it is?' Heidi gulps, her meek voice trembling.

'I think so,' Faith replies, wiping her perspiring brow with the tattered sleeve of her top. 'It's a pit of molten rock.'

CHAPTER 23

'Why did I have to follow them to that stupid house?' Kyle complains to himself as the huge Viking ship rocks from side to side on the violent waves.

On the main deck, twelve wooden oars, on either side of a weather-beaten white sail, row in unison. Although, when hesitantly boarding the boat, Kyle noticed that no one was actually rowing. An elaborately carved, formidable sea serpents head, rests at the front of the vessel, its eyes ablaze with crimson flames.

The young boy huddles behind a wooden crate, his arms clutched tightly across his knees, which are pulled closely to his chest. The colour has drained from Kyle's face, and he now looks rather pale. 'I can't take much more of this,' he mumbles groggily to himself, holding his stomach as he crawls unsteadily towards a hatch that leads to a lower deck. Realising there's no ladder between the two tiers, Kyle lowers himself through the hatch, dropping hard onto the tough glass floor below.

He gasps, his queasiness slightly subsiding as his attention switches to the dreadful sight laid out before him through the ship's glass base. Thousands of human bodies, of all ages, sizes and races, float beneath the waves. The darkness that looms at the deepest depths of the raging water conceals the ocean bed. The limbs of the victims are bound by sturdy, tarnished chains, securing the prisoners captive beneath the surface. Escape is impossible; the offenders doomed to be forever drowning for their earthly sins.

'Sick!' Kyle exclaims in disgust, a cold shiver trembling down his spine as he witnesses several people tugging on their restraints, struggling to break free, but to no avail. Having surrendered, others remain motionless, realising that all hope has spent.

'Well, I guess they must deserve it for some reason,' Kyle says, attempting to make himself feel better as he turns his gaze away from the horrific sight.

Across the opposite end of the lower deck sits an impressively polished, wooden table. As Kyle wobbles his way across the swaying glass floor, he licks his lips as the contents of the table come into focus. Bread rolls, chicken legs, cheese, fresh fruit, crisp clear water, everything associated with the finest medieval banquet lays spread out before him. A look of confusion crosses his face, wondering why the food is so conveniently placed there. He lifts a warm bread roll, inspecting it closely before raising it to his nose and taking a suspicious sniff.

'seems okay,' he says joyfully, the aroma of freshly baked bread making him drool as he takes a seat at the table.

CHAPTER 24

'This is totally freaky,' Roxanne mutters under her breath as the three friends emerge from the darkness, still clutching onto the overcrowded lift. Walls of lava surround them, bubbling with immense heat. Thousands of molten faces groan in despair and as they peer out from the scalding, liquid walls.

'I can't handle much more of this heat,' Heidi complains, Faith steading her as she begins to wither like a wet lettuce.

'I need off this contraption,' Roxanne whimpers, sweat pouring from her forehead like a shower.

They continue downwards, travelling deeper and deeper through the vast castle. Faith eyes suddenly brighten. 'Oh, thank goodness,' she pants as the end appears in sight. As the friends begin to leave the flowing walls of lava behind, walls made from cool stone slabs replace them, which feel like paradise to the three roasting girls.

Roxanne wafts her white top up and down, allowing the air to cool her skin, while Heidi fans her blushing face with her hands. 'I thought I was going to die... seriously,' Heidi wheezes, inhaling deeply as the lift comes to rest on the cold ground. 'I thought the sauna at the swimming pool was bad, but that was something else!'

'I guess this is as far as it goes,' Faith says, gazing around the basement they have been transported into. The stone, moss covered walls exude a damp, stale fragrance, which fills the spacious, square room. Heidi wrinkles her nose as she notices three skeletons, crumpled and slouched against the walls; their mouths hanging open and a blackness filling their desolate eye sockets.

The girls' attention turns to a tall stone door, embedded into the wall across the far side of the cellar. Faith glances above her. 'Looks like this might come in handy,' she says, unscrewing the silver skull from the top of the lift.

'You think this leads to the next level?' Roxanne asks hopefully as they approach the door, noticing a skull shaped indentation carved into its centre.

'Fingers crossed,' Faith replies as she carefully slots the skull into the hollow.

'We're doing pretty well,' Heidi says enthusiastically, her fingers tightly crossed. 'I mean... only four levels to go, right?'

'Hopefully...' Faith responds as the door begins to rumble. 'If all my research was correct.'

'It better be,' Roxanne mutters under her breath.

The girls jump back, Heidi latching securely onto Faith's arm as the stone door proceeds to crumble before them. Heidi's long blonde hair flails in a fierce breeze as chunks of rubble fly away, as if a powerful vacuum cleaner sucks from behind the wall.

'Stand back!' Faith commands as the wind dies and a sheet of darkness appears beyond the doorway. 'Hold onto my hands,' she instructs her young friends. 'We'll all go together. Hold tight and don't let go.'

Heidi shrieks, covering her mouth with her hand as the monk suddenly appears in a burst of blue light, standing before them within the doorway.

'Oh, I wish he wouldn't do that,' Roxanne gasps to herself, her hand on her rapidly beating heart.

The monk stands motionless. 'The path that lies ahead shall lead you to the next hurdle of your journey,' he declares, his dusty hood shielding his face with shadows, only his pupilless yellow eyes gleaming from the darkness.

'You mean… the next level?' Faith asks softly.

'That is correct, my child,' the monk responds. 'Although, I come to you with a warning.'

Roxanne nudges Heidi in the ribs. 'I really do hate this place,' she sighs under her breath.

The monk continues. 'The doorway that I stand before shall let you pass. However, there is one condition. The individual first to enter, shall become a sacrifice to the darkness, required to open the gateway to the next level in which you seek.'

A look of confusion crosses Heidi's face. 'Let me get this right,' she says, holding her up index finger as she gazes thoughtfully at the ground. 'The first one of us to go through that door, will… what? Die?'

The monk rises off the ground, hovering within the doorway. 'May God be with you,' he says, only a moment before vanishing in a flash of intense blue light.

'Well, that's just fantastic,' Roxanne utters, throwing her hands into the air as she turns and paces away from the door. 'Now what are we supposed to do? I mean, he didn't tell us that part, did he? Why do we always have to figure it out for Christ's sake?'

'Roxanne!' Heidi gasps, flustered. 'I don't think you should say that down here?'

'Huh?' Roxanne responds, puzzled as to what her best friend is declaring.

Heidi raises her eyebrows. 'Taking the lord's name in vain, stupid.'

'Oh... right,' Roxanne replies sheepishly, her finger pressed against her lips, realising that they need the forces of light on their side, so it's probable best to remain respectful.

'Oh my God!' Heidi squeals, making a dash across the damp basement floor. Roxanne shakes her head, rolling her eyes at her best friend's hypocrisy, as Heidi skips towards the opposite end of the room. 'We can use this guy,' she calls back to her friends. She stands beside one of the cold grey skeletons that leans against the wall, its mouth hanging open. She reaches out, grasping the skeleton's skinny arms with both hands. 'Blimey, you're heavy for a pile of old bones,' she puffs as she begins to drag the skeleton towards the door. Amazingly, the skeleton remains intact after what has probably been hundreds, even thousands of years. 'Whoops,' Heidi gasps as the corpse's arms both suddenly detach from the shoulder sockets. She flings them aside in disgust.

'Ouch!' Roxanne exclaims, rubbing her leg as one of the scraggly arms whacks her. Heidi spins around. 'Sorry, Roxy, I didn't see you skulking behind me.'

Roxanne kicks the arm away with annoyance. 'I wasn't skulking.' She pauses to rub her leg once again. 'That's the last time I come to your rescue.'

'I don't need rescuing, thank you very much,' Heidi jokingly retorts as she grabs the skeleton by its skull and continues to drag.

'Yeah, whatever,' Roxanne smirks, folding her arms as she watches her friend struggle with the pile of bones.

'This chap's just big boned, that's all,' Heidi pants as she proceeds towards the doorway.

Faith watches as Heidi and her skeleton friend reach the door. 'I take it you assume this heap of old bones can be the sacrifice?' she asks.

'Damn right I do,' Heidi reciprocates with a sigh of relief, dropping the skeleton before the door. As the bones crash onto the hard ground, the skull snaps away from the spine.

'Well, that's a start,' Roxanne says as the cracked skull rolls into the darkness that fills the doorway. Heidi bends down and grabs the ribcage. She glances up, expecting some help.

'Well...' She says as Roxanne stares blankly back at her.

'Oh right, sorry,' Roxanne says, moving forward and taking hold of the skeleton's scrawny ankles.

'In you go,' Heidi says optimistically as she and Roxanne swing the headless skeleton from side to side before releasing it into the gloomy exit.

Bright sparks of red lightening flash in the blackness beyond the door as the pile of bones evaporate into dust and then disperse. The girls watch from a safe distance as the darkness gradually lightens, becoming a soft, warm, pearly light.

'That did the trick,' Heidi says, wiping chalky dust from her palms.

Faith looks rather stunned by Heidi's quick thinking, but thankful, nonetheless. 'Good job, Heidi,' she praises. 'I think it's now safe to enter.'

The girls stand side by side before the glistening entrance, their hands linked.

'I hope that dead guy worked in our favour,' Roxanne says hopefully, her grip tightening around Heidi's hand, as the three friends step warily into the light. As the serene radiance consumes them, they leave the depressingly gloomy castle and the first level of Hell behind.

CHAPTER 25

Kyle jolts in his chair as the boat abruptly slams to a halt. 'Ooof, have I crashed?' he asks himself, clambering unsteadily to his knees. 'I'm so stuffed,' he groans, rubbing his stomach as he drops a half-eaten bread roll onto a large silver plate on the table before him. As the ship ceases to sway, Kyle wobbles down the room towards the hatch in the ceiling through which he first entered. 'That food was so nice,' he says, thinking out loud as he hauls himself up through the opening and back onto the upper deck of the ship. The motionless oars bob slightly on the now tame ocean.

The boat has docked at a grungy, steel harbour. A turnstile is situated between two thick pillars, which are, as usual, ablaze with fire at the peaks. Beyond the turnstile, a path surrounded by a mass of spiny, dead trees leads from the harbour.

A cold shiver runs down Kyle's spine as he watches a group of ravens soar overhead in the stormy sky, squawking as they flap down into the ghostly forest. 'Where are you, Emilio?' he chunters under his breath as he steps from the boat and begins to make his way down the metal pier. He gasps, his trainers skidding on the shiny, slippery surface as he walks cautiously along. 'Guess I'll have to crawl under,' he says, reaching the sturdy barrier that blocks his path. Moments before he has the chance to proceed, a heavily armoured guardian steps from behind one of the smouldering columns. His body kit is slightly different to the ushers that Kyle encountered earlier. This demon is dressed head to toe in black steel. A black mask conceals his face, which in Kyle's opinion is probably a good thing.

'I... I think I left something on the boat,' Kyle chokes timidly, his heart racing as he backs slowly away. The guard lifts his black steel-clad hand. A deadly, spiked ball attached to a sturdy chain is nailed through his wrist.

'I'm sorry, I'm sorry. I'll leave,' Kyle says, holding his hands out in protest. The Hell warrior suddenly swings the heavy spiked ball at high speed, seriously bending the metal turnstile as it strikes with great force. Realising that the mighty guard is unlikely to compromise, Kyle's retreat quickens and he prays that he can hide on the Viking ship. He spins around as he decides to make a dash for the boat. 'Wait! Come back!' he yells, halting at the end of the pier as the ships mast sinks beneath the water. 'Uh oh,' he groans as the boat vanishes beneath the dark ocean waters, leaving him stranded.

CHAPTER 26

Kyle's palms become clammy with anticipation as the pier beneath his feet begins to rumble. He turns his head and shrieks in horror as he witnesses the guard charging in his direction, his destructive weapon swinging furiously. The young boy screams as the beast gains on him, the hurtling sphere of death glinting in the light of the rising moon. Diving into the gloomy water is the only solution that floods Kyle's mind. As he prepares to take the plunge, Kyle's trainers slip on the wet metal of the pier, causing the boy to fall backwards, landing flat on his back. The solider growls as he attempts to swerve the human obstruction. Kyle huddles himself into a ball, shielding his head with his hands as the bulky guard trips over him uncontrollably.

The knight howls as he slides along the shiny pier and plummets into the dark ocean waters. Kyle keeps his eyes fixed on the end of the dock as he shakily returns to his feet. The ocean surface begins to settle once more as Kyle cautiously cranes his neck, revealing a view of the water. He flinches backwards as the water suddenly breaks. The guard roars fiercely, casting the heavy, spiked ball onto the pier. Kyle falls to the ground once more as the threatening ball slams into the pier with a clunking of metal.

Two corroded iron chains rise out of the murky ocean behind the struggling, armoured fiend. Kyle shuffles backwards, keeping his eyes locked on the sight before him. The heavy chains wrap violently around the guard, one gripping tightly around his solid, reinforced neck, while the second clamps his arms together, making escape impossible. The determined chains drag the demon below the water's surface once again. The sound of the spiked ball being dragged along the iron pier makes Kyle cringe. With one final splash, the Hell soldier's instrument of death follows him into his final resting place beneath the dark waves.

Kyle sits in silence for a few moments, astounded by the rapid events that have just taken place. He glances nervously behind him to make sure that the knight was alone. Suddenly, the sound of water breaking from the end of the pier regains his attention. He gasps in fear as he turns to see yet another chain extending from below the waves, reaching for him, ready to drag him to his watery grave.

CHAPTER 27

A glass tunnel, surrounded by water, is the first sight to greet the girls as they step from the sheet of darkness. Emerging silently out of the dark doorway, their eyes vigorously scan their new environment. They remain speechless as they witness hundreds of bodies floating all around them. Sturdy iron chains bind the limbs of the individuals, securing them within the dark waters.

Heidi covers her mouth with her hand, staring at the shockingly inhumane sight. A middle-aged lady reaches her one free arm towards the tunnel, her long, straggly grey hair becoming tangled in the chains that bind her as she struggles, hoping in vain for the girls to rescue her from the watery prison in which she is captive.

'This is awful,' Heidi gasps, turning away in repulsion. 'Why are these people treated this way?' she asks despondently as Roxanne puts her arms around her shoulder comfortingly.

'I think...' Faith says softly, averting her gaze from the dismal waters. 'I think they must have done wrong on earth and are now paying for their sins.'

Roxanne glances around the glass tube. 'They must have done some pretty terrible things to deserve this,' she says, observing a young man who constantly chokes due to the chain that wraps securely around his throat.

The girls walk cautiously along the tunnel, which seemly stretches forever. They link arms to gain a feeling of security as they proceed. Heidi cringes once again, attempting not to look at anything other than the ground as the friends pass underneath countless chained bodies. Every one of them doomed for an eternity of suffering beneath the miserable, violent waves.

'How much longer do you reckon we have to walk?' Roxanne grumbles as they continue arm in arm along the underwater passageway.

'Looks like it might be a while,' Heidi groans, puffing as the tunnel's end blurs in the distance, stretching far beyond her eyesight range.

Faith flinches, turning her head sharply to her left as something on the outside the of tube catches her eye. 'What the...?' she gasps, horror-stricken by the spectacle that looms towards the fragile glass tunnel.

CHAPTER 28

Holy cow!' Roxanne exclaims, her gaze also alighting upon an immense shape. The girls stand, transfixed. Their eyes follow a gigantic fish as it swims over the transparent tunnel. The monstrous fish's metallic turquoise scales glint as it glides through the choppy waters. Hundreds of wiggly tentacles protrude from the beast's wide tail and razor sharp fins, floating in the water like wet spaghetti. A lower set of needle-pointed, brown teeth jut from its jaws, creating the illusion of a wickedly evil grin. A pair of marble sized, pitch-black eyes search for prey as the fish navigates the dark waters with ease.

The girls continue to observe as the mighty fish stops abruptly. Its spiny tentacles begin to grow, extending towards a cluster of chained people. The victims squirm and struggle as the tentacles caress each one of them up and down their bodies, as if searching for something. The body of a bedraggled, elderly man remains entirely motionless as the tentacles begin to prod him vigorously. Heidi grabs Faith's arm in fright as the enormous fish suddenly lurches towards the old man, gobbling him up in one fell swoop.

The friends stand still, gawping, their mouths hanging open.

'That was seriously freaky,' Roxanne blurts after a few moments of silence, while Heidi's small hands remain clenched tightly around Faith's forearm.

'I'm never going to do another wrong thing in my life, ever,' Heidi tells herself as she and Faith follow Roxanne, who proceeds along the tunnel ahead of them. 'Even if I step on a worm or something,' she continues, staring at the ground in a daze, 'I'll pray for forgiveness and bury it and everything, because I'm never coming to Hell again for as long as I live.'

'Heidi, that doesn't even make sense,' Roxanne announces, glancing over her shoulder, one eyebrow raised at Heidi's nonsensical ranting.

As the girls continue their tedious journey along the water surrounded walkway, they watch the gigantic fish swim relentlessly around the tunnel, scouting for its next victim. Their pace begins to slow, their feet tiring. They are seemingly getting no further with each step they take.

'Girls, look,' Faith says excitedly. Heidi and Roxanne take their gaze from the floor, where they have been staring sluggishly for the past twenty minutes.

'About damn time!' Roxanne exclaims as the adventurous gleam returns to her eyes. Another glass tube is positioned vertically at the end of the tunnel, leading up to the ocean's surface.

'I'm guessing that's our escape route,' Faith tells the other two as she squints into the distance and notices a doorway in the vertical tube.

'Yay! Come on slow coaches,' Heidi squeals as she takes off down the tunnel.

'Heidi, wait!' Faith yells after her, but Heidi is too excited at the thought of leaving the passage to take any notice.

'She'll be OK,' Roxanne puffs as she and Faith dash after her.

Heidi stops in her tracks as the vertical tube comes into focus. 'Wow, a boat,' she says energetically, clapping her hands as she notices a small, wooden craft located through the opening in the tube. Roxanne and Faith join their friend before all making their way across to the boat.

As the girls approach, a sliding door snaps shut, sealing the boat within the glass tube. The sight reminds Roxanne of a ship in a bottle that her grandparents have on the mantelpiece in their living room.

'Oh, I knew it was too easy,' Roxanne groans, hitting her fist on the tough glass.

'Look,' Heidi says, noticing a panel of square buttons on the sliding door. Each one of the buttons is inscribed with a tiny black and white illustration.

'This must be some kind of electronic locking system,' Faith declares, running her finger gently across the panel.

A distant booming sound from behind grabs the girls' attention.

'What the heck was that?' Roxanne asks, her voice trembling. The three friends squint into the distance in the direction from which they came. Their eyes open wide in alarm as they instinctively cling to each other for dear life, as a colossal tidal wave hurtles along the passage towards them.

CHAPTER 29

Kyle quickly pulls his head back behind the pillar that he now hides behind, a deadly chain missing him by a mere millisecond.

'I've got to get out of here,' he tells himself, sweat dripping from his brow as he stares into the dismal forest that spans behind him. A mass of sturdy chains now accumulates at the end of the pier, reaching from the dark waters like a giant, iron octopus.

Kyle's attention suddenly fixes on a small path, leading from the back of the pier and into the depths of the forest. He catches a glimpse of the monk who glides behind a cluster of shadowed trees. Kyle once again takes a sly glance around the pillar. The chains writhe at the water's edge, anticipating the young boy's moves. In order to catch up with his guide, Kyle knows that he must reach the forest as quickly as possible.

After one final peek, Kyle makes an abrupt dash for the narrow path. A couple of chains dart towards the fleeing boy, nipping at his ankles like pincers. To escape the shackles of death, Kyle dives into the dead foliage at the end of the path, the thin branches and crispy leaves crunching under his weight as he lands heavily.

Peering out from being the twigs, Kyle nervously watches as the clan of deadly chains recedes beneath the waves.

'If I never see another chain again it will be too soon,' he breathes with a huge sigh of relief. He suddenly jerks his head, staring into the forest behind him as he remembers the monk. 'I have to find Emilio.'

Carefully emerging from his hiding place, the sound of snapping twigs resonates as he cautiously tiptoes along the path and into the forest. Looking up through the trees, Kyle can see the grey storm clouds racing across the blustery sky. A flock of ravens fly overhead, squawking eerily as they swoop through the forest, searching for food.

Kyle's eyes vigorously scan the surrounding area as he descends through the shadowy woodland. 'Emilio?' he calls quietly, his hand cupped around his mouth, to avoid excessive echo. Shadows of all shapes and sizes appear to hide and whisper as the young boy creeps fearfully onwards. After passing behind an old tree stump, he halts in shocked surprise. He finds himself standing before a girl, huddling timidly in the bushes. This girl looks to be about 18 years old, and appears to be as human as himself. Her long, wavy red hair, rests halfway down her back. Her Smokey eye make-up and pale complexion makes her appearance rather striking. She wears a mud splattered white blouse and stonewashed pale blue jeans.

Kyle silently stares at the girl, thinking that she is the most beautiful girl that he has ever seen. The girl stares back, neither sure of what to say or do. After a few awkward moments, the girl opens her mouth. 'Are... are you... a real boy?' she asks, guardedly rising to her feet while maintaining her distance.

'Yeah... I'm real,' Kyle replies hesitantly, looking the girl up and down. 'Are you real?'

The auburn headed girl nods. 'I was on my way to a friend's birthday party,' she informs Kyle. 'I was walking right outside the creepy old house when I suddenly blacked out. Then I woke up here only a few minutes ago, wherever here is. I always knew there was something strange about that house.'

'You don't know where we are?' Kyle asks.

'I have no idea,' she replies, tears forming in her eyes as she glances around the dark forest. 'I thought I was dreaming, but after pinching myself a few times I guess I'm not, am I?'

'No, you're not dreaming,' Kyle answers in a hushed tone as the chilling resonance of squawking birds drifts on the breeze. 'I think I was in that same old house, so were my sister and her friends. They did some kind of spell or something, and that's how we all ended up here.'

The girl looks surprised. 'The Wiltmore street house?' Kyle nods. 'Wait... a spell?' the girl continues, sounding rather confounded. 'What kind of spell?'

'A spell to send them to Hell. Which I guess worked,' Kyle replies. 'Now they have to destroy the Devil... I think.'

Kyle sits the girl down on a bed of crisp leaves as he explains about his journey through the abyss so far. He tells her all about the monsters and about his monk companion who helped him to reach this point.

The girl continues to look stunned as Kyle's tale concludes. 'This sounds like a story from some freaky horror novel or something,' she says, running her hands agitatedly through her flowing red hair.

'What's your name?' Kyle asks.

'Jasmine. What's yours?'

'My name's Kyle,' he tells her, getting to his feet and assisting Jasmine off the foliage. 'We better keep moving,' he says as they begin to walk carefully along the leaf cluttered path. 'The monk that I told you about, I saw him go this way. He must be helping us.'

The young boy's eyes brighten as Jasmine slips her hand into his. They creep hand in hand along the dirty pathway, carefully stepping over fallen branches as they proceed. The trees seem to murmur and groan as they pass by. Small shadows scurry and hide in the dark crevasses of the wilderness, sending a chill down Kyle's spine. He realises that his new friend is older than he is, but he just can't help feeling that he must protect her.

As the full moon begins to rise into the darkening sky, the forest path illuminates with a subdued silver sheen.

'I'm sure Emilio came this way,' Kyle murmurs under his breath as he and Jasmine continue along the path, clutching onto each other tightly, every small sound making them jump.

'Who's Emilio?' Jasmine asks.

'Emilio is my monk. Well, that's what he used to be called… when he was alive.'

The two new companions continue to tiptoe along the trail, crunching the brown, dried leaves as they tread. The wood seems to fall darker by the second as they descend deeper and deeper through the moonlit trees. Their pace slows as they step out into a circular opening. Gangly, bristly trees surround the entire space, casting a spooky atmosphere into the arena.

'Where to now?' Kyle asks, staring around for any sign of a visible path. Before Jasmine can reply, they both leap backwards in horrified surprise, as a giant eagle-like bird abruptly lands before them. The new friends stand motionless, not daring to utter a single word as the king-sized bird of prey eyes them suspiciously. Its fearsome black eyes glimmer in the moonlight as it taps its immense clawed feet on the dirty ground. The monstrous bird stands as still as a statue, deadlocked on Kyle and Jasmine, as if anticipating a chase.

Jasmine's piercing scream breaks the silence as a second creature unexpectedly pounces from the dark trees. The bird squawks loudly, flapping its bulky wings frantically as a four-legged animal, the size of a large dog, locks its jaws around the bird's thick, feathery throat. Kyle grabs hold of Jasmine's hand as they watch the nightmarish performance unfolding before their unbelieving eyes.

'A wolf,' Jasmine whispers, her voice breaking as she begins to slowly back away down the path along from which they came, Kyle mimicking her moves. They cringe as the loud snapping sound of the bird's neck breaking resonates through the trees. The bird falls silent, its struggle for life ceasing. The wolf drops its kill on the ground, licking the blood from its lips with satisfaction. Before the beast can devour its meal, the sound of scuffling feet makes its ears to prick to attention. Kyle and Jasmine freeze to the spot, praying that they will be camouflaged within the darkness. The wolf takes a couple of steps forward, its eyes shining a dazzling emerald green.

'Uh oh!' Kyle exclaims under his breath as he and Jasmine become illuminated in the beast's headlights. They stand motionless in the beam as if physically unable to move. The wolf suddenly begins to change before their eyes. Its teeth are the first to grow, extending into long deadly incisors. Its shoulders begin to arch. The sound of cracking bones fills the air as the creature's legs grow larger and stronger. The young companions observe in terror as the horrific transformation concludes. A colossal, fearsome werewolf now stands before them, snarling viciously as it turns its attention to its new prey.

CHAPTER 30

'Back away, slowly,' Jasmine says in a shaky, hushed voice. She takes a tentative step backwards, tugging Kyle's hand when he fails to move. Once Kyle's feet start working again, the friends cautiously edge their way backwards along the path, keeping their eyes firmly fixed on the horror movie monster. The beast stands motionless, as if playing with its dinner, snarling at its retreating meal from a distance, thick gooey saliva dripping from its pursed jaws.

A flock of ravens, soaring across the dark sky, momentarily captivates the werewolf's attention. Without uttering a single word, the friends turn and dash along the path. Not daring to look back, Kyle stumbles on the loose, uneven terrain, as he tries to keep up with his longer legged friend. They gain speed through the sinister forest, using their hands to protect their faces from the spiny branches which scrape and scratch as they pass, as if attempting to halt their escape.

'What the...?' Jasmine puffs, out of breath, as she and Kyle stand before a gigantic tree that blocks their route.

'We must have taken a wrong turn!' Kyle cries, glancing around the shadowy cul-de-sac for an alternate exit.

'Shush,' Jasmine hushes her young companion as she pulls Kyle into the shadows that surround the tree. She holds her finger to her lips, motioning for him to be as quiet as possible. 'I think we're being stalked.'

The two friends huddle close in the gloom. Their ears prick as the sound of snapping twigs reverberates from the dark path. Their heavy breathing is all that can be heard in the silently still air. Their hearts pound in their chests as the anticipation grows heavier with each second that passes. They remain motionless, hoping to be concealed within the shadows.

Their breathing suddenly softens in unison, almost ceasing altogether, as a dark silhouette emerges from the dark trees. A jade glimmer sparkles in the murkiness as the werewolf halts in the centre of the path. Kyle and Jasmine watch as the beast lowers its shabby, devilish head, sniffing the ground.

'It's picking up our scent,' Jasmine whispers shakily.

The wolf sharply raises its head towards the round, silver moon as it releases a tremendous, skin crawling howl. The whites of the friends' eyes glint, shining in the moonlight. The terrifying beast lowers its head, turning in their direction. They sit in the gloom, too petrified to move, or to even breathe. The wolf pads along the forest path, getting closer and closer to the hiding youngsters. Jasmine lets out an unintentional, quiet gasp, as the Hell hound stops within inches of her. Its long, dripping snout sniffs at her hair, its stale breath vaporising on her face. She shuts her eyes tightly as the werewolf howls once more, opening its gruesome, saturated jaws in the direction of her head.

Realising that he must act quickly, Kyle leaps to his feet, dashing to the large tree that blocks their escape.

'I'm over here you stupid mutt!' he bellows, waving his arms in the air while jumping up and down on the spot. The werewolf sharply fixes its gaze on the frustrating distraction, its bright green eyes narrowing menacingly. Jasmine opens her eyes, yelping when the beast's heavy paws stomp on her legs as it dashes towards Kyle. Having no strategised plan of action, Kyle freezes to the spot in terror.

'Kyle, move!' Jasmine screams, jumping to her feet as the werewolf pounces at the small boy. He stares in a horrified trance as the creature leaps towards him. He dodges to the side at the very last moment, grimacing when the wolf's long claws clip his shoulder as it soars past him. Jasmine hurriedly joins her friend as the crazed wolf crashes head first into the thick tree.

'Quick,' Jasmine screeches, grabbing Kyle by the hand as the werewolf slouches dizzily against the stump. She jumps in shock, halting in her tracks as a gaping hole opens in the tree, ferociously swallowing the hairy beast in one fell swoop.

The friends stare in bewilderment as the hole snaps shut, the tree trunk becoming solid once again. They creep slowly forward, gripping onto each other's arms tightly. They freeze again as the great tree begins to rumble. The sound of splitting bark echoes through the night sky as the trunk begins to split. The bark cracks and bends, forming an oval doorway.

Once the air falls silent and the tree falls motionless, Kyle and Jasmine tiptoe towards the opening. A winding staircase, made from intertwined twigs and sticks appears through the opening.

'Do you think we should go down?' Kyle asks Jasmine, hoping, as she is older and wiser, that she might take charge.

Jasmine peers into the cavity. 'I guess,' she says unreassuringly. 'I haven't exactly got to grips with this place yet, but my feelings are that we should get out of here as soon as we can. That said, I'm not exactly keen on the idea of following that wolf.' She carefully peers inside the tree trunk. 'I can't see or hear anything down there. For some reason, it feels like we're meant to go down. Maybe your monk opened it for us to escape?' Kyle seems unsure, but reluctantly nods in agreement. Jasmine takes his small hand and steps one foot across the threshold. 'Just take it easy and be quiet.'

She winces as the meshed steps of twigs creaks under her weight. The occasional burning torch hangs from the bark inside the tree. In Jasmine's opinion, flaming torches are not the most appropriate lighting solution within a space made entirely of wood, but she realises that they face bigger issues. She looks warily over the wobbly, wooden handrail to get a better awareness of where the stairs lead.

'Oh, you have to be joking!' she exclaims under her breath, slowly retracting her head back over the railing.

'What is it?' Kyle asks, his voice lowered as nervousness once again possesses him. He moves next to Jasmine, who silently stares ahead of her in a state of revulsion. They both gasp as the doorway abruptly seals, generating a loud splintering resonance as it closes.

'Jaz, what were you looking so worried about?' Kyle asks apprehensively, desperate to acquire an answer.

'I saw something moving at the bottom of the stairs,' she whispers. 'It was yellow and black and looked like...'

'Looked like what?' Kyle asks impatiently. Jasmine flinches as a rustling comes from below.

Jasmine gulps, the pit of her stomach turning. 'It looked like a massive spider.'

CHAPTER 31

The three girls sit in the wooden boat, looking bored and unsure of what to do. The glass tunnel is now sealed and surrounded by water.

'I still can't believe I worked out that really tough locking system so quickly,' Heidi announces, looking rather chuffed with herself.

'Yeah,' Roxanne sighs, 'and I can't believe you're still going on about it.'

'Jealous much?' Heidi retorts.

Roxanne rolls her eyes as she turns her attention to Faith. 'How much longer do you think we will be stuck in here?' she asks, realistically knowing that Faith is none the wiser than she is.

'I hope it's not too much longer,' Heidi chips in. 'I really need to use the little girl's room.' Faith simply shrugs, feeling dejected.

The girls sit silently for a few minutes more. Roxanne twiddles her thumbs while Heidi fiddles with her long blonde hair.

'I'm going to play the game eye spy,' Heidi proclaims, breaking the monotonous silence.

'Okay... I'll play,' Roxanne reluctantly agrees.

Faith looks confused. 'How do you play?' she asks Heidi.

'Well, I give you the first letter of an object that I can see and then you have to guess what that object is.' Heidi looks thoughtful for a second, attempting to think of an object that will cause her opponents great difficulty to guess.

'Come on, Hei,' Roxanne complains impatiently. 'Waiting for you to decide is even more tedious than doing absolutely nothing.'

'Okay, I got it,' Heidi announces. 'Eye spy with my little eye, something beginning with the letter W.'

Roxanne sighs heavily, gazing at her friend with an unimpressed expression. 'Water?' she asks unenthusiastically.

'Aaawww,' Heidi groans, folding her arms, disheartened by the fact Roxanne guessed correctly and her turn is over so quickly.

'You have a go, Faith,' Roxanne says, hoping that Faith can be more imaginative. Faith nods in agreement and scans the area for a slightly more inconspicuous object.

'Eye spy with my little eye, something starting with the letter... F' she stares into the ocean waters, horror shining on her face.

'Fish!' Heidi screams turning to face the direction in which Faith stares in horror.

The three girls crowd together as they witness the ferocious, armoured fish, swimming at top speed towards them along the connecting, water filled tube. Ready for destruction. Ready to devour them all.

CHAPTER 32

It's going to eat us!' Heidi wails, almost jumping onto Roxanne's lap, throwing her arms around her friend's neck. Roxanne pushes Heidi off her knee as she leaps to her feet, frantically running her hands across the glass tubing.

'Roxy, there's no way out!' Heidi yelps, certain that her grave is going to be a watery one.

Faith stares at the oncoming, terrifying monster. 'There will be any second now!' she squirms, starting to gnaw at her fingernails as the huge fish approaches the fragile tunnel.

All three girls scrunch their eyes tightly as the gigantic fish looms swiftly upon them, Heidi gripping onto Roxanne for all she's worth. Heidi screams, toppling backwards off the boat as a powerful thud vibrates through her body. She sits upright, sloshing her long hair from a pool of water, which now accumulates beneath the small boat.

'Heidi, get in,' Roxanne commands, leaning over the side of the boat and attempting to pull her friend back on board. Heidi shrieks as she jumps onto the wooden seat inside the craft, coming face to face with the gargantuan fish. The hideous fish glares through the glass with its small black eyes. Water gushes through a large crack in the vertical tube, caused by the monster's heavy collision.

'We're rising,' Faith informs her quivering companions as the small boat begins to ascend, bobbing on the water.

'I wonder where it leads,' Roxanne says inquisitively, looking up and noticing that the tube disappears into a cloud of darkness.

The girls wait apprehensively as water continues to rise. As the bobbing vessel reaches the halfway mark, the Hell fish slowly reverses. The tentacle ladened beast charges full pelt into the damaged tunnel for a second time. Heidi peers over the edge of the craft as a loud shattering noise comes from below. She yelps as the boat swiftly shoots upwards as water floods the tube from below.

'Hold on tight,' Faith manages to yell, her stomach feeling weightless, as if on a roller coaster at a fair ground.

The girls screech as they soar into the uncertain shadows above. Their cries echo as the glass tunnel comes to an end and the small boat shoots into a spacious, rocky cave. The cave fills with the water from below, transforming it into a mini glistening lake. The boat bobs on the surface as the tunnel seals and the water ceases to rise.

Using their hands as oars, the girls steer the boat towards the edge of the pool. Faith in the lead, they unsteadily haul themselves from the swaying vessel. The cavern that they now find themselves in appears to have a single exit.

'Come on,' Faith instructs her young friends as she jogs towards a large hole, a few feet up in the wall. Roxanne and Heidi join her underneath the passageway.

'It looks like we can fit through,' Faith tells them, peering into the darkness that fills the opening.

'You've got to be kidding,' Heidi says, backing away from the wall.

'Hei, we don't really have much of a choice,' Roxanne tells her.

'But I get claustrophobic,' Heidi whimpers, her brow perspiring as she becomes tense. 'I went potholing once and almost screamed my lungs out because I got stuck. After that I swore I'd never crawl through anything, ever again.'

'Heidi, we have to, we have nowhere else to go,' Faith says.

'But... I can't.' Heidi continues to moan. 'Even sleeping on the bottom of bunk beds freaks me out. This one time I...'

'I don't care!' Faith yells, interrupting Heidi's ranting. 'We *are* going through, end of story.' Heidi looks miffed, taken aback by Faith's outburst.

Loose stones fall to the damp ground as Faith scrambles into the opening.

'Okay, the quicker we do this, the quicker it will be over,' Roxanne says to Heidi, placing a comforting hand on her arm.

'Fine,' Heidi sighs, rolling her eyes as she traces Faith's footsteps.

'Just follow Faith,' Roxanne instructs as she assists her friend into the hole. Heidi mutters something under her breath as she disappears inside the passage. Roxanne can just make out her friend's feet vanishing into the darkness as she too clambers up the wall and enters the confined space.

Heidi continues to grumble as the three companions scramble through the narrow, pitch-black tunnel. Suddenly, Faith stops moving and the line of crawling girls comes to a standstill.

'Faith, what are you doing?' Heidi shrieks, beginning to panic.

'It's a dead end!' Faith exclaims, running her hands across the walls all around her and realising that there's nowhere else to go.

Heidi's heart starts beating rapidly and her breathing becomes heavier at the thought of being imprisoned. 'I need to get out!' she screeches in alarm, hysterically shuffling about in the restricting passageway.

'Ouch, Heidi, stop kicking me,' Roxanne scolds as her friend's feet jab her on the side of her head.

'I told you this wasn't a good idea,' Heidi whimpers uncontrollably as claustrophobia takes control of her rationality. 'I can't breathe, I need to get out. Roxanne, go backwards, I have to get out!'

Unexpectedly, an extremely welcome light fills the tunnel.

'The wall in front of me wasn't solid,' Faith announces. 'It just slid out of place as I ran my hands across it.' As Faith shuffles onwards, Heidi wipes her grubby hand across her sweating face with relief, her panic slightly subsiding, but on the brink of return. Faith's mouth drops open in surprise as she exits the tunnel, getting to her feet and finding herself standing in another cave.

'Faith, help,' Heidi calls, laying on her stomach, half out of the passage and her arms outstretched. Faith bends down and grabs Heidi by her hands, tugging her entirely out of the tunnel and helping her to her feet. Noticing that neither of her friends are paying a scrap of attention to her, Roxanne figures that she'll make her own way out of the passage.

As Roxanne hoists herself from the damp ground and rises to her feet, the sight that enthrals Faith and Heidi seizes her attention also. The cave they have now entered is much the same as the one that they came from, although with a few major differences. This cave is not waterlogged, and a tall wooden door is situated on the opposite wall. A small iron cage hangs low from the slimy ceiling in the centre of the grotto. A raven, the colour of night, perches on top of the cage, is if its protector. Several dry, old bones appear to be the only contents within the metal prison.

'Do you think that's...?' Roxanne whispers in Faith's ear, trying not to alarm the menacing looking bird. Faith nods, realising that the pile of bones must be the remains of the second monk. Heidi moves in closer, attempting to eavesdrop on her friends' conversation.

'We have to get to them,' Faith whispers back to Roxanne.

'Get to what?' Heidi blurts out, and not at all quietly. Roxanne slaps her hand across her own forehead in dismay as Heidi's voice echoes around the cave.

The raven squawks loudly, flapping its wings as it soars into the air. Faith hastily whispers something to her young friends. Roxanne and Heidi dash towards the opposite end of the room, while Faith stands back against the wall.

'Woohoo! Over here you stupid fat bird!' Heidi shouts, waving her arms to get the raven's attention.

The bird's squinty black eyes glare at the schoolgirls as they jump in the air and clap their hands loudly, causing an unwanted commotion. The raven loses interest in Faith as it hovers in the direction of the two leaping girls.

'What now?' Heidi whispers from the corner of her mouth as the bird approaches.

Roxanne tries to think. 'I guess we just have to keep it occupied until Faith...' she screams, rolling across the floor as the agile bird dives at them unexpectedly, narrowly missing her head.

Roxanne sits upright against the wall, rubbing her grazed arm. The next thing she knows, Heidi also tumbles along the ground towards her.

'Ooof,' Heidi puffs, crashing into Roxanne with a thud. 'This ground is even more uncomfortable than it looks,' she says, sitting up while holding her back in agony. Her attention returns to the air as the evil bird hovers threateningly above them. The two frightened girls shuffle along the wall as the raven flaps ever closer. They come to a halt as they find themselves huddled in the corner of the cave, trapped by their predator, with nowhere to hide.

CHAPTER 33

I think it's gone,' Jasmine whispers into Kyle's ear as the pair crouch anxiously behind a large rock at the base of the hollow tree. As Jasmine cautiously raises her head to get a better view, Kyle suddenly yanks her back down.

'I think it's coming back,' he says under his breath, as the distant sound of something heavy rolling across the ground gets closer. They both peer vigilantly around the rock that they conceal themselves behind. They observe as the huge spider returns, leaning on a round boulder and pushing it around the floor.

'Jaz, what's it doing?' Kyle asks, confused.

'I have no clue,' she responds, also looking bewildered at the spider's strange actions. 'We'll have to wait here until it's gone again, and when we have a chance, we have to move quickly.'

A hole in the ground, the size of a manhole, lies a few metres away from the friends' hiding place and could be the only suitable means of escape.

Kyle retracts his head behind the rock while Jasmine watches in silence as the arachnid performs its extraordinary dance with the boulder. She gasps in disbelief as the strong spider rolls the stone into the opening in the ground. She withdraws her head behind the rock in dismay.

'What's up?' Kyle asks, not witnessing what has just taken place.

'That hole,' Jasmine replies in a whisper. 'We might not be able to use it anymore.'

As the spider retreats down a passageway, made entirely of tree bark and intertwined branches, Kyle and Jasmine speedily depart their hiding place.

'Quick, Kyle,' Jasmine whispers. 'We have to move this stone so we can get out of here.' The comrades flatten the palms of their hands against the boulder and push as hard as they can. The stone sphere wobbles slightly, but it's too heavy for them to dislodge.

Jasmine grabs Kyle and pulls him behind the boulder, concealing themselves as the spider emerges once more. They shuffle around the boulder as the spider moves across the room. They lean against the round rock, waiting for the terrifying arachnid to leave. They can hear it clicking and rustling, but they dare not look in fear of being spotted.

A look of disgust appears on Jasmine's face. She raises her hand and wipes away a blob of gunge, which has splattered onto the top of her head. Fear suddenly pounds in her chest. She gulps hard, tilting her head slowly backwards. She screams, leaping away as the spider peers down from on top of the boulder. Kyle hastily scrambles away from the boulder, clinging onto Jasmine, a few feet from the deadly spider. Their hearts thud as the spider remains eerily motionless, its four tremendous black eyes glinting with evilness as it stares at the terrified friends.

Jasmine attempts to back away at an incredibly slow pace. She shrieks, diving out of the way, Kyle leaping in the opposite direction, as the arachnid suddenly springs towards them. Kyle puffs as he lands hard on the ground, becoming winded. Jasmine stares around helplessly as she finds herself trapped at the perimeter of the room. The spider advances towards its human prey, hungry for a fleshy snack. Jasmine shrieks as the eight-legged beast speedily jumps one hundred and eighty degrees, shooting a thick gluey web that covers her from head to toe, pinning her to the wall.

Jasmine struggles to break free from her constricting, sticky prison, but the web is thick and tough and she can barely move. The spider skulks closer and closer, its huge fangs protruding from its salivating jaws.

'Hey!' Kyle shouts from behind the monster. He throws a jagged chunk of rock that smacks down onto the spider's bulbous body with a squelch. The hungry beast backs away from Jasmine as it turns its attention onto its new, more irritating target.

Kyle turns and runs back towards the staircase that first led them into the room. He grinds to a halt, his eyes widening in shock as the spider springs onto the wall before him. It clicks its long fangs together menacingly as the frightened boy hurriedly retraces his steps. He stops upon reaching the boulder. A gurgling sound from behind him causes his skin to crawl. He gasps in shock as he spins around. The tree spider's mouth hangs open. Thick goo drips from its fleshy jaws as it creeps unnervingly towards him.

Kyle gulps, flattening himself against the stone as the creature approaches. The air falls deadly silent as the spider stands incredibly still, blood-lust filling its row of black eyes. The terrified boy glances down to see a loose stone besides his feet. He quickly leans forwards and scoops the rock in his small hands. The spider appears to glare with annoyance as Kyle extends his weapon above his head for protection.

The arachnid pounces unexpectedly. Kyle barely manages to release the rock in time before dropping to the ground to avoid the monster's attack. The large stone connects with the tree spider's gruesome head, disorientating the beast and causing it to fall off balance. The dizzy arachnid slams hard into the large boulder, clinging to it as the round rock becomes dislodged and rolls out of the hole in the ground. Kyle watches as the stone rolls. A squelchy, bursting sound fills the tree as the heavy boulder squashes the arachnid beneath.

Kyle pauses for a brief moment, making sure that the spider can't move from underneath the boulder. After noticing a forming puddle of thick, green blood, evidently from the spider's squashed abdomen, he dashes across to his imprisoned friend.

'Jaz, are you OK?' he cries as he reaches the mass of sticky cobwebs. Jasmine is unable to reply as the web seals her mouth tightly shut. Kyle glances around for a way to release his friend. Dashing across to the wall, he grasps hold of a substantial, protruding twig. Bending it with all his might, the branch suddenly flings across the room as it snaps with a loud crack. After retrieving the branch, he returns to Jasmine.

'Don't worry, Jaz, I'll get you out!' he tells her confidently as he commences to prise the tough, gooey cobwebs from his captured companion.

CHAPTER 34

'Faith, help!' Heidi screeches from her huddled position in the corner of the cave, as the raven dives at the two schoolgirls. The bird squawks with infuriation as a large bone hurtles through the air, soaring past its snapping beak.

'You're going to have to move,' Faith yells to her young friends as she reaches inside the cage, retrieving yet another bone and flinging it at the raven. Roxanne grabs Heidi by the hand. Both girls scramble to their feet as the feathered fiend becomes distracted by Faith's bone tossing skills.

'What are we going to do?' Heidi asks nervously as the raven dodges yet another flying bone. As Faith reaches for the skeleton's humerus to use as a projectile, an inscribed bronze plaque beneath the bones catches her eye. Roxanne and Heidi watch as Faith wipes the plaque free from bones. Faith stares inquisitively as she begins to read the inscription aloud.

'Control thy mind, defeat thy foe.' Heidi appears confused as she stares blankly into the cage.

'What does it mean?' Roxanne shrieks, leaping to the side as the raven dives for her once more.

'I don't know,' Faith replies, grabbing the skull to use as a weapon. The bird squawks, flapping away as a burst of blue light flashes around Faith. Roxanne and Heidi tumble to the ground, as if propelled by a powerful force field. They gawp silently from the ground, as their seemingly unconscious friend rises into the air, a blue glow pulsating around her. The two schoolgirls watch in amazement as

Faith hovers in mid-air. Heidi suddenly recalls the memory of watching a television show where a magician made his assistant float, and she was certain that she could see the wires. But is certainly no illusion. The vivid blue light that surrounds Faith begins to pulsate, beating faster and faster before shrinking away, as if entering Faith's body. Once Faith has absorbed the luminosity, her eyes flash open with a sparkle of blue rays.

'Faith... are you OK?' Roxanne asks curiously as she and Heidi watch nervously. Faith remains silent as the raven once again soars viciously towards the girls. Faith's eyes swiftly fixate on the plunging bird. Roxanne and Heidi jump, shrieking as the raven suddenly combusts into a frenzy of black feathers. The raven's screech of anguish wafts on the humid air as a mass of singed feathers flutter to the damp ground.

Heidi's mouth hangs open in bewilderment as a single feather settles on the top of her head.

'Faith!' Roxanne cries as the older girl falls from the air and drops wearily to the ground.

'How do you feel?' Heidi asks as she and Roxanne crouch beside their friend.

Faith places her hand on her forehead as she sits upright. 'A little light headed... and a bit nauseous,' she replies, holding her uneasy stomach.

'Wow!' Heidi exclaims as she turns to see the final black feather settle on the ground. 'That bird just went... poof! How did you do that, Faith?'

'Hei, give her a sec,' Roxanne says, placing a caring hand on Faith's knee.

'It's alright,' Faith replies, pushing herself unsteadily to her feet. 'The feeling's starting to wear off.' She walks across to the pile of feathers. 'A strange feeling built up inside me. It was so powerful that I was unable to control it. It just felt right, and I somehow knew that I could destroy the raven with my thoughts alone.'

'That's powerful stuff,' Roxanne says in awe.

'For some reason, I get the feeling that I can't just do it whenever I feel like it. I don't understand it,' Faith responds confoundedly. 'The best way I can describe it is that I now feel like a drained battery.'

'Yeah, but a rechargeable one,' Heidi interjects, as this is the second time that Faith has performed such a profound act.

Momentarily, something across the opposite side of the humid grotto catches the girls' attention. The figure of the monk, standing before the large door vanishes as quickly as it had appeared. Heidi marches across to the sealed wooden door as she notices a camouflaged, circular lever positioned next to it.

'I think we wind this up,' Heidi yells back to her friends as she grabs the handle tightly with both hands.

'Hang on, Hei,' Roxanne says, dashing across to join her. 'It will probably take the strength from both of us to shift this thing.' The two girls grip the handle and begin to heave.

'Heidi, pull harder!' Roxanne orders, her face turning puce with the strain from rotating the stiff lever. As the heavy door rises from the girls' vigorous winding, they become aware of wooden spikes that protrude from the base of the door.

'Hurry up, Faith,' Roxanne yells as the door reaches its limit, only a few feet off the ground. 'I don't know how long we can hold it for.' Faith wobbles, still feeling rather dizzy from using her powers, and staggers towards the intimidating door. She stops at the foot of the exit, not daring to pass underneath as she stares at the row of hanging spikes.

'Faith!' Heidi shrieks as her arms become weak and the door begins to lower. Realising that this is the only way to move onwards, Faith drops to her hands and knees and passes quickly through the gateway.

'What now?' Heidi pants. 'One of us alone can't hold it open.' Before either of them can think of a solution, the wooden handle suddenly snaps in half. The girls gasp in horror as the door begins to drop, soon to seal them within the cave that will become their grave.

CHAPTER 35

A squat iron box slides briskly underneath the doorway, jamming the falling door and disabling it from closing entirely. With elated surprise, Roxanne and Heidi approach the door.

'Are you two OK?' A familiar voice asks from beyond the doorway.

'Yeah, we're OK,' Roxanne replies, dropping to her knees. She peers through the space between the ground and the spikes that protrude from the door, which have become wedged on the lid of the iron box. Faith assists Roxanne as she squeezes through the gap on her stomach, flattening herself as much as possible so as not to scrape her back on the wooden spikes. As Heidi lowers herself to the ground to follow her friend, she hears Roxanne gasp, followed by the sound someone makes when they are hungry and have seen a delicious snack.

Dragging herself through the tight gap, Heidi's mouth drops open in surprise. The spacious room that they have entered is filled from floor to ceiling with hundreds of crates, boxes and barrels. A few of the crates are slightly open and the contents catch Heidi's eye as Faith helps her from the ground.

Roxanne stands by one of the crates. 'Go on, Roxy, open it,' Heidi says excitedly, her mouth watering at the thought of what she expects to find inside.

'You have to be kidding me!' Roxanne exclaims as she peers inside the slightly ajar box.

'Roxanne, don't be a tease, open it so I can see too,' Heidi scolds impatiently. Roxanne slides her fingers underneath the wooden lid and lifts it off completely. Faith's eyes light up eagerly.

'Wow!' Roxanne exclaims joyfully. 'I've never seen so much junk food in all my life.' The now open box that stands before the girls is packed to the brim with delectable snacks. Crisps of all flavours, doughnuts of all varieties, bottles of fizzy drink, pastries, sweets, chocolates, biscuits, every scrumptious thing they could ever imagine.

'Just in time too,' Heidi says as she places her hands on her hips. 'I think I was about to waste away from starvation.'

After rummaging fiercely through the crate, the three friends slouch against a pile of boxes while they enjoy some much-needed nourishment. They chat about their lives back home, their families and their friends. Faith tells her young companions about her pet cat named Mittens, who takes up most of the space on her bed at night. Heidi giggles, cramming a custard tart into her mouth as Roxanne relays a few select stories to Faith, about fun and mischievous times she and Heidi have shared.

'I once pushed Roxy down some stairs... by accident, of course,' Heidi chuckles, between sips of drink from an unlabelled can. 'Her head went straight through the plaster wall at the bottom. Her mum wasn't best pleased.' Faith looks shocked while trying not to laugh.

'The wall was shoddily built, and luckily I have a tough head,' Roxanne retorts, nudging Heidi as she is about to take another sip from her can. Fizzy drink slops all over Heidi's chin and spills down her neck.

'Oh, that does it!' Heidi bellows, jumping to her feet. She yanks the lid off one of the crates and grabs a large gooey pastry, topped with thick icing and colourful sprinkles. Roxanne shields her head with her hands as the sticky bun soars through the air, splatting in her hair.

'Heidi, you cowbag,' Roxanne laughs as she also springs to her feet. She reaches into a barrel and retrieves a handful of delicious treats. 'Food fight!' she shrieks as she catapults the snacks at her friend.

'Ouch! Watch it, Roxy,' Heidi scolds. 'I think you threw a bar of chocolate.'

'Oh, it was a chocolate key,' Roxanne informs her as a glistening, golden key lies on the ground at Heidi's feet. 'It looks like those chocolate coins you get at Christmas time, but in the shape of a key.'

Faith tilts her head inquisitively as the key glimmers. 'I don't think it is chocolate,' she says thoughtfully, crawling towards the golden object. 'It's a real key, a real golden key.'

'What would a random key be doing in one of these boxes?' Roxanne says as Faith pick up the key.

In the distance, a sudden and tremendous roar thunders from somewhere beyond the room of treats.

'That didn't sound inviting,' Roxanne whispers as the three girls stare over the containers of food, peering into a gloomy tunnel that adjoins the next cave. Heidi gulps hard as they all realise that they must continue onwards, and in order to progress, they must face the source of the terrifying roar.

CHAPTER 36

So, they can't know that you're here?' Jasmine whispers to Kyle, confused, as they peer through the hole in the ground, once plugged by the tree spider's boulder. Below, they watch Heidi, Roxanne and Faith lingering by the crates of junk food.

'No, I already told you,' Kyle whispers back. 'If they see me, the earth will be taken over by evil, or something like that.'

Jasmine looks concerned. 'And it was your monk who told you this?'

'Yeah...' Kyle answers, mystified at Jasmines questioning.

'How are you even sure that you can trust him?' she asks, sitting away from the hole. 'I mean... I haven't even seen this so-called monk.'

'I'm not lying,' Kyle declares defensively, keeping his voice low so that his sister and friends won't overhear their conversation.

'No, I believe you,' Jasmine reassures her young friend. 'I just mean... I wouldn't one hundred percent trust anyone, or anything, down here. But unless we can prove otherwise, I suppose we should follow what he advises.'

The boy and girl return their gaze through the hole. They watch silently as the three girls huddle together, walking towards a murky tunnel that leads from the room that they occupy.

Kyle turns to Jasmine as his sister and her friends vanish into the gloominess of the tunnel. 'We have to follow them,' he tells her. 'We can't risk losing them.' Jasmine nods in agreement. 'Help me down,' Kyle says as he swings his legs through the hole. Jasmine manoeuvres herself behind her young friend, holding him underneath his arms as she helps to lower him safely through.

Kyle's feet gently touch down on top of a pile of the wooden crates. He gasps, wobbling unsteadily. The crates sway beneath his feet as he reaches up to help Jasmine down.

'Whoa!' she exclaims as she lands heavily alongside Kyle and the crates sway further. They hold each other upright as the boxes settles back in place.

'We have to be quiet,' Kyle whispers as he climbs carefully down the tower of wooden containers, helping himself to some choice snacks as he descends, placing them into his pockets for later sustenance. 'And we mustn't lose them.'

After helping Jasmine back to solid ground, the two friends creep towards the black tunnel. They attempt to remain as hushed as possible as they peer into the murkiness.

'Can you see them?' Kyle whispers into Jasmine's ear. Jasmine squints into the gloom, shaking her head, as the only thing that greets her is a sheet of darkness. She takes hold of Kyle's small hand and they begin to skulk side by side down the dark passageway.

'I'm scared of the dark,' Jasmine pants nervously as they become completely consumed by blackness. Neither end of the tunnel can be seen by the naked eye. They continue to walk, occasionally stumbling on loose pieces of rock, hidden in the dark. Suddenly, a speck of light appears in the distance. As the circle of light grows with every step the nervous friends take, the silhouette of the three girls come into focus.

'There they go,' Jasmine says as the figures are consumed by the white light.

'We better get a move on,' Kyle responds, quickening his pace.

Their steps slow once again as they reach the exit of the tunnel. Jasmine's mouth drops open in astonishment as her eyes adjust from the darkness. Below them, a gigantic pit is filled with thousands of cavities. Obscenely obese individuals occupy each crater, as if wedged and unable to free themselves from the ground. At the far end of the pit, a gargantuan giant stands guard. The guardian of the slobs stands tall, towering high above his overweight captives. His moist, green skinned body, is stout and flabby, only a tatty black loincloth just about covering his modesty. In the centre of his wide head, one large, blinking, red eye, keeps watch over his prisoners. Sturdy black chains protrude from a cliff wall behind the beast, securing him in place as if the job has been forced upon him.

'Can you see them?' Kyle gulps as Jasmine leans carefully forward to get a better look. Her eyes scan the pit before her, but the mass of flabby figures cause too much of a distraction.

'There!' Kyle exclaims, pointing as the girls appear in view. The three girls can be seen hurriedly making their way through the chasm, keeping their distance from each of the putrid bodies as they traverse the pit.

'Come on,' Jasmine instructs as she realises how the girls got to the bottom of the chasm. She moves closer to the end of the crater. She swings her legs over the edge, placing her feet firmly onto a solid wooden ladder that leads to the very bottom. As Jasmine descends, Kyle clambers over also. Jasmine gives him a helping hand from the ladder as he reaches the bottom. Turning around, they come face to face with the hoard of festering slobs.

'Don't get too close,' Jasmine warns as they creep along a rocky path in the centre of the cavity. The plump mutants struggle on either side, groaning and drooling as mounds of junk food spills from yet more crates that are placed all around them. In front of Kyle and Jasmine, one of the beast's plump necks stretches from the continued pressure of attempting to reach the delicious food.

Jasmine watches in disgust as the slobs stuff their faces with every treat that they can reach. They continuously gobble the food, as if forever hungry and never satisfied.

'This is sick,' Kyle says, scrunching his nose as morsels of food drop from the ravenous drooling mouths. Tiptoeing past row upon row of gluttonous beasts, the two friends continue to pursue the girls who are now almost out of sight.

'Hang on,' Jasmine instructs, tugging Kyle behind a rock as the girls can be clearly seen ahead.

'What are they planning to do?' Kyle asks worriedly, peeking from behind the rock. His sister and her two friends stand motionless before the soaring guardian. They have reached the end of the path. They must continue onward, but with the colossal giant blocking their way, it's duel or die. Do they have a choice?

CHAPTER 37

O kay, what now?' Roxanne mutters from the corner of her mouth as the friends stare nervously up at the towering giant. The monstrous beast looms high above them, sludge dripping down his slimy green skin.

Faith glances to the side as something catches her eye. The ghostly apparition of the monk fades from before a large, black iron cage. Inside the cage, hundreds of small bats with piercing blue eyes sit on perches, the occasional squeak coming from amongst them.

'I think that might help us in some way,' Faith tells her young companions, both of whom continue to gawp at the bulky guardian. 'Follow me,' Faith instructs, slowly sidestepping towards the bat cage. Hesitatingly turning their attention away from the colossal beast, the two schoolgirls mimic their friend's actions. The giant roars, bearing its sharp fangs as a ball of fire shoots from its central red eye. Heidi screams as the fireball scorches the ground before them. Faith crashes into the other two girls as she stumbles backwards in shocked surprise.

'Ooof,' Heidi puffs as she lands hard on the rocky ground, Roxanne tumbling on top of her.

'We can't get past!' Roxanne exclaims, heaving herself off her friend to notice that a line of blazing fire now surrounds the cage.

'We have to,' Faith replies nervously. 'That cage must be our way out, somehow. It's precious enough for the monster to protect, so we have to reach it!'

As Heidi clambers to her feet, the three girls stare helplessly at the prison of bats which is now shielded by flames. The school girls exchange anxious glances as Faith closes her eyes tightly, concentrating intently on the situation at hand. Heidi's attention turns to the immense tyrant as he growls with annoyance. As Roxanne nudges her in the ribs, Heidi's gaze quickly reverts to Faith. Vibrant blue shimmers emit from Faith's body, surrounding her with an electrified aura.

Roxanne and Heidi watch in wonder as the cage begins to glow, an aqua sheen illumining the black iron bars. Heidi's mouth drops open in amazement as two of the bars begin to bend in opposite directions. The sound of straining metal irritates the giant further. A second burst of fire shoots from its single red eye, soaring directly towards Faith. Roxanne and Heidi scream, hurling themselves to the ground as the ball of fire soars past them. Moments before disaster strikes, Faith holds her arm out straight, her glimmering blue palm turned towards the oncoming fireball.

'Faith!' Heidi shrieks in distress, expecting her friend to burn like a match as the fireball slams into Faith's hand. To the young girls' utmost surprise, the smouldering sphere of raging flames immediately transforms into a solid ball of rock upon encountering Faith's palm. They watch in astonishment as, with a sharp rising of her arm, Faith sends the now dense orb flying high into the air, smashing through the rocky roof of the high cave.

The enormous cyclops roars in sheer rage as Faith collapses to the ground. Roxanne dashes to her side, quickly followed by Heidi. Roxanne's vision becomes fixed on the cage as hundreds of small bats scatter from the open bars. The towering giant writhes and thrusts in his restraints, frantically attempting to break free as the bats swarm towards him.

The girls observe, Heidi watching squeamishly through her fingers, as the cluster of bats flies speedily into the giant's gigantic, gaping mouth.

'What's going on?' Faith asks groggily, slowly propping herself on one elbow. Her attention suddenly focuses on the giant.

'He's going to blow!' Heidi shrieks as the chained guard begins to shake violently. Before they can move, the monster's belly bursts open, like an inflated paper bag being popped with great force.

The three girls squeal, shielding their heads with their arms as the swarm of bats shoot like miniature rockets from the monster's stomach. As the vigorous fluttering fades into the distance, the girls' attention returns to the now hollowed beast. The cyclops roars pitifully, dropping wearily to his knees and then becoming silent. Behind the girls, the festering mob wails and groans as they witness the recent demise of their guardian.

'Look,' Heidi announces, pointing directly into the gaping cavity in the monster's gut.

'Do I have to?' Roxanne answers, her eyes reluctantly following in the direction that her friend is pointing. To their astonishment, a golden door in the cliff-side can now be seen through the belly of the beast. A large keyhole carved in the centre.

'Does this mean what I think it means?' Faith asks dizzily as she fully returns to consciousness. 'We actually have to... climb through that?'

'No time like the present,' Heidi declares, heaving herself to her feet and jogging towards the gory opening.

'Heidi, wait a second!' Roxanne yells after her friend, but it's too late. Heidi reaches up, grabbing a handful of the giant's lumpy flesh. She heaves herself up and into the blood dripping cavity. Holding her nose, and with a look of disgust on her face, she quickly squelches her way through the monster's entrails. Fortunately, it only takes a few seconds to pass through the revolting tunnel before making it to the other side. She breathes a sigh of relief as she reaches the dazzling door. 'Faith, you do have that key we found... right?' she calls back, her voice sounding strange as she holds her nose while shaking excess gore from the soles of her boots.

Faith reaches into her trouser pocket and retrieves the golden key. 'Don't drop it in all that gooey mess,' she warns before flinging the key in Heidi's direction.

Heidi catches the key, barely managing to hold onto it as the key slips through her blood smeared fingers. Faith offers Roxanne a helping hand into the erupted belly of the beast, before she too clambers up and through.

'I've never smelt anything so putrid,' Faith gags as she emerges. Roxanne squeals as she attempts to brush away a few gory entrails that cling to her navy jeans, only to make it worse from the blood that covers her hands.

'I can't really tell if I got anything on mine,' Heidi says, looking down and checking out her red trousers.

'This place really doesn't get any better,' Roxanne moans as Heidi slips the large key into the keyhole. The door opens inwards as the key clicks inside the lock. A look of uncertainty appears on Faith's face as darkness once again greets them beyond the doorway.

'Why are there so many dark doorways in Hell?' Heidi asks no one in particular.

'Do you two hear that?' Faith asks, ignoring Heidi's question as a faint scratching sound can be heard in the gloominess. The three friends hold their breath. They each lightly step into the opening of the tunnel as silently as possible. They stop, listening as intently as they can for any sound within the darkness. Heidi takes another tentative step forwards, looking rather confused.

'I can't hear any...' her words are cut short as an enormous, rotten hand suddenly reaches from the darkness. The grotesque hand hastily wraps around the three girls, clutching them tightly. Their petrified shrieks fade into the distance as the hand wrenches them at a great speed into the uncertain depths of the black doorway.

CHAPTER 38

'What on earth was that?' Jasmine gulps as she and Kyle rush from behind the rock that concealed them from sight.

'Jaz, what just happened?' Kyle asks worriedly. 'I couldn't see properly.'

Jasmine pauses for a moment, thinking of a cover story that won't be quite so shocking to her young friend. 'They went into that passageway behind the dead monster... I... I think a bat flew out and startled them.'

Kyle looks relieved as he hears Jasmine's explanation. 'Well, we'd better hurry, we don't want to lose them,' he says, heading speedily towards the hollowed giant. Jasmine appears nervous as she too reaches the devoured monster, slouching before the exit.

To their complete surprise, the giant's bulky corpse begins to crumble before them. Its moist flesh commences to melt into a congealed slime, its gigantic skeleton disintegrating into a chalky dust.

'I didn't fancy crawling through that, anyway,' Jasmine announces, taking Kyle by the hand as they both nimbly step across the pool of dissolved remains.

'It's a shame we don't have x-ray vision or night goggles,' Kyle says as he and his nervous companion approach the pitch-black entrance of the tunnel. 'Do you think that we should just start walking?' he asks, turning to notice a worried expression across Jasmine's pale face. 'What's wrong?' he asks as Jasmine's uneasiness begins to infect him also.

They both stand silently still as a faint sound from inside the tunnel can be heard in the distance.

'Kyle,' Jasmine whispers from the corner of her mouth. 'Prepare yourself for...' Before she can finish her hushed sentence, the distant sound becomes frighteningly louder, like the sound of long fingernails being scraped along a chalkboard at lightning speed. Kyle's eyes widen in stunned horror as the decaying hand reaches from within the gloom. Jasmine's scream fades from the entrance as the foul hand grasps them, propelling them through the passageway.

The stench of decaying flesh makes Kyle feel queasy as he struggles to break free from the tight grip of the hand. The feeling of motion sickness overwhelms his stomach as the pair hurtle at top speed.

The two friends suddenly, and unexpectedly, tumble from the tunnel. They roll across an uncomfortable gravelly ground before slowing to a halt. Gradually raising their heads, Kyle and Jasmine realise they have entered a completely new realm of the underworld. The surrounding area is stony and dirty. Dank, derelict, boarded houses sit each side of a long street that stretches ahead of them. Broken stone and marble statues scatter the ground. Rain falls hard, soaking everything as far as the eye can see, the occasional flash of purple fork lightening illuminating the dull, stormy sky.

'This place is spooky,' Kyle says in a whispered tone as he picks himself off the hard ground, brushing his light blue jeans free from gravel and dried dirt.

'Now that is bizarre!' Jasmine exclaims, bewildered, running her fingers through her long, red hair. To her surprise, her head is thoroughly dry. She looks confused as the torrential rain continues to pelt, covering her, and everything else in sight.

Kyle also touches his head as he notices Jasmine's confusion. 'This rain doesn't get you wet!' he exclaims, feeling his clothing, which also remains bone dry. 'Wow,' he continues, amazed by this discovery. 'This is so cool. I wish the rain was like this back home.'

Jasmine continues to look mystified. 'It is kind of cool,' she replies. 'Cool, but rather pointless.'

A sudden gust of wind blows Jasmine's hair into a wild jumble of red strands. The friends' mouths drop open in harmony as they witness the terrifying sight before them. A colossal, whirling tornado spins ferociously at the far end of the long street. The grey twister slithers like a snake across the ground, uprooting statues and thrusting them high into the night air. The frightened couple watch in fear, helpless as the cyclone begins on its destructive path towards them.

CHAPTER 39

'This is not good!' Roxanne exclaims, staring out from the downstairs window in one of the sturdier houses situated on the dark, stormy street. Heidi and Faith rush to join their friend. From behind the windowpane, the girls watch the terrifying tornado spinning out of control at the far end of the gloomy avenue.

'Okay,' Roxanne says to the other two, focusing her attention away from the world outside, 'we need to find whatever it is that we're looking for, and fast!'

'Do we even know *what* we're looking for?' Heidi asks, her eyebrows raised as she gazes around the spacious living room. Faith appears puzzled as she too surveys the room for any clues.

'I have no idea,' she replies to Heidi's question. 'I don't even know if we *should* be looking for anything. As I said, another monk appeared for a split second in this window, that's why we came in. There must have been a reason for him guiding us in here.'

Behind them, the sound of footsteps on the vinyl flooring startles the girls. They huddle silently, watching the dark kitchen doorway with nervous anticipation as the plodding looms closer. As the source of the footsteps comes into view through the doorway, the girls' expressions change from worried to relieved confusion. A teenage boy and teenage girl stand in the kitchen doorway. The chandelier suspended in the centre of the front room illuminates their faces as it occasionally flickers with a dull yellowy glow. The girls remain silent, not exactly knowing what to say, or what to expect.

'Are... are you new?' The boy asks timidly, the girl holding onto his arm uneasily. The young couple gingerly take a step into the room. The three girls look at each other in bewilderment.

'New?' Faith finally replies, sounding mystified.

The boy and girl move a fraction closer. 'Well,' the girl says, a slight quiver in her voice. 'It's only been us here for...' she raises her eyes to the ceiling as if she is trying to recall, 'I can't actually remember how long it's been. It seems like forever. I can hardly remember my life on earth anymore.'

'What did you do to end up here?' Heidi asks inquisitively.

The girl seems annoyed with herself. 'Gary and I burgled a few houses,' she says glancing regretfully at her companion, who reciprocates her remorseful look. 'We were hard up for money, and we knew stealing was wrong, but it felt like we didn't have a choice. The last time we did it, the police caught us in the house of an old couple. We both panicked and fled through the back door and into the street. That's when the lorry...' Heidi doesn't know quite what to say as the girl pauses, unable to continue.

Gary places his arm around her, comfortingly. 'That last night is the only real memory either of us have of our previous lives,' he says sombrely. 'Wendy can't even remember her own family.'

'That must be awful,' Faith gasps, imagining the thought of not being able to remember her friends and family.

'This is why people shouldn't break the law,' Heidi blurts out. Roxanne nudges her in the ribs. 'What?' Heidi snaps at her friend. 'It's true.'

'It seems like they've learnt their lesson,' Faith tells Heidi, attempting to raise the current level of compassion as she walks slowly towards the young couple. 'So, you're trapped in this house, forever?' she asks curiously.

Gary and Wendy exchange troubled glances. 'That's not the worst part,' Wendy informs the girls.

At that very moment, the windows and door of the house begin to shudder.

'The tornado!' Roxanne exclaims as Heidi races to the window once again.

'That's the worst bit,' Gary says, looking uneasy as the roof also starts to shake.

'What do you mean by worst?' Faith yells, the noise from the violent gale reaching a crescendo. Heidi squeals as the twister spins closer and closer with each passing second.

'Every few hours the tornado comes,' Wendy shouts, moving in closer as Heidi re-joins the huddle. 'It tears everything on this street to pieces, including the people who are stuck in these houses.' Heidi looks horrified as Wendy continues to explain the situation. 'After the cyclone has destroyed everything and everyone, things piece back together and return to normal. As we are unable to leave, all we can do is sit and wait for it to happen over and over again, forever.'

Heidi screams as the large window suddenly shatters into hundreds of sparkling shards. The imposing wind gusts around the room. The girls hold onto each other fretfully, having no idea how they can escape the certain doom of the ferocious, spiralling tornado.

CHAPTER 40

'We must do something. We have to get out of here!' Faith yells as the girls remain huddled. Gary and Wendy linger motionless, knowing that nothing can be done to influence the outcome of the traumatic situation.

'Where's a monk when you need one?' Heidi bellows as the friends stare around the room, in search of something, anything that might help.

'Faith!' Roxanne shrieks as a blue hue attracts her attention. In a dusty corner of the room, a pile of old bones rests in the shadows. 'That's why we were lured in here.' She makes a dash towards the dark corner of the living room.

Faith and Heidi pursue Roxanne as they too realise that the bones of the third monk lie across from them.

'Go on, Faith, touch them,' Heidi pleads, her long blonde hair blowing frantically in the violent gale. Faith crouches in the shadows. She closes her eyes as she hurriedly places her open palms directly onto the pile of bones. But, it's already too late. Before Faith can begin to glow, the entire roof of the house lifts off with an almighty snapping of timber.

The group of helpless friends have no time to utter a single word before they too are ripped out of the house with tremendous force. Roxanne flies through the air, screaming when she catches her leg on the shattered wall of the house as she exits. Heidi's intense screams are muffled by the ferocious commotion of the cyclone. Her long hair wraps around her face, leaving her blind, as she soars through the stormy night sky. Not that the sense of sight would help her situation at any rate. Faith too remains helpless. Even if she were able to concentrate, would she even wield enough power to assist?

Silence reclaims the street as the tornado's supremacy begins to fade, the spiralling wind dispersing into the miserable, rain filled sky. Five bodies lie motionless on the rocky ground. Gary and Wendy lie hand in hand, as they always do. Faith, Heidi and Roxanne have been separated by the fierce gale. The raindrops caress their silent, still bodies. The entire street is plagued with hundreds of motionless people, every single one of them, dead.

Chapter 41

As the blustery wind begins to cease, Kyle and Jasmine's uncontrollable twirling slows as they drift deep inside the depths of the cyclone. Their eyes remain tightly shut, not daring to witness the horror that surrounds them. The friends remain hand in hand, completely disoriented, as their feet surprisingly touch down onto solid ground once again.

'Can I look now?' Kyle asks shakily, still gripping onto Jasmine's hand with his remaining strength.

'I think we're safe,' Jasmine replies wearily. 'Well… as safe as we can be in Hell, I suppose.'

A bright, open space, is the first thing to greet Kyle's blurred vision as he reluctantly opens his eyes. The two friends now stand in the centre of a spacious, circular room. Its bright lighting and light beige walls, ceiling and floor exude a peaceful atmosphere, compared to where they have just come from. Their new scenery is entirely the opposite of what they expected.

'Hey,' Kyle blurts, stepping away from Jasmine as he notices a stone slab protruding from the wall beside them. Jasmine follows her young companion across to the large plaque. She gazes down in surprise as the ground directly beneath her feet lowers slightly, followed by a clicking sound. Five tiles, each one a different chalky colour, rest beneath the plaque on the wall. As Jasmine retracts her foot, the pale blue tile on which she stood raises back inline.

'I don't get it,' Kyle says, confused, while he studies the stone slab before him. Jasmine's attention also turns to the plaque. She appears flummoxed by a drawing scrawled upon it. All the colours of the rainbow are painted in a sort of chart. An elaborate sketch of a 3-headed beast has been painted next to the chart of colours. The first head is that of a vicious werewolf, baring its deadly fangs. The central head seems to be some bizarre species of bird. Its beak is long and thin, similar to a flamingo's, only longer and more lethal looking and the bird's feathers are a deep blue. The third head is Jasmine's worst nightmare, a snake. Its head is thick and scaly. A long, black forked tongue protrudes from its venomous jaws. The painting of the strange 3-headed creature is bright and eye catching, although none of the heads have eyes, just black sockets.

Jasmine shudders as she backs away from the wall. Glancing back to the ground, she takes notice of the coloured tiles once more. The blue tile that she stood on is situated next to a pale pink tile. Next to that, a light green one, then a yellow and lastly a red.

'I guess we must be missing something,' Kyle says, looking at Jasmine with a helpless expression on his young face.

The sound of a sliding mechanism from above suddenly grabs their undivided attention. A wide section of the roof shifts to one side, leaving a hollow in the ceiling.

'Well, we better find whatever it is we're missing, and quick,' Jasmine whispers nervously as something begins to lower from the opening in the centre of the room.

They stare upwards, horror stricken as the three-headed abomination from the painting descends before them. Four sturdy barbed wires lower the apparently dormant monster into the room.

Jasmine grips onto Kyle's arm. The friends stand immobile, not daring to make a sound. The cumbersome brute touches down and rests motionless in the centre of the room. For a moment nothing happens, as if the room has been frozen in time.

Kyle's eyes widen in terror as the beast begins to twitch. 'Uh oh,' he utters in horror, as the monster gradually awakens from its slumber. Kyle presses himself flat against the wall as the fiend's three heads roar, squawk and hiss in unison like a chaotic choir. As the youngsters stare in fright, the unnerving wild animal noises resonate through the tension filled air. The creature's eyes are hollow and black, precisely as depicted in the drawing.

'There aren't any doors!' Kyle exclaims, realising they are trapped within the solid circular room. Before Jasmine can respond, the serpent's long black tongue shoots from its deadly jaws, promptly wrapping around the friends' waists. Jasmine screams, struggling to break free from the tight grip of the moist tongue. It's no use, her arms are pinned against her body and she is unable to budge, even an inch.

'Help me!' Kyle yells in panic to no one in particular, as there is no one around who can aid them. The situation seems hopeless. The snake's eye hollows glow a bright yellow as it tugs the suffering friends closer towards its ravenous, formidable jaws.

Jasmine gazes pitifully at her young companion, her eyes tearing as she accepts her fate. 'I think this is goodbye.'

CHAPTER 42

'Jaz, what can we do?' Kyle shrieks, panic stricken by the three headed Hell beast.

'I can't move!' Jasmine screams in reply, struggling frantically to break free. As Kyle too thrashes furiously, the slime from the snake's black tongue lubricates his left arm and it slips free. He hastily begins to pound the serpent's grotesque tongue with his small, clenched fist. He hits as hard as he can, but it's no use. The serpent doesn't flinch, not even slightly.

Both the wolf and the bird heads snap at the confined friends as the snake reels them closer, lifting them off the ground.

'I think we've had it!' Jasmine whimpers, accepting her doom. As his punching didn't help, an alternative idea floods Kyle's head. He cranes his neck forwards, his mouth wide. The snake hisses in pain as Kyle sinks his teeth into the slimy black tongue with vigour.

Jasmine squeals as the tongue hastily unravels from around them and they fall to the ground. She puffs as she lands heavily on the floor. Kyle spits out a mouthful of black goo as he quickly heaves himself to his feet.

'What are we going to do?' Kyle asks, wiping away the remnants of gunk from around his mouth with the back of his sleeve.

Jasmine grabs her young friend by the hand and sprints to the painted stone slab and floor tiles. 'We have to figure this out,' she tells him in a panic as she studies the plaque intensely. 'This has to be the answer, and we have to do something quickly!'

The friends once again study the painting of the demon. Kyle glances behind them to make sure that the real thing is still recovering from his attack. Something suddenly strikes Jasmine as being rather odd. The painting depicts the monster's three heads as having black pits in place of its eyes, although she recalls the snake's piercing yellow eyes. She turns curiously back to face the large monster. To her surprise the beast's six eyes are hollow and dark.

'Kyle, we have to discover the eye colour of each head,' she whispers in his ear so that the creature is none the wiser to their plan.

'Huh?' Kyle responds inquisitively. 'Why do we need to know that?'

'I'll explain once we find out,' she answers, glancing uneasily at the roaring Hell beast. 'Here's what we're going to have to do,' she says, moving in closer, shielding her face as she once again whispers into Kyle's ear.

The creature's three heads fall silent, each of them watching suspiciously as the two friends secretively converse below, the binding wire stopping it from moving closer. The beast growls with irritation as Kyle abruptly dashes to the left-hand side of the room. He stands underneath the head of the werewolf and begins to hurl abuse as loudly as he can. The attention of the bird is distracted as Jasmine mimics Kyle's taunting from the centre of the room.

'Come on, you brainless bird!' she yells, waving her arms frantically over her head. The bird opens its long beak, shrieking an ear-piercing screech as a ball of fire grows within its open jaws.

Jasmine's eyes widen in horror, taken aback by the sight of the flaming ball. The bird's eyes illuminate with a blue sparkle as the fireball shoots from its open beak.

'Jasmine!' Kyle yells as the flaming sphere soars towards his friend. Jasmine leaps to the side, tumbling across the floor as the spot where she had been standing becomes scorched in flames.

'One to go,' she reminds herself as she scrambles quickly to her feet and joins Kyle. 'Here pooch!' she hollers, dancing a little jig as she attempts to aggravate the werewolf. The wolf snarls, bearing its blood-stained incisors. The beast's eyes shine a deep red as it becomes enraged by Kyle and Jasmine's relentless provoking.

'Yellow, blue and red,' Jasmine repeats to herself, grabbing Kyle by the arm and speedily making her way across to the multi-coloured floor panels.

As they reach the tiles, Jasmine hastily steps on the yellow panel. The yellow tile sinks an inch before clicking into place. She then presses her foot onto the blue tile, which also clicks into position. Lastly, she treads onto the red square. To her surprise the panels shift back into their original positions.

'Did anything happen?' Kyle asks, glancing around the room while keeping one eye fixed on the chained monster.

'I don't think so,' Jasmine responds in a deflated tone. Suddenly, Kyle shoves his friend hard. The snake's long black tongue slams into the wall where she had been standing just a split second before. As the tongue withdraws into the serpent's deadly mouth, the companions stare around the room, attempting to figure out their next move.

'Maybe we have to stand on them in the correct order,' Kyle suggests, thinking aloud as he studies the painting. He continues to talk to himself. 'The wolf is first, and he has red eyes.' Kyle quickly moves to the red tile, stamping onto it and causing it to descend and click into place. 'Jaz, what colour eyes did the bird have?' he inquires as he sees that the bird's head is in the centre. Jasmine jogs to the blue floor panel and steps onto it.

'Hopefully this will work,' Jasmine mutters to herself as she then stands onto the yellow tile.

The friends pause in suspense as the last tile clicks into position. They glance uneasily at each other, as all three heads begin to wail in an unholy chorus. The thick wire that binds the creature start to vibrate uncontrollably. The huge beast roars in defeat as the shackles rip from its bulky body. Kyle and Jasmine duck, covering their heads as gooey fragments of monster soar through the air.

As the room falls silent, the traumatised companions uncover their heads, staring around the room in bewilderment. The once serene room is now splattered with a dark green ooze, like a gory finger painting. The sturdy wire drops from the opening in the ceiling, splashing upon impact with the slime covered floor. Jasmine and Kyle remain speechless as a square platform, which reminds Kyle of a magic carpet, mysteriously descends from the opening above them. As the lift comes to a halt, the friends step vigilantly towards it. They tiptoe across the grisly clutter, Jasmine being careful not to get any additional monster remains on her trousers.

'Do you think we should get on?' Kyle asks nervously as they reach the lift, which hovers above the ground like an impressive magic illusion.

'I don't think we have much choice,' Jasmine responds unenthusiastically as she heaves herself up onto the floating platform. Kyle springs up beside her, causing the lift to sway.

'I don't have a great feeling about where we're heading,' Jasmine whimpers as the lift begins to rise, transporting them into the unwelcoming darkness above.

CHAPTER 43

The dismal street remains silent and still as the heavy rain continues to fall. The scattered bodies lay cold and lifeless alongside the mass of debris, which blows around in the now gentle breeze.

The chunks of broken buildings begin to lift off the ground, swirling around and fitting back together like a gigantic 3D jigsaw puzzle. The widespread corpses also begin to shift. They rise off the wet ground, gliding through the night sky as they each become airborne. The destruction of the fierce tornado pieces back together as the bodies re-enter the buildings from where they came. The walls rebuild and the shattered windowpanes remould without so much as a scratch on them, as if they had never been broken.

Faith's, Heidi's and Roxanne's lifeless bodies float upwards, swooping through the opening in the top of the house. The corpses of Gary and Wendy join the three girls, all settling on the living room floor. As tables and chairs mend themselves, the roof re-attaches and the house becomes a whole once more. In a matter of minutes, the demolished street is entirely repaired.

Gary and Wendy begin to stir. As they both sit upright, returning to normal as they always do, they notice the three girls face down on the floor. Wendy crawls towards Roxanne and turns her motionless body over.

'Hello,' she calls softly. 'It's alright now, you're OK.'

As Heidi comes too and shuffles onto her back, Gary wipes her long, blonde hair from across her face. 'Oh, my poor head,' she whimpers as Gary helps her to sit up.

'It's your first time,' Gary says. 'Don't worry, you'll get used to it.'

These words snap Heidi from her vertigo. 'I don't think so!' she exclaims as she stands up quickly, her head spinning with dizziness as she does so. 'I am *never* going through that again. *Never!*'

Wendy looks at Gary doubtfully. 'We only have a few hours until the next one comes,' she reminds their new companions as Roxanne and Faith also return to consciousness.

Heidi's eyes glint as she remembers something important. 'The bones!' she yelps, rushing to the shadowy corner of the room. 'Roxanne, help Faith,' she commands while checking that the old bones are situated where they were before the tornado's attack.

Gary and Wendy assist their dizzy acquaintances to the corner of the room. They guide Faith over to the pile of bones that Heidi guards like precious treasure. Upon reaching the bones, Faith kneels, groggily placing her hands upon them. The group stands back, watching as bright blue sparkles begin to emit from the ancient skeleton.

Faith becomes engulfed in radiant sapphire shimmers as the monk's power washes over her entire body like a magical tidal wave. A blue aura remains around Faith as the illuminating colour seeps into her like a sponge soaking up water. Gary and Wendy watch in amazement as Faith appears to be lifted back to her feet by a strong, invisible force. The four youngsters spectate as Faith's feet leave the floor. She hovers slightly above the ground, her eyes closed and the fuzzy aura vanishing as it absorbs into her body. Moments later and Faith's feet gently touch onto solid ground once again. A couple of seconds pass before her eyes open in a flash of blue crackles.

'Faith, how do you feel?' Heidi asks, approaching her friend with caution.

Faith looks down at her hands. Blue sparks crackle across her palms and down her fingers. 'I feel… potent,' she replies with vigour.

'Huh?' Roxanne asks, seeming confused.

'She means powerful,' Heidi explains, moving closer to Faith. 'Faith, we need to find a way out of here.'

'You can't leave this house now,' Wendy pipes up. 'Once you're in here, there's no escaping. Like us, I'm afraid you're now trapped, forever.'

CHAPTER 44

Like Hell we are!' Heidi blurts, heatedly. 'We haven't come all this way to get stuck in here with you two.' Gary and Wendy gaze solemnly at the ground. Heidi gasps, realising how her words must have sounded. 'I'm sorry,' she apologises. 'I didn't mean it like that. The reason we have come here in the first place is to destroy the Devil himself... or herself... or itself... or whatever it actually is.' Gary and Wendy listen intently as Faith interjects, relaying the tale of how, and why, they were transported into the Abyss.

'So, does that mean if you succeed... we will be freed?' Wendy asks hopefully.

'To be honest,' Faith says, 'I'm not exactly sure *what* will happen. All I do know is that it will change the human world and everything in it. But I have a feeling that you will be just fine.'

Roxanne turns away and walks across the room. 'Well, I guess we'll see what happens *when* we succeed!' she says while beginning to search for a way out of the house.

'Wait a second,' Gary says, something suddenly returning to his memory. 'There's a door in the basement,' he tells the girls. 'Neither of us has been down there for... well, for... years I suppose.'

'Oh yeah, that's right,' Wendy says, also recalling the door. 'We tried to open it hundreds of times when we first ended up in this horrible house, but it wouldn't budge an inch, so we finally gave up.'

'The door is only small,' Gary continues, 'more like a solid metal hatch really.'

Roxanne walks back to Faith. 'Do you think *you* can open it?' she asks optimistically, hoping that Faith's powers could be the answer.

'I won't know until I try,' Faith replies. She turns to Gary. 'Will you take us to it?' Gary nods before taking his girlfriend by the hand and leading the three friends into the kitchen.

'Down there,' Gary points to a dusty wooden door at the far end of the gloomy pantry.

'Can we come with you?' Wendy asks as the three girls move towards the door.

Heidi steps closer to Wendy. 'Of course you can,' she says understandingly. 'But you have to be careful. You think it's bad in here, well... it's much worse out there. Trust me.'

The couple glance nervously at each other as they follow the three girls through the creaky basement door and down the cold stone steps.

'I'm guessing this must be it?' Faith asks, spotting a round, iron hatch half way up the back wall of the basement. Gary nods as he and Wendy stand close together, waiting with anticipation.

Roxanne and Heidi stand back, giving Faith space to concentrate. They wait silently as Faith closes her eyes and takes a slow, deep breath.

'What's she doing?' Wendy whispers curiously, leaning towards Heidi.

'Shush,' Heidi quietly replies, her finger pressed to her lips. 'This could be intense.'

They all stand in a hushed group, observing as Faith prepares. Wendy gasps as apparitions of blue flames scorch Faith's feet. With her eyes remaining closed, Faith places the palms of her hands onto the solid hatch. The skin on her hands shifts to a pale blue shade. The colour begins to transfer onto the small door. Moments later, the entire hatch is glowing with a blue hue that now begins to sparkle.

The others move aside as Faith takes a few steps backwards, her eyes still shut tight. Sapphire flames manifest around the edges of the door and sparks of intense blue electricity crackles at Faith's fingertips. Everyone, apart from Faith, covers their heads as the iron door flings off its hinges in a burst of blue bolts. Heidi screams, shutting her eyes and bracing for impact, as the door soars directly towards her. After a moment of silence, Heidi opens her eyes while turning back to her powerful ally. Heidi's eyes open wide in surprise as the heavy iron door hovers in mid-air, merely inches from where she stands.

Faith's eyes are now wide open and shine a bright blue. She appears to concentrate with ease, staring at the hatch door, seemingly unfazed by Heidi's near-death experience. The friends watch in complete silence as Faith waves her hand majestically before the solid metal door. The hatch door begins to wither and melt, transforming into liquid metal and splashing onto the ground, forming a shiny puddle.

Once the task is complete, Faith closes her radiating blue eyes. After a couple of seconds, she reopens them, her eyes now her natural shade.

'Faith, are you OK?' Roxanne asks, concerned, placing a hand on her friend's shoulder.

'Strangely, I feel fine,' Faith replies, sounding surprised. 'I don't feel weak like I did the previous times.'

Heidi seems eager at her friend's reaction to the incredible progressing power. 'That might mean you can use your powers easier from now on,' she says optimistically, rubbing her hands together excitedly.

'Let's hope so,' Faith answers with a slight smile, enthusiastic about the prospect of using her powers to assist them when hopelessly in need.

The group turns their attention to the opening in the wall, realising that they now have a possible escape route.

'I feel quite daring now that Faith has our backs,' Heidi announces proudly, walking to the doorway. 'Give me a leg up, Roxy,' she instructs her best friend. Roxanne obliges, grabbing hold of Heidi's ankles and shoving her into the opening above. A narrow, dark tunnel leads from the doorway. Heidi squints, waiting for her eyes to adjust to the dimness. The space around her is uncomfortable and cramped, with just enough room to turn around. 'Not another one of these,' she grumbles to herself, recalling the last time she was almost trapped in such a confined space. 'Give me your hand,' she says, turning and leaning from the dark hole in the wall. Heidi grasps Roxanne by the wrists and tugs her up into the passageway, with some assistance from Faith who hoists from below. Roxanne then takes Heidi's position and helps Faith into the gloomy tunnel.

A loud slamming sound comes from the entrance of the passage as Faith slides her feet through. 'What was that?' she gasps as all light vanishes from the tunnel. She attempts to turn herself around in the restricted space. Unable to successfully manoeuvre herself, she kicks her feet behind her. The soles of her shoes clang on a second metal shutter, which appears to have manifested from thin air and now seals the hole.

'Guys, are you OK?' Roxanne calls.

'Maybe we really aren't allowed to leave,' Wendy's muffled voice replies from the other side. 'Don't worry about us, we're used to it. If you complete your task, we'll hopefully be set free.'

Determination gleams in Faith's eyes. 'We *will* complete it, and when we do you will be saved,' she assures the abandoned couple.

With Heidi leading, the girls crawl in single file through the darkness. Gripping onto each other's ankles, so as not to lose one another, they continue along the uncomfortably claustrophobic tunnel.

CHAPTER 45

I guess we have to go through sometime,' Kyle whispers to Jasmine as the friends stand in a narrow room in front of a hefty, wooden door. The lift that brought them here now fits into the floor. The only exit to the room is the door that they stand before.

Worried expressions cross the friends' faces as they both grasp the door's bulky handle. Constant screams and wailing can be heard from the other side. The persistent screams fade in, one by one, becoming louder and then ending abruptly. Stomach churning groans of misery accompany the screams like a depressing choir.

'Okay,' Jasmine says, taking a deep breath. 'Let's do it.' They push hard on the heavy door. As it slowly opens, the friends' mouths drop open as the horrific scene confronts them.

A vast, circular pit is situated in the centre of the spherical cavern, only a narrow ledge running the grotto's perimeter, giving very little space to traverse safely. The pit is filled to the brink with stinking, tar-like sludge, reminding Kyle of a gigantic mud wrestling pit. Thousands of bodies slop in the cavity, unable to break free as the filth appears to hold them in place like cement.

A thick black fog lingers far above the putrid, sludge filled crater. The friends gaze upwards as the faint sound of screaming comes from above. As the shrieks become louder, a group of bodies plummet through the dark mist. Mud splatters through the air as the helpless individuals splash hard into the pit of thick muck. Jasmine gasps as the people return to the surface, steaming dirt soldering to their skin.

A second door is situated in the wall of the cave, opposite to where the friends stand.

'Follow me,' Jasmine instructs Kyle, attempting to keep the quivering in her voice to a minimum so as not to worry her young companion. 'Stay close to the wall, and whatever you do, don't fall in.'

Jasmine steps onto the narrow ledge that leads around the perimeter of the pit. With their backs flat against the uneven wall, they shuffle carefully along. Jasmine shudders at the horrific sound of the tortured victims as she slowly and carefully sidesteps, not daring to stop for fear of losing balance.

'This is easier than I thought it would be,' Kyle announces, feeling relieved as the exit becomes nearer with each step they take. Jasmine's attention suddenly turns to the mud below Kyle's feet. Her heart leaps into her throat as a rotting corpse abruptly lurches from beneath the rancid slop, unexpectedly latching one of its decaying hands around Kyle's ankle. Kyle yelps in horror, attempting to grip the wall as the mangled body tugs on his jeans. Jasmine clutches onto her young friend's hood, yanking him back while praying that her efforts won't send them both toppling into the festering pool.

'Jaz, don't let me go!' Kyle screams, terrified for his life as the slimy carcass tightens its grasp on his leg. Using both hands now, Jasmine clasps onto her friend with as much vigour as she can muster, not daring to move for fear of slipping into the mud below. It's a tug of war, with Kyle's life literally in her hands.

CHAPTER 46

I can't take much more of this!' Heidi panics, the dark tunnel becoming increasingly claustrophobic, seemly closing in around them as the three girls continue to crawl blindly in single file. 'Ouch!' Heidi complains, rubbing her head as she unexpectedly crashes into the end of the tunnel. She frantically runs her hands across the cold stone wall before her. 'I can't go any further!'

'This better not be as far as it goes,' Roxanne says, alarmed at the thought of being trapped in the confined space.

'Wait a sec,' Heidi instructs her friends as something above catches her eye. A tiny white dot glints in the corner of the tunnel. Upon closer inspection with her fingertips, Heidi realises that the small light shines from the centre of a round button.

Knowing there is no other option, and being quite curious, Heidi puts her finger to the button, concealing the light from sight. A clicking noise comes from beneath the girls as the button is pressed by Heidi's inquisitive finger. The girls' shriek, their stomachs feeling weightless as the bottom of the tunnel immediately drops like a trapdoor.

They only fall a few feet before hitting a hard surface. Although the room that they have fallen into isn't bright, the girls' eyes take a few moments to adjust. They find themselves in a long, gloomy corridor. Large lights hang from the ceiling, flickering on and off while swaying side to side as if a strong breeze blows through the passageway, although the air is still.

The black marble floor is shiny and polished. The hallway stretches in front of them with an open doorway situated at the far end. Metal shutters drape from ceiling to floor on either side of the corridor, like a desolate street comprised of closed shop fronts.

As the girls clamber to their feet, Faith grabs hold of Heidi to stop her from making any sudden movements.

'We should move carefully,' Faith tells her friends. 'Something unexpected is likely to happen when we least expect it. You know what this place is like.' Roxanne nods with compliance before they begin to walk cautiously down the hallway.

'This is so tense,' Heidi whispers, feeling unnerved by Faith's words of warning as they tiptoe along the silent corridor.

'This can't be good,' Roxanne says as a clicking sound echoes through the passage, followed by the steady rising of the metal shutters.

The girls halt in their tracks, crowding together as solid steel bars can be seen beyond the lifting metal covers. Heidi's eyes open wide, her body trembling with terror at the sight that lies before them. Prison cells are situated on both sides of the room. Some are vacant, while others hold horrors from the worst of nightmares. The girls stare around the hallway, frozen to the spot with sheer dread. The shutters appear to have been sound-proof. Roxanne's eyes fix upon a man who screams in anguish as he is consumed by flames. The smell of singed hair and cindering flesh fills the passage, making the girls feel nauseous. Roxanne watches as the man crashes around his cell, forced to remain in the confined space as he burns eternally, with no hope of ever extinguishing his torture.

A middle-aged woman, begging for help, captures Faith's attention. The woman pleads frantically, her arms stretched through the bars of her cell. Unsure what to do, Faith remains motionless, Heidi griping tightly onto her arm. The friends scream as bolts of lightning suddenly strike the imprisoned woman from all sides, with an intense electrifying explosion. The whites of Faith's eyes glint as they reflect the bright electricity bolts. The woman screams in agony as the electricity scorches her skin. Rancid smoke fills the cell and the odour of burning flesh invades the friends' nostrils even more so than before.

As the lightning bolts cease, Faith remains speechless as she witnesses the sizzling, charcoaled corpse of the woman draped motionless across the prison bars. Faith turns away in disgust as the body vanishes in a cloud of grey smoke. Her eyes lock onto the sight that seizes Heidi's attention. Opposite the cage of the burning man, a group of three people occupy a larger cell. Instead of metals bars, this prison has a thick sheet of glass that blocks the escape of the captives.

The three individuals, one middle-aged man, a young man in his early twenties and a woman in her early thirties, huddle together in one corner of the room. The prison in which they sit is overgrown with weeds and plants. Twigs and branches sprout from the solid brick walls that construct three of the cell walls. The people stare nervously around the room, as if searching for something with their eyes.

Suddenly, the woman shrieks, terror filling her eyes as she springs to her feet. She hurdles over foliage while dodging the protruding branches with ease, as if she has performed this exact routine a million times before. Heidi,

Faith and Roxanne's attention is now firmly fixated on the glass-fronted cage.

Heidi's skin crawls as a gigantic king cobra slithers from a hollowed tree stump. She dashes across to the glass panel. 'Run!' she yells, banging her small fists on the glass. The two men don't appear to hear her thumping while keeping their eyes locked on the serpent. Heidi stops pounding as the snake suddenly freezes. It rises off the ground, supporting itself with its lower body. Heidi gasps as the snake turns its scaly head towards her, its small, evil eyes gleaming bright red. The younger man sees his chance and darts in the woman's tracks while the snake's attention is elsewhere.

Faith grabs Heidi and pulls her away from the cage as the snake focuses once again on its prey. The middle-aged man searches for a way to bypass the serpent, but that time has passed as the reptile is now far too close. The man huddles in terror in the corner of the room, his arms shielding his face.

Heidi gasps, louder this time, as the towering snake springs forwards, thrusting its long, poisonous fangs deep into the man's arm. The younger man and woman witness the horror from the opposite end of the cage, not daring to utter a single word. They continue to watch as the scaly serpent relentlessly bites its helpless, cowering victim. Faith covers her mouth in shocked disgust as the snake finally slithers away through a hole in the ground. The man's face, arms and neck are covered in deep, oozing, puncture wounds. He appears stunned as he sits motionless.

'Come on,' Roxanne says. 'I can't watch anymore, let's get out of here.' Taking Heidi by the hand, Roxanne walks alongside Faith towards the open door at the end of the corridor. Heidi glances back, quickly wishing that she hadn't, as she witnesses the man rolling on the floor in an uncontrollable seizure, foaming furiously from the mouth.

As the girls close in on their escape route, the door slams shut before them, followed by the sound of a lock clicking.

'Damn it!' Heidi shouts angrily, dashing up to the sealed doorway and striking it with a forceful kick. 'Ouch,' she groans, hobbling away. 'I should really learn not to do that.' A keyhole is carved into the door, but with no key available it seems impossible to open.

A whirring noise comes from the opposite end of the passage. Looking back to where they had first entered, the girls see a violet cloud of mist beginning to take form.

'Quick, over here,' Faith instructs, tugging a limping Heidi towards one of the vacant cells. Faith speedily shoves her two younger companions into the cage before entering it herself. She closes the iron barred door as softly as she can behind her, holding Roxanne and Heidi back as she peers through the bars. She squints as something solid begins to form within the swirling purple mist.

Faith gulps with nervousness as the haze subsides. 'Over there,' she commands, pointing to a bed that is fastened to the back wall of the prison cell.

'Hurry up!' Heidi squeals, nervously jumping up and down on the spot, beginning to panic as Roxanne attempts to squeeze herself under the bed. Heidi's patience fails her and she shoves Roxanne's legs under before squeezing in next to her.

The sound of heavy footsteps emanates from the hallway as Faith drops to her knees by the side of the bed and attempts to force her body into the already jammed space. Realising that she can't possibly fit, she knows she must find a separate hiding place. Springing back to her feet, Faith whips a thin white sheet that covers the mattress and wraps it around herself before slumping in the corner of the room. Hearing Heidi's gasp of horror, Faith peeks from underneath her disguise. A janitor, dressed in navy blue overalls, washes the corridor floor with a wet mop. The worker has the body of a human man, but the head of a slobbering bulldog. The beast mops the already gleaming marble floor as it continues down the hallway and past the cell that the friends conceal themselves within.

'Keys!' Heidi quietly exclaims to Roxanne, noticing a bunch of silver keys dangling from the janitor's belt. The canine cleaner's furry ears prick to attention as it hears Heidi's faint uttering. Roxanne promptly places her clammy palm across her friend's mouth to stop her from making any further noise. The creature plods towards the iron bars, his eyes glinting as they scan the seemingly empty cell.

To Heidi and Roxanne's total surprise, Faith suddenly flings away the sheet that camouflages her. The evil pooch snarls savagely, saliva dripping from its open jaws as Faith leaps to her feet.

'Faith, what the Hell are you doing?' Roxanne whispers with uncertainty. Faith crouches besides the bed, whispering to her young friends as the fearsome dog throws open the cage door furiously.

Faith turns to face the beast as the iron door crashes against the wall, taking a chink of plaster from the wall. A look of horror appears on her face as the dog reaches into its pocket and retrieves a black truncheon equipped with a crown of spikes embedded into the top end. It appears that the half man, half hound, janitor is also the prison's security guard.

'I hope this works,' Faith whispers to herself, doubting the fact that any of them will get out of the prison alive.

CHAPTER 47

'I can't hold on much longer,' Jasmine panics, her arm muscles exhausted from fatigue. Kyle too is becoming weak from the good versus evil tug of war. On the contrary, the putrid corpse that grasps at Kyle's ankle doesn't appear to be surrendering anytime soon.

Kyle realises that he must act now, before it's too late. With all the strength he has left in his body, he leans precariously forward. Jasmine's face turns puce as she tugs her tilting companion with all her might, the young boy's sole hope from plummeting into the stinking mud pit. Kyle thumps the undead on its bony skull as hard as he possibly can. Kyle topples backwards, slamming flat against the wall as the corpse groans in agony, releasing its tight grip from around his leg, Jasmine holds her arms out to steady herself as she teeters dangerously on the edge of the stinking pool.

'Right, let's move,' she commands, flattening herself against the wall and carefully beginning to shimmy towards the exit. Kyle imitates Jasmines moves, following her footsteps. He keeps his eyes fixed on the bubbling mud at his feet, so as not to be caught off guard by any further unpleasant surprises from below.

Jasmine breathes a huge sigh of relief as she steps into the archway of the exit. 'Give me your hand,' she says as Kyle edges around the doorframe. She takes her young companion's outstretched hand and helps him into the safety of the entranceway.

Taking a few moments to catch their breath, the friends examine the new area before them. They stand in yet another hallway. No doors or exits are visible.

'Well, that's just great!' Kyle groans, sensing that they face a dead end.

'There has to be something,' Jasmine says, pacing further into the passage. After a few steps she halts abruptly.

'What's the matter?' Kyle asks from the doorway. Jasmine looks down at her feet.

'I... I can't move,' she gulps, attempting to lift her feet from the floorboards. The boards that she stands on begin to ripple as she leans forward and attempts to prise her leg from the ground.

'The floor is just an illusion!' Jasmine shrieks as she realises that she is unable to break free. 'I'm sinking!'

CHAPTER 48

'Give me your hand,' Kyle yells, dashing across to his submerged companion.

'No!' Jasmine shrieks, but it's already too late as Kyle also falls victim to the floor illusion.

'I'm so stupid,' he gasps in exasperation, realising that his actions were far too hasty as he begins to descend alongside his friend. They both fight to free their feet, but with no avail as they only sink faster with each struggle. Jasmine attempts to think of a plan, but with only her upper body now above the ground level, she knows that there is nothing she can do.

'What are we going to do?' Kyle whimpers, unable to move his arms as they accidentally become wedged in the supple floor.

'On the count of three, take a deep breath and hold it, okay?' Jasmine instructs as they rapidly descend. As they sink up to their chins, Jasmine begins to count. 'One... two... three.' The two friends take a deep breath, closing their eyes as they become completely submerged beneath the rippling floorboards.

It feels like sinking through extremely thick custard, Kyle thinks, even though he has never experienced such a thing. They continue to sink with their eyes tightly shut, their limbs unable to move and the air in their lungs depleting. A waft of warm air suddenly caresses Jasmine's ankles. As her legs become free once again, she kicks in mid-air, just in case anything nasty lurks below. She squeals as the weight of her lower body suddenly pulls her free from the flexible floor.

She only drops a couple of feet before falling on her knees in something soft. She gradually opens her eyes as she hears Kyle drop besides her, taking a deep breath of air as he does. Shielding her eyes as they adjust to the lighting, Jasmine can distinguish a bright yellow ball hovering above her. She soon comes to realise that the ball is a huge sun, suspended high in the bright blue, cloudless sky.

'Whoa, are we in Egypt?' Kyle asks, rubbing his eyes and staring around the barren region. A vast desert surrounds the friends, the occasional cactus dotted sporadically. A group of turkey vultures circles high in the warm, dry air. The bird's heads are red and almost entirely bald, except for some sparse black bristles. Their grey flight feathers glint a dazzling silver as they catch the sun's powerful rays.

'It's boiling out here,' Kyle whinges, wiping the back of his hand across his clammy forehead. Jasmine gets to her feet, dusting sand from her trousers. She once again shields her eyes with her hand as she gazes around the seemingly everlasting desert. As she squints, a shape comes into focus on the horizon.

'I think that's a pyramid,' she informs Kyle, pointing into the distance.

'I can't see anything,' Kyle replies, his eyes following Jasmine's extended finger.

'It's a long way off,' Jasmine says. 'Look harder and you'll just be able to make it out.' Kyle pushes himself to his feet. He stands beside Jasmine, blocks the intense sunshine from his eyes with his small hand and strains to peer into the distance.

'Oh yeah, I see it now,' he says as a blurry triangular silhouette appears in view.

'No time to dillydally,' Jasmine says with a big huff as she strides forward, determined to reach the pyramid as soon as possible in order to protect her fair complexion from the intense heat. Kyle groans, reluctantly tracking his friend's sandy footprints, knowing that they have a long, exhausting trek ahead of them.

CHAPTER 49

Faith stands motionless, staring into the menacing eyes of the slobbering beast. 'Come on,' she whispers impatiently, her eyes narrowing as the canine-headed security guard stares silently back at her. Heidi gasps, peering from underneath the bed as the fiend raises his spiky truncheon, stepping closer to Faith.

'Remember what to do,' Roxanne whispers into Heidi's ear as Faith paces backwards, the monster gaining on her. Faith steps up onto the creaky bed, pressing herself flat against the wall, with nowhere left to run. As the creature reaches the foot of the bed, the schoolgirls speedily reach out, deftly grabbing his ankles.

'Now!' Roxanne yells. Upon hearing Roxanne's confirmation, Faith darts forwards, pushing forcefully on the beast's hefty chest. With a growl of helplessness, the prison guard topples backwards, crashing to the ground with an almighty thud.

Faith assists her friends to their feet as they hurriedly scramble from beneath the bed. Roxanne promptly straddles the guard's chest, making sure that her knees pin his arms firmly to the ground. The guard's slow reactions to this invasion tells Roxanne that he must have hit his head pretty hard on the marble floor. Now that the guard is immobile, Faith and Heidi attempt to unfasten the set of keys that hang from his belt.

'Got them!' Heidi yells gleefully as she yanks the keys free from the leather strap. Dizziness subsiding, the dog's grotesque mouth snaps at Roxanne's flailing legs as she swiftly dismounts his chest. The fleeing girls make a dash for the locked door. Heidi skids to a halt as she arrives first. She holds up the bunch of sparkling silver keys. 'There are thousands of keys here!' she exaggerates, jangling the mass of clinking metal.

'Heidi, just get it open!' Roxanne shrieks, glancing over her shoulder to witness the stunned, yet furious guard, struggling to his feet. Heidi selects a key at random and attempts to place it into the lock. The key doesn't fit. She takes the next one. That too doesn't match the opening.

Roxanne begins to sweat as she notices the guard bending down and retrieving his deadly cudgel. She darts back to the cell, slamming the door shut and sliding the heavy lock into place, allowing them a few more seconds to escape.

Back at the door, Heidi tries the last key. 'None of them fit!' she squeals, attempting to force the final key into the lock. Faith takes a closer look as Heidi continues her attempt.

'Heidi, you have the key upside down!' she cries, grabbing the set of keys from her young friend.

'No need to snatch,' Heidi mutters as Faith begins to try each key again.

'What's the hold up?' Roxanne pants as she returns. Suddenly a click emits from the door as Faith selects the correct key.

'Come on,' Faith urges as she strains to pull open the heavy door. 'Go!'

'Whoa,' Heidi utters in surprise as she teeters on the edge of the doorway. Leading from the base of the door, a narrow metal slide vanishes into darkness below. 'It's like one of those really steep slides at a water park.'

'We need to go, now!' Faith shrieks, turning as the cell door crashes open behind them, the drooling brute standing in the doorway.

'You first,' Heidi says to Roxanne as she steps backwards, standing on Faith's toes as she retreats from the uncertain blackness. Roxanne rolls her eyes before sitting on the ledge, her legs resting on the smooth metal slide.

'Heidi, quick!' Faith insists as the security guard steps into the hallway and begins stumbling towards them. Heidi shuffles in behind Roxanne, clamping her arms securely around her friend's waist. Faith speedily joins the human train, gripping Heidi around her stomach.

'Go on!' Faith yells as the line of girls remains motionless, the infuriated guard steadily approaching from behind.

Roxanne cranes her neck to look at Faith. 'But...' she whimpers, uneasy with the thought of plunging into the darkness that awaits them.

'We don't have time for buts,' Faith replies fretfully, attempting to nudge Roxanne forwards. Heidi shuts her eyes tightly as Roxanne begins to slide, dragging her and Faith along for the ride as she disappears over the edge.

'Don't let me go!' Heidi yells, her voice echoing as they plummet into the mysterious darkness below.

CHAPTER 50

'There's a light!' Roxanne yells after a few moments of sliding at top speed through complete blackness. Heidi doesn't respond and keeps her eyes firmly closed as the friends hurtle towards the speck of light that rapidly increases in size with each passing second.

A few moments later, the conjoined girls shoot from a black hole that hovers in mid-air above a sandy ground. The girls become detached from one another as they land uncomfortably on the hot sand. Heidi spins on her side, her eyes still shut tight as she rolls uncontrollably.

She screams at the top of her voice, her eyes shooting wide open in pain as she spins into a large cactus. Luckily for her, the cactus has minuscule needles, but dreadfully sharp ones nonetheless.

Roxanne sits up where she landed, taking note of her vicinity and realising that her friend's cries were nothing to be too concerned about. 'Well, you have always said you wanted to see what acupuncture feels like,' she says with a snigger, hauling herself off the sandy ground whilst watching Heidi pluck tiny cactus needles from her arm.

'Oh, how funny you are,' Heidi retorts sarcastically, wincing as she continues to pick the short, sharp spikes from her skin.

Still smirking, Roxanne turns, curious to see where Faith landed. Her mouth drops open in surprise as she walks slowly forwards, staring up as she stands beside Faith.

'Whoa!' Heidi exclaims, forgetting the pain in her arm as her attention focuses on the sight that captivates her friends. 'I've always wanted to visit one of these,' she declares, moving next to Roxanne. A gigantic pyramid looms before them, stretching into the cloudless, bright blue sky.

'What's that?' Roxanne enquires, pointing to a patch of swirling grey mist, far up the side of the pyramid.

Faith shields her eyes from the dazzling sun. 'It's another monk,' she informs her young friends. The monk slowly raises his hand, beckoning the girls towards him.

'You've got to be kidding me!' Roxanne sighs, wiping her moist forehead with her sleeve. 'There's no way on earth I'm climbing all the way up there.'

'Well, it's a good thing we're not on earth then, isn't it,' Heidi ridicules as she strides towards the towering stone triangle. She screams, covering her head with her arms as a turkey vulture soars out from behind a giant cactus. 'Don't look at it!' she squeals in warning. 'It'll peck your eyes out.'

'I think we have bigger problems to worry about, Hei,' Roxanne scoffs as she and Faith follow their friend. Heidi waits for Roxanne and Faith to join her before continuing onwards. After a couple of steps, Heidi screams for a second time, leaping backwards as a large egg hits the soft sand before her. To the girls' surprise, the egg didn't shatter on impact. Looking up into the bright sky, they realise the vulture that startled Heidi is responsible for the egg, as it hovers high above them.

'Look,' Roxanne says as the egg begins to bury itself underneath the warm sand. The girls step apprehensively backwards as the ground beneath their feet begins to rumble. The desert surface breaks and something begins to appear.

'Uh oh,' Faith murmurs as a set of sand-coloured pincers rise from the grains. The girls gasp as an enormous scorpion arises from beneath the desert. This scorpion is like no other. It is formed entirely from solid sand. A bulbous tail stinger, filled with a bright green liquid, flails in the humid air as the predatory arachnid fully emerges.

'Why does everything have to be so bloody difficult,' Roxanne says.

'We can avoid it if we run,' Faith whispers as they all take a careful pace backwards. Suddenly, an unexpected hoard of eggs slams into the surrounding desert, creating a giant ring around the three girls.

'Stupid birds!' Heidi yells as a kettle of vultures circles above.

'Oh, this is just fantastic,' Roxanne moans as the eggs disappear beneath the sand. 'Now what do we do?' Both Heidi and Faith remain silent, watching fearfully as an army of deadly sand scorpions begin to break through the desert ground.

CHAPTER 51

Faith topples backwards as she stumbles on something that juts from beneath the sand. Upon landing on the ground, Faith's hand makes contact with something tough. Roxanne and Heidi gawp as a shimmering blue light flows up Faith's arm.

'Look,' Heidi says, nudging Roxanne, 'monk bones.' As Roxanne's eyes follow the direction of Heidi's pointing finger, she realises that Faith's hand is placed on top of a skull, barely protruding above the sand.

Faith's eyes close as the exuberant blue glow caresses her entire body, sinking deep within every fibre of her being. Heidi and Roxanne squint, shielding their eyes with the backs of their hands as the blue hue becomes brighter and more intense. Heidi gasps as Faith jolts backwards, her eyes flashing open with an explosion of indigo light. Faith raises her open palms towards the sky. An intense funnel of blue beams emits from her body, shooting high into the warm air.

Entranced by the spectacle before them, Heidi and Roxanne forget about the sand monsters that approach from behind.

'Aaahhh!' Roxanne screeches as something firmly grips her ankle. 'Get it off,' she cries, turning to see a sand scorpion's large claw clutching her leg. Heidi hesitates for a second before striking a fierce kick at the creatures extended pincer. The scorpion hisses as Heidi's stern wallop disintegrates its claw. As Roxanne becomes free, she and Heidi stare into the sky as a hoard of dark storm clouds gather from all directions. A strong gust of icy wind wafts Heidi's long hair, blowing a mass of blonde strands across her eyes. Roxanne wipes her hand across her face as a droplet of water splashes onto her cheek.

Faith drops to her knees as the bright blue light fades from around her. As she returns to her normal self, the sky falls dark and a pattering of rain hits the sand. As Heidi and Roxanne help Faith to her feet, the light shower abruptly transforms into a heavy downpour. The army of scorpions extrude high pitched shrieks as the droplets of cool rain cover them like a soggy blanket. The girls observe in wonder as the sandy monsters melt away like ice-cream on a hot summer's day.

As the scorpions form giant lumps of wet sand, the dark storm clouds begin to disperse.

'It's bright again,' Roxanne says as the sun shines onto her face, warming her skin once more.

'Faith, your hair!' Heidi exclaims, taking hold of Faith's sopping ponytail. Whipping her hair around, Faith gasps as she sees that the lower portion of her ponytail is now a navy shade of blue.

'Strange,' she remarks, looking quizzically at her hair. 'It might fade, or if not, I'll just colour over it when we get home.'

Heidi seems reassured by Faith's mention of returning home and instantly feels more at ease. 'Okay, come on you two slackers,' she orders as she trudges through the mushy sand and towards the great pyramid.

CHAPTER 52

'That rain was a stroke of luck,' Jasmine says, wringing excess water from her long red hair.

'Yeah,' Kyle replies, out of breath as he jogs a few paces to catch up with his friend. 'I thought we were goners when all those massive scorpions hatched everywhere.'

'Not far now,' Jasmine tells him as the intimidating pyramid looms upon them.

Just a few minutes later and they reach the foot of the almighty stone structure. A golden plaque is nailed onto one of the stone blocks that make up the building. Jasmine squints at the tiny inscription that is etched on the shiny rectangular plate.

'Only one may undertake the challenge of the ancient conqueror,' she informs Kyle, reading aloud from the plaque. Next to the writing, a small oval indentation is strategically placed. Looking closer, the friends can see that a small red laser beam shines from inside. 'Let me do this,' Jasmine says, cautiously placing her thumb into the egg-shaped groove. The friends wait in silent anticipation, anxious with the thought of the ancient conqueror in their heads, whatever that may be.

After a few long moments, a buzzing sound alarms. Jasmine takes Kyle by the hand, stepping backwards as one of the large stone slabs begins to shift. A chalky dust fills the air as the stone block moves inside the pyramid, creating a doorway.

'Be careful and don't touch anything,' Jasmine warns as she leads them through the gloomy opening.

They step from the warm atmosphere of the desert and onto the outskirts of a large, sparkling, hexagonal room. Every inch of the spacious room is paved in gold. Jewels and riches scatter an enormous golden table at the far end. A tall, golden coffin stands on its end in the centre of the room. Four oversized, medieval looking weapons hang on the wall, including a blood-smeared spiked ball that dangles from a solid gold chain.

'Wow!' Kyle exclaims as his eyes set upon a shiny golden sword with a ruby incrusted handle. He moves forwards, walking towards the huge glistening weapon. 'Ouch!' He exclaims, rubbing his head as he slams into an invisible force.

'What's the matter?' Jasmine asks, glancing around, confused.

'I can't seem to get into the room,' Kyle explains, pressing his hands onto an unseen wall. 'This has happened to me before,' he grumbles.

A bewildered expression crosses Jasmine's face as she holds her hands outstretched and paces forward.

'Hey!' she exclaims as she passes her friend. 'That was easy enough,' she half smiles, nevertheless confused as Kyle remains unable to enter the room the way she has managed to.

Suddenly, the sound of small metal objects landing on a hard floor seizes Jasmine's attention. Slowly turning to face into the large room, she notices a pile of long golden bolts at the foot of the coffin. Right before her eyes, the thick bolts that hold the upright coffin lid in place unscrew themselves one by one. As they begin dropping to the ground, Jasmine backs away, uneasy about what might emerge from the great tomb. A stunned expression crosses her face as she pushes up against the invisible wall that Kyle remains stuck behind. Spinning around, she comes face to face with her young companion. They are separated by the invisible force, Kyle on the outside of the vast chamber and Jasmine within.

Jasmine's eyes widen as she turns back around. She watches as the final bolt plummets to the ground with a heavy clinking of metal. She realises that the coffin is soon to open. She also knows that whatever is lurking inside is not going to be pleased to see her.

CHAPTER 53

The girls reach the halfway mark on their climb up the great pyramid. Heidi gasps, her foot slipping on a loose sand stone. Roxanne yelps, worried for her own safety as she feels her friend's hand gripping tightly onto ankle to stop her tumbling to the sandy earth below.

'Be careful,' Roxanne scolds, tugging her leg away from her friend's grasp.

'Stop fooling around you two,' Faith reprimands, not quite knowing what's taking place below her. 'We have to remain focused, we're almost there.'

The friends carefully persist with the treacherous climb towards the opening, high up in the pyramid's wall.

'My arms ache, big time,' Heidi whines as they approach the cavity. Faith clambers onto the ledge and positions herself to assist her friends in joining her.

'Thank the Lord for that,' Heidi puffs, resting for a moment on the pyramid side while Faith gives Roxanne a hand up and onto the ledge besides her. They both return and grab Heidi by her wrists, hauling her onto the platform along with them. 'Okay, let's just take a break here for a while,' Heidi pants as she crumbles into a heap in the opening.

As the sheltered cavity in the wall of the Pyramid is shielded from the scorching sun, the girls reach the mutual decision to rest for a brief while. They shuffle around for a few moments, attempting to get comfortable. They settle upon each other and their eyelids begin to close. After only a few minutes they each fall into a restful, relaxing and much needed sleep.

Meanwhile, inside the lower section of the pyramid, Jasmine waits apprehensively for the coffin to open.

'Maybe *you* have to open it?' Kyle suggests from behind the unseen wall. Jasmine gulps, timidly taking a step forward. As she moves further into the room, something behind the coffin catches her eye. A segment of the wall at the back of the room is cracked. As she moves past the coffin, she can see what lies beyond the wall.

'Hey,' she yells back to Kyle, briefly forgetting about the coffin, 'there's a set of stairs behind this wall.'

As she searches for a way to pass through to the other side, the creaking of a stiff door opening startles her. Her eyes widen as she turns around to see the coffin door wide open. Standing behind the tomb, Jasmine shivers at the thoughts of what lurks inside. Taking notice of the expression on her young friend's on-looking face, she understands that a fearsome predator must inhabit the tomb.

Kyle appears to be frozen to the spot, his mouth hanging open and his eyes wide with sheer terror. Jasmine hesitantly takes an apprehensive step towards the coffin. She glances up as the heavy sarcophagus suddenly teeters backwards. She gasps as the coffin falls in her direction. She manages to dodge in the nick of time as the tomb crashes onto the gold paved floor, shattering a row of the gleaming tiles as it lands.

As she gathers herself, Jasmine's expression mimics Kyle's as she stands before a towering, golden knight. Her feet feel heavier than stone as the bulky knight turns to face her, its golden armour clanking as it rotates. The look of horror remains on Jasmines pale face as she stares into the hollow blackness of the knight's shiny helmet. She screams as a deep roar bellows from within the knight's pitch-black helmet, causing her hair to thrash around in the sudden strong gust.

The menacing knight slowly turns and paces towards the back wall. He raises his heavy arm as he arrives at the row of lethal weapons that hang there. Jasmine exchanges petrified glances with her excluded companion as the warrior lifts the massive, razor-sharp sword from its receptacle.

Jasmine moves backwards in stunned silence as the soldier clanks the heavy golden blade on the ground. The intense scraping of metal fills the air as the knight drags the deadly weapon in her direction. With nowhere to run to, and no escape from the room, Jasmine fears that all her previous efforts to stay alive may have been in vain.

CHAPTER 54

As the knight looms upon her, Jasmine cowers fearfully, the image of being sliced in half racing through her mind. Her eyes open wide as the reinforced warrior raises the huge sword. Due to the weapon being extremely heavy, Jasmine is able to evade the knight's slow attack, dodging to one side as the sword clanks onto the golden floor with a shower of fiery sparks. He takes a second swipe, aiming for Jasmine's throat. Fortunately, she foresees the knight's attack and quickly rolls out of harm's way.

Nimbly leaping to her feet, the red head dashes across to the invisible wall that protects her friend.

'I don't know what to do!' she shrieks, a quiver in her voice. Kyle looks bewildered, wishing more than anything that he could help his distressed friend, but he has no idea how she can survive this situation.

Jasmine turns her head to keep a watchful eye on the knight as he returns to the wall of weapons. Jasmine watches as he ungracefully slams the huge sword back into its holder. Her eyes express dread as the warrior grasps a horrifyingly enormous ball and chain. The heavy spiked ball crashes to the ground as the knight rips the chain from the wall.

Jasmine gulps as she turns to face her enemy. She has absolutely no idea what she can do to progress beyond this seemingly impassable situation in which she is trapped. A twinkle of light reflects in her eyes as the knight moves menacingly towards her. As she pays closer attention, Jasmine notices that a large circular hole is embedded in the knight's armour, directly in the centre of his chest. The perimeter of the hollow is encrusted with sparkling diamonds.

An idea suddenly springs into her mind; she just prays that it works. She sprints to the long jewel scattered table, quickly avoiding the knight's hurtling mace as she goes. Upon reaching the table, she hurriedly uses her hands to spread out the shimmering mound of precious stones. Her eyes scan over the gems as they disperse across the shiny surface.

'Ah-ha!' she exclaims as the object that she's searching for catches her eye and she seizes a large sparkling diamond with both hands. Her bright eyes reflect in the glistening jewel as she holds it aloft. She screams in shock as the armoured giant's reflection shows within the hefty jewel, followed by the intense sound of the heavy mace smashing down onto the lengthy golden table, precious stones dispersing in all directions. As the knight in shining armour is unable to strike a second attack in such quick succession, Jasmine realises that this may be her only chance. Taking a deep breath, she races up to the towering golden brute. Standing on the tips of her toes, she reaches and thrusts the giant diamond into the hollow set in his chest.

Jasmine loses her balance, toppling backwards as the knight makes a sudden jolt. Her face turns puce as she lands hard on the ground, becoming winded. She watches apprehensively from the floor as the diamond begins to glow a dazzling bright white. The enormous knight drops his weapon, falling motionless, as if his batteries have suddenly run out.

Jasmine glances at her young friend, who looks confused from behind his invisible wall. Slowly rising from the golden floor, Jasmine keeps her suspicious gaze fixed on the armoured guardian, who stands frozen before her. She remains motionless, waiting for something to happen, but nothing does. She scratches her head in bafflement. To her astonishment, the knight also raises his colossal arm at the exact same time Jasmine does. At first, she seems mystified by the knight's action, but as she lowers her arm, the knight replicates her exact moves.

'What's going on?' Kyle yells from behind the invisible wall. Jasmine holds her finger to her lips, gesturing for him to be silent while she concentrates. Kyle observes as the warrior mimics her action once more. Jasmine turns to face the direction the knight is facing. She bends forwards with her hand open. A look of achievement lights her face as the knight also bends, placing his large hand around the handle of the mace. Jasmine then closes her hand and stands back upright. Again, the knight imitates her action. She lifts her right leg, moves it forward and then places it back onto the ground. Kyle watches from afar as the knight takes a step forward. Jasmine replicates the actions with her left leg, then again with her right. She stops stepping as the knight stands within a few feet of the cracked wall.

She takes a deep breath, begging that her plan works as she thrusts her left arm backwards. She shrieks as the knight flings the chain backwards, the deadly spiked ball crashing to the ground beside her. She carefully positions herself to match the knight's stance with exact precision. After taking a final deep breath, Jasmine forcefully hurls her arm forwards. Just as she figured, the knight copies her moves with complete accuracy.

The fragile wall crumbles as the weighty spiked sphere impacts with great force. Jasmine's eyes shine with triumph as the set of stairs can now be clearly seen through the large hole in the wall. Realising that she must discontinue the knight's copycat tactics, she deliberately falls stiffly forwards, careful to cushion the blow with her hands upon landing.

Just as she hoped, the knight also topples forwards. As he crashes face first onto the hard ground, the large diamond shakes loose from the indentation in his chest. Jasmine springs to her feet as the glistening jewel rolls across the golden floor. To her glee the knight lies thoroughly motionless.

'You did it!' Kyle exclaims in shocked delight as his small hands suddenly pass through the invisible veil and he enters the room.

'Come on,' Jasmine instructs her young friend, striding towards the gaping hole in the wall and climbing through. Once on the other side, she helps Kyle as he struggles to clamber across.

'I take it we go up then,' Kyle says, now standing before an upward winding staircase. The two friends start slowly up the cold stone steps. Hand in hand they creep, trying to remain as quiet as possible so as not to alert their presence to anything sinister which may be lurking above.

CHAPTER 55

Heidi yawns, stretching as she wakes from a peaceful rest.

'Ouch,' Roxanne groans, waking abruptly as Heidi's foot crashes into the back of her head.

'I was having such a nice dream,' Heidi informs her companions as she props herself up and leans against the cool passage wall. 'I dreamed that I was back at home. Mum was baking biscuits. Me and Kyle were helping out and he wasn't annoying me like he usually...' she suddenly stops, midsentence. 'Kyle!' she exclaims. 'We have to find him!'

'We will find him,' Faith assures, rising to her feet. 'Until we do, the monk will make sure that he's OK.'

Heidi seems comforted by Faith's constant support. She grasps Faith's helping hand and is gently assisted to her feet. 'Come on, Roxy,' she orders, stepping over her friend as she heads down a short tunnel that leads inside the pyramid.

Once Faith helps Roxanne to her feet, they join Heidi at the inner entrance of the passage. The girls stand side by side, staring out across the wide-open interior of the immense pyramid. A long wooden bridge stretches from the shadowy doorway which they occupy. The bridge is fastened in place by thick, sturdy looking ropes, which are firmly fixed onto platforms at either end. Directly above the bridge, a horizontal wooden ladder oddly stretches across the ceiling. Peering over the rocky platform edge, the girls gasp in horror. In a pit far below the bridge, thousands of long, razor-sharp spikes protrude from the ground, a mass of human bones scattered amongst them. Amid the human remains, the occasional carcass of varying creatures slump in gory piles.

'We certainly don't want to fall down there,' Heidi announces, backing away from the brink.

'You think?' Roxanne retorts sarcastically, but with a lump in her throat, as she tiptoes carefully onto the bridge. She freezes, a look of concern flashing across her face as the bridge begins to creak.

'Maybe we should use these handle bar things,' Heidi suggests, pointing above Roxanne's head.

Faith studies the ladder from afar. 'It doesn't look altogether safe in my opinion,' she remarks, eyeing clumps of mould that have formed along the wooden ladder. Something nudging her in the back suddenly gains Faith's attention. Being captivated by the sight before them, the girls fail to notice that the opening to the inside of the pyramid commences to seal itself with a sliding brick wall, forcing Faith onto the bridge as it sets into position behind her. Heidi and Roxanne glance over their shoulders as Faith pushes into them.

Seeing the wall and realising that they have no option but to cross the room, Roxanne turns her attention back to the slightly swaying bridge. Slowly and carefully starting across the bridge, she holds tightly onto the thick roped rails for support. Heidi follows closely behind while Faith completes the line, joining the proceedings in last place.

The ancient bridge continues to groan as the girls proceed towards the opposite end of the room. A snapping sound that echoes through the vicinity induces a look of dread on Heidi's suddenly pale face. Looking ahead, she witnesses the ropes beginning to spilt and tear.

'Heidi, no!' Faith commands, attempting to grab her friend as Heidi panics and begins to run along the dangerously fragile bridge, overtaking Roxanne in an ungainly manner. 'Jump and grab the bars,' Faith yells at the top of her voice as the brittle ropes disintegrate under the pounding weight of Heidi's thundering footsteps. Roxanne and Faith leap as hard as they can, grasping the overhead ladder tightly. Completely disorientated, Heidi hesitates as the bridge crumbles beneath her feet. Realising that she will never reach the end in time, she jumps, reaching for the bars above. But it's already too late. Roxanne's heart leaps into her mouth as the bridge completely falls away and her best friend plummets into the pit below.

CHAPTER 56

'Faith!' Roxanne shrieks, desperate for her friend to use her powers to save Heidi. Little does Roxanne know that Faith's influential attention is already fixed upon their plunging companion. To Roxanne's utmost relief, Heidi's descent begins to slow. An indigo aura encases her as she hovers only a few feet above the bed of deadly spikes.

Heidi remains stunned in shock, her eyes scrunched tightly shut. Hanging from the horizontal ladder above, Roxanne holds her breath in terrified suspense, her face becoming puce from the strain of hanging in mid-air. Behind Roxanne, Faith restrains herself from blinking, not daring to take any chances on losing her concentration.

Terrified that she isn't strong enough to hold on for much longer, Roxanne has no choice but to swing her way to the end of the ladder. Behind Roxanne, Faith's eyes suddenly glaze, transforming into deep blue pools. She hangs effortlessly, no tension straining her body as she levitates Heidi with the power of her mind.

Upon reaching the final rung of the ladder, Roxanne releases her throbbing grip, falling to the platform below. Turning, she holds a deep breath as she witnesses her best friend floating upwards and towards her.

'Heidi,' Roxanne calls softly as her friend hovers next to the ledge on which she stands. Heidi opens her eyes in disbelief at the sound of Roxanne's voice.

'I thought I was dead,' she whimpers, staring wide-eyed at the vast drop beneath her.

'Give me your hand,' Roxanne instructs, holding her arm towards Heidi, gripping onto a rock with the other hand to prevent herself from falling. Heidi slowly reaches, accepting her friends helping hand. Roxanne grips tightly as Heidi's fingers intertwine with her own. She gently pulls and Heidi floats with ease to the safety of the ledge.

The very moment Heidi's feet touch down safely onto solid ground, the blue hue surrounding her quickly disperses. Faith's eyes blink, returning to normal. All of a sudden, she begins to panic as her mind and body return to reality. She pants in alarm, her arms feeling the pressure of supporting her bodyweight as she dangles from the ladder. Gritting her teeth, she begins to grab each handlebar in turn, swinging towards the safety of the ledge.

'Come on, Faith, you can do it!' Heidi yells supportively as Faith looms upon the platform, breathing heavily and her face red from the rising tension.

Heidi sighs with relief, wiping her moist forehead with the back of her hand as Faith drops safely next to them.

'Thank you!' Heidi says emotionally, flinging her arms around Faith's neck. 'This is the second time you've saved me and this time I thought I was a gonner for sure.'

'I'm glad you're both alright,' Faith replies breathlessly, wearily crumpling to the ground.

'Faith, are you ok?' Roxanne asks, worried as she crouches beside her friend. To her surprise, Faith unexpectedly leaps to her feet, crackles of blue sparks emitting from her fingertips. The two schoolgirls gaze in amazement as the blue tip of Faith's ponytail begins to spread, her hair soaking up the navy colour like thousands of micro sponges.

Roxanne and Heidi kneel in silence as the sparkles from Faith's fingers fade away.

'Faith, are you OK?' Heidi asks as she and Roxanne get to their feet. 'What just happened?'

'I feel... fine,' Faith announces, sounding a bit startled. 'I feel more than fine, in fact I feel downright invigorated.'

'I like your hair that colour too,' Heidi tells Faith with a smile. Faith looks confused.

'Your ponytail is now completely blue,' Roxanne informs her perplexed friend. 'The top of your head is still brown though. It looks pretty cool.'

A nearby scratching noise suddenly redirects the girls' attention. A murky doorway at the far end of the high platform hides anything that may be lurking beyond. The friends cautiously make their way towards the opening as the intriguing scraping sound becomes more intense.

Poking her head around the edge of the doorway, Roxanne's eyes follow an extended, upwards ramped pathway, adjacent to where they stand. At the foot of the narrow path is a seemingly solid wall. At the opposite end, a gigantic ball, which seems to be made entirely of dirt, rests at the top.

Realising that they must press onwards, the girls carefully step into the slanted aisle, keeping their eyes fixed on the large ball of dirt at the summit. They jump in shock as a heavy stone shutter drops within the doorway through which they entered, sealing them on the ramped passageway. Heidi coughs and splutters as a cloud of dust and dirt soars into the air from the weighty impact. With nowhere else to turn, the girls walk hand in hand up the path towards the huge sphere of mud. They halt in their tracks as the same scratching sound can be heard once again, only this time at a much closer proximity.

Heidi shrieks, squeezing her girlfriends' hands as a large beetle suddenly rises from behind the ball. The shiny black beetle rests on the great boulder of mud, staring down the path at the imprisoned girls.

'This doesn't look good,' Faith states as the gigantic bug teeters forwards, gently rolling the large boulder towards the edge of the ramped passage.

'Does it ever look good?' Roxanne asks while Faith closes her eyes, concentrating her thoughts. After a few focused moments she reopens her eyes, staring intensely up at the beetle. She looks puzzled when nothing happens. Faint blue sparks momentarily crackle in her eyes before dying out almost immediately.

'Faith...' Roxanne murmurs as the beetle shifts the heavy ball of earth forwards. The girls freeze in the centre of the path as the ball topples in their direction. As the passage is too narrow to dodge the boulder, and with Faith's powers unable to aide them, the confined girls are helpless.

CHAPTER 57

R un!' Faith yells as the great rolling ball picks up speed. 'Run where?' Heidi shrieks hysterically as the three of them turn and dash down the path. Faith is unable to respond to Heidi's question, as she herself doesn't know the answer. Upon reaching the end of the passage, Roxanne notices something strangely helpful about the wall that blocks their way.

'We can climb this,' she informs the other two without hesitation. Small ridges protrude from the wall, enabling them to clamber high above the speeding boulder, if they have enough time.

Roxanne hurriedly leaps onto the wall. Heidi mimics her friend's actions as she too grabs hold of a small platform on the wall and heaves herself up. To evade the rolling ball of filth, Faith frantically searches for any vacant platform that she can use. Roxanne and Heidi's limbs flail chaotically as they scramble as fast as they can.

'Hurry up!' Faith shrieks, bobbing agitatedly on the spot as she waits impatiently for her young friends to advance. But it's now too late. As the ball hurtles towards her, all Faith can do is to wait for the inevitable impact. She closes her eyes tightly, crouching and folding her arms for protection as the dirt boulder crashes into her with immense force. Heidi gasps as the huge ball thumps into Faith, sending her smashing through the tough wall below them. Fortunately, she and Roxanne have managed to scale the wall far enough to avoid the collision.

Roxanne puffs as she releases her grip, dropping to her knees as she lands hard on the rocky ground. Heidi quickly follows, crashing to the floor and rolling around ungracefully. Roxanne helps her friend to her feet before they both turn their attention to the shattered wall.

'Faith?' Heidi calls softly as she and Roxanne step towards the mound of rubble that was once the wall. Beyond the debris lies a sparse corridor with another wall at the far end. The destroyed ball of soil and shattered wall conceal Faith below. Heidi and Roxanne both shriek, quickly shielding their heads with their arms as a hoard of bricks and grime soars into the air. They gasp in unity as they uncover their heads, staring at Faith who stands taut before them. She stands in the centre of the debris, not moving a muscle, her hands rigid at her sides. Her now full head of blue hair shines a with a deep alluring hue, as if light radiates from each and every strand. Faith stares blindly forwards, her eyes bright sapphire pools. Energetic sparks of blue electricity discharge from her tense fingertips.

'Faith?' Heidi says, hoping to get a reaction. Faith remains in a powerful trance and doesn't reply. The two nervous schoolgirls exchange confused glances. Their attention quickly returns to Faith as she suddenly withers into a heap on the ground.

Stumbling over the rubble, Roxanne and Heidi notice that their friends' half-open eyes have returned to their natural state.

'What happened?' Faith asks groggily, the words rasping in her throat as she speaks.

'You don't remember?' Roxanne asks, sounding surprised.

Faith gazes at the ground, a thoughtful expression on her face. 'I remember… I remember trying to find a space on the wall to climb up. I couldn't find one, and as I turned around the boulder was getting closer and closer… and… that's the last thing I can remember.' Heidi and Roxanne once again exchange baffled glances.

'Are you not hurt?' Heidi asks. 'I mean, that ball of… whatever it was, must have hit you pretty hard.' Faith glances down, checking her body. Not a scratch in sight. She hurriedly searches her fleece pocket. Luckily, the dagger is still hidden securely inside. Both of the schoolgirls had almost forgotten about the dagger.

'It seems that I'm OK,' she informs her young companions, still feeling rather dazed as she places the dagger back into her fleece pocket.

'Well, call me confused,' Heidi blurts out. 'But I guess it's a good thing. I mean that you're alright, that is.'

The three girls suddenly fall silent as a rumbling emits from the wall at the far end of the passage that they now inhabit. They watch as the wall slides to the side, creating a gloomy exit ahead. Roxanne and Heidi help Faith to her feet. The threesome hold hands, Faith in the middle of the uneasy schoolgirls as they timidly approach the new doorway. They flinch as a light flickers inside the opening, flooding the room beyond with brightness. They continue cautiously forwards, not knowing what to expect as they head towards the dazzling white light.

CHAPTER 58

Kyle and Jasmine both squint, shielding their eyes with their backs of their hands as a bright light suddenly fills the room that they occupy. 'I thought we were going be trapped in darkness forever,' Jasmine says with relief as her vision adjusts. 'We must have been sitting up here for at least twenty minutes after that door locked behind us.'

The two friends slouch against a large white wall at the back of a bare room. Even the door they entered through has completely vanished. 'How the heck do we get out of here?' Kyle asks anxiously, realising there are no exits from the claustrophobic room.

They saunter leisurely around the perimeter, running their hands along the walls to find any possible hidden passages. 'Well, that was useless,' Jasmine states as they find nothing helpful.

'Hey look, Jaz,' Kyle says, tugging on her white blouse. She turns around to see what her young friend is trying to show her. They watch attentively as large red letters begin to manifest on the right-hand side of the huge white wall.

Jasmine takes a few steps towards the wall as she attempts to figure out the writing. 'It's backwards,' she tells Kyle, recognising that the letters are appearing in reverse. She begins to read the words as Kyle moves alongside her. 'How many... legs... does,' Jasmine pauses, waiting for the next word to appear.

Meanwhile, on the other side of the white wall, Faith, Heidi and Roxanne are in a very similar position to Jasmine and Kyle.

'Hold it still, Hei,' Roxanne orders her friend. The three girls have their arms wrapped around a heavy wooden pole. With all their might, they attempt to hold it steady against the white wall.

'We need more blood,' Faith informs her struggling companions from the front of the line. The girls unsteadily manoeuvre the pole to a large stone well, positioned to the side of the room.

'Okay, on three,' Faith commands as they stumble towards the well which is full to the brim with thick bubbling blood. Roxanne scrunches her face in disgust, wishing that she had a free hand to cover her nose as the foul stench of warm blood wafts up her nostrils.

'It smells like a slaughter house,' Heidi says, trying to hold back her gag reflex as best she can.

'Come on, girls, we don't have much time,' Faith trembles, turning to see the back wall progressively closing in on them. After carefully dipping the pointed end of the pole into the blood, the friends fumble their way back to the wall.

'What's the next word?' Heidi asks from the back end as they lift the huge blood dripping stake.

'We have to write the words... 'it have',' Faith explains, reading from a small instructional plaque, fastened to the wall. 'And let's hurry. This thing is too heavy.'

'I'm confused,' Kyle says, scratching his head in wonderment. 'How many legs does... does what have?' he questions impatiently. Jasmine too looks rather muddled as to why the writing has abruptly stopped mid-sentence. The pair pay close attention once again as more backward letters suddenly begin to appear.

217

'It have,' Kyle blurts once the writing has finished.

'Very good,' Jasmine praises him, patting him on the back.

Kyle's self-satisfied expression returns to that of uncertainty. 'I still don't get it. How many legs does *what* have?' he says again.

Before their very eyes, five square shaped panels manifest on the white wall, protruding underneath the gory writing. The buttons are labelled from one to five.

'I think we press one,' Kyle says as he and Jasmine step towards the wall.

'But, which one?' Jasmine replies.

Kyle looks nervous as Jasmine takes a second step towards the wall. 'You do it, Jaz,' he says, his words quivering as they leave his mouth. Jasmine cagily reaches her hand towards the button engraved with the number three. Kyle closes his eyes tightly as Jasmine pushes the button. After pressing it, she immediately steps back in line with her young friend.

As the buttons vanish, the smeared red writing begins to drip, running down the once pristine white wall. Jasmine takes Kyle by the hand, backing away as the blood splats onto the ground and begins to spread across the floor. They back against the far wall, huddling together as the blood settles into the centre of the room.

'What's going on?' Kyle whimpers as the blood begins to tremble like a plate of wobbly jelly. The friends watch in shocked silence as the gore commences to rise. The blood begins to clot, becoming thicker and more solid as it takes shape. Muscles begin to appear, wrapped in wispy blue veins that sprout from within. Kyle stares in a mesmerized trance, while Jasmine places her hand across her mouth with repulsion, scarcely able to look at the gruesome sight that forms before them.

'What is it?' Jasmine whispers fearfully, hardly daring to breathe as she speaks the words. Too horrified by the gruesome materialization before him, Kyle remains silent. A large beating heart pulsates in the centre of the mass of blood, veins, and muscle, suddenly followed by a second that appears directly next to the first.

'I feel a little faint,' Jasmine pants, wiping her moist forehead with the sleeve of her white blouse. Kyle's concentration abruptly switches to his friend as he hears a loud thud next to him.

'Jasmine!' he cries, witnessing his friend, collapsed in a heap on the ground beside him. 'Jaz, wake up,' he begs, kneeling alongside her and shaking her by the shoulders.

Immense worry etches on Kyle's young face as Jasmine fails to respond to his vigorous efforts. Turning around, his eyes widen as he observes the mass of blood and gore that continues to develop, becoming larger and more deadly looking with every passing second. He gulps in horror, his bright eyes glinting in terror as three horse-like legs become distinguishable from the bloody bulk. He shudders with fear, flattening himself against the wall as a blood curdling howl echoes throughout the inescapable room. 'Why did she have to choose three legs?'

CHAPTER 59

Heidi quivers. 'Did you hear that?'

'I think anyone within a five mile radius heard it,' Roxanne replies in a sarcastic yet worried tone.

'But what the dickens was it? That's what I wanna know,' Heidi quickly retorts.

Roxanne raises her eyebrows. 'Dickens?' she asks sounding rather bemused. 'My mum says that word.'

'I know,' Heidi replies. 'That's where I got it from. She's always saying it when I'm over at your house.' Roxanne and Faith gaze silently at Heidi.

'Okay, moving on,' Roxanne says, turning her focus to Faith. 'What do you suggest we do now?' Before Faith can reply, Heidi suddenly shrieks, causing her two friends to jump in shock. Spinning around to face Heidi, both Roxanne and Faith gasp as they come face to face with one of the monks. The three girls stare into the darkness of the monk's hooded face.

'He scared the living daylights out of me,' Heidi whispers behind her hand.

'You have done well on your quest thus far,' the monk begins, directing his words at Faith. 'Through your triumphs and your determination, you have succeeded to gain the power and strength of our long forgotten brotherhood.' The mysterious figure floats gracefully towards the three friends. 'You must now submit your belief to your brother,' he now directs at Heidi. 'For the accomplishment of your task now rests on his shoulders alone.'

'Kyle?' Heidi squeaks. 'Is he okay? Where is he? What do you mean our task rests on his shoulders?' she rambles, bombarding the monk with as many questions as she can before having to draw breath.

'Beyond the wall you stand before,' the monk continues as he once again rises off the ground, 'is where your brother will accomplish either victory or feel defeat... for you all.'

Heidi marches a few paces forwards, standing almost directly underneath the floating monk. 'That's not good enough!' she bellows hysterically, worried for the safety of her younger brother, as well as for herself and her friends. Roxanne puts a hand on her anxious friend's shoulder.

The monk looks down at Heidi. 'His actions, and his alone, will determine the outcome of your selfless expedition,' the monk says as he commences to fade.

'But what's going on?' Heidi cries, begging to know more information. 'Tell me!'

'Everything shall become clear once your sibling succeeds... or fails,' the monk's words waft on the still air as his silhouette fades away entirely.

Roxanne and Faith comfort their stunned friend as she stares at the ground in dismay.

'At least we now know that your brother's still alive,' Faith says softly, attempting to make the situation a little better for Heidi.

'Yeah, but for how long?' Heidi answers, a tear running down her ivory cheek. 'And for some damn stupid reason, our lives now depend on him!' she explodes, striding purposefully across to the wall covered in blood dripping letters. 'Kyle!' she yells at the top of her voice. 'Can you hear me?'

Beyond the wall that separates the siblings, Kyle frantically attempts to awaken his unconscious companion. 'Jasmine, wake up, wake up!' he pleads, continuing to shake her. Jasmine lies comatose on the hard ground and doesn't react to her young friend's efforts. Kyle is too preoccupied to hear the muffled cry of his sister from the adjacent room.

He suddenly freezes, not daring to move as the sound of hooves can be heard pacing behind him. He remains completely motionless, trying hard not to breathe heavily, but his thudding heart makes the task almost impossible. A look of absolute terror glimmers in his eyes as a waft of warm breath ruffles his hair from behind. Each and every hair on his neck stands, a shiver shooting down his spine as the stale breath surrounds him, like evaporating steam from a boiling kettle.

A large three-legged beast stalks Kyle menacingly from behind. The Hell creature is oddly shaped. Its three horse-like limbs giving it the appearance of an old fashioned three-wheeled car. Matching the hoofed legs, the animal's torso is hard and lumpy and covered in dark coarse hair. Although still covered in bristly fur, its broad shoulders and hefty arms are more similar to that of a muscle bound human. The brute's head resembles that of a horse, only much darker and more sinister in appearance, its blunt yellow teeth chattering eerily. Its eyes are pitch-black spheres and its nostrils drip with gloopy, putrid slime.

A look of doomed dread fills Kyle's helpless eyes as the monster snarls. With no escape from the confined room, and having no means to defend himself, Kyle kneels timidly in prayer, hopeful that God must exist after all, and awaits his almost certain, untimely and extremely painful demise.

CHAPTER 60

We have to do something!' Heidi exclaims hysterically. 'Who knows what's happening to my brother behind this wall!'

'I know what you're saying,' Roxanne says sympathetically. 'But there doesn't seem to be much we can do. The monk said it's up to Kyle.'

Tears of frustration drip from Heidi's eyelashes. 'But he's all alone and what if he does fail? I'll never see him again and we'll all die down here.'

'I'm sure he'll be fine,' Roxanne replies, doubting her words even as she speaks them.

The two friend's attention suddenly turns to Faith as they realise that she has fallen silent, where she would usually be offering comforting words to back up Roxanne. They stare in awe, mouths hanging open as they watch their friend standing mightily, hovering a few inches above the ground. Her hair once again shines bright blue and is no longer tied into a neat ponytail as it blows around her head in an intangible gale. Her eyes have returned to deep blue pools of power and crackling electricity emits from the tips of her fingers.

Roxanne takes Heidi by the arm and steps backwards, giving Faith the space she needs. Heidi gasps, covering her mouth with her hand, overwhelmed by the sight of two intense beams of sapphire light that discharge from Faith's eyes. The friends gaze in amazement as the rays of light penetrate the huge white wall before them.

A howl of torment from beyond the partition makes the hairs on the schoolgirls' arms stand on end. As quickly as it possessed Faith's being, the power swiftly departs from her body and she descends back to the ground.

'What just happened?' Heidi asks as she and Roxanne move apprehensively towards their friend.

'I think I might have helped Kyle,' Faith replies, the remaining dazzling blue shimmers fading from her navy hair.

Heidi looks pleasantly surprised. 'How do you know that?' she asks enthusiastically, her fingers crossed in hope. 'And how did you know what to do?'

'I don't know,' Faith says, struggling to untangle her now wavy blue hair that drapes untidily over her shoulders. 'It's as if I have some sort of intuition. I didn't consciously do anything this time. It's like… the power took over me and knew how to help.'

'But you think he's OK? I mean… you feel it… right?' Heidi asks optimistically, hoping for Faith's reassurance.

Faith stares hard at the ground. 'I believe your brother is alright,' she answers after a few moments. 'I'm not sure why, or what exactly just happened, but I honestly believe he's safe.'

A doorway suddenly manifests within the white wall, not entirely unexpected as things like this seem to occur often and they are getting used to the sudden surprises. The ghostly door shimmers like the surface of a rippling lake. Roxanne and Heidi move either side of Faith, the three girls standing before the gleaming mirrored doorway, their reflections staring back at them. They gaze in distress, speechless by what they witness. Their mirrored selves are altered, each one dark and twisted in her own special way.

Faith stares at her image in the reflective doorway. Her doppelganger's pitch-black hair blows in a none existent wind, her deep black eyes glinting with a shine of pure evil as she grins wickedly.

Heidi's mirrored image looks old and frail, possibly how she would look in seventy years from now. 'I look terrible!' Heidi exclaims, running her fingers through her beautiful blonde hair. Her reflection mimics her exact actions, combing her bent, arthritic fingers through her wispy, dull hair, breaking the fragile strands between her crinkly fingertips. Her reflection's actions are much slower, as if even raising an arm causes her much difficultly.

Roxanne stares hard at her seemingly normal reflection. Nothing seems different or unusual. While she watches, her reflected body begins to turn to wood. Rising from her feet, all the way to the top of her head, her reflection transforms into a solid wooden figure, reminding Roxanne of the queen on an elaborate chess set.

'Roxy, you've turned into a tree person!' Heidi exclaims in shocked disbelief as her friend's reflection stands rigid.

The three friends stand gawping silently at their sorrowful mirrored images within the door before them.

'What do we do?' Heidi asks after a few moments of complete silence.

'Well, I think it's some kind of doorway or portal,' Faith says.

'So, I guess Kyle is OK,' Roxanne says to Heidi comfortingly, before turning to Faith. 'And it seems that you did help him after all.' Faith slightly smiles, pleased that she was able to help, but at the same time rather worried that she had no conscious control over her increasing powers.

With no alternative, the three friends step slowly towards the shimmering doorway. Their unnerving reflections beckon them onwards, calling them closer.

'I really don't know about this,' Heidi whimpers as they get within touching distance of the mirrored doorway.

'As usual we don't have much choice, Heidi,' Faith replies, not taking her eyes from the frightening images before them.

'Why do we look like this?' Heidi asks no one in particular, transfixed by their gruesome doubles.

Roxanne removes her gaze from the horrific sight before glancing around the perimeter of the shiny doorway. 'How do we get through? Is there a handle anywhere?' Before her friends can reply, their frightening reflections lunge from within the mirror, grabbing their human equivalent tightly by their clothing and yanking them through the apparitional doorway and into the next level of the Abyss.

CHAPTER 61

I hate this place,' Kyle mumbles to himself in a hushed breath. He remains kneeling over Jasmines unconscious body, his eyes tightly closed and his fingers in his ears.

He realises that whatever monstrosity was breathing down his neck is no longer doing so, but he doesn't dare open his eyes to find out why. After a few more uncomfortably silent moments, the young boy hesitantly opens one eye. As he does, the blurred vision of his friend lying flat out at his feet is the first sight to greet him.

Curious to see what had been behind him, Kyle cautiously rises to his feet, slowly turning around as he does so. He screws his nose, disgusted at the gruesome spectacle stretched out before him. The menacing Hell beast lies in a gory mound. Its vicious head and bulky torso have been blown to smithereens and its entrails now smear the large white wall as if a crazed artist has unleashed their fury with a tin of crimson paint.

Kyle's revolted expression switches to that of victorious anger. 'You think you can get the better of me?' he yells furiously, trying to get his hands to stop shaking. 'Now you're the one who's dead,' he says smugly, kicking the corpse with a slight hesitation, half expecting it to come back to life as his toes nudge the bulk.

He suddenly freezes upon hearing a shuffling behind him. He decides not to waste any time in finding out what now lurks in the room. 'Jasmine!' He exclaims, glee filling his innocent eyes as he spins around to find his friend standing facing him. 'I tried to wake you,' he tells her, throwing his arms around her. 'But you wouldn't wake up. I thought you were dead.' Jasmine doesn't reply, or even react to Kyle's interactions, she simply stares at him. 'You should have seen this monster, it was...' he turns to get another look at the bloody mess behind him. 'Actually, I'm not too sure what it was.'

A look of infuriation appears on Jasmine's once friendly face. 'Sasbian,' she snarls, continuing to stare into Kyle's eyes.

'Huh?' Kyle asks, confused. 'What are you talking about, Jaz?'

'Sasbian was his name. He was my loyal servant,' Jasmine replies, her voice becoming raspy as she speaks.

Kyle seems even more bewildered. 'Jaz, what are you going on about?' he asks again.

'First thing's first.' The girl says, taking a step towards her young companion. My name is not Jasmine and I am not who you think I am.' Kyle begins to panic, beads of sweat forming on his forehead as he steps backwards.

His so-called friend takes another pace in his direction. 'You remember your friendly monk?' she asks, lips curled in a sneer.

'Emilio? Yeah, I remember him,' Kyle responds, his mind racing with thoughts that don't piece together.

'Well... I *am* Emilio,' the girl tells him. 'I am also, as *you* know her, Jasmine; a lost mortal from earth like yourself and your sister.' The girl smiles evilly, her eyes transforming into deep black pools.

'Who are you?' Kyle whimpers, now afraid for his safety, and from the one person he thought he could trust with his life.

'My name is Jazelle, Angel of darkness and devoted servant to my master, the dark lord.' Jazelle continues to look deep within Kyle's eyes as she relays her story. 'I was formally devoted to the one *you* call... God.' A spark of light glimmers within her now pitch-black, soulless eyes. 'I was an Angel in the kingdom of light for centuries, devoting everything I was to the higher power within the heavenly realm. I began to get bored, weary from being overlooked by your so-called Lord; always too busy creating the perfect afterlife for you worthless mortals to consider our opinions. That is when my saviour sensed my true calling and came for me, leading me to an entire new beginning where I would be appreciated and granted freedom. The dark lord accepted my defiance of 'God' as a true sign of subordination, granting me control over the eternal damnation of his victims within the underworld. It wasn't long before the darkness expelled the final flicker of light from my being and I finally became a truly fallen Angel.'

Kyle takes another step away from the demon woman, gasping as his foot skids on a patch of blood. 'I don't understand,' he says nervously. 'I mean... why did you pretend to be my friend all this time?'

'Your entire journey has led to this point, and I knew it was destined to end here,' Jazelle begins to explain in a wicked, hissing voice. 'I was alerted to your presence from the moment your sister and her friends successfully conducted the ritual of Hades. It was my understanding that I should befriend you and gain your trust.' Kyle looks hurt, feeling emotionally violated by the demon woman's trickery. 'I intentionally kept you and your friends apart, and I assured your safety until you reached this room.'

'But... why?' Kyle splutters mournfully, a single tear dripping from his lower eyelid and splashing onto his cheek.

'From the moment you entered this room, your sister and friends relied on you to defeat my trusted companion, Sasbian. If you failed, you would have died and your sister and friends would have become trapped on the opposite side of that wall, spending all eternity in Hell. The most powerful black magician to ever have lived, and died, laid a potent curse upon that room. Their own distorted thoughts and memories would have driven them to the point of insanity. No amount of white magic would ever have freed them.' Jazelle averts her eyes from Kyle, looking thoughtful. 'The older girl must have more power than we believed possible,' she says to herself with dissatisfaction.

'Power?' Kyle asks timidly.

'Enough!' The demon woman bellows in a strong commanding voice, swiftly raising her arms towards the ceiling. Kyle stumbles backwards, leaning on the blood-stained wall as a great veil of thick black mist consumes Jazelle completely.

The boy's eyes widen in horror as the fog disperses. Jazelle stands before him. Her hair, now as black as her eyes, stands tall as if she is hanging upside down. Her entire body is covered in a tough, shiny black material and sharp black nails protrude from her fingertips, causing her veined face to appear pale and sickly.

'As your friends were kind enough to ruin our hard constructed plans, there is no more use for you,' Jazelle informs him, her chapped insipid lips smirking as she raises her hand. Kyle huddles in the corner of the room, his face glowing orange as it reflects a fireball that develops within Jazelle's open palm.

Unexpectedly, the intimidating demon woman suddenly closes her hand, extinguishing the ball of fire. She gazes contemplatively at Kyle. 'On second thoughts, I have a feeling that you may come in useful when your sister and friends arrive at my master's lair, *if* they make it that far.'

She strides purposefully towards Kyle, grabbing him firmly by the arm and yanking him rapidly to his feet. 'Enough with this façade,' she growls. 'You'll see your sister soon enough, and when you do, it will be the last time you ever see each other.'

Kyle remains in a speechless daze as the demon woman thrusts her free arm into the air, summoning a stormy fog. Kyle's eyes race with terror and uncertainty as the fog rises around them, concealing them inside a funnel of gushing black mist and miniature dazzling lightning strikes. In severe panic, Kyle stares around within the swirling fog, frantically attempting to prise himself from Jazelle's grasp. His eyes begin to feel heavy and his head begins to feel light. All of a sudden, everything around him falls into darkness and he loses consciousness.

The gory corpse of the demon horse combusts into a frenzy of roaring flames as the churning fog begins to disperse. As the dark mist completely evaporates, Jazelle and her young captive are nowhere to be found. Only time will tell where she has taken him and what malicious plans she has in store.

CHAPTER 62

Moments after being snatched by their gristly doubles, the girls are forcefully thrust through the other side of the mirrored door.

'Watch it, old me!' Heidi snaps, stumbling on loose rocks and stones as her wicked reflected image heaves her from the doorway.

Turning around, the girls catch one last glimpse of their grinning, malicious doppelgangers before the shimmering mirror fades away to nothing, just a bricked wall left in its place.

'Ouch, the ground's burning my feet,' Heidi complains, jumping up and down. Faith glances down as she too feels intense warmth on the soles of her feet. The vast amount of loose rocks and shingle smoulders beneath their feet, exactly like an enormous barbeque.

The three roasting girls hastily scan the land that they have been cast into. They stand on a heated pebbled beach. Waves of scalding lava crash onto the shoreline, sizzling as they return to join the steaming molten ocean that stretches as far as the eye can see. Crossing is certainly not an option. Ahead, a tall brick wall with a single opening is the only obstacle that awaits them.

'Let's get to it,' Roxanne says, boldly speeding towards the shadowy entrance in the wall.

'Let's not be hasty,' Faith suggests as she and Heidi swiftly pursue their hot-footed friend.

'Faith's right,' Heidi says, grabbing Roxanne by the shoulder and spinning her around to face her. 'We can't just go rushing into anything around here. Especially not now we're getting closer to our goal.'

Roxanne raises one eyebrow. 'I was only walking quickly because the ground's burning my feet.'

'Well, I know what you can be like,' Heidi retorts. 'You can be rather impetuous at times.'

Roxanne raises both eyebrows this time. 'Heidi, if you're determined to use long words at inappropriate times like this, make sure they're words that I can understand.'

'If you two are quite finished?' Faith interrupts, gently pushing both girls onwards, 'my feet are scorching.'

As the threesome reach the gloomy doorway, Heidi rushes across to a large rusty plaque that is nailed to the wall. Her eyes promptly scan the engraved writing, assuming that there will either be a cryptic riddle or a message of doom etched within. 'You're not going like the sound of this.' She begins to read the inscription aloud as her two companions huddle around. 'Dromm's labyrinth of nightmares past hast many paths to chance. Upon proceeding beyond the flaming torches of mayhem, there shall be no turning back. Forever you may remain imprisoned in a place of incomprehensible torment. Go forth and determine your fate.'

Roxanne shoots Faith a nervous sideways glance as Heidi steps away from the rusting plaque. The girls don't utter a word, standing side by side before the shadowy opening. Faith takes a deep breath as she warily leads her young friends into the mysterious labyrinth.

CHAPTER 63

I t's the same thing over and over again,' Roxanne states, becoming weary after an hour of trudging along path after path, each one surrounded by tall bricked walls.

'We're never going to get out of this place,' Heidi grumbles, promptly sitting down and resting against one of the uncomfortable walls. 'We must have missed those flames of mayhem, but all this walking is mayhem enough for my poor feet.' Roxanne and Faith sit beside their friend, also needing to rest their aching legs.

'That's so much better,' Roxanne says, releasing a huge sigh of relief as she relaxes against the wall. 'My feet are killing me!'

'Allow Dromm to do the killing,' a ferocious, gruff voice bellows from afar.

The girls leap to their feet, no longer noticing the soreness of their soles, as the skin crawling voice echoes through the labyrinth. Standing a couple of hundred feet away, a colossal beast glares forebodingly down the path. The monster stands upright on two hairy, grey hoofed legs. Its bulky torso glistens as the sunlight that filters from above the high surrounding walls reflects from hundreds of shiny turquoise scales. The creature's head looks similar to that of an alligator, only much fiercer. Its small black eyes stare menacingly as it snarls at the frightened girls, revealing its sharp blood-stained fangs.

'Back away slowly,' Faith whispers. The three petrified girls creep backwards, step by step, as inconspicuously as they can. Roxanne glances at her feet as she treads on a twig, which snaps under her weight with a loud crack. She quickly returns her gaze ahead at the sound of Heidi's cry.

'Run!' Faith shrieks, turning to dash in the opposite direction of the stampeding brute. 'Heidi, move!' she exclaims, panic stricken as she crashes into her gob smacked friend. Roxanne quickly grabs Heidi by the arm, spinning her around as Faith shoves her onwards, willing her to run as fast as she is able.

With the creature hot on their tracks, the girls hurtle back along the same long path that they have spent the last while trudging tirelessly.

'What is it?' Heidi squeals in terror, glancing over her shoulder to see the monster gaining, its fearsome jaws snapping hungrily.

'I think that's Dromm, the guardian of this level,' Faith puffs, propelling Heidi forward.

The terrified girls continue to sprint along the path, Heidi wincing from pain that shoots up her calves. Loose dirt and stones shake at their feet as Dromm heavily pursues them, gaining with every passing second. Knowing that the path continues straight on and has no turnings, the fleeing friends are sure that it's only a matter of time until the hideous creature has them in its slimy grasp.

CHAPTER 64

'Faith, can't you do anything?' Roxanne pleads as she continues to drag Heidi along the path.

'I don't have time to concentrate,' Faith pants, panic stricken and out of breath.

'Tell the powers to do something by themselves, like last time,' Heidi calls over her shoulder as Roxanne yanks her onwards.

'It's not that simple,' Faith wheezes, pushing Heidi forward.

'Stop shoving,' Heidi complains. 'I can't run any faster!'

The pursued girls' attentions lock onto something up ahead as they hurtle down the path.

'It's a monk!' Heidi exclaims, her eyes focusing on the distant figure. 'He'll save us.'

The girls gain extra momentum, dashing as fast as they can towards the monk. Heidi gasps as she turns her head to witness the gap between themselves and the charging beast decreasing by the second.

'Your souls are mine!' Dromm roars as he closes in. Heidi squeals in panic as she returns her gaze to the hooded figure.

'Help us!' Roxanne yells as they get within a few feet of the monk. To the girls' dismay, the monk fades and vanishes moments before they reach him. They screech to a halt, baffled by the monk's sudden disappearance.

'Holy crap!' Heidi shrieks, fearing for her soul as Dromm charges at them, death gleaming in his fearsome black eyes.

Before the girls even have time to think, the section of path they stand on suddenly crumbles underneath their weight. Dromm skids to a standstill as the girls vanish through the ground. He bellows with frustration as the friends' terrified screams diminish into the uncertain darkness below the labyrinth.

The petrified, shrieking friends plunge through the dark for what seems to be an eternity. After an entire minute of constant falling, Heidi opens her eyes, only to be greeted by a black veil that surrounds her. She can't even see her hand as she waves it in front of her face. She suddenly realises that she feels no wind, and her hair isn't blowing around, as it would be normally be if she were truly falling.

'Roxanne... Faith?' she calls nervously, frightfully eager for a rapid response as she hovers in mid-air. The only reply is the echo of her own voice, resonating far into the concealing gloom. She gulps, butterflies churning in her stomach as she senses that she may be alone, and possibly stuck in the endless obscurity, forever.

CHAPTER 65

'Girls?' Faith calls, trying to remain calm as she floats motionless in the pitch black wilderness. Gulping tensely, her heart begins to race as she becomes progressively more uncomfortable with each silent, passing second.

Something to one side suddenly seizes her attention. Squinting in the darkness, Faith stares as a distant white light shines brightly. The light begins to pulsate, expanding in size as it captivates Faith's gaze. She can't tell if she's moving towards the light or if it's moving towards her.

The light shines brighter as it grows larger with each fleeting moment. Before long, Faith's eyes close involuntarily as the dazzling white light intensifies. Through her closed eyelids, Faith can see the darkness being entirely consumed by the illuminating light. She draws her knees to her chest, fastening her arms securely around them, reminding herself of a foetus in the womb.

A few moments on and the bright light begins to fade. Faith continues to huddle in the same position. Slowly opening her eyes as the brightness dies away, she gasps in astonishment as her blurry vision adjusts to her new surroundings.

'What's going on?' she murmurs in a state of disbelief as she lies on a lawn of dewy grass. A gigantic mansion, shrouded in shadows, looms before her, reaching into blackness. Sudden flashbacks from her childhood leap into Faith's mind. She recalls the time when she was around eight years old. She used to have a recurring nightmare of this exact house. She reminisces that she would be trapped inside the huge mansion. A hefty masked man wielding a deadly hammer would pursue her, attempting to murder her. In her dream, she never did escape the house. She would wake up before discovering the exit, or being trapped by the mad man.

After a few stunned moments, Faith picks herself off the ground, the moist grass leaving a damp patch on her clothes. She takes a look around, trying to spot her friends, but soon realises that she is utterly alone. Surrounding the mansion, darkness stretches for what seems to be forever. The overwhelming sense that trudging into the adjacent darkness will achieve nothing, chokes her. She takes a deep breath and cautiously paces towards the mansion's chunky stone steps that lead to the ominous doorway.

Subdued lighting can be seen through the downstairs dirt smeared windows as Faith quietly makes her towards the dark wooden doorway. Halting as she reaches the door, she notices an ancient looking scroll, tied with black ribbon, placed at her feet. Crouching, she retrieves the parchment. She unfastens the ribbon and carefully unravels the fragile paper, making sure not to tear it.

'Through these gates of nightmares, you shall pass,' Faith begins to read quietly to herself. 'Your courage and determination have led you this far, but do you have enough strength to see you through to the conclusion? Only you can save yourself now. Succeed to find the glimmering exit and your journey is almost at an end. Fail and your journey has only just begun, as here you shall stay forever more.'

Faith's mind races with an array of nightmarish thoughts as she places the scroll back on the stone step. She grips the door's oversized bronze handle and quietly lifts the heavy latch, wincing when the door creaks as she slowly pushes it ajar. Wanting to make as little noise as possible, she squeezes herself through the slightly open door before softly closing it behind her. As soon as the latch falls into place, the door evaporates into the air, leaving a solid stone wall in its place.

Faith gulps, trying to recollect the details from of nightmares from all those years ago. Upon turning around, she is greeted by a dull, square shaped entrance hall. Tatty pictures of dead flowers hang lopsided from the grimy, once white walls. One picture is different. Faith stares at a great, unnerving portrait of herself, suspended on the focal point of the back wall. She is dressed in an old fashioned, white ball gown. Her hair is styled in ringlets and curls. The portrait has been slashed through the centre and dried red marks stain Faith's dress, as if the picture bled when sliced.

In the centre of the room, a filthy spiral staircase leads upwards into what Faith remembers to be the library. How ironic, she thinks to herself as she reflects on her career choice in the mortal world. No other doors lead from this room; the only way from here is up.

After taking a few steps towards the stairway, Faith stops dead in her tracks. She looks up at the ceiling as heavy footsteps can be heard thudding above. Another memory suddenly flashes into her mind. She gasps worriedly as she remembers that the hammer wielding foe of her childhood nightmare lies in wait at the top of the staircase.

CHAPTER 66

Faith struggles to recall her nightmare as she moves onto the first step of the winding staircase, knowing full well that her enemy is lurking above. She creeps silently up the stairs, hardly daring to breathe as she advances. The opening to the room above awaits her and with no door to separate the stairway and the library, Faith must try to remain out of sight.

Nearing the top, she crouches, peering cautiously up into the library. The occasional flickering candle, burning in tall, old-fashioned holders, pierces the otherwise completely dark room. Faith gazes nervously around the space. No movement can be detected and all is quiet. She can just about make out a door, which appears to move in the soft glow of the dancing candlelight.

Faith warily enters the room, praying that the floorboards don't creak under her weight. She stops, standing motionless, not knowing whether to aim directly for the door, or to sneak behind the bookshelves. Her memory of her childhood nightmare is so distant that the details are extremely hazy. Across the far side of the room, a shadowy cumbersome figure rises from behind a large wooden desk. This makes Faith's decision easier and she quickly steps behind one of the tall shelves, crammed with hundreds of dust covered books.

She peers through the rows of publications, remaining extremely silent as she watches the large silhouette bend forward, reaching towards the floor.

'It's him,' Faith whispers to herself as she recognises the immense rectangular hammer that the shadowy figure lifts from the ground. She stares in horror as the awkward murky shape trudges back and forth at the far end of the room. She waits for him to leave, but after a few minutes she recalls that he almost never leaves the library. She will have to sneak past him if she is ever going to escape.

Carefully stepping to the side, Faith prepares herself to slink inconspicuously past her childhood enemy. She gasps, shuddering as the wooden boards creek beneath her feet. Her gaze quickly refocuses back to the shadowy man as he slowly lifts the heavy hammer. Faith begins to breathe heavily, overcome with panic as the brute plods towards her hiding place.

All of a sudden, Faith feels a shooting pain flow up her right leg. She looks down to see a large black rat gnawing at her ankle. Covering her mouth with her hand to suppress a scream, she shakes her leg, flinging the rodent from her foot. The rat scampers around the shelf. Faith hears a loud thud as the masked man slams down his hammer, crushing the rat as it attempts to flee past him.

Faith once again peers through the mounds of dusty books. She screws her nose with repulsion as the maniac bends and retrieves the squashed rat by its tail. His menacing laugh reverberates throughout the library as he haphazardly flings the corpse in Faith's direction. She squeals meekly in disgust as the carcass slams into the shelf, directly on the gap from which she peers, droplets of blood splattering her in the face.

Faith wipes the traces of blood from her cheek with the back of her sleeve as the masked thug turns, heading for the door. Faith releases a deep sigh as the rat at least bought her more time. As she sighs, her breath stirs the thick layer of dust that covers the old books before her. She feels a tickling sensation in her nostrils as she accidentally inhales the dust. She holds her nose, desperately trying not to sneeze. The bulky silhouette opens the door, slamming it behind him as he leaves the room. Faith finally loses control and sneezes, continuing to hold her nose as she tries to remain as quiet as possible. She freezes with anticipation, her hands across her nose and mouth, praying that she wasn't heard.

Dread fills her eyes as the door flings open. She gulps nervously as the silhouette of the large man re-enters the library.

'I hears you, Miss Faith,' the tyrant says in an unintelligent voice as he trudges slowly in her direction. Wherever she runs, she is bound to be spotted and very possibly flattened by the hoodlum's deadly weapon.

'I sees you,' he mumbles forebodingly, catching a glimpse of Faith's blue hair, which shines in the revealing candlelight.

Chapter 67

Faith gasps in terror, frozen to the spot, not knowing what to do. She can't help but stare at the large silhouette as it moves towards her, emerging from the darkness and into the orange candlelight. Her mouth drops open with horrified recognition as the monster from her scariest nightmare stands in the eerie light of the flames, shadows dancing around him. The top of his overly wide head is half covered in a black leather mask, small jaggedly cut holes unveiling his truly wicked eyes. His disfigured, drooling mouth remains exposed, revealing his grotesquely rotten teeth.

Faith closes her eyes, concentrating on the image of blue electricity. She imagines her enemy surrounded by cracking blue power, burning and disintegrating before her. She opens her eyes, staring at brute. Nothing. She holds up her palms, willing the blue energy to respond to her demands. Nothing.

'Me gonna bash you good,' the masked man says in his dim-witted voice as he slowly advances. He chuckles as he raises his hammer, ready to strike if Faith decides to make a dash for the door. Realising that her powers are seemingly useless within her nightmare, Faith has other ideas in mind as the fiend looms upon her. As he reaches a few feet of her hiding place, Faith places the palms of her hands on the shelf and pushes with all her might. The masked mutant groans as the heavy bookshelf topples forward, crushing him under its immense weight as it lands hard on top of him.

Faith realises this maybe her only chance for escape. She speedily dodges the fallen shelf and heads for the open door. She jolts to a halt as she passes the apparently unconscious fiend. She notices that he dropped his hammer, which is now lying unattended at his side. Faith stoops and grabs the handle with both hands, panting as she struggles to move the extremely heavy implement from its resting place. She shrieks as a strong, grubby hand grasps her ankle. Squirming away, Faith releases her grip on the hammer and races through the open door.

Scurrying down a long, dimly lit corridor, Faith gawps as she passes a selection of monstrous paintings of explicit torture that hang on the eroding stone walls. More candles in bronze holders protrude from the walls, illuminating the path with an eerie orange glow.

She quickens her pace, heading for a wooden door at the end of the spooky passage. Upon reaching the end of the corridor, she grabs the round brass handle and the door opens with a timid creak. Before she can see what the room has in store for her, the masked man's insidious laugh flows from the opposite end of the candlelit passage. She turns to see him waddling his way towards her, dragging the hammer along the ground behind him. Faith quickly backs into the room, slamming the door shut behind her.

'Damn it,' she groans, searching for a lock, but to no avail. She turns to face into the room, eager to distance herself from her bloodthirsty foe. Stares around the enclosed area, Faith notices that she occupies a small square room, much different from the rest of the mansion. The walls and ceiling are made entirely from mirrors. A hoard of stuffed animals and porcelain dolls clutter the floor. Some of the toys are small and some are large, like prizes at a fairground.

Faith suddenly catches her reflection in the mirror opposite. 'What the heck?' she whispers to herself in bewilderment. The mirror reflects her image as an old-fashioned doll. She wears a long white dress and matching knitted bonnet, tied under her chin.

Upon hearing the scraping of the dragging hammer, Faith's attention suddenly refocuses on her aggressive stalker. She quickly scans the room for an exit, but the only door in the room is the one through which she entered. With no other option, she dashes to a corner of the room and hastily sits down. She figures that she's fully clad as a life size doll for a reason. As the door creaks open, Faith slumps in the corner, staring straight forward and trying to calm her breathing.

'You go squish like rat,' her creepy adversary chortles as he heaves his weapon into the compact room. He stands motionless, staring into the mirrored space, baffled by all the toys, as if he has never ventured into this room before. 'I sees you no more, where you gone?' he says, scratching his head densely as he stares at the toys.

The masked man suddenly realises that he can see himself in the mirrored walls. The dreadful reflection seems to antagonize him considerably. He raises his hammer, smashing it down onto a pot doll, dressed as a baby, which instantly smashes to smithereens. He kicks a small stuffed elephant before violently stamping on a brightly multi-coloured, knitted rabbit.

His reflection surrounds him as he moves into the centre of the room. He bellows wildly, striking one of the walls with his hammer. Faith gasps, her eyes lighting as a wooden door appears behind the shattering wall of glass shards.

The rampant fiend abruptly stops as he hears Faith's intake of breath. 'There's you are,' he says, recognising Faith's blue hair sprouting from underneath her bonnet. Faith can't possibly run for it, he will attack before she can even get to her feet. She concentrates as the brute staggers towards her, slobbering with crazed excitement as he closes in for the kill that he has been waiting all these years to achieve. Something seems different. Faith's eyes widen in horror as she realises that in the dream, she didn't have the powers and this must be why they wouldn't work in the library. She sits motionless amongst the jumble of toys, attempting to think of a solution. The only solution appears to be allowing the hunter to finally capture his prey.

CHAPTER 68

Faith remains sitting in the corner of the room, paralysed with fright as the tormenting man lifts his hammer high above his head, ready to land the killing blow. She looks up as the extreme weapon comes into contact with the fragile mirrored roof. She quickly grabs a large brown teddy bear, using it to shield herself as the glass breaks.

Thousands of shiny mirrored shards plummet to the ground. Faith cringes as the glass rains down, penetrating the cuddly bear that she protects herself with. Once all the glass has fallen, Faith tosses the toy aside, leaping to her feet. The masked man cowers in pain, hundreds of glass splinters protruding from his bulky torso. Faith realises this is her only chance for escape. Dodging past him, she opens the newly found door and races up a flight of solid stone steps beyond.

A gust of wind blows through her long blue hair as she nears the top of the cold stairs. She glances down at her clothes. Her outfit has returned to normal. Continuing upwards, she can see bright twinkling stars as she approaches an archway that leads outside the mansion. She stops as she arrives at the opening. She now stands on a small balcony at the very top of the building. Plummeting to the ground is her only chance, there is no other way. She peers over the veranda railing, hoping that the drop isn't as far is it appears. What she sees below is not what she expected. A shimmering black hole floats a few feet below the balcony. She watches, captivated as bright blue sparks flash within the portal.

Her concentration is abruptly interrupted as the masked man's freakish laugh echoes up the dark stairway. The sound of his hammer being dragged up the steps of stone soon follows. Faith shivers as she senses her foe clomping his way towards the secluded balcony.

'Is this the way out?' Faith asks herself uncertainly. She can't possibly escape the crazed hammer man in such close quarters. Jumping is her only means of escape; she just prays that it's the right decision.

'I gots you now, Miss Faith,' the ogre's voice drones from beyond the darkness of the archway. Faith clambers up the metal railing. She swings her legs over, holding tightly to the rails as she leans apprehensively towards the swirling black vortex. She closes her eyes tightly, not daring to see where she's heading as she drops from the veranda. The whirling black hole immediately closes in a flash of blue power as Faith vanishes within it, leaving no trace of her presence at the nightmare mansion.

CHAPTER 69

'Where am I?' Roxanne wonders in a daze as she awakes from unconsciousness. The last thing that she can remember is being helplessly suspended, surrounded by a vast darkness. She shivers as she lies on an uneven rocky surface. Cold water half covers her body as she slumps uncomfortably on the ground.

She slowly levers herself off the rocky terrain, her back aching as she moves to an upright sitting position. It takes her eyes a few moments to adjust to the gloomy area. As she rests in the puddle of cold, fresh water, she becomes conscious of the fact that she now sits in a large dank cavern.

Droplets of tepid water drip from the moist, stalactite clustered roof, splashing into the numerous pools of water situated on the bed of the cave.

'What am I doing here?' Roxanne asks herself, gazing around the dismal grotto. A faint sound of someone sniggering echoes through the darkness. Roxanne slowly gets to her feet, her eyes swiftly scanning the vicinity as a multitude of strange noises emit from within the shadows.

'This feels familiar,' she murmurs under her breath as she catches glimpses of squat goblin shaped shadows that cackle wickedly as they hide in the gloom.

She turns around, not completely surprised to find a passage leading from the cave behind her. It's as if she has been here before and her subconscious knows what to expect. She hastily makes for the rocky passageway, attracted by a blue glimmering that exudes from within. As she heads for the opening, she keeps one eye on the mischievous shadows, apprehensive as to what they might look like in the light, or if they would even exist at all.

Pale blue, twinkling lights shine on Roxanne's face as she reaches a gemstone encrusted passage, cautiously stepping inside. The sparkling tunnel is bright, even though no source of light can be seen, as if it doesn't hold true to the real world. Roxanne paces her way through the twinkling channel, the feeling of serene calmness washing over her body as she travels. As she departs the beautiful passageway, Roxanne finds herself in a more spacious cave. This cave floor is entirely flooded with deep, crystal-clear water.

Roxanne appears baffled as she teeters on the brink of the deep icy pool. There appears to be no way around, and even if there was, there are no exits so it would be pointless.

'Looks like the only way is down,' the girl huffs, crouching and placing her hand into the water. 'You have to be kidding me. It's freezing,' she complains, retracting her chilly hand. She suddenly pauses as a distant shape through the slightly rippling water catches her gaze. She gulps hard, her breath freezing in her throat as an enormous shark swims far below the water's surface.

CHAPTER 70

Shuffling away from the edge of the pool, a long forgotten memory engulfs Roxanne's mind. She remembers that when she was around seven years old, her dad took her to the opening of a new aquarium. She loved to stare at all the beautiful and strange fish, but most of all she wanted to watch the shark feeding in the large outdoor tank.

The shark attraction was closed after the trainer, who was feeding the fierce creatures, accidentally fell into the tank. The spectators, including young Roxanne, watched helplessly as the man was eaten alive by the vicious, blood-thirsty fish.

The memories flood into Roxanne's head in graphic detail, as if it happened only yesterday. The shark that Roxanne has glimpsed within the waters of Hell is the megalodon, a humongous version of its close relative, the great white. She remembers watching a video online about the megalodon shark which terrified her to the very core. Back on earth, the megalodon has been extinct for millions of years, but here it is, right below Roxanne's feet. She doesn't know what to do, but what she does know is there's no way on earth, or in Hell, that she's diving into shark infested waters.

Her hand touches something as she scuffles even further from the pool. Glancing down, she sees a small paper scroll tied with a black ribbon. She cautiously picks it up, loosening the bow and carefully unravelling the old paper.

'Six feet under is where thou shall rest if you do not descend beyond,' Roxanne already dislikes the sound of this as she continues to read aloud. 'Not through the earth, air, nor through fire. The element of life holds the key that you most desire. Lying on its stationary bed is where thou shall head.' Roxanne looks rather confused. 'Where's Heidi when you need her,' knowing that her friend, even though rather ditsy most of the time, does have a good head on her shoulders when it comes to this kind of thing.

'Earth, Air, Fire and water,' she mutters to herself. 'Water must be the element of life that holds the key, whatever the key might be.' She rereads the inscription on the scroll. 'Six feet under is where thou shall rest if you do not descend beyond. Lying on its stationary bed is where thou shall head.' She ponders for a second. 'Oh great,' she grumbles. 'I'm guessing whatever it is I need to find lies on the bottom of this pool.'

Warily returning to the poolside, she peers apprehensively into the motionless water. Through squinted eyes, she can just about make out the bottom of the deep pool. What appears to be an opening is implanted into the pool's bed, like an oversized plughole. Roxanne figures that her aim is to make it safely through the hole, far below the water's surface.

'There's no way I'm going down there,' she says to herself, getting to her feet and stepping away from the edge of the flooded cavern. She turns to leave, hoping to find an alternate route. She screams, jumping on the spot as the shadowy monk stands inches from her face.

'You must face your ultimate fears,' the monk advises her. 'Only then can you be strong enough to succeed.'

'But there's no way that I'll get past that shark,' Roxanne says, turning her head and looking at the deep pool. 'Anyway, I don't even think I can hold my breath long enough to...' She stops as she turns back around, only to find that the monk has vanished as quickly as he had arrived. 'It's so annoying when he does that,' she grumbles, rolling her eyes.

Roxanne sighs pitifully as she once again peers into the clear pool. No movement can be seen below. Perhaps she does have a chance, if she swims quickly. Attempting to remain as inconspicuous as possible, she sits on the side of the pool, gently dipping her legs into the chilly water. Her heart involuntarily quickens, thudding in her chest, making it more difficult to control her breathing. All she can picture is the immense shark swimming towards her at top speed, clamping its fearsome jaws around her feet and yanking her to her watery grave.

'I can't believe I'm doing this,' she shivers, feeling like crying as she carefully lowers herself in, trying hard not to make any ripples on the surface as she descends.

Knowing that she must keep her eyes open, she ducks her head under the water for a quick test try. This water feels somewhat different than she expected, but she can't quite figure out why. She gasps in shock as the huge shark darts between two mountainous rocks at the bottom of the vast pool. Instead of coughing and spluttering, no water filters into her throat. To her utmost surprise she realises that she is able to breathe, just as if she was on land.

With her eyes open, she is able to see every little detail of the waterlogged cavern. The rocks are covered in brightly coloured, luminous corals. For a moment she becomes lost in the serenity of the beautiful pool. She quickly remembers the blood thirsty fiend and bounces back to reality. She inhales a deep breath, still unable to believe that she can actually breathe under the water. Gently kicking her legs, Roxanne heads towards a cluster of rocks, realising that the massive fish can't possibly squeeze itself between them. Swimming in this water comes so naturally to Roxanne. She glides, as if she was a bird flying through the still air.

Making it safely to the first cluster of rocks, she keeps a watchful eye on anything that stirs below. With no sign of the shark, Roxanne edges around the rocks, keeping close and trying to remain concealed for as long as possible. Her heart pounds as an enormous, crimson jellyfish floats just a few feet from her, its long, deadly tentacles trailing behind like the tissue paper from an exploded party popper.

After scouring the vast waters for any sign of the humongous shark, Roxanne tentatively swims away from the protection of the rocks, keeping her eyes fixed on the noxious appendages of the jellyfish as they sway hypnotizingly in the almost motionless water. After swimming a few metres into open water, Roxanne's heart leaps into her mouth as a large, swiftly approaching shape, emerges from the corner of her vision.

CHAPTER 71

Roxanne averts her gaze from the jellyfish, turning to witness the somewhat distant shape of the gigantic shark swimming in her direction. Its wide, pitch-black eyes reflect the bright corals as it zooms like a torpedo towards her. The girl's legs feel numb with terror and horror fills her eyes as the shark advances, far too quickly for her to dodge its attack. Almost certain that she will never make it to the hole in time, an alternative idea pops into her head. As crazy as it may seem, she has to act quickly if she's going to have any chance of survival. She turns her body effortlessly, facing the giant jellyfish. With a strong kick, she thrusts herself towards the deadly, swaying tentacles. She gasps, accidentally swimming too close for comfort, but somehow managing to avoid becoming tangled in its poisoned feelers and she safely passes the floating blob.

She gulps, praying for her plan to work. Hovering behind the protection of the floating jellyfish, she maintains a safe distance as the shark pelts towards her, death gleaming in its hungry eyes. The immense, razor jawed fish seems to disregard the presence of the jellyfish as it bursts through the array of lethal tentacles without contemplation.

Roxanne speedily swims upwards as the shark ploughs through the jellyfish's defence system at top speed. As the venom instantly infects its bulky body from head to tail, the shark becomes paralysed. The enormous fish spins out of control, crashing into the rocky wall of the water filled cavern. Roxanne observes intently as the shark begins to sink, unconscious from the brutal impact.

Thankful that the plan succeeded beyond her wildest dreams, Roxanne quickly swims towards the opening in the ground. Upon reaching the hole, she grabs the rim and manoeuvres through with ease.

Her scream echoes as she plummets a few feet onto a hard concrete ground. Sitting upright, she rubs the back of her head in a dizzy state of bafflement. She looks up to where she fell into the room only moments before. The water filled cave, which should be situated directly above her, has vanished. An elaborately carved, white ceiling takes its place. The circular room that Roxanne finds herself slumped in is relatively spacious, but there are no signs of a door or any openings, which doesn't surprise her. Thick white pillars placed evenly throughout the room stretch from floor to ceiling.

'Hmmm,' she mumbles to herself in confusion, looking around as she clambers to her feet. 'Oh, that's odd,' she remarks, realising that she is now bone dry, not a drop of water to remind her of her time in shark infested waters. Ever so gradually she cautiously wanders into the centre of the large room, expecting something sinister to leap out from behind each column that she passes. She comes to a stop upon reaching a large, rectangular stone slab that lies on the ground. Kneeling down, she observes some text, etched into the solid surface.

'Beneath thy feet must thou reach, it is I alone whom blocks your way.' Roxanne continues to read the inscription as she runs her fingers over the writing. 'The unsighted serpent is the key. Employ her wisely to set thou free.' Roxanne sits back, looking confused, 'I really do hate riddles,' she grumbles, slouching uncomfortably on the ground.

She suddenly notices a grubby white statue across the far side of the otherwise bare room. Heaving herself upright, the girl curiously makes her way across to the sculpture. The statue is of a bald lady, who stands upside down on her hands. Replacing her legs, a thick, scaly tail, similar to that of a snake, stretches high into the air. For as long as she can remember, snakes have always been one of Roxanne's biggest phobias. She turns her nose up as she notices that the reptile woman's eyes and mouth have been stitched shut.

'It's only a statue,' Roxanne tells herself as she turns away, not entirely believing the words that leave her mouth. She begins to make her way back to the stone slab, when an unexpected rumbling seizes her attention. She gasps, slowly turning to face the statue again as the rumbling intensifies.

'This isn't good,' Roxanne murmurs nervously, witnessing the sculpture shuddering, as if a powerful earthquake disturbs it from below.

Roxanne shrieks, shielding her head with her arms as the statue explodes like a grenade. Dust soars into the air as debris crashes loudly to the ground. Roxanne hesitantly removes her arms from her head, not wishing to view what may await her vision.

'This *really* isn't good,' she utters to herself in a hushed whisper, her eyes wide with terror as the half woman half reptile creature stands before her. Alive.

CHAPTER 72

Roxanne stands extremely still, holding her breath and remaining as quiet as possible. The serpent woman lingers, almost motionless, as if waiting for a chase to commence.

Roxanne wrinkles her nose as the settling dust from the explosion of plaster irritates her nostrils. Unable to control the tingling sensation, a loud sneeze shoots from her mouth. She cringes as the noise echoes through the spacious room. The girl prepares to make a run for it, but pauses as she notices the creature's lack of reaction. The serpent woman remains in the same motionless position as before, with not so much as a flinch.

Roxanne suddenly notices that the strange creature has no ears. *That's why she never reacted to the sound, because she didn't hear it,* Roxanne thinks. Feeling rather confounded by this extraordinary organism, Roxanne slowly begins to back away. As she takes her first step, the serpent lady twitches, as if sensing Roxanne's presence for the first time. Roxanne continues to retreat, quickening her pace as the monster appears to come to life with every fleeing step that she takes.

Roxanne shrieks as the merciless creature abruptly charges towards her, effortlessly sprinting on her hands with more ease than an Olympic track star. The terrified girl turns, dashing as fast as she can in the opposite direction, afraid to look back. She screams for a second time as she catches her heel on an uneven section of the cemented floor. She tumbles uncontrollably to the ground, rolling on her side before crashing into one of the sturdy pillars with a thud.

Roxanne lies still for a moment, her head spinning with intense dizziness as fragments of plaster crumble from the column beside her. After a few seconds, she recalls where she is. She turns her head sharply, expecting the horrific snake lady to be looming over her, ready to extinguish her young life. To her utmost surprise, the monster stands stationary in the centre of the room. Roxanne looks mystified, confused as to what's happening, and her woozy head isn't exactly helping the situation.

'Oh, I get it!' she exclaims to herself as wisdom flashes like fireworks. 'It reacts to movement by sensing vibrations in the ground.' She now feels that she will be safe as long as she remains still, but she can't just stay in the same spot forever. She detects the fact that the creature stands before the stone slab in the middle of the room.

Beneath thy feet must thou reach, only I stand in your way, she thinks to herself as she recalls the inscribed riddle. *The unsighted serpent is the key*. Even though she is not sure how, Roxanne realises that the snake lady is the answer to her escape. Reaching out her hand, Roxanne carefully grasps a small chunk of plaster, which rests at the base of the column that she crashed into. Aiming carefully, she hurls the piece of rubble onto the large stone slab.

Roxanne remains motionless as the serpent woman raises her tail high into the air, smashing it violently onto the fragment of plaster. Dust soars into the air as a large crack tears down the centre of the stone plaque. Roxanne gasps with excited astonishment as she finally understands the situation, and better yet, the solution. She hastily throws another portion of plaster, and yet again the creature slams its vicious tail onto the already fractured slab. This time the plaque splits in half, shattering and falling into darkness. A black hole in the ground is now all that remains. This is Roxanne's chance, but nevertheless she must take extreme caution, as one swipe from that tail would most certainly be fatal.

She seizes a larger chunk of debris. She brings back to mind the time she and Heidi entered the shot-put competition at their school's sports day. She takes aim and tosses the plaster chunk as far and as accurately as she can. The rubble crashes to the ground across the far side of the room, chipping into smaller pieces as it hits the cement with force. The vibration attracts the serpent woman's attention and she darts away from the hole, leaving the exit unguarded.

Hurriedly scrambling to her feet, Roxanne sprints towards the opening in the ground. The snake lady senses the girl's rapid footsteps and immediately backtracks, realising that she has been deceived. Upon reaching the dark hole, Roxanne hesitates as the fear of plummeting into another uncertain terrain takes over. A black mist, flashing with blue lightening, swirls within the pit.

Leaning over the whirling vortex, Roxanne gulps, unaware of the fast approaching, rampant Hell beast. Her eyes open wide in horror as the unexpected sight of the serpent woman's tail catches her eye. She shrieks as the heavy tail slams onto the ground, barely missing her shoulder. She wobbles uncontrollably as the ground shakes beneath her feet. Fortunately for her, she topples forward, plunging into the portal and vanishes from sight.

CHAPTER 73

Urg, my tummy feels a bit queasy' Heidi complains, rubbing her stomach gently as she sits upright. Expecting a response from her friends, Heidi appears confused as silence greets her from the neighbouring gloom.

'Roxy... Faith?' she calls out as she slouches on a hard surface, surrounded by far-reaching darkness. She begins to feel increasingly worried when her second call receives no reply. Sweat beads forming on her temples, she gazes around the extremely murky environment, attempting to pinpoint any clue of what her next move should be. As her eyes begin to adjust to the blackness, silhouettes of numerous objects begin to take shape all around her. She gulps hard, shrinking back against the ground as a dismal figure gradually appears, standing motionless in the dark. The large individual grasps something which moves slowly back and forth, but Heidi is unable to distinguish what that something is.

Without a hint of a warning, an intense white light abruptly blinds Heidi's vision. Instantly screwing her eyes tightly, Heidi shelters her face with the back of her hand. As the bright spotlight begins to fade, a jolly, yet chilling laugh causes Heidi to jump to her feet in sheer horror. To her utter dismay, the large figure that she saw through the murkiness is now illuminated in full view.

The unsettling laugh emits from inside a giant blow-up clown. The clown's bright green hair stands tall, almost as if he has suffered an electric shock, Heidi thinks. His orange and yellow striped jumpsuit comes complete with fluffy red pompoms down the middle. His oversized yellow shoes, tied with thick red laces makes Heidi think of chewy sweets from her childhood, making her stomach rumble. The clown holds a single blue balloon, which wafts on the ever so slight breeze.

Heidi stands frozen to the spot, terror shining in her eyes as she stares captivatingly at the frightful clown. Memories from when she was a toddler flood her mind. She closes her eyes, wincing as she recalls a family outing to a travelling funfair one crisp autumn afternoon. She remembers that she was about 3 years old. She rides on her dad's shoulders as he makes his way through the crowd of visitors. She can hear the crunching of fallen leaves under his heavy brown boots as he treads.

Her dad lifts her off his shoulders as they reach her mum. Her baby brother, Kyle lies fast asleep in the pram that she gently rocks back and forth. Heidi cringes as she recalls looking up at the attraction they stand before; the Funhouse. Above the entrance, a grotesque painted face of a clown, with its unnerving false smile, beams down at her.

Heidi reopens her eyes, her memories beginning to blur. All that she can remember is that she's had a fear of clowns ever since that day, and has never set foot near another funhouse again. She glances back towards the inflatable clown, who continues to laugh in an intimidating fashion. Beside the clown, a dark archway suddenly illuminates.

'Oh, you have to be fricking kidding me,' Heidi whimpers, whishing the ground would open up and swallow her as she reads the large multi-coloured letters above the arched doorway; 'Funhouse'. She inhales a deep breath, expelling a heavy sigh as she prepares to enter the house that she is certain will *not* be as much fun as advertised.

'Well, this is just great,' she complains, creeping cautiously towards the dazzling entrance. She keeps her eyes fixed on the creepy clown's jolly, yet menacing, face as she approaches. His repetitive laughing sends shivers shooting down her spine. She pauses in her tracks. She holds her breath, her heart rate increasing as she convinces herself that the clown just winked at her. Taking another deep breath, the girl shakes the dreadful thoughts from her mind and she continues onwards. Passing the clown, she shrieks, jumping in fright as his balloon bursts with a loud bang. 'Don't do that,' Heidi scolds, thumping the clown on the arm in anger, a new sense of courage taking hold as adrenaline pumps through her veins.

The clown's continuous chortling grows fainter as Heidi gingerly enters the funhouse, walking warily down a seemingly endless corridor. The path is dimly lit with a row of tiny purple bulbs running along either wall. She huffs, noticing the lights fading into the distance before her. Her feet ache and this hallway is extremely long, much longer than she'd like it to be.

As she continues along the path, something in the distance seems to be walking directly towards her. She gulps nervously, her heart beginning to pound and her pace slowing. Realising that turning back is not an option, she prepares herself to run and dodge the figure as she gets closer and closer with every step that she takes.

'Oh!' she exclaims to herself in relieved surprise, getting close enough to see who the figure is. 'It's just me,' she says, staring at her reflection. She now comprehends that the passage isn't as long as it first appeared. A large mirror is positioned at the end, giving the illusion of an endless corridor. Written on the mirror, in what appears to be red paint, are the words '*touch me*'. Warily reaching out her hand, Heidi touches the mirror. To her astonishment, her hand penetrates the glass.

'Eeewww, it feels like jelly,' she says, wiggling her fingers inside the gooey mirror. She gasps as she feels something slide into her hand.

'What the?' she comments, retracting her hand from the mirror to see that she now holds a small scroll. Inquisitively unfastening the black ribbon that secures the scroll, allowing it to flutter to the ground, she carefully unfolds the delicate paper and begins to read aloud. 'To find your way out of here, you must defeat your greatest fear.' Heidi gulps, not liking the sound of this at all. 'The key to freedom lies behind the phoney smile, only then may you discover Kyle.' Heidi suddenly gains a glint of determination in her eyes. 'Kyle must still be alive!' she exclaims with joyous relief. 'Now it's up to me to save him.'

Her confidence swiftly subsides as the spine-chilling laugh of the clown abruptly echoes down the corridor from behind her.

'No way!' she exclaims in horror as the clown from outside reflects within the mirror. The once inflated rubber clown walks along the passage and is as lifelike as any clown Heidi had the displeasure of meeting back on earth. The girl gasps, spinning around to see the newly animated assailant trudging towards her. Replacing the burst balloon, a shiny meat cleaver is grasped in its white-gloved hand. Its permanent cheerful expression remains fixed on its bright white face as it plods closer and closer, chuckling hysterically.

'Well,' Heidi says nervously as she turns back to face the mirror, 'here goes nothing.' Without hesitation, she closes her eyes and leaps through the liquefied mirror and into the beginning of her worst nightmare.

CHAPTER 74

Heidi opens her eyes as the sensation of stepping through jelly disperses from her body. She is now confronted by a large gloomy building that looms ahead of her. A green flashing sign reading 'Hall of Mirrors' hangs above the doorway.

'Oh, I hate the hall of mirrors,' Heidi grumbles, recalling the time she had a panic attack after becoming lost inside a hall of mirrors while with Roxanne on holiday. 'I have a strange feeling this isn't going to be as straight forward as it seems,' she says as she meanders towards the entrance.

As she gingerly pushes open the door, the spine-chilling laugh once again bellows from behind her.

'I knew it!' she exclaims, spinning around. Her breathing deepens as the awful clown begins to emerge from the rippling mirror that she herself passed through only moments before. 'Hall of mirrors here I come,' she says to herself, thrusting the door open and darting inside.

Through the doorway, a passage entirely decorated with glistening mirrors greets the school girl. She wastes no time in dashing down the shimmering corridor, almost forgetting to be watchful of any traps that may be set. All she can think about is that horrific clown with its false smile painted across its face.

'Huh?' she gasps in confusion as she reaches a dead end. She pushes on the mirrored panel before her, but it doesn't budge. She quickly turns and presses on the surrounding panels, praying that one of them gives way. 'Oh crap!' she exclaims hysterically as the clown's laughter echoes along the glass corridor. 'Quick, Heidi, think,' she urges herself as multiple images of her colourful pursuer reflect in the surrounding mirrors.

She speedily darts from one mirrored panel to the next, pushing each one in turn, eagerly hoping that a hidden doorway with be revealed at any moment. When each panel refuses to dislodge, she yields and hurriedly makes her way back to the dead end.

'Stay back!' she yells as the hideously jolly clown skulks closer, the razor-sharp cleaver raised threateningly above its head. On the ground, a few feet from her, Heidi spies a small red button in the centre of the path. She obviously missed it in her state of panic. Her enemy is now too close for her to back-track. 'Step on it,' Heidi whispers to herself with anticipation as the clown advances in her direction. 'Come on, you stupid clown, step on it.'

She waits silently, trapped at the end of the corridor like a caged animal ready for slaughter. As the chuckling clown approaches, its oversized yellow shoes depress the red button. Heidi jumps in shock as a loud horn sounds and a jet of thick mist shoots from the ceiling above her pursuer. She presses herself against the back panel as the clown becomes smothered in the cloud of fog. She squeals, surprised as the mirrored panel suddenly dislodges, causing her to tumble backwards as the section of wall rotates like a tall turnstile.

As Heidi falls flat on her back, the reflective panel settles back into its original position, clicking back into place and separating her from the colourful attacker.

'That was a stroke of luck,' she sighs with relief, heaving herself off the ground. The mirrored wall seems to be soundproof as the clown's laughing can no longer be heard on the other side. Heidi's foremost hope is that the monster isn't clever enough to figure out how to continue its hunt.

'Whoa!' Heidi exclaims, turning to face into the area that she now occupies. She stands on the perimeter of an expansive square room. The walls, ceiling and floor are all painted black. Countless pictures of indiscriminate objects are drawn on the four walls in luminous paint of many different colours. A sealed hatch is embedded into the ground in the centre of the room, a small control box fixed next to it.

Heidi looks perplexed as she walks across and inspects the control panel. It comprises of four rows of numbered buttons. The rows are labelled, 'North', 'East', 'South' and 'West', each row having five buttons numbered '1-5'.

'Ooh a riddle,' Heidi says, noticing an inscribed plaque nailed to the front of the hatch. Kneeling besides the trapdoor, the girl begins to read the text. 'To save your soul, employ the elements to gain control. The bright northern star lights the way to the western flood.'

Heidi sits on the floor, pondering the riddle. The bright sketches on the walls grasp her attention as she notices that some of them may be of use to her. Each picture has a number from one to five painted within its centre. The scrawlings appear to be completely disorganised. A vase with a single flower, a bright green tree with pump red apples hanging from its branches, a teddy bear, a unicorn and many other random objects. Heidi spots a drawing that resembles the planet earth. She has an idea in mind as she continues to scan the wall. She smiles as her eyes fix upon what appears to be a drawing of a tornado, spiralling out of control. In close proximity is a painting of a flame. She claps her hands in delight as the final illustration that she sees is of a fluffy cloud that expels large droplets of rain.

'I'm so clever,' she congratulates herself while making a mental note of the numbers on each picture. 'North is earth, so that's number three. East is air, number...one. South is fire, number three again and West is water, which is number... five,' she says, thinking out loud as she keys in the code on the control box. A look of bafflement appears on her face as a message saying 'Invalid', illuminates on a small LCD screen attached to the panel. She grabs the handle of the door and tugs doubtfully. Her fears are confirmed as the door remains locked and sealed tight. 'This is going to be tougher than I thought,' she groans.

It's not long before she realises what she may have overlooked. Glancing around, she notices that all the four walls are almost identical. The drawings are exactly the same, only the numbers are different for each illustration.

'This isn't fair,' she complains, lying flat on her back as her head begins to throb. 'This is far too complex, even for me. There are millions of different combinations that it could be,' she exaggerates in exasperation, her brain feeling utterly drained.

She abruptly sits bolt upright as she detects something that she wasn't previously aware of. Despite the numbers being different, one wall has an extra painting. The image of a golden star is painted above all the other illustrations on that one wall.

'The northern star,' Heidi gasps, knowing that this must be of some significance. After thinking silently for a moment, it finally clicks. 'North to West,' she says eagerly. 'I have to match each element to the corresponding wall that faces in that direction, starting in the North and ending in the West.'

She begins on the wall with the golden star; she figures that this wall must face north so she makes a mental note of the number on the picture of planet earth. On the east-facing wall, she observes the number on the tornado painting, the flame on the south and the rain cloud on the western wall.

'This better work or else I'll be stuck in this room forever,' she says, keying in the code '1,4,1,5'. She heaves a huge sigh of relief as the control panel flashes green, followed by a clicking sound.

Heidi leans across to the door, grasping the handle and heaving. The door opens silently, revealing a mesh of colours in the room below.

'A ball pool,' Heidi gasps as she peers through the now open hatchway. The ball pool was the only part of the carnival funhouse that she actually enjoyed when she was younger, although that may soon change. The pool of brightly coloured, plastic balls is situated roughly thirty feet below the opening through which Heidi peers.

'It's not that far,' she tells herself, attempting to remain calm and not to let fear overcome her. She carefully swings her legs over the side, perching on the edge of the opening. She turns herself around, gripping the ledge firmly and carefully lowers herself through. She squeals as she dangles from the doorframe, her legs swinging uncontrollably in mid-air. As her arms are not physically strong enough to pull herself back up, the only way from here is down.

Her grip weakens as she hesitates, but she finally gives in to the inevitable and releases her fingers from the ledge. Her shrieks echo as she plummets into the pool, plastic balls flying in all directions as she lands. Luckily, even though the pool of balls isn't very deep, the bottom of the pit is conveniently lined with soft sponge to break her fall.

'That wasn't too bad,' Heidi pants, dragging herself from the ball pool, not wishing to stay in there for too long as anything could be lurking in wait beneath the bright colours. 'This better not be another puzzle, my head can't take it yet,' she says setting her eyes upon a wall, which is filled with dozens of brightly painted red doors. The doors are all different sizes and are spaced across the wall at different heights. A wooden ladder rests in the corner of the room, obviously as an aid to reach the higher doors.

Heidi checks around for a riddle or a clue as to which door to open, but she can't see anything of interest. Apart from the ball pool and the wall of doors, the room is otherwise bare. She silently stands facing the doors, pondering which to open first. From behind, a loud thudding and the sound of scattering plastic balls makes her gasp and jump in shock. A chill runs down her spine, as she knows that someone or something has just landed in the pool of balls behind her.

CHAPTER 75

Heidi turns slowly around, fearful about what she might see. Before her, the hundreds of bright balls sit unmoving in the pit. She stands motionless, scarcely daring to breathe.

'Roxy?' she calls softly, instantly feeling stupid for even thinking it could be her best friend. She gulps nervously, watching as the balls begin to part, something stirring from below.

'Oh no!' she gasps in disbelief as a large white hand rises through the balls, instantly followed by the hideous laughter that she thought she had escaped in the mirrored hallway.

She spins back around and dashes across to the wall of many doors. She grabs the handle of one of the doors at random, yanking it open. She looks surprised as a solid brick wall greets her. *Is there no way out?* she thinks to herself as she slams the door shut and proceeds to open the one next to it. 'Another wall?' she says frantically, crashing the second door to a close. After speedily opening each door on the lowest level with no success, she realises that she must aim higher. She glances towards the ball pool as she hurries across to the set of ladders. The clown's intense green hair now protrudes through the balls, both its hands gripping onto the edge of the pit as it attempts to pursue its terrified young victim.

Attempting not to allow terror to overcome her, Heidi grabs the lightweight wooden ladders and hurriedly makes for one of the elevated doors. She rushes up the steps of the ladder, reaching the first door and wastes no time in flinging it open. She screams, losing her balance and toppling backwards as a hoard of brightly coloured, paper streamers spring out of the doorway. She squeals, shielding her head with her arms as she tumbles through the air, expecting to hit the hard ground with force. To her astonishment, instead of landing on the tough marble flooring, she settles into something soft and comfortable.

She turns her head inquisitively to see what broke her fall. Her eyes open wide in horror as she stares into the freaky smiling face of the killer clown. Lying in the arms of her foe, she yelps in alarm as the clown's large hands squeeze her tightly while once again emitting the horrible, blood-curdling chortle. Heidi can't think of anything else to do apart from to punch the clown on its large red nose. The clown's laughter wavers as Heidi struggles to loosen one of her arms and wallops the clown on its nose with all the strength that she can muster. She strikes for a second time and the clown's grasp relents, dropping the girl as it protects its aching nose with its oversized white hands

Heidi promptly gets to her feet and dashes back to the propped ladder. She moves it slightly to the left, positioning it between two unopened doors. She leaps the rungs, two at a time as she ascends to the top. The door to the left of her has a large lock where a key is obviously required in order for it to open. She selects the door to her right, prising it open as quickly as possible. Three round red buttons numbered from 1-3 are all that occupy the inside of the doorway.

'This better not be a trick,' Heidi says doubtfully, hesitantly pushing the first button. She looks up as a sound comes from above. She watches as a tile in the ceiling flips open, releasing a mass of gooey mess. The green slimy substance splats directly in front of where the clown stands, still protecting its painful nose. Heidi looks confused as she turns her attention back to the buttons and presses the middle one. She again gazes upwards as another sound emits from the ceiling. From the same opening, a shiny metal spike descends. It clicks into place and stops as it protrudes through the hole.

'The key lies behind the phoney smile,' Heidi reminds herself as she suddenly remembers the words written on the scroll. Her focus swiftly returns to the clown as the creature regains focus and removes the meat cleaver from its baggy jumpsuit pocket. As the make-up covered monster takes a step towards the ladder, the sticky green gunge bonds its oversized shoes to the floor like superglue. Heidi now realises what must be done as she turns her awareness back to the buttons.

'Take this you freak of nature!' she cries, thumping her fist on the third and final button. As the button is depressed, the heavy spike releases from its locked position and plummets towards the ground. Heidi covers her eyes with her hands as the sharp spear pierces the immobile clown. She jumps in shock as the clown pops like a balloon, sending a deafening echo bounding throughout the room.

Thousands of pieces of colourful confetti surge from within the monster, dancing in the air as they flutter to the ground. All that remains of the unsightly clown are its gigantic yellow shoes and its stripy suit. Something rests upon the ground between the remains, catching Heidi's eye as it glistens amongst the settling confetti.

'The Key!' she exclaims as she hurries down the ladder. Carefully avoiding the gooey mess, she leans forward, retrieving the key before returning to the ladder. She scampers up the steps towards the locked door, eagerly inserting the key and unlocking it with anticipation.

'Whoa,' she utters as the door creaks open to reveal a large cylindrical corridor, which is bathed in subdued purple light. At the end of the passage, a misty black portal, with flashes of blue lightening, swirls enticingly.

'Get me out of this un-fun house,' she mutters to herself as she clambers into the passageway and stands upright. She walks down the corridor, gazing around at the pretty, twinkling violet lights as she proceeds. A look of puzzlement appears on her face as the passage begins to move. She topples to the side as the entire cylinder swivels, getting faster and faster with every rotation.

'I feel sea sick... without the sea,' Heidi complains, holding her stomach as she tumbles, unable to stand upright in the revolving channel. She releases a loud gasp of dismay as a second sensation fills her with dread.

'The tunnel's shrinking!' she cries as the passage slowly begins to seal itself. 'I have to get out of here, fast.' Still incapable of standing, Heidi resorts to dragging herself by her elbows along the turning path. 'I'm so dizzy,' she groans with frustration as she continues to roll uncontrollably.

Her breathing becomes heavy as exhaustion takes over. 'I can do this,' she tells herself sternly as she focuses on the whirling portal. She squeals as the tunnel begins to feel extremely tight and claustrophobic. A few moments are all she has left before she is crushed to death by the contracting passageway. She knows that she must give it her all. She tugs herself towards the exit with almighty determination. Fortunately, her willpower pays off as she finally reaches the end, thrusting herself into the crackling portal moments before the tunnel seals completely behind her.

CHAPTER 76

The constant sound of a ticking clock stirs Heidi from her deep slumber. She rubs her eyes with the palms of her hands as she wakens. She lies on a soft, comfortable bed. Silky white satin sheets envelop her completely. She stretches, flinging back the covers and sits upright, swinging her legs over the side of the bed. She sits in a light and airy room with pale wooden flooring and stone walls, rather like a converted attic of a farmhouse.

Her attention focuses on two more beds across the opposite end of the room. The covers are bulked up, as if bodies lie beneath. Heidi steps down onto the creaky wooden flooring and tip-toes nervously towards the pair of beds opposite her. She freezes, remaining silent as something stirs under the covers of one of the beds.

'Roxanne!' Heidi exclaims with delight as her best friend drowsily emerges from beneath the duvet. 'What happened to us?' Heidi asks, running to her bleary eyed friend and draping her arms heavily around Roxanne's shoulders.

'Heidi!' Roxanne squeals as she arouses. 'You don't even want to know what happened to me,' she tells her tightly clutching friend.

'Likewise,' Heidi replies. 'It was my worst nightmare come true.' Before any more words can be spoken, a familiar groan comes from the final occupied bed.

'I recognise those voices,' Faith says, rubbing her head as she sits up in her bed. Roxanne and Heidi dash over to their friend, plonking themselves down next to her and giving her a great big hug at the same time.

'What happened to us all?' Faith asks as her head finally stops spinning.

'Well, I was in a 'fun house',' Heidi informs her friends, gesturing inverted commas with her fingers when she says the word 'fun'. 'I was being hunted by a gigantic killer clown.' She shudders at the memory of her nightmare.

'And I had to swim through a deep pool, being hunted by a massive shark before battling a blind, deaf and dumb snake lady thing,' Roxanne adds.

Faith raises her eyebrows. 'Well mine seems rather tame compared to those,' she laughs, groggily.

The girls' conversation ceases as they hear a scuffling noise coming from below them. Looking to the left, Faith spots a flight of wooden stairs that appear to lead to the ground floor.

'Come on,' she whispers, taking her young friends' hands and creeping towards the steps. They cringe as the floorboards creak with each step they take. As they reach the lower floor, they see that the downstairs room is entirely empty, with a single door leading to what must be the outside.

'Come on girls,' Faith says quietly. 'We have to keep moving, we must be close to the centre or we wouldn't have been split up like that... I imagine.' Faith leads her companions down the final couple of steps and strides towards the closed door. Heidi screams, grabbing Roxanne firmly as the monk unexpectedly appears in front of the door in a dazzling flash.

'I've said it once and I'll say it again, I really wish you guys wouldn't do that,' Heidi says, placing her hand on her pounding heart.

'You three girls have done well to succeed to this point of your journey. The powers of darkness grow ever stronger, invading your souls as you progress towards your final destination. One of you shall soon be tested.' The girls gaze worriedly at each other as the monk continues. 'Can the increasing energy be controlled, or will it override your senses and everything you hold true. Only time will give you the answer.'

Heidi raises her eyebrows. 'And what's that supposed to mean?' she asks with attitude, becoming rather fed up with having to work everything out for themselves. The monk vanishes as quickly as he appeared, without giving Heidi the answer that she wanted. 'Rude,' she mutters, rolling her eyes, expecting that outcome nonetheless.

'I wonder what he meant by that,' Roxanne ponders.

'Let's not worry about it yet,' Faith replies. 'We have to get moving and let's try to stick together. I don't want us to get separated again.' Faith cautiously opens the door, squinting as a stream of light from outside passes over her face.

'Oh great,' Heidi moans as Faith opens the door fully to reveal high-bricked walls before them. 'We're still in that blasted maze.'

Heidi follows dejectedly as Roxanne and Faith step through the doorway. The girls are faced with the option of going left or right. Looking to the right the girls see a pair of flaming torches in the distance.

'Wait a sec,' Roxanne says, suddenly remembering something from when they first entered the maze. 'There was something about... the torches of... mayhem. But I can't remember if we should be looking for them or avoiding them.'

'I don't think we have a choice,' Faith quivers as she looks to her left.

'Oh no!' Heidi exclaims in horror as she also looks left. 'It's Dromm!' The huge mutated guardian of the maze clomps its way down the path towards the friends.

'We can't go back,' Roxanne says, turning to see that the doorway has vanished.

'Run!' Faith orders, shoving the young friends to the right as the immense brute suddenly charges towards them, its fearsome jaws snapping ferociously.

'I have serious deja-vu,' Heidi pants as Roxanne pushes her to run faster. 'I don't know about this,' she says as they approach the flaming torches that stand at the entrance to a larger room.

'We have no other option,' Faith cries as they dash past the torches of mayhem and through the entryway.

The space they now occupy is completely bare, and not surprisingly, there are no other exits leading from the room. The girls look around desperately, realising they're trapped.

'We've come the wrong way!' Heidi shrieks in alarm as Dromm hurtles towards them at top speed, eager to devour his helpless, meaty dinner.

CHAPTER 77

The three girls huddle together in terror. Roxanne and Heidi close their eyes tightly while Faith attempts to use her powers to stop the Hell brute. After what seems to be a long time waiting for the beast to attack, Roxanne timidly reopens her eyes.

'Faith, you're doing it,' she says as Dromm stands at the entrance, attempting to beat down an invisible wall with his colossal fists.

'I'm not doing anything,' Faith replies, confused. Heidi also opens her eyes, curious about what's taking place. 'That inscription you remembered,' Faith says, turning to Roxanne. 'It mentioned something about 'once you pass the flaming torches you can't go back. Perhaps it's now sealed off.'

'That's all very well,' Heidi says as Dromm stomps angrily away, 'but now we're trapped in here. Although, saying that, something is bound to happen like it usually does.'

Before Faith can respond, a rumbling from behind them grabs their attention. The girls turn slowly around, stepping backwards as the far wall begins to split and crack down the centre.

'Told you so,' Heidi says as the wall separates, revealing a creepy archway made entirely from bones and skulls. Through the horrifying mass of remains, a flight of steep stone steps leads down into uncertain darkness.

'Is that what I think it is?' Heidi asks, pointing to a small pile of bones that lie on the ground in the middle of the doorway, slightly separated from the rest of the ancient remains. Faith looks excited, realising that another pile of monk's bones is situated just a few feet from where she stands. If Heidi had not pointed them out, she might have missed them completely.

'Wait a minute,' Roxanne says as her eager friends hurry towards the bones. 'The monk warned about handling energy.'

Heidi looks confused. 'So?' she asks, unable to comprehend what her friend is trying to say.

'So,' Roxanne says, rolling her eyes. 'Maybe we should consider *not* touching *these* bones... or Faith not touching them, I mean.'

'Stop trying to be clever, it doesn't suit you,' Heidi smirks. 'We need this charge of power. There might not be many left and Faith needs to be as strong as possible.' Roxanne sighs, accepting that Heidi is most likely right in her thinking.

'It will be fine,' Faith assures her young friend. 'I have a peculiar feeling that the Devil's lair is somewhere down there,' she says, glancing towards the dark archway. 'I have to be at my most powerful if we are going to have any chance of succeeding. We've come too far to fail.'

Roxanne moves in next to Heidi as Faith crouches, ready to absorb another portion of the monks' powers. Roxanne waits in nervous anticipation as Faith carefully places the palms of her hands on the heap of old bones. As expected, the bones begin to glow with a bright blue hue. The sapphire shimmer absorbs into Faith's hands, flowing up her arms and through her entire body. The glow intensifies as her hair shines with a dazzling blue radiance.

Heidi and Roxanne jump backwards in surprise as Faith swiftly releases her hand from the bones. She abruptly springs to her feet in a commanding and powerful stance, her arms taut at her side and her fingers spread wide.

'Faith, are you okay?' Heidi asks nervously as Faith stares ahead, seemingly looking straight through her. Roxanne's mouth drops open in horror as Faith's eyes suddenly roll backwards, being replaced with completely black pools. The two friends hold onto each other tightly, recoiling as the vivid blue colour drains from Faith's hair. From the roots to the tips, the stunning blue sheen is overridden by blackness until her entire head is covered in pitch-black locks.

'What's going on?' Heidi whispers from the corner of her mouth, not wanting to take her gaze from Faith's terrifying transformation. Roxanne's lips quiver, unable to reply, as she too is captivated by Faith's alteration. Thin blue veins sprout across Faith's face as her complexion turns pale and her lips become dry and begin to crack.

'Faith…' Heidi says tensely. Faith stands motionless, breathing heavily as she stares unnervingly at the two frightened girls. 'Are you… okay?'

'Your venture has been for nothing, and now your pathetic souls will fuel the master's dark universe,' Faith croaks in an evil rasping voice.

Roxanne releases Heidi's arm as she takes a vigilant step towards Faith. 'Faith, what's going on? she asks, trying to remain calm, but her voice trembling. Faith disregards the question and extends her arms sharply towards her young friends. Roxanne and Heidi soar backwards, crashing to the hard ground as a burst of black power discharges from the palms of Faith's hands.

The schoolgirls tumble across the floor before coming to rest on the uncomfortable ground.

'Heidi, are you alright?' Roxanne asks as she sits upright as quickly as possible, her head spinning and disoriented.

'I'm OK,' Heidi replies, hitching her trouser leg to reveal a graze on her calf. 'Where's Faith?' she gasps, concerned as the two girls look towards the gateway of bones and Faith is nowhere to be seen.

CHAPTER 78

T his is bad,' Roxanne says shakily as she clambers to her
feet. She suddenly recalls the mirrored doorway that
showed their sinister reflections. 'Faith's reflection came
true,' she tells Heidi, who had also just realised the same
thing. 'That means that ours might…'

'Roxanne, stop!' Heidi cries, covering her ears. 'I don't
want to think about it, I can't.'

Roxanne puts her arms comfortingly around her
frightened friend. 'It will be okay,' she says, attempting to
sound sincere. 'We just have to find Faith and do
something.'

'But do what, Roxy?' Heidi asks, uncovering her ears.

Roxanne thinks for a second before answering. 'To be
honest, Heidi… I have no idea, but we have to try something,
anything to get her back.'

Heidi grips Roxanne tightly by the hand as they both
walk apprehensively towards the archway of bones. The
unwelcoming flight of cold stone steps greets them as they
reach the gloomy entrance.

'You first,' Heidi says, retreating a few steps backwards.

'I don't think so,' Roxanne promptly responds, raising
one eyebrow disapprovingly. 'We'll go together.'

The girls lock arms as they pace nervously down the
stairs, keeping an eye open for anything sinister in the
shadows, which now includes their friend. They creep
cautiously through the tense dankness, attempting to

remain composed as they enter the fifth level of the underworld.

The humid, shadowy passage begins to widen as they descend deeper. A mesh of fiery colours can be seen through the blackness in the distance. A choir of severe cries and screams wail along the passage, sending chills down the girls' spines.

'What the…?' Heidi gasps in horrified disbelief as they approach the end of the tunnel. The passage expands into a huge cave. Blazing torches illuminate the room in a blistering heated glow and the walls drip with moisture. Hundreds of sturdy wooden tables fill the entire vicinity. People of all ages lie on the table tops, strapped down with blood-stained razor wire while cloaked demons perform a vast array of stomach churning tortures on their selected victim.

Roxanne covers her mouth, rapidly feeling considerably ill as one of the torturers uses a rusty implement to slice the scalp of a young woman before viciously ripping her long brown hair clean off her head, leaving her skull exposed. The victim screams in sheer anguish, but remains conscious throughout her torture.

'I can't watch,' Heidi whimpers, shielding her eyes with her hand. Before anything else can happen, Roxanne swiftly seizes Heidi by the arm, yanking her behind a section of the rocky passage that juts from the wall.

'What're you doing?' Heidi whispers before noticing that Roxanne has her finger pressed to her lips, signalling for her to be quiet. The friends cautiously peer around the rocky edge. Two of the cloaked guards walk towards them, their faces concealed by heavy hoods. Roxanne and Heidi keep well hidden in the murkiness so as not to be noticed.

The guards halt before they reach the girls, turning to the left hand wall of the passage. The friends gasp as the torturers remove their robes and hang them on a row of hooks that look as if they have been carved from bone. Beneath the clothing, the two guards are cold, grey skeletons, their eye sockets smouldering with black flames.

The girls duck back behind the protruding section of wall, hiding in the shadows as the skeletons march past them and vanish into the gloom.

'We have to go through,' Roxanne says, peering back into the torture chamber.

'Are you thinking what I think you're thinking?' Heidi asks, hoping that her friend has an alternative plan.

'Follow me,' Roxanne replies, quietly making her way to the cloaks that hang on the wall.

'I thought so,' Heidi groans, hesitantly following her friend. 'I'm really not sure about this. What if we get caught?' she asks worriedly, her legs trembling as Roxanne hands her one of the cloaks.

'We have no choice,' Roxanne whispers as she slips on the cloak and fastens it securely. 'It's either this or wait here until we starve to death, and I'm already really damn hungry. Now put it on.' Heidi sighs heavily as she follows Roxanne's instructions, fumbling with her cloak before fastening it tightly around herself.

'Now,' Roxanne says as she gets ready to put up her hood. 'Calmly follow me. Keep your head down and try to blend in.' Roxanne places the hood over her head and her face becomes blanketed in darkness. Heidi hurriedly mimics her actions. As she follows Roxanne to the entrance of the torture chamber, she fears the demons might hear her thumping heart.

'Remember what I said, and keep quiet,' Roxanne instructs as she takes a deep breath and steps into the humid cave. The awful screaming and crying makes the girls feel physically sick as they tread slowly past row upon row of gruesome torture tables. The gut wrenching stench of stale blood and burning flesh fills their nostrils. Heidi quickly stops herself from covering her mouth in disgust as she unwillingly witnesses a middle-aged man having his teeth extracted, one by one, with rusty pliers. The helpless man splutters, choking as his mouth fills with blood.

The girls continue, passing unnoticed by the busy, agony-inflicting torturers. Roxanne gasps in shock, pausing for a brief moment as a young girl, around the age of six or seven, lies on one of the tables. The girl cries for help, struggling as she attempts to break free. The sharp razor wire cuts into her wrists and ankles. As Heidi crashes into Roxanne from behind, the girl's torturer looks up from the far end of the table as he prepares a vast array of blood-stained contraptions.

'This sow is mine,' he snarls as Roxanne and Heidi promptly continue onwards. They walk with their heads down, trying to keep a low profile as they aim for an immense, wooden door.

'What are we supposed to do now?' Heidi asks through gritted teeth as she notices that the door doesn't have any handles.

'I'm guessing we push,' Roxanne answers, flattening the palms of her hands against the door. 'I can't open it!' she puffs, the door not budging an inch. Heidi moves alongside her friend and helps to push, but the door remains tightly sealed.

'You can't go through there,' a gruff voice bellows from behind them. The girls gulp, slowly turning around to see a hoard of hooded torturers standing facing them. 'No one enters the master's lair,' one of the guards barks. 'You should know the rules. Unless...' Heidi gulps for a second time, perspiring in panic under the heavy grey cloak. 'These two are impostors!' The guard yells, pointing his bony finger in the direction of the two frightened companions. Roxanne and Heidi exchange horrified glances from the darkness of their disguises, images of their impending torture flashing through their minds as the mob of irate hooded skeletons advance towards them.

CHAPTER 79

'Roxy, what are we going to do?' Heidi asks, her lip quivering in terror as the mass of cloaked figures gains on them. Roxanne's mouth turns numb, unable to speak as she notices blood smeared tools of death in each of the torturers' cold, fleshless hands. The two terrified girls stand motionless, sick to the stomach as the thought of this being the gruesome end to their long journey fills their heads. There's nothing they can do, but wait, wait for their inevitable, eternal torture.

The hefty wooden door behind the girls abruptly explodes open. Huge chunks of wood slam hard into Roxanne and Heidi's backs, sending them flying in opposite directions. Roxanne groans as she lands hard on the rocky ground. She quickly sits upright, rubbing her head as her vision stops spinning and she can once again see straight. A look of shock appears on her face as she witnesses the hooded gang of guards standing motionless, as if petrified on the spot.

'Faith!' Roxanne exclaims, turning her head to see her pale and evil looking friend standing in the shattered doorway, her black hair blowing in a non-existent gale. Faith remains silent as she walks slowly across to Heidi, who lies unconscious on the ground. Roxanne watches, unable to catch her breath as Faith bends forwards and scoops Heidi into her arms like a rag doll.

Roxanne timidly heaves herself to her feet as Faith completely blanks her and walks back through the devastated doorway, Heidi draped lifelessly across her arms. Roxanne glances back at the dumb struck demon hoard. She apprehensively pursues Faith, keeping a safe distance, but at the same time not wanting to lose sight of Heidi.

The spacious, circular room that she enters is lit by one single spotlight in the centre. No walls can be seen as the circumference of the room is submerged in shadows. Roxanne freezes, silently watching as Faith steps into the light and places Heidi on the ground. She then turns towards Roxanne, raising her arms into the air. Roxanne ducks as a powerful bolt of black energy soars in her direction. She soon realises that Faith wasn't aiming for her as she turns to witness the broken doorway seal itself, the splinters of wood piecing back together in their original positions like a complex jigsaw being solved too easily.

Roxanne remains quiet as Faith turns, stepping over Heidi and vanishes into the darkness beyond the spotlight. Roxanne hesitates for a few moments to ensure that everything seems as safe as possible before dashing to her friend.

'Heidi?' she whispers, gently shaking her friend by the shoulders. She sighs with relief as Heidi stirs, slowly opening her eyes.

'What happened?' Heidi asks groggily as her friend helps her to her feet. 'Was I knocked unconscious again?'

'Got it in one I'm afraid,' Roxanne responds, brushing her friend's long blonde hair from in front of her face with her fingertips.

'Where are we? How did we escape those millions of demons?' Heidi asks nervously as only silence emits from the darkness that surrounds them.

'Faith burst open the door and she carried you in here,' Roxanne informs her. 'I followed, but she just disappeared into the dark.'

A second spotlight suddenly flashes on in the direction that Faith vanished.

'Kyle!' Heidi shrieks as her younger brother becomes illuminated within the bright beam, his wrists and ankles tied with black rope to a vertical wooden board that has small casters fixed to the base, reminding Heidi of a knife throwing trick she once watched on a TV talent show. Kyle seems to be out cold and hangs limply. Heidi abruptly halts in her tracks shortly after making a dash towards her brother as Faith appears from the darkness next to him.

'Faith, what on earth is going on?' Heidi yells hysterically, her head spinning with confusion.' A look of shock appears on Heidi and Roxanne's faces as Jazelle steps from the gloom next to Faith. Jazelle and Faith look almost identical, black electricity crackling at their fingertips. They each grasp the board that Kyle is strapped to and slide him into the darkness and out of sight.

'Faith belongs to us now,' Jazelle says, her voice wispy and sinister.

'Who are you? Roxanne asks timidly, taking Heidi by the hand.

The evil woman looms formidably from edge of the darkness. 'My name is Jazelle. I falsely helped your brother to reach this point, and all for good reason. You must witness his death in exchange for your audacity of attempting to destroy the underworld. To think, such insignificant humans having the nerve to enter our abyss, believing they have the power to make a difference.

Pathetic.' She turns to look at Kyle. 'Now you can watch him die, before we destroy you also. Foolish little girls.'

Roxanne holds Heidi back as she attempts to charge for Jazelle, shouting and swearing in fury, unable to control her emotions any longer.

'On second thoughts,' Jazelle says gruffly, turning to Faith. 'Deal with them first!'

Heidi stops yelling as Faith steps towards them, her hands raised. 'I can't move!' Heidi cries in panic as she tries to dodge Faith's dark power.

'Neither can I!' Roxanne exclaims as she attempts to move her legs, but they remain stuck to the ground as if they have been bolted down. Roxanne's eyes widen in horror as she glances at her feet. The tips of her black shoes begin to turn tough and brown.

'I'm becoming wooden!' she exclaims in horror as her feet gradually turn to wood.

Heidi suddenly remembers her sinister reflection, and knows that hers too will become reality. She looks down at her hands as a tingling sensation ripples through them. The skin on the back of her hands begins to weaken, becoming old and frail. She feels the same sensation filling her entire body. Her beautiful long blonde hair starts to thin, becoming wispy and sparse. The skin on her pretty face begins to sag as deep wrinkles rapidly set in.

'Heidi, we... we... have to do something!' Roxanne stutters as she witnesses her best friend's gruesome transformation. Heidi, now starting to hunch, turns her elderly head pitifully to look at Roxanne. Her eyes look cold and heavy as she stares dejectedly at her friend, not having the energy to respond.

'Faith, you don't want to do this!' Roxanne cries, attempting to reach any remaining morsel of humanity inside their friend, her arms stiffening at her side as she yells. 'If you do this, we have come all this way for nothing! Don't let them control you. Be strong and let's finish what the monk's once started. This is why we came. Faith, can you hear me?'

Roxanne's pleading appears to wash over Faith as she ignores her words and continues her dark magic. There is nothing else that they can do. Heidi crumples to the ground as her old knees can no longer support her weight. Roxanne stares at the ground miserably as she is almost entirely consumed in a wooden shell. A single tear rolls down her cheek, splashing onto the ground as her head transforms to wood and she becomes a solid timber statue.

CHAPTER 80

Faith's evil grin abruptly vanishes from her wicked face as a monk suddenly appears behind her, his hand pressed firmly on the top of her head. Bright blue energy pours from the monk's hand and into Faith's body. Jazelle propels backwards, disappearing into the darkness as the monk blasts her away with a powerful explosion of white lightening from his free hand.

An intense shade of blue begins to overrule the blackness of Faith's hair. From roots to tips, the stunning blue colour floods, banishing the black and leaving her head flowing with dazzling sapphire locks. Her complexion brightens and her lips fill with moisture once again. The darkness of her eyes evaporates as a sparkling blue replaces it. Once Faith's humanity has been restored, dazzling beams of light shoot from within her chest, flowing into Heidi and Roxanne. Heidi's almost lifeless, withered body immediately begins to tighten. Her straggly hair bouncing as it revitalises, becoming thick and full. As if being reborn, Heidi can actually feel her muscles repairing as she becomes youthful and vibrant once again. The wooden statue of Roxanne begins to crack and splinter. Thick chunks of bark chip off and drop to the ground. As the pieces of wood flake away, Roxanne can be seen within. As the remainder of the bark splits from her body, Roxanne drops to the ground.

As the intense power continues to pour into the schoolgirls, their hair begins to mimic Faith's. Commencing from the roots, each hair on the friend's heads absorbs the same bright blue colour until their entire scalps are covered with gleaming sapphire hair.

Heidi springs to her feet, energised like never before. Roxanne closely follows.

'Heidi... your hair!' Roxanne exclaims in surprise, turning to see her friend's flowing blue tresses. Heidi pulls her hair in front of her face as she notices Roxanne's brilliant blue locks.

'Your eyes!' Heidi exclaims as she looks back to notice that Roxanne's eyes glint with a dazzling blue tinge.

They both turn their attention to where Faith stands. The monk continues to float behind her, his hand pressed securely on the top of her now entirely blue head. Recognising that his work has been successful, he releases Faith from his powerful grasp. She drops hard to her knees, gasping for breath as if she has just run a marathon.

'We don't understand,' Heidi tells the monk, glancing at Roxanne's dumbfounded expression.

'The increasing power was too great for Faith's body to control,' the monk begins to explain to all three girls. 'The power erupted within her and the dark forces that dwell within the Abyss took advantage of the situation, turning the power against her. I had no choice but to dispel a portion of her power; it was essential to retain her mortal soul.'

'But... what about us?' Roxanne asks, still mystified by their unanticipated transformation.

'The paramount conclusion for this situation was to share the power equally between the three of you,' the monk informs the two astounded girls.'

Roxanne and Heidi look at each other elatedly. 'Does this mean we can do stuff?' Heidi asks eagerly. 'Like... float things with our eyes?'

'You must not waste your extraordinary gift,' the monk warns sternly. 'You are not educated to harness the power inside of you. Use it only when you must.'

'B... But...' Heidi stutters. But it's too late as the monk abruptly vanishes in a cloud of blue smoke. 'Bye then,' she says to herself as the mist disperses.

'Faith?' Roxanne says softly, approaching her friend who cowers on the ground.

Faith looks up, a tear dripping down her cheek as her breathing slows. 'How can you even look at me?' she sobs. 'I almost killed you... if it wasn't for the monk I would have.'

Heidi walks over as Roxanne crouches in front of Faith. 'It wasn't you,' Roxanne comforts her. 'It wasn't your fault.'

'But I could see and feel everything!' she tells them as Heidi kneels beside Roxanne. 'I knew I was speaking. I knew exactly what I was doing, but I couldn't do anything about it. I felt like I was a puppet on strings.'

'You were,' Roxanne tells her. 'You were being controlled, and we don't hold anything against you... right Heidi?' Heidi looks at Roxanne, still unsure about the whole situation, but she nods in agreement nonetheless.

'Kyle!' Heidi suddenly exclaims, jumping to her feet as she remembers her younger brother.

'Heidi, be careful!' Roxanne warns as Heidi dashes into the darkness. Roxanne sighs with relief as Heidi quickly reappears, dragging the board and Kyle with her. Roxanne too gets to her feet, running across to help untie the young boy from the board as he begins to regain consciousness.

Faith slowly heaves herself to her feet and paces sheepishly towards the others.

'Kyle, can you hear me?' Heidi asks, hurrying to loosen the tight rope that binds him.

'Heidi?' Kyle says groggily as he opens his blurry eyes. 'Is that really you?'

'It's me,' Heidi answers softly, stroking her brother's moist hair. 'Don't worry, we're here now and everything's going to be fine.'

'Jasmine... Or whatever her real name is, tricked me and kept us apart,' Kyle tells his sister as his senses come back to him.

After the girls assist the boy from the board, Kyle recounts the story of his journey. He informs them of how Jazelle disguised herself, first as a monk and then as Jasmine. He tells them about the monsters that he faced and how much he longed to see Heidi again.

Heidi and Roxanne take it in turns to tell Kyle about their gruelling trek through the deep, dark Abyss. Faith stands silently to the side, still overcome with guilt from the recent events.

'We would have never made it here if it wasn't for Faith,' Heidi tells Kyle as she notices Faith's awkward posture.

'That's right,' Roxanne chips in. 'She saved our lives on more than one occasion,' she says, glancing at Faith and smiling. Faith smiles back, thankful that her friends honestly do forgive her.

'Now we can help each other,' Faith says as she re-joins her friends. 'We now share the power and we can end this once and for all... together.'

'But what do we do now?' Kyle asks, noticing the blackness that surrounds the spot lit floor.

'I guess we choose a direction and hope for the best,' Roxanne replies.

The four friends compose themselves, huddling apprehensively in a group before walking cautiously into the ambiguous darkness before them.

CHAPTER 81

I hope we're going the right way,' Kyle whispers as the four friends pace deeper and deeper into the darkness.

'Is anyone else starting to feel really cold?' Heidi asks as a sudden change in the temperature causes goose bumps to creep up her arms.

'Whoa!' Roxanne exclaims as through the gloominess, a huge grotto carved entirely from ice glints in the light of a giant, purple flamed lantern, which rests at the cave's entrance. The group walks cautiously through the blackness and towards the massive ice cavern, the temperature dropping with each step they take.

'Ooohhh, that's kinda pretty,' Heidi comments as they reach the huge purple flame, dancing within the glass walled lantern. Roxanne and Kyle roll their eyes while Faith peers into the large entrance of the cave.

'See anything?' Roxanne questions her. Faith shakes her head, standing away from the opening.

'What's that?' Kyle suddenly pipes up, dashing across to the thick wall of ice. The three girls quickly join the boy, not wanting to take their eyes off him for a second, just in case.

'This doesn't fill me with much confidence,' Faith gulps as thousands of skeletons appear in view, frozen within the thick ice that forms the cave's exterior.

The group of friends exchange sudden nervous glances as an immense roar echoes from deep within the ice cavern. A second roar follows, accompanied almost instantly by a third, and sounds to be getting closer.

'Monsters are coming,' Kyle says, tugging his sister's jumper. Heidi puts her arm around her brother as she and her friends furiously look around for a place to hide. The barren area that they occupy appears to be vacant of any hiding spots. The frost covered ground stretches all around, vanishing into uncertain distant darkness. Deep growling grasps the attention of the group.

Without uttering a word, Faith hurriedly leads her young companions behind the lantern, praying that the huge flame will help to conceal them from the approaching beasts, whatever they may be. Heidi shivers as they huddle behind the lantern, the purple flame emitting an icy coolness rather than warmth.

Observing from beyond the cold purple flame, the friends watch the shadowy entrance with nervous anticipation. A dark purple glow begins to shine from the darkness within the ice cavern, becoming more vivid with every passing second. Deep growling suddenly accompanies the purple light, causing the hairs on the back of Kyle's neck to stand on end. Recognition fills Faith's eyes as something large slowly emerges from the cave.

'Isn't that...' Roxanne's words are cut short as Faith promptly nods, looking at her with wide eyes. A single beast steps from the darkness of the ice cavern. Three vicious dog-like heads sprout from a thick neck upon its gigantic muscular canine body. Purple flames burning from within the Hell hound's six eyes light its path. A bright purple ooze drips from its three snarling jaws like cold violet lava.

'That's the dagger dog!' Heidi exclaims with realisation. Roxanne elbows her friend, signalling for her to stay quiet. But it's already too late. The six-pointed ears of the devil dog prick to attention in unison. The three horrifying heads turn in the direction of the purple flame that aids to hide the trembling friends. Faith's mind races, attempting to determine a plan of escape, but merely a void greets her.

A strong vibration within her fleece snaps Faith back to reality. Fumbling to unzip her inside pocket, Faith's fingers wrap around the cold handle of the dagger which shudders violently. Her young friends watch apprehensively as Faith retrieves the dagger, the vibrations sending shockwaves through her entire body, causing her teeth to chatter uncontrollably.

To everyone's astonishment, the silver dog-headed handle now resembles the monstrosity before them with even greater likeness. The eyes and mouths of each silver head glows with a bright purple light, replicating the Hell beast's three cold flaming heads. Faith grips the shaking handle with both hands, praying that she doesn't drop it.

The group watches, mesmerised as the immense guardian of the ice cavern roars in anguish. The purple light of the dagger glows brighter, expanding from the handle. The demon hound turns to face the terrified youngsters. Starting from its three howling heads, the creature's body begins to disintegrate like chalk. The grainy substance floats through the air as if being sucked into a whirlpool. The friends watch as the dagger within Faith's grip absorbs the eroding beast. The ear-piercing howling fades away, turning to silence as the final particles disappear within the bright violet light that surrounds the dagger's handle. The vibrations begin to slow and the purple light decreases and fades.

The now motionless dagger pulsates with an intense red glow, and for some reason, fills Faith with a surge of positive energy. She suddenly places her hand on her forehead, closing her eyes tightly.

'What's wrong?' Roxanne asks worriedly. 'Heidi?' she says, sounding even more concerned as Heidi copies Faith's actions. Kyle stands back, watching as Roxanne suddenly mimics her two friends.

'Whoa!' he exclaims to himself as each of the girls suddenly begin to glow with an intense indigo radiance. As the colour begins to fade away, the three girls appear even more vibrant than before.

'I feel we're almost at the end,' Faith says. Roxanne and Heidi both agree, feeling exactly the same sensation as their friend. Heidi and Roxanne move either side of Kyle, linking arms as they follow Faith warily into the disturbing ice grotto that now lies unprotected.

The anxious youngsters creep through a long ice passage that slopes downwards, reminding Heidi of one of those tunnels you find in zoos and large aquariums that pass beneath the water, and when you look up, you're surrounded by ocean wildlife. But all she can see now are skeletons encased within the ice all around her. The occasional purple flaming torch illuminates the path in an eerie, flickering glow. The violet flames exude a frosty bitterness rather than heat, maintaining the ice caves wintry chill.

The four friends continue down the passage, huddling together to stay warm as they descend. After a few minutes of trudging, the constricting passage opens into a wide space. The area looks exactly how the friends imagined the inside of an ice cavern would look. The walls are constructed of solid, jagged ice and thick icicles hang from the high roof.

'Let's just hope those don't come loose,' Heidi gulps, craning her neck backwards, getting a full view of the deadly looking ceiling. A colossal throne constructed entirely from human bones and bound with skin occupies the centre of the large room.

'That's so gross!' Heidi exclaims, cringing as she notices that the skin moves, as if breathing. Seconds after Heidi speaks, the doorway through which they entered promptly ices up, sealing the friends within the frozen tomb.

'Looks like we're stuck once again,' Heidi grumbles, not even sounding surprised this time.

'Faith,' Roxanne whispers, nudging her friend with her elbow as something catches her gaze. A heap of bones lies to the side of the cave, stacked against the icy wall.

Faith glances to the spot where Roxanne signals with her eyes. 'There are a lot of bones in these walls,' she says. 'Do you really think they could be the final monk?'

'Well, there's only one way to make sure,' Roxanne replies, grabbing Faith by the arm and marching her across to the pile of bones. Eavesdropping into her friends' conversation, Heidi speedily darts in their direction, dragging Kyle with her.

'What are you doing?' Heidi asks, all of a dither. 'Don't you even remember the last time she did that?' Faith stares solemnly at the ground.

'But we need all the power we can get,' Roxanne responds, knowing that they have little choice.

Heidi moves in closer to Roxanne. 'But what if she goes mental again?' she whispers.

'Don't worry, Heidi,' Faith answers, overhearing Heidi's not so quiet whispering. 'Now that we all share the power, it's only right that we share this final portion too.' With her right hand, Faith gently takes Roxanne and Heidi's right hands. The three girls glance nervously at each other as they kneel beside the pile of bones.

'Here we go,' Faith says, taking a deep breath before placing their hands onto the cold skeleton. Waves of blue light pour into the girls' hands, flowing up their arms and into their bodies as they absorb the ultimate power, the energy distributing evenly between them. After a few moments the pile of bones ceases to glow and the last remaining particles of blue light sink into the girls' skin. Once the power has been fully drained, the three potent friends sit back and relax, as if they have each just received the best massage that money can buy.

'Did it work like it was meant to?' Kyle asks, half expecting his sister and friends to grow really tall or extremely muscular or something.

'Yes... yes, Kyle it did,' Heidi replies as she looks intently at her hands, which crackle with blue electricity. 'We're ready now... right?' she asks Faith as they all rise to their feet. Before Faith can reply, a deep rumbling seizes the group's attention. They all gaze slowly upwards to witness the hoard of lethal icicles trembling.

'Everyone, stand as far back against the wall as you can,' Faith instructs. 'I think this is it... I think it's time to face the Devil.'

CHAPTER 82

The friends stand with their backs flat against the icy wall as the shaking intensifies.

'My back's soaking!' Heidi complains in Roxanne's ear before shrieking as an icicle crashes in front of her, shattering into a thousand twinkling shards.

'Everyone, stay against the wall,' Faith commands as the rumbling becomes louder. Suddenly, everything ceases and the room falls quiet and still once again. The friends stand for a few moments in complete silence, waiting and watching for anything threatening to manifest.

'You think that's it?' Heidi asks optimistically. 'I mean… did we do something without realising it?' Roxanne gives Heidi an unconvinced glance before redirecting her vision to the centre of the room. A black mist slowly begins to appear, swirling above the disturbing gory throne. The friends stay back, joining hands as a solid presence starts to take form within the thickening mist.

Two thick, hairy, brown legs drape over the edge of the chair, complete with tough clattering hooves. The black fog slowly reveals a broad crimson torso, its pair of immensely muscular arms resting upon the pulsating, skin bound supports. A scratching sound emits from the long, curly black fingernails as they caress the gory throne.

'He looks just like people say!' Heidi exclaims in horror, feeling her heart beat faster and faster with every passing second.

Faith's eyes widen as the Devil's formation concludes. 'Well… almost,' she says as the friends observe the terrifying faces of Satan. The great beast that sits before the group has three heads, which sprout from its tremendously wide and veiny neck. The central head has the appearance that is common knowledge from many story books on earth. Its face looks like it's constructed from thick, red leather. Fractionally above its pointed ears, smooth black horns protrude upwards. Its narrow eyes glint with a fiery orange glow as its vampire looking mouth sneers at the friends.

The head to the right is covered in dense brown fur. It appears to be an extremely evil, terrifying goat's head. Its eyes are wide and blacker than night. Its brown horns curl down by the side of its narrow face and its mouth is filled with blunt, rotten teeth. The head on the left is the most disturbing of all. It is comprised entirely of smooth jet-black skin, with no eyes, nose or ears. Its only feature is an oversized grotesque mouth, which hangs open, dark crimson blood oozing over a black tongue and dripping down a pointed chin.

Faith suddenly breaks from her mesmerized trance as the dagger in her pocket begins to vibrate. She reaches inside her fleece and grabs the knife forcefully so as not to drop it. Heidi and Roxanne glance over as Faith removes the glowing red blade. The Devil's three heads gasp, in what can only be described as trepidation, as they observe the powerful implement within Faith's grip.

Faith's amplified senses tell her that this is the absolute correct timing, right down to the very second. Influential power takes over her body as she lifts her arm behind her head, and, with all her strength, flings the dagger towards the immense beast of darkness. Kyle gasps, clutching onto Roxanne's and Heidi's arms as the dagger penetrates the

Devil's hefty chest. To Faith's utter shock and dismay, the Devil raises his throbbing hand and seizes the knife.

'This doesn't look promising,' Roxanne utters through gritted teeth as Satan forcefully rips the dagger from his chest, the wound healing almost instantly. The ground trembles as he heaves himself from his throne of flesh, standing tall and menacing. Towering above the friends, Hell's ruler must stand at least forty feet tall. He drops the dagger at his feet in disgust. All three evil heads snarl and hiss at the cowering group of petrified friends.

Faith attempts to use her powers to halt the now slowly advancing brute, but to no avail.

'Roxanne, Heidi, help me... help me to stop him!' Faith commands. The three girls concentrate with all their might. Blue sparks begin to crackle around the beast's body as the girls' energy collaborates. Their concentration is abruptly cut short as the Devil stomps his enormous hooves with infuriation.

'This is never going to work!' Heidi shrieks as she topples backwards, slamming hard into the wall of ice as she is shaken off her feet by the earthquake caused by the dark lord's thundering stamping.

'You have to do something!' Kyle cries, nimbly avoiding a plunging icicle. Faith stares blankly at the ground, with no alternative plan left in her head. The group huddles nervously together, sheer terror causing their minds to fall blank. The distressed friends are left helpless at the mercy of Satan himself.

CHAPTER 83

W e need the knife thing,' Heidi says to Roxanne as she quickly realises that Faith is on the verge of giving up the fight.

'And how are we meant to get it?' Roxanne retorts, looking across to see the shining red blade protruding from underneath one of the Devil's mighty hooves.

'Damn it,' Heidi moans. 'This isn't going to be as easy as I thought.'

Roxanne looks stunned. 'You thought this was going to be easy?' she asks with a flabbergasted expression across her face.

'Wait!' Heidi suddenly exclaims, pointing her finger in the air. 'I have another idea.' Faith snaps from her trance as she hears Heidi's impulsive outburst. As Kyle is dragged into the conversation by his sister, Faith strains to hear what her three young friends are discussing, but the Devil's tormenting snarls drown their voices.

Faith watches in astonishment, her heart in her throat as Heidi dashes to the far right side of the cave.

'Woohoo!' she yells, jumping up and down with her arms flailing above her head. Kyle then copies her, standing a few feet from his sister. He bends forward and grabs a large piece of shattered icicle from the ground.

'Take this no brains,' he yells aggressively, hurling the chunk of ice. The ice rock soars into the air, cracking Satan in the ribs with a soft thud. By this time, all three terrifying heads fixate on the exasperating siblings. This is now Roxanne's time to shine. Making absolutely sure that the three heads of the Devil are preoccupied, she hurries across to the lodged dagger. She kneels on the ground in front of the hairy hoof and clasps the handle with both hands.

'Roxanne... hurry,' Heidi pleads through clenched teeth as the Devil's heads become more infuriated with each passing moment. One of the Devil's hulking red arms swipes at the brother and sister.

'Roxanne!' Faith cries as the grotesque bleeding black head notices the girl at his feet. Roxanne stops tugging as something drips on the top of her head. She slowly tilts her head backwards, looking nervously above her. She gasps in horror as the evil black head dribbles blood as it sneers at her menacingly. As if from nowhere, a jagged piece of ice smashes into the side of the black head. Roxanne quickly glances behind her to see Faith poised with a second block of ice, ready and waiting.

Roxanne uses all her strength to yank the dagger from under the beast's colossal weight before speedily returning to Faith. Noticing that the extremely risky task has been successful, Kyle and Heidi swiftly re-join their friends. Roxanne hurriedly explains the remainder of the plan.

Kyle stands back, keeping one eye on the monstrous fiend of darkness as the girls take their positions. They stand close, each with an upward facing arm outstretched, their fingertips toughing one another's. The dagger lies across their open palms, the blade facing towards the appalling demon. Kyle watches in awe as his sister and friends concentrate intently on the powerful artefact.

'Sebynyw pwul selah, bys, sebynyw sleh, sebynyw hlep!' the devil roars in a gruff, disturbing voice, each head taking turns to speak a word at a time. The girls pay no attention and continue to focus on the task at hand.

'Quick!' Kyle yells as two bright balls of glowing fire begin to form within the open palms of the Devil. The girls' eyes fix on the lustrous dagger, penetrating deeper within its fibres as it begins to shimmer with a bright blue outline. Their eyes sparkle in unison with a bright sapphire glow as the dagger suddenly soars from their open hands. They direct the blade with their controlled stare as it rockets directly towards the bleeding head of black skin.

All three wicked heads roar as the knife strikes the head on the left, piercing deep within its skull. Kyle observes as his friends continue their intense application of their powers. The black head begins to glow bright blue before exploding in a frenzy of bone and gore. The powerful girls don't even flinch as they become splattered with Satan's entrails.

The dagger hovers above the weeping, severed neck. The red head growls, snapping its teeth in the direction of the dagger. The girls' concentration is suddenly disrupted as the Devil abruptly clamps its jaws around the glowing knife. They stare in bewilderment as the beast swallows the ancient artefact in one swift mouthful. The girls stare at each other, their mouths open in shock. Their plan appeared to be going so well, but now it seems to have backfired.

'He was meant to do that... right?' Kyle calls to his stunned friends.

'What do we do now!?" Roxanne blurts in Faith's direction, ignoring Kyle's question.

'I...I...' Faith stutters, unable to think straight as it appears their plan requires serious redirection.

'I think we need to move,' Heidi states, horror shining in her young eyes as she stares up at the beast. As the others follow Heidi's gaze, they witness a forming black mist swirling high above their heads. The Devil appears to be concentrating intently on manifesting the thickening fog.

'I don't know what he's doing,' Faith says, 'but we have to stop him!'

The three friends stare at the ground in unison, their bodies rigid as they stand in a powerful stance. Kyle watches, mesmerised as his sister and friends become engulfed by a blue wave of power. The girls suddenly grab each other's hands, rapidly throwing back their heads as gleaming blue beams of power shoot from their eyes. The dazzling beams strike Satan directly in his muscular chest, penetrating deep within his soulless body. The two remaining heads snarl angrily as he raises a bulky arm. With ease, he places his huge palm across his chest, blocking the brilliant blue light.

'Watch out!' Kyle yells as the sapphire beams are abruptly overtaken by a crimson glow and are repelled in the direction of the girls. But it's too late. The blood-red beams of energy zap the three friends directly in their eyes, causing them to drop to their knees, shrieking in pain.

The central ferocious head of Satan emits a booming laugh of triumph while the terrifying goats head cackles and hisses viciously.

'Are you okay?' Kyle yells, frantically sprinting to the girls.

'My eyes!' Heidi squeals. 'They burn, they burn!'

Kyle!' Faith yelps, stretching her arms blindly in front of her. 'Kyle, place my hands on top of your sister and Roxanne's heads, now!' Kyle doesn't ask any questions as he speedily moves alongside Faith, grabbing her hands and pulling them in Roxanne and Heidi's direction. Faith stumbles on her knees as Kyle yanks her arms so that she can reach her suffering companions. He hastily places Faith's palms onto the tops of Roxanne's and Heidi's heads. As he does what Faith instructed, a blue shimmer surrounds Faith's hands almost immediately. The blue light appears to penetrate her young friend's scalps. At the same time, the top of Faith's head also glows blue. Moments later Faith retracts her hands and all three girls open their eyes.

'Oh... my eyes... they're okay,' Heidi states as she rubs them with palms of her hands.

'Faith, how did you know what do to?' Roxanne asks, felling extremely relieved that Faith was able to cure their painful blindness.

'I guess it was just one of those things,' Faith replies. 'I just... knew.'

The girls suddenly refocus their attention on the Devil's actions. They all gasp in horror as they realise that that black leathery head has somehow re-spawned. The reassembled beast continues to concentrate on developing the black fog that becomes increasingly dense with every passing second.

'Whatever it's creating must be highly powerful,' Faith informs the others quietly.

'But how do we stop it?' Heidi asks, her voice quivering, fearing that Faith is none the wiser than she is.

Kyle kneels besides his sister, linking arms with her to feel any sort of comfort in this terrifying situation. The group of perplexed friends huddle together, unable to figure a solution to their ultimate problem. They look above them as the heavy black fog begins to rumble, flashes of bright red lightening crackling within.

The three heads of Satan Bellow in victory as a cluster of carmine lightning bolts shoot from the fog, vaporizing the group of youngsters in a brutal instant.

CHAPTER 84

Roxanne gently stirs from a deep and relaxing sleep. She slowly opens her eyes and begins to stretch. Turning to her bedside cabinet, she retrieves her cartoon character covered alarm clock that she bought as a souvenir when she and her family visited Disney world in Florida a couple of years back.

She flings her covers back and swings her legs over the edge of the bed. Yawning, Roxanne opens her cupboard and removes a white jumper and navy denim jeans from their hangers.

'Good morning, sleepy head,' Roxanne's mum, dressed in a sky blue apron and a pair of bright yellow washing up gloves which compliment her African complexion perfectly, greets her daughter cheerfully as Roxanne makes her way down the stairs.

'Hey, Mum' Roxanne replies, tying her navy blue hair in a bun on the top of her head as she plods down the steps.

'Sleep well?' her mum asks as she clatters around in the spacious, open-plan kitchen.

'Yeah, I guess so,' Roxanne replies, thinking hard. 'I had some really weird dreams... scary dreams, but I can't remember them very well. Also, why is my hair blue? I don't remember dying it.'

Roxanne's mum ignores her daughter's question as she retrieves a plate from one of the low kitchen cupboards.

'Well, the breakfast I'm preparing will make you feel better,' her mum says as she fills the kettle with water from the tap. Roxanne isn't especially excited. She knows that her mum only ever prepares toast or cereal for breakfast. She can't even heat milk in a pan without boiling it over.

'Mum, can I quickly use the phone to call Heidi?' Roxanne asks, patting her jeans pockets. 'I don't know where my mobile is.' Roxanne remembers that Heidi was in her frightening dream last night and she has a feeling that she needs to speak to her best friend. Roxanne's mum hums loudly to herself as the kettle boils noisily and she doesn't appear to have heard her daughter's question.

Roxanne shrugs and steps into the hall. She lifts the cordless phone from the receiver and dials Heidi's home number; her mum would kill her if she phoned a mobile number from the landline. Almost immediately, a familiar voice answers Roxanne's call. 'Can I speak to Heidi please?' Roxanne asks politely as Heidi's mum's voice greets her.

'I'm sorry, Roxanne, but Heidi has just popped into town with her father. I'll get her to give you a ring when she gets in, she won't be long.' After thanking Heidi's mum, Roxanne sighs with relief. Everything seems normal. The strange feeling she has in her gut about something being wrong must be the after effects of the nightmare she had last night.

'Breakfast is served,' Roxanne's mum announces, placing a delectable plate of homemade pancakes on the table. 'What are you waiting for?' she asks as she notices the baffled expression on her daughter's face.

'Erm... nothing.' Roxanne responds as she takes a seat at the breakfast table. 'It's just that you've never made pancakes in your life, not even on Shrove Tuesday.' Her mum simply smiles sweetly before returning to the kitchen. Roxanne dips one finger in the thick red sauce that flows over the stack of pancakes. She pulls a repulsed face as she licks her fingertip. 'Mum, this sauce is gross, what is it?' Her mum is humming to herself once again and doesn't reply.

As Roxanne sits at the table, staring at her breakfast, her mind seems to clear slightly. She just knows that she must speak to Heidi. Something feels wrong, but she can't put her finger on what. For some peculiar reason, she also keeps thinking about Faith, the friendly librarian that occasionally helps them with their school work, but again she has no idea why Faith would be in her thoughts.

'I'll eat my pancakes cold. I have to go see Heidi,' Roxanne calls as she quickly leaves the table. She speedily heads into the hallway and begins to slip on her shoes. She gasps in surprise as she turns to face the front door and finds her mum standing in the way.

'Maybe you should wait until later. Heidi's out with her father at the moment,' she informs Roxanne, while blocking the front door.

'How do you know that Heidi's with her dad?' Roxanne asks, looking puzzled.

The warm smile suddenly drops from Roxanne's mum's face. 'Woops,' she says sheepishly, her mouth transforming into a menacing grin. Roxanne begins to back away, but her mum has other ideas. She forcefully grabs her daughter by the scruff of her neck and propels her out of the hallway. Roxanne screams as she soars through the air before crashing hard into the breakfast table. As the clattering and smashing of utensils, plates and glasses fills the still morning air, Roxanne's mother looms in the doorway that links the kitchen and hallway.

'What's.... what's going on?' Roxanne asks shakily, pulling herself to her feet, using the back of a dining chair for support.

'Still not figured it out, dear? Her mum replies in a sarcastic tone.

'Mum, have you gone nuts!?' Roxanne shrieks, wiping away a small trickle of blood that seeps from the top of her head.

'Allow me to answer that question.... with this,' her mum responds as she removes a glistening kitchen knife from her flowery overall pocket.

Roxanne becomes suddenly dizzy, her head throbbing as if under immense pressure. She cups her head in her hands as her thoughts clear and the memories of her time in Hades flood her mind. She shakes the dizziness away as the brain fog clears her mind becomes unblemished.

'You're not my mum,' she says, glaring at the demon that portrays her mother.

'Thankfully, you are correct,' the demon snarls, her eyes transforming into deep red orbs. 'What mother would want such a disappointment of a daughter?' Roxanne sees red and grasps the heavy, stainless steel toaster from the kitchen top. She yanks the plug from the socket and throws the toaster forcefully at her mum's evil doppelgänger. The hefty implement cracks the demon woman hard on the side of the head, knocking her unsteadily to the ground.

Knowing that she only has seconds to react, Roxanne pelts full charge towards the front door. She hurdles over the unmoving image of her mother. She shrieks as a strong hand grips her ankle and she lands hard on the carpeted hallway.

'Let me go, you bitch!' Roxanne shouts before using her free leg to kick her mum's evil twin hard in the face. Roxanne cringes as the demon's head crashes hard against the wall with a sickening thud; however, she is relieved when the woman's grip loosens from around her ankle. Roxanne scrambles to her feet, and without a second glance, rips open the door and dashes out of the house.

CHAPTER 85

'M ittens, what's wrong with you today?' Faith asks, keeping a safe distance from her brown and white cat who sits at the bottom of the stairs, hissing and scratching at the air. Each time Faith edges closer, Mittens works herself into a frenzy, going berserk; very uncharacteristic of this usually soft and friendly feline. 'Mittens, I really have to get to work so stop being so silly, it's only me.' The cat pays no attention to her mistress, beginning to roll around in a ball at the foot of the stairs, screeching hysterically.

Faith realises that something is clearly wrong, but is mystified as to what. Retreating to her bedroom, Faith opens her wardrobe and retrieves a long sleeved, green jumper. She returns to the top of the stairs. Hissing continuously, Mittens bares her teeth as Faith reappears above her. Faith cautiously descends the cream carpeted stairs, nervously holding the jumper at arm's length before her.

'Sorry, my little baby,' Faith apologises in advance before tossing the woolly jumper over her crazed pet. As the shape of her cat struggles beneath the fabric, Faith leaps over Mittens and down the last couple of steps, hastily vacating the house before slamming the front door behind her.

'What was all that about?' Faith asks herself, wiping her brow with the back of her hand. The dismal autumn sun shines down on Faith as she stands in the front doorway of her house, a mild chill wafting in the air. Staring across the deserted red and brown leaf strewn road, Faith senses that something isn't altogether normal. She raises her right arm, rolls back her black fleece sleeve and checks her watch. 'Typical,' she complains, tapping her fingertip on face of the watch as the hands rest motionless. A rustling sound suddenly grabs Faith's attention. She gasps in horror at the bizarre sight that lies before her eyes. It appears that the entire neighbourhood's felines are assembling in the middle of the street.

'What the Hell is going on?' Faith whispers nervously, flattening herself against her front door. She stares wide eyed into the street as cats of all colours and sizes emerge from every nook and cranny. She watches as a large ginger and white tom cat crawls from underneath the car of the house across the road. A scruffy black and white moggy leaps from her next door neighbour's green wheelie bin. As more and more cats appear, Faith wonders why on earth all of these animals are grouping on her street like a fluffy army. Realisation suddenly dawns as she stares into the snarling faces of the raging, hissing pets. They *are* an army, and they are ready to go to war.

CHAPTER 86

'Nice Kitties,' Faith says soothingly, holding her hands in protest before her as the hoard of fury critters advances. By now, Faith realises that something is very wrong and that being outside at this moment is probably not the wisest of ideas. Without removing her attention from the snarling and spitting crowd, Faith slowly reaches a hand behind her, grabs the door handle and gently pushes open the door. The cats hiss and growl, their spines arching threateningly as Faith hastily steps backwards into her house before slamming the door and locking it securely. Surely her own loveable pet will be easier to handle than the gang of enemies outside.

Faith turns around to find her green jumper ripped to shreds at the foot of the stairs. Faith takes this as a very bad sign. Gulping nervously, she edges slowly into the doorway leading into the kitchen.

'Mi... Mittens...' she calls softly, her voice quivering. She never thought that she would be scared of her own pet. The house is quiet, which makes Faith even more on edge. A sudden deafening crash makes her scream, the large kitchen window exploding into hundreds of glistening shards. Faiths eyes open wide in horror as the hoard of felines leaps through the window and into her kitchen, seemingly unfazed by the glass splinters that protrude from their little furry bodies.

Faith backs out of the room as the hissing cats gather in the kitchen. As she makes it to the stairs, the pack of aggravated predators once again stalks its prey like a cornered mouse. Faith glances at the front door, quickly dismissing the idea of returning to the street. She creeps backwards and up the stairs, not taking her eyes from the cats below as she silently moves. She prays that the terrifying felines won't follow. To her dismay, the cats squeeze themselves onto the staircase, like morning commuters to work shoving their way onto a crowded train. With each careful step Faith takes, the mob pads up the stairs towards her, their eyes dark and filled with sheer hatred. After arriving at the upstairs landing, Faith's pace quickens as she heads towards her bedroom. She slips through the doorway and closes it just as the cats reach the top of the stairs. The bedroom door has no lock. *But they're only cats,* Faith thinks to herself, *they can't open doors... right?* She decides not to take any chances. Grabbing her bedside draws, she pulls them in front of the door, just in case. Everything is silent. *Perhaps they have lost interest,* Faith wonders as she quietly perches on the edge of her bed. Her pounding heart is the only sound that can be heard as she strains to perceive any noise from the hallway beyond her bedroom.

A few moments later, Faith's heart rate begins to slow and her breathing becomes steady. She wonders why everything is so very quiet. She half expected the hoard of cats to scratch down her bedroom door. *Are they waiting for me on the landing? Trying to fool me into a false sense of security?* she ponders, feeling her face becoming hot again at the very thought.

A shadow suddenly casts on the pastel pink carpet at Faith's feet, blocking the warm sunlight that filters into the room through the white net curtains that hang in front of Faith's bedroom windowpane. Turning her head and staring at the window, the whites of Faith's horrified eyes shine in the sunlight. Beyond the netted drapes, the silhouette of a small furry creature looms, pressed up against the glass.

Faith stands, keeping her eyes static on the window. Loud scratching and hissing from behind abruptly grasps her attention. She had almost forgotten about the cats on the landing, but now the entire situation springs to the forefront of her mind as the rampant moggies begin to violently claw her bedroom door to pieces.

CHAPTER 87

Faith's heart once again begins to race uncontrollably as she frantically searches around her room for anything substantial to use as a blockade. As her king-sized bed is the largest and heaviest object available, she grasps the base of the chocolate brown, faux leather bed and begins to tug with all her might. Her face turns puce, the vein on her forehead protruding from the pressure as she continues to heave, but the bed refuses to move more than a few centimetres. After a few exhausting moments, Faith admits defeat and releases her grip. She stands in the centre of the room, panting and thinking hard, trying to conjure up a plan.

She yelps, dropping to the floor, covering her head with her arms as her bedroom window suddenly shatters.

This is it, I'm done for, Faith thinks to herself, quivering on the floor, expecting at any moment to be mauled to death by the posse of frantic felines. To her surprise, nothing happens. Timidly lowering her arms that shield her head, she hears her name being called from outside. A rock lies on her bedroom floor, surrounded by shards of sparkling glass. It takes a moment for Faith's senses to alter before she slowly rises to her feet and cautiously heads towards the shattered window.

'Faith!' a vaguely familiar voice yells from below as she reaches the window. Faith hesitates for a second as she sets her gaze upon the person who yells her name from her back garden.

'...Roxanne?' Faith murmurs to herself, sounding rather confused, wondering why the schoolgirl who frequents the library, with her blonde best friend, is here at this moment. Faith's head suddenly begins to throb, as if she has been inflicted with a terrible migraine. As she holds her head in her hands, recent memories flood her mind as if a mystical dark veil has been abruptly lifted.

Suddenly, recalling everything that has happened since she and her young friends entered the Abyss, Faith's mind becomes lucid once more and she hurriedly readies herself to climb out of the broken window. Below, Roxanne wards off a small gathering of cats. She flings a long, wooden broom around her as the felines attempt to close in from all directions.

'Faith, hurry up!' Roxanne pleads at the top of her voice as she bends down, picks up a large stone and hurls it at a black cat that balances on nearby tree branch.

Faith speedily pulls the duvet from her bed and throws it over the glass scattered window ledge. Quickly, but carefully, she swings her legs over the windowsill, trying not to put too much pressure onto the duvet in case she gets any sharp surprises.

'Down the drainpipe,' Roxanne yells from across the other side of the garden as she continues to fend off the crazed pussies. This plan of action had already entered Faith's mind and she grasps the black piping with her right hand. She gulps, pausing for a second before reaching across with her left hand, swinging from the window ledge as she acquires a secure grip on the drainpipe with both hands. Her feet come to rest on the bracket that fixes the pipe to the wall of the house. Glancing down, Faith gasps as she witnesses a pair of cats waiting patiently on the grass directly below where she clings to the side of the house. The cats stare up at her, licking their lips hungrily as a glint of evil shines in their piercing black eyes.

Faith yelps, her heart jumping into her mouth as her feet slip from beneath her. She tightens her hold on the drainpipe, but it's no use and she begins to descend. The awaiting cats go berserk with anticipation, hissing and clawing at the air as their prey slides in their direction.

CHAPTER 88

Stay back you mangy beasts!' Roxanne bellows, swiftly swatting the demented moggies with the hefty wooden broom that she wields inelegantly. The pair of fur-balls flee in opposite directions, hissing frantically as Faith lands hard on the grass.

'Faith, are you okay?' Roxanne asks, placing a hand on her friend's shoulder.

'I'm fine. Thank you, Roxanne. What's going on? It took me a while to remember everything that's happening. I didn't recall anything until I saw you and then it all came flooding back like a tsunami.'

'The same thing happened to me with my...mum,' Roxanne explains. 'All I can say is that it was a *very* weird morning,'

'What about Heidi and her brother?' Faith enquires, suddenly wondering why Roxanne is unaccompanied.

'I went straight to their house after getting my memories back." Roxanne informs Faith as they gaze around the vicinity on the lookout for any cats that may be on the prowl. 'The front door was open so I went inside but no one was there, so I left and that's when I saw all the cats, and then you in the window.'

After a few moments of consideration, the girls decide that the best plan of action is to head to the library where Faith works. They don't know *why* this is the best plan, but it's the only one that they can think of.

'Maybe Heidi had the same idea,' Roxanne wonders out loud as they walk at a steady pace through the cold, deserted streets. Not a person, or cat, in sight. All the houses appear dark and abandoned, reminding Roxanne of a zombie movie that she watched with Heidi a few weeks back.

'...Perhaps,' Faith replies, not really listening to Roxanne as she walks with her arms wrapped tightly around herself, her head down as the cold breeze ruffles her long, navy ponytail.

Hey, that's not usually there,' Faith hears Roxanne exclaim in surprise. Faith raises her head to witness a gigantic inverted crucifix, made entirely from stone, resting in the centre of the town square. A huge sealed doorway appears to be carved into the centre of the structure.

'I don't even want to know what fits inside that,' Faith murmurs, a chill running down her spine.

'Maybe we should take a closer look,' Roxanne suggests as she begins to pace slowly towards the towering monument.

Faith speedily grabs her young companion by the arm. 'I really think that we should head for the library, with *no* detours,' she insists nervously, directing Roxanne away from the menacing construction. As the girls turn to walk in the opposite direction, a deep sound of stone rubbing against stone causes Faith to sigh detectably.

'Oh, I couldn't see that one coming,' Roxanne mumbles with a roll of her eyes as the friends turn back around to see the heavy door slowly opening, as if stirring from a deep slumber. The girls glance at each other, undecided if they should make a run for it or wait out of curiosity. They stand in the same spot, seemingly frozen with anticipation. The sound that emits from within the strange tombstone is not at all what either of them had expected.

'Does that sound like a...?' Roxanne says.

'A baby crying,' Faith finishes, walking cautiously towards the now open doorway.

Roxanne stands a few paces behind her friend as Faith peers inside the obscure structure.

'Oh my gosh, it *is* a baby!' Faith exclaims as Roxanne joins her. Looking inside, the friends witness a small cradle made of stone. The cradle slightly sways as if being rocked by an unseen mother.

'Just because it sounds like a baby, it doesn't mean that it is,' Roxanne warns as Faith steps one foot inside, making sure that she doesn't enter the crypt entirely, as it might be the last thing she ever does. Roxanne stands against the open door, not at all sure that she would be able to stop it from closing if it wanted to.

Within the cradle, a dusty grey cloth conceals a lump that rests motionless beneath. Faith takes a deep breath as she reaches into the crib. Lightly grasping the tattered cloth, she slowly retracts the covers and gasps in horror at what she reveals beneath.

CHAPTER 89

A seemingly nutrition deprived baby girl, clothed in grey rags, lies uncomfortably on the cold stone cot, sorrowful whimpers escaping her chapped lips and her helpless eyes bleary with tears.

'This totally creeps me out,' Roxanne shudders, peering over Faith's shoulder.

Faith turns to Roxanne with a concerned look dispersed across her face. 'What should we do?' she asks, realising that Roxanne is unlikely to have a helpful answer to her question even before it departed her mouth.

'Leave it,' Roxanne replies without a second thought. 'Let's get the Hell out of here, that thing's freaking me out.'

'But it's only a baby,' Faith says softly, gazing sympathetically at the snivelling infant.

'And just what do you propose we do with it?' Roxanne asks abruptly. 'I'm guessing it's been put in this coffin for a reason, and to be honest I don't really want to find out what that reason is.'

'Let's just get her some food,' Faith replies as she leans into the crib. 'I'm sure one of the shops will have some milk or something.'

'Faith, no!' Roxanne exclaims, but it's too late as she witnesses her friend retrieving the wrinkled baby from its stone bed before walking past Roxanne and into the fresh air of the town.

'It's only a baby,' Faith repeats, looking down at the helpless child. 'Not everything down here is going to be evil.

Take us for example. We might be able to help...' Before Faith is able to complete her sentence, she flinches in surprise as the weight suddenly becomes heavier in her arms. Roxanne gasps, staring into Faith's arms. Peering down, Faith gasps as the baby commences to grow at a rapid rate.

Shock stricken, Faith drops the child. The expanding baby girl lands hard on the pavement, causing her to cry loudly. Faith abruptly steps back, observing the baby as she expands on the ground. Its shrill blubbering resonates deeper as it develops its new shape.

'I think it's time we leave,' Faith says, finally agreeing with Roxanne as they both begin to back away. Neither of the girls can take their eyes from the growing child as the tattered clothing rips from its ever increasing body. They stare with gob-smacked expressions as the infant continues to transform before them. As the body twists and bends on the hard pavement, the sound of cracking bones makes the girls shudder.

The friends continue to stare as the shape before them stops writhing, becoming a mass of motionless skin and bones. Roxanne grips Faith's arm as the shape begins to move again. As they pace slowly backwards, Roxanne and Faith realise that the baby girl has grown into a much older woman. But this is no ordinary woman. Rising unsteadily to her feet, the woman's old, wrinkly skin reminds Roxanne of an oversized prune. Her wispy black hair rests lifelessly half way down her arched back, her spine protruding amongst jet strands. Standing as upright as she is possibly able, the frail woman slowly turns in the direction of the girls, her neck cracking loudly as she moves. The friends gasp in horror as they see the face of the bedraggled lady. Her skin is sallow and crinkly like an overused, deflated balloon. Her hollow, dark pitted eye sockets stare unresponsively and her mouth hangs open in a twisted and frightening expression, exposing her jagged, rotten teeth. The decrepit woman raises her thin, feeble arms into the air. The musty blanket, that was covering her as she lay as a baby, soars from the crypt, wrapping itself securely around her, forming a makeshift tattered gown.

'We *really* have to leave,' Roxanne urges, tugging at her friend's black fleece as Faith remains frozen to the spot in horror at the sight before her.

The old woman gradually rises off the ground, her toes pointing towards the pavement as she hovers mid-air. The girls' eyes widen as bright orange flames combust from the scraggly woman's feet.

'Run!' Faith yells, her legs discovering mobility once again. The friends flee as the floating woman drifts forebodingly after them. The terrified friends dash down a criss-cross of deserted streets, running as fast as their legs will carry them. A few minutes later they sprint through the town park, trampling the beautiful flower beds that lay in their direct route of escape.

'I'm getting a stitch,' Roxanne complains, hunching over as they reach the open iron gates at the park's exit.

'I think... that's the least of your worries,' Faith stammers, gasping for breath.

'The witch!' Roxanne exclaims, panic stricken as the bedraggled woman floats through the entrance to the park, scorching the grass and flowers with the fires that engulf her feet, as she drifts in the direction of the girls. 'How did she get here so fast?'

Roxanne stands upright, taking a deep breath, readying herself to abscond once more. Before the friends can take even one step, the woman raises her feeble arms. The heavy iron gates immediately slam shut, sealing the friends in the park as the witch advances on her targets.

CHAPTER 90

The girls stare frantically around the enclosed park, trying to spot any potential means of escape, but it appears hopeless.

'Our powers!' Roxanne exclaims, as if a light switch has just been flicked to the 'on' position in her brain. 'I forgot that we have powers. It must be the memory fog that we both experienced.' Faith's eyes suddenly alight as the memory floods her mind also. Without uttering another word, Faith takes Roxanne by the hand. As if a blanket of concentration has fallen upon them, they transfix their vision on the intruding female with precise precession. Whirls of brilliant blue light begin to swirl around the girls' feet. The blue shimmer rises and it soon engulfs the friends in a misty sapphire casing. The girl's close their eyes in unison as they summon the power from the depths of their very souls. With their eyes remaining shut, they are unaware that the witch has advanced to within a few feet of them. She once again stretches her thin, bony arms towards the friends, her dark eye sockets now glimmering with fire.

As if communicating telepathically, the friend's eyes flash open with a bright blue spark of power. The swirling energy that surrounds them abruptly blasts outwards in all directions, like a destructive energy bomb, engulfing the surrounding area. Grass and flowers are ripped out by the roots. Wooden park benches shatter into smithereens and the sturdy iron gate is blown forcefully apart.

After a few moments, the bright blue discharge fades away and the girls' eyes return to their natural colouring.

The two friends drop to their knees as the overwhelming lack of physical energy overwhelms their bodies.

'I thought... this feeling.... of being drained... had stopped,' Faith pants as she attempts to catch her breath. Before Roxanne manages to reply, she suddenly remembers the reason they had used their powers so fiercely to begin with. Looking up, she notices that the witch hovers motionless, only a few feet from them, her head hanging limply backwards like a circus's best contortionist. The blast seems to have stunned the witch, but most likely a temporary solution.

'I don't think that was... enough to... stop her,' Roxanne gasps, heaving herself to her feet before helping Faith to stand upright. Faith stumbles, her head feeling dizzy as she stands.

'We better hurry,' Roxanne urges, tugging at Faith's black fleece as she turns to notice the wide-open iron gates. Regaining all of their senses, the girls turn and flee from the park as they hastily make their way towards the library.

CHAPTER 91

W e can't just stay in here forever,' Heidi whispers to her younger brother, lowering her voice when movement somewhere in close quarters can be heard. Heidi and Kyle kneel silently in complete darkness, the gut wrenching odour of stale food wafting into their nostrils with every breath they inhale.

'I'll have another look,' Kyle whispers back.

'Okay, but be quiet,' Heidi orders, the palms of her hands beginning to sweat with nervous anticipation. Kyle carefully places his hands on a tough plastic surface directly above his head and presses gently.

'I think there's more of them now,' he groans in a hushed tone, peering through the narrow opening that he has created.

The siblings hide inside one of the large black bins that rest against the wall in the food court of the town's shopping centre. The fast food counters inside the mall have all been destroyed. Slush machines leak brightly coloured liquid that gush over the white tiled flooring. Trays, utensils and napkins scatter the ground as a hoard of crazed town residents overturn the tables and chairs with an almighty clatter.

'Why are they doing this?' Kyle asks his sister, knowing all too well that she is as clueless as himself. 'And that's my teacher, Ms Cutters, smashing that shop window with her forehead. They're like zombies, but they look like normal humans.'

'I think they're far from being human,' Heidi replies, manoeuvring herself next to her brother and peeping through the opening. 'Any brainwaves on how we get out of this one?' she asks, not sounding entirely hopeful. 'It's just a matter of time until they ransack this bin, and then we're done for.'

The entire rabble of zombie residents abruptly freezes to the spot and the vicinity falls silent. The individuals stare uncertainly around the room, as if they sense a great threat approaching. An ear piercing screech suddenly emits from outside the shopping mall, becoming louder as the cause of the dreadful sound soars through the wide open doors.

'No way!' Kyle exclaims in disbelief. 'A dragon, a real live dragon!' A small emerald coloured dragon, about the length of a car, flies into the shopping centre, its giant wings knocking over carts and trollies as it swoops in. Waving broken table legs and knives in vexation, the crazed individuals holler nonsensical rantings towards the hovering scaly beast. A tubby, middle-aged woman pelts a bottle of tomato sauce into the air, which crashes into the winged reptile's dark green, armoured back. Almost immediately, the dragon rotates one hundred and eighty degrees in mid-air. Without hesitation, the creature opens its fearsome dripping jaws, expelling an intense blast of red hot fire. The woman screams in anguish as she becomes engulfed in scorching flames, instantly melting her cream coloured trousers and sea blue knitted cardigan to her charring flesh.

The blazing victim flees in distress, dashing frantically around the food court as the foul smell of burned hair and skin wafts throughout the vicinity. She stumbles clumsily over shattered pieces of glass and wooden remnants of broken chairs. Tripping, she grabs onto the nearest body, a young, smartly dressed man who immediately becomes ablaze with bright, dancing flames.

Though not having their entire faculties about them, the zombie residents realise that the situation has worsened at a critical rate and they begin to scarper in all directions.

While the brightly burning bodies infect their surroundings and fellow inhabitants with fire, the deadly dragon moves swiftly through the heated air, swooping low and ripping off the limbs and heads of the rampaging escapees with great ease.

An elderly, white haired gentleman has somehow managed to avoid attacks from both the ground and from the air. Even though violently insane, the man is astute enough to know that the exit is blocked by the fire breathing monster and that he must find a place to hide. Through his bloodshot eyes, he blearily makes out the shape of something large and black across the far side of the room.

'Oh no!' Heidi whispers, her eyes widening and reflecting the gleaming flames. 'That lunatic is heading this way!'

CHAPTER 92

H old the lid down tight,' Heidi instructs as they close the lid of the bin, sealing them inside the foul smelling darkness. Gripping the handle indentation, the siblings pull firmly while they wait in silence.

Their grasps tighten as the lid of the bin begins to tremble. They know that only inches away, the crazed man is attempting to uncover their hiding spot. A sudden immense warmth forces the brother and sister to release their grasp on the lid as they tumble against the back of the bin. Outside, the insane man combusts into a frenzy of suffocating flames as the dragon soars overhead, torching the ground with fire as it flies.

The mythical creature extends its deadly talons, ready to capture its charcoaled pray. The howling, smouldering gentleman drops to his knees, avoiding the aerial attack by mere centimetres. Annoyed by the failure of the onslaught, the dragon breathes a fiery puff of dark smoke from its dripping nostrils. As the armoured beast prepares a second attack, it uses the bin as a platform to rebound from, like an Olympic swimmer upon reaching the end of the pool before returning to the starting position.

The force from the rebounding dragon causes the large wheelie-bin to slam into the wall before toppling unsteadily forward. Kyle and Heidi hold back their screams as the bin hits the ground, the mound of rotting rubbish sweeping them through the flapping lid as if they are riding a stinking avalanche.

Tossing a slimy black banana skin from his face, Kyle gasps in horror as he witnesses the immense winged reptile pinning its sizzling meal to the ground with its giant clawed feet. The brother and sister sprawl on the heap of festering waste, observing mutely as the dragon devours the blackened corpse, chunk by chunk. The rest of the town's folk have fled the shopping centre, leaving a mass of destruction in their wake. The few smouldering bodies that populate the food court will be more than enough to appease the mighty dragon. Even so, the youngsters know that they have to remain unnoticed if they are to stand any chance of escape.

Tumbling from the top of the mound of litter, the clanking of an empty tin can acquires the attention of the feeding creature. The brother and sister lie utterly still, staring into the dark eyes of the fearsome animal. As the staring competition continues for what seems to be an age, the siblings wonder if the dragon has even seen them. Maybe it senses by movement or sound.

Disturbing the terrifying silence, a large black rat scurries from inside the bin and across the tiled flooring, unaware of the situation that it becomes mixed up in. The scaly menace fixes its evilly dark eyes on the scampering rodent as it becomes yet another distraction. As the rat hurries ignorantly past the brute's leathery feet, the dragon suddenly lurches, snapping its jaws towards the furry creature. With a hasty reaction, the rat swiftly dodges the attack, darting towards the back of the room, away from the overturned bin and the vulnerable teenagers.

'...Now,' Heidi orders in a trembling whisper, scrambling uneasily to her feet as the dragon pursues the fleeing rodent with vigour. Once upright, Heidi quickly helps to steady her brother as his feet skid on the mountain of slop beneath him. Without so much as a second glance, the siblings dash behind the dragons back and through the open doors that lead from the food court and into the main shopping centre.

Meeting the same fate as the food court, the rest of the mall has been destroyed. The terrified youngsters dash past shattered windowpane after shattered windowpane, crunching the glass shards beneath their feet as they hurtle down the aisle and towards the exit. Fortunately for them, the crazed residents seem to have abandoned the premises entirely.

Bursting through the door that leads into the shopping centre car park, they screech to a halt. Shielding their eyes from the bright sun, they notice that the car park is completely unoccupied. A shiver runs down Heidi's spine as she succumbs to the overwhelming feeling of solitude.

'So... what do we do now?' Kyle asks, the light breeze ruffling his messy hair. Heidi releases a heavy, dejected sigh, tucking her intense blue hair behind her ears with her fingertips.

'Roxanne must be somewhere. Her front door was open and I'm guessing that wasn't her real mum with red eyes lying unconscious in the hallway.' She looks at her brother with a look of hopelessness in her eyes. 'I just don't know what to do.'

CHAPTER 93

'Okay, let's try again. We have to concentrate,' Faith instructs as she and Roxanne sit hand in hand across a small table inside the library, a single open book resting between them.

'It's not easy to think clearly when there's hundreds of demented people trying to get in and kill us!' Roxanne exclaims, endeavouring to block out the loud cries and banging on the door, caused by the hoard of deranged town's folk who have the building surrounded.

The girls close their eyes and begin to breathe with controlled, deep breaths. The blaring crashing and banging fades to the back of their minds as they focus intently.

'I think we should go home,' Kyle suggests as the siblings stand in the car park of the shopping centre, trying to think of a plan. 'Mum and Dad might be back by now and they can help us.'

'Kyle, I've already told you. Mum and Dad aren't here. This might look like the place we live, but it's not real. It's all just an illusion.'

Kyle frowns as he slumps against the closed door of the shopping centre. 'Well, your idea of looking for the others in the mall wasn't so great either. I reckon we should...'

'Shush,' Heidi suddenly dictates.

Kyle halts mid-sentence, waiting. 'What? I can't hear anything,' he blurts after a few moments of silence. Heidi ignores her brothers questioning. She places her hands over her ears and screws her eyes tightly as she strains to block any outside interference. Her eyes suddenly flash open with relieved recognition.

'Roxanne?' she says, sounding confused, her hands still pressed firmly on the sides of her head. Kyle looks perplexed as his sister talks to herself. 'Roxanne, is... is that you? Say something again.'

Roxanne and Faith ignore the relentless pounding and crashing from outside as they concentrate attentively on their goal.

'Heidi... Heidi can you hear me?' Roxanne asks again as the faint voice of her best friend wafts into her mind.

'I can hear you. Is it really you, Roxy?' Heidi replies as her friend's voice becomes clearer, as if an aerial in her brain has been suddenly adjusted.

'Heidi, are you safe? Where are you? Faith interrupts as she also tunes into the telepathic conversation.

'Faith, is that you?' Heidi asks, sounding even more baffled and slightly worrying that her mind may be playing tricks on her.

'We're in the library in the middle of town,' Faith continues. 'As we now share the power between the three of us, I thought that a book on meditation and spiritual techniques might help us to contact you. Thank God it worked. But we have a problem. It appears that most of the town's people have followed us and they have the place surrounded.'

Kyle quietly observes his sister who seems to be having a conversation with thin air, although to his better judgement, he assumes there is more to this situation than meets the eye. As the breeze rustles the trees beyond the walls of the car park, he hears the mention of fire and the word 'dragon'.

'Get things ready and we'll be there in five minutes,' Heidi says before releasing her hands from over her ears. She turns to her brother with a look of hope gleaming in her eyes. 'We have a plan.'

CHAPTER 94

Why can't we just run,' Roxanne whispers as she and Faith poke their heads around the library's fire escape door, the deep orange setting sun shining into their eyes.

'Because we have to get rid of these.... people.... these zombies, 'Faith whispers back. 'We can't have them chasing us all over town.'

'But do you think this plan will actually work?' Roxanne asks as they step gingerly outside, leaving the door open so they can return inside the library.

'I hope so,' Faith replies, peering cautiously around the edge of the building. 'Okay, they're still at the front door,' she relates to Roxanne, witnessing what appears to be over a hundred of their neighbours, friends and relatives wielding machetes, iron poles and any other implement that will cause severe damage. 'I'll keep a look out. Just be quick and don't get spotted.'

Clutching a large plastic water jug and section of hosepipe, Roxanne carefully tiptoes towards a smashed in silver car, parked on the grass verge opposite the library. Fortunately, the Library's staff room and maintenance cupboard were exactly the same as the factual ones, so Faith knew what implements could be found in there.

Roxanne keeps low as she dashes across the road, looking all around her for any signs of movement. Ducking behind the grimy car, she shuffles her way towards the petrol cap. Reaching up, she grasps the cover and turns, praying that no key is required. She sighs a breath of relief as the tension releases. After unscrewing the cap, Roxanne carefully inserts the section of hosepipe, which Faith trimmed to size with small gardening sheers from the maintenance cupboard, into the fuel tank. She screws her nose as the strong aroma of petrol wafts into her nostrils. Placing the other end of the pipe between her lips, Roxanne gently begins to suck. She suddenly splutters, spitting a mouthful of petrol into the plastic jug. Wiping her mouth with the back of her sleeve in disgust, she watches the dark liquid slosh from the hosepipe and into the clear container.

Faith shuffles agitatedly on the spot, willing her young friend to hurry, while keeping one eye on the rampaging townies.

'Phew!' Faith exclaims to herself as Roxanne pops up from behind the car, an entire jug full of petrol in her tight grasp.

'Faith, give me a hand,' Roxanne pants, fumbling her way back across the road. 'This is really heavy!' Faith meets Roxanne halfway, assisting her with the heavy jug as they head back towards the library. Making sure to close the door securely behind them, they re-enter the open fire escape doorway.

The two girls carefully pour a puddle of petrol around the main door to the library, leaving a long trail down the main aisle. Using mugs from the kitchen, they splatter the rows of books with the flammable fluid before dashing to the front of the library and tossing the empty jug aside as they prepare for the next part of their plan. Standing on chairs, they can just see through the high windows. The resident mob groups tightly together as they relentlessly attempt to gain entrance to the library.

'Come on, Heidi,' Roxanne whispers nervously, wiping her oily hands on her trousers.

'There... look!' Faith exclaims, pointing into the sky. As Roxanne's gaze follows Faith's finger, she can make out a large, dark object silhouetted by the setting sun. Below the dark object they watch as a couple of shadowy figures dash along the main road in the direction of the library.

'We have to move!' Roxanne exclaims, her heart racing as she clambers from the seat and sprints back to the fire exit. Faith takes her position at the main door to the library.

'Let's pray this works,' Faith says to herself apprehensively, inhaling a deep breath as she takes hold of the key that fits securely in the door lock. She grits her teeth as she slowly turns the key. Taken by complete surprise, Faith crashes to the ground as the door immediately bursts open with great force. As her head stops spinning, Faith leaps back to her feet and dashes towards the fire exit where her friend waits, the hoard of crazed townies tumbling haphazardly into the building behind her. Luckily, Faith managed to yank the key from the lock as she fell backwards.

'Faith, come on!' Roxanne yells as Faith turns back, shoulder barging a large bookshelf as hard as she can. The crashing of books and heavy wood distracts the zombies and places a temporary barrier between themselves and their attackers.

The girls quickly leave the library through the fire exit, slamming the door shut before heaving a heavy bin in front to block any possible escape.

Roxanne peers around the stone wall of the library. 'Come on, come on!' she chants to herself, as, in the distance, Heidi and Kyle continue to run for their lives.

'Remember what to do!' Heidi pants furiously, sweat dripping from her shiny forehead as the siblings continue to pound the street. Kyle nods in response as he gulps for air.

Even with a great head start, the enraged dragon gains ground with every passing second, its fleeing snack almost within reaching distance. Fortunately, breathing controlled bursts of fire at such a high speed is an impossible task for the mighty beast.

'Okay... on my command,' Heidi orders, the library looming before them, which now houses the entire zombie pack as they attempt to discover Faith and Roxanne.

The hunting beast begins to descend, preparing for the kill. Its razor sharp talons flex with excited anticipation as it swoops towards its vulnerable pray. Turning her head, Heidi yelps with horror as she witnesses the winged fire breather only a few metres behind them.

'Okay... okay.... now!' Heidi cries as they reach the path that leads to the main doors of the library. The brother and sister instantly throw themselves flat onto the tough tarmacked ground with an uncomfortable thud. Due to the high speed chase, the dragon is unable to alter its path. Soaring through the open library doors, the scaly beast crashes into the hoard of zombies within, emitting a blast of fire as it collides.

'Yes!' Roxanne exclaims, clapping her hands together in triumph as bright orange flames shine through the library's windowpanes. She and Faith speedily dash to the front of the building and assist the siblings who now hold the large doors shut. Faith hastily slips the key into the lock and turns it, sealing the captives to their certain fiery doom.

'How did you learn to contact me telepathically?' Heidi asks as Roxanne wraps her arms around her best friend.

'It was Faith's idea,' Roxanne begins to explain. 'She just figured that there might be some kind of 'connection' between us now, as we all share the power.'

'Nice going, Faithy,' Heidi says as she gives Faith a hug also. Faith feels rather proud of herself and somewhat closer to the two girls, now this ultimate union has been achieved.

'Maybe we should go now,' Kyle interrupts, looking worried as the library burns furiously beside them. The crashing and screaming inside makes him cringe and he wonders why his sister and her friends don't seem overly bothered. *Are they becoming too confident because of the powers they have?* He wonders.

The friends turn to leave the blazing scene when both Faith and Roxanne abruptly freeze to the spot. The sibling's eye lines follow the terrified stares of their friends. Down the main street, far in the distance, an advancing blurry figure of a woman can be seen, bright orange flames scorching the ground beneath her hovering feet.

CHAPTER 95

W hat the Hell is that?' Heidi gasps, shielding her eyes from the setting sun.

No time to explain,' Faith replies, dumbfounded by the fact both she and Roxanne forgot all about the baleful witch.

Roxanne tugs at Heidi's arm as she turns and flees in the opposite direction of the oncoming horror.

'Where... where are we going?' Kyle winces, holding his stomach as a stitch kicks him in his side. His question goes unanswered as the racing huddle pelts along the main street.

An idea suddenly shoots into Faith's head. 'Down here,' she bellows, turning from the main road towards Oakland Avenue. Her pace slows as they reach a quaint little building, finished in white paint.

'The museum?' Roxanne asks as the friends halt outside the narrow wooden door.

'This is where I found the dagger, remember?' Faith says, stepping forward and grasping the door handle.

'Stole the dagger, you mean,' Heidi blurts as Faith opens the door and steps inside the murky building. Faith searches the wall in the hallway and presses the light switch.

'So... what are we doing here exactly?' Roxanne asks as the grimy light bulbs flicker on. Faith pauses to respond while Kyle shuts the door behind them.

'When I came in here the last time, there was a cabinet full of ancient weapons. I thought we could use them to protect oursel...' she hesitates, sighing dejectedly as the friends enter the main room, only to find that the area has been completely ransacked. All of the glass cabinets have been destroyed and all the weapons are missing.

'I guess those crazy people had the same idea,' Heidi says, scouting the room for any left overs.

The seconds pass as the friends stand in complete silence, not one of them having anything useful or constructive to add. What breaks the subdued atmosphere is the unnerving sound of the front door opening, and then slamming to a close. The friends continue their mutual silence as they congregate at the back of the room, watching the doorway that leads into the hall with tense anticipation, Heidi's nervous gulping the only sound.

Roxanne's grip suddenly tightens around Faith's arm as an orange glow shines through the archway that leads into the inescapable room that the group occupies. The friends gasp in horrified accord as the scraggly witch floats formidably into the room. She halts, hovering on the spot, the black hollows of her eye sockets appearing to glare at the terrified youngsters. The friends have nowhere to run and the witch blocks their only escape route.

Faith glances at Heidi and Roxanne, who instantly seem to connect with her on a deeper level. The three girls hastily hold hands, complete concentration replacing fear. As they apparently stare into the witch's evil soul, sparks of sapphire power begin to shine within their focused eyes and crackle over their joined hands. All of a sudden, the crackles and shimmers fizzle and die. The girls blink in surprise as their eyes return to normal and the feeling of fear regains their senses. Faith gasps at the realisation that their telepathic session must have temporarily drained their powers.

'What do we do?' Kyle whispers, his voice breaking with panic as the sinister witch raises her frail arms with intent. The girls look at each other, expressionless. Gliding menacingly towards the petrified friends, sparks of almighty dark magic flash from the witch's fingertips as she prepares the attack.

CHAPTER 96

The terrified friends flatten themselves against the wall with the intention of staying alive for as long as possible. Faith recalls that people sometimes say 'your life flashes before your eyes' just before you die. But for Faith, what comes to the forefront of her mind is her time in Hell and how far they have all come, just for it to end like this.

Becoming instinctively protective over his sister, Kyle springs towards the witch, his small fists clenched furiously as he readies a strike.

'Kyle!' Heidi exclaims in horror as her younger brother is catapulted across the room with an almighty burst of black power. He slumps on the ground as he impacts the far wall.

Before any further reactions can take place, the witch lunges forward, forcefully wrapping her surprisingly strong arms around the horrified girls. The three friends tremble in a state of bewildering shock as an almighty surge of energy rushes through their entire bodies. A bright blue haze surrounds the foursome as the witch extracts the hard gained power from the three girls. As if draining a battery of its charge, the scrawny enchantress greedily absorbs the lucent sapphire power.

Unable to move, or to even think, the friends remain helpless as they sense the potent energy draining from their bodies, feeding the witch's hunger for power. Their bright blue hair fades and is replaced with their natural colourings. As the final spark of power drains into the witch, the girls drop to their knees, their legs becoming too heavy to support their weight.

As Faith's exhausted mind returns to reality, she hardly dares to raise her head, realising that she may only have seconds left before losing her mortal life and being sentenced to spend an eternity in Hell. The surprised voice of Heidi is what first alters Faith's perception.

'Who... who are you?' Heidi's voice can be heard asking. Faith is taken aback as the tone in Heidi's voice is not what she expected. She sounds curious, but also relieved. Looking up to join her young friends gaze, Faith is greeted by a beautiful young woman. The transcendent female smiles down at the three stunned friends, her warm blue eyes sparkling. Even though the interior of the museum is somewhat dreary, the girl's long silver hair glimmers as if she radiates a glistening light.

The young woman leans forward, holding out a hand in Faith's direction. Her old fashioned, white gown drapes on the ground as she waits for Faith's acceptance. Faith glances at her young friends as she cautiously welcomes the mysterious woman's helping gesture. Their eyes cease to part as Faith heaves herself to a standing position before releasing her grip on the girl's hand.

'Do not be alarmed,' the young woman says affectionately. 'I have much to tell you.'

CHAPTER 97

Heidi and Roxanne rise slowly to their feet, keeping their eyes fixed on the unusual girl.

'I... I don't understand,' Faith says, unable to divert her fascinated stare.

The young woman glances at all three girls warmly. 'Then, I think that I should explain,' she says, gesturing for the girls to take a seat on a padded bench near the archway.

'What about my brother?' Heidi asks as the trio lower themselves onto the seat, not quite daring to assist him just in case all is not as it seems. The dazzling, silver haired girl turns to look at Kyle, who remains slouched against the wall.

'I am sorry about what I did to your brother,' she says remorsefully. 'But he will be just fine, and you will see him again very soon.' With that, she raises her hand into the air. Heidi gasps in horror, as, right before her eyes, Kyle combusts in an astonishing flash of white light.

'What have you done with him? Heidi screams, jumping to her feet with alarm as the light fades and her brother has vanished.

'Do not fret, he is now safe,' the girl says as she refocuses her attention on her three new acquaintances. Roxanne gently tugs on Heidi's black jumper. Heidi sits back down as the young woman begins to speak.

'My name is Isabel. I lived on earth, many years ago. I was twenty three years of age when I was sentenced to an eternal damnation in Hades.' She pauses, collecting her thoughts as she recalls her human life on earth. 'I studied the art of white magic from a young age. I always felt that I was connected to the universe on a deeper level than most human beings. I kept this fact a secret from everyone, even my own family. That kind of thing would not have been tolerated in my time. You would be hanged or drowned if suspected of witchcraft, even if you used your magic to help people. I sensed what the monks were planning and it was I who helped them to create the ritual of Hades and blessed the gemstone dagger that you now possess.' She points to Faith's black fleece top which conceals the dagger within her inside pocket. 'The townsfolk gained knowledge of the ritual and of I as its creator. I was burned at the stake for witchcraft, my soul banished to the underworld where I was to remain for all eternity, unable to speak or to use my magic. The only chance to break the curse was to obtain the almighty power of light, but this was impossible, until you three arrived.'

'So... this was all planned or something?' Roxanne asks, breaking the silence.

'You were chosen for this mission before you were even born,' Isabel says to Faith, who remains sitting in confused silence. 'You and I share the same bloodline, Faith. You have powerful natural abilities that you are unaware of. This is why you were selected and how you have made it this far on your journey. The crucial energy that you have induced throughout your voyage is enormously powerful, but do not be fooled, this power alone is not enough to accomplish the task at hand.' Isabel steps closer to Faith who remains looking dumbfounded. 'It was your mission to deliver the monks power to me.' Isabel holds out her hands towards the friends. A lucent, silvery shimmer ejects from her palms and circles the three girls'.

All of a sudden, the entire room implodes in a bright flash of pure white light, engulfing everything and everyone within. Heidi grasps Roxanne's hand as tightly as she can, afraid that her first instinct may have been correct and that they are now being subjected to the same terrible fate as Kyle.

As the luminescence dissipates, the familiar surroundings of the museum greet them. The girls blink in unison, banishing the remaining bright spots from their vision.

'You two, your hair!' Heidi exclaims, noticing Roxanne's now untied, flowing silver locks, glimmering with radiance. Faith too has been granted the same transformation. Heidi pulls her own long hair over her shoulder to be greeted with the same dazzling radiance.

'Now that I have been restored to my former self, I have bestowed upon the three of you the same power of light that I myself yield,' Isabelle informs them. The three girls glance at each other curiously.

'So... this means what, exactly?' Heidi queries.

'Back on earth, I was one of the most powerful witches of light and love,' Isabelle begins to explain. 'And now, the three of you are just as powerful as I. This is the conclusion that you have been destined for. Together we have the ability to abolish this abomination and relieve the mortal world from all evil for all eternity.

Faith rises to her feet, mimicked closely by her young, silver haired companions. 'But, how do we use this power, and know when to use it?' she asks their new mentor.

'Your inner instincts will guide the way,' Isabelle says as she gazes warmly at the friends. 'Roxanne, Heidi, Faith...

the time has come.' With those final words, Isabelle serenely closes her eyes, raises her arms and claps her delicate hands above her head. Once again, the small room fills with the blazing white light, concealing everything in sight. After a few seconds, the light fades, leaving the museum silent and unoccupied.

CHAPTER 98

'W'e're back,' Faith gasps as the overwhelming brightness fades and she realises that they no longer inhabit the museum in their fictional home town. Heidi shivers as the icy chill from the Devil's dwelling runs once more down her spine. Other than Satan's gory throne and the bloody mess caused by the explosion of the black head, the ice cave appears deserted.

'This is where we were before we came to our Hellish hometown,' Heidi informs Isabelle.

'The Devil was here,' Roxanne continues. 'We managed to destroy one of its three heads before we were banished, but it just grew back.'

Isabelle gazes around the room at nothing in particular. 'The dark force is nearby,' she states, her body tingling with ultra-fine sensations that seem to come from within her very being. 'It is aware that we are here, I can sense it.'

'The dagger!' Heidi exclaims as a red glow pulsates from within Faith's black fleece top, like a bright heartbeat. Faith reaches into her inside pocket and retrieves the ancient artefact, which shines with a ruby hue.

'It's coming,' Isabelle whispers. 'Don't be surprised if it takes an alternate form from that which you met before. Satan can, and will, play on fears and trickery. Be prepared.'

The girls ready themselves, backing against the cave's glacial wall. Faith clenches the glowing dagger in her perspiring palm, not daring to let it out of her grasp for even a second.

'Kyle!' Heidi exclaims in shocked delight as her brother appears in the carved archway within the icy wall. Isabelle hurriedly holds her arm outstretched when Heidi attempts to dash towards her brother.

'Remember what I told you,' Isabelle says, keeping her narrowed eyes firmly fixated on the young boy across the chilly room. 'The sinister and powerful force of Satan is very clever and will deceive you whenever possible. That is not your brother.'

Upon failing to fool the girls into a false sense of security, the apparition of Kyle dissolves into wispy black fog and vanishes from sight.

'Do not worry,' Isabelle comforts as she notices Heidi's tear filled eyes. 'Your brother is safe. I made sure of that.'

'Where is he?' Heidi asks, shaking her phantom sibling from her mind. 'Where did you send him?'

Before Isabelle has a chance to respond to Heidi's questioning, the girls' attention becomes distracted as the entire frozen cavern begins to rumble.

'Watch out!' Faith screams, grabbing Roxanne and Heidi close as an avalanche of deadly icicles and heavy blocks of ice crash to the ground, surrounding them with shattered mirrored fragments. The three friends glance tensely above them, astonished by the fact that they are somehow managing to avoid the continuous fatal cascade. Isabelle stands next to them, unfazed by the proceedings, her eyes now completely white. Directly above them, the girls witness the deadly falling ice which rapidly melts, vanishing from sight as if plunging into an invisible, red hot furnace.

'It's some kind of protective force field,' Faith whispers to her young friends as they huddle together and watch Isabelle's compelling magic at work.

After a few tense moments of being caught in the icy downpour, the room ceases to shake and the air falls silent once more.

'Thank you,' Faith says, placing an appreciative hand on Isabelle's shoulder.

Heidi suddenly looks thoughtful. 'But how come our powers didn't kick in like you said they would?' she asks.

'There was no need. I had the situation under control,' Isabelle calmly replies, her eyes returning to her normal blue shade. 'This was easy compared to what is coming.'

The girls' eyes widen with recognition as a gruff, sinister voice echoes throughout the cave. 'Sebynyw pwul selah, bys, sebynyw sleh, sebynyw hlep!'

'Ready yourselves my friends,' Isabelle insists, taking a long, deep breath. 'Satan is here.'

CHAPTER 99

Sebynyw pwul selah, bys, sebynyw sleh, sebynyw hlep!' the Devil speaks once again in surround sound, attempting to distract the foursome.

'What does that mean?' Faith asks, turning to look at Isabelle as the Devil's words succeed to divert her attention.

'Satan speaks an ancient language,' Isabelle informs her.

'Do you understand it?' Heidi asks, her voice quivering.

'Yes. I understand all languages,' Isabelle replies. 'It's a component of my gift.'

'Well?' Roxanne interrupts.

'Satan says that we will fail and we will die,' Isabelle explains to her new friends. 'The words of Satan can alter your subconscious mind and make you believe what it says, with devastating consequences.' Isabelle closes her eyes, waving the palm of her hand before herself and the girls.

'What was that'? Heidi asks, wiggling a finger in her ear as a tingling sensation invades her head.

'Now we can only perceive each other's words,' Isabelle informs them. 'The voice of Satan can no longer intrude our minds.'

The group falls into silence as wisps of black mist seizes their attention. They watch as the dark intensifying vapour oscillates above the gut wrenching throne that bleeds with anticipation. The mist transforms into a thick, swirling, pitch-black fog, red sparks of power pulsating within.

'This is the very essence of Satan,' Isabelle whispers to her nervously awaiting companions. 'It is the most powerful form of evil that rules all of Hades. This is not going to be an easy task.'

Heidi gasps, clutching tightly onto both Faith and Roxanne as a gigantic, bloodshot eyeball appears in the centre of the swirling fog. The friends watch uneasily as streams of black vapour disperse from the main cloud, attaching to the surrounding glacial walls, forming immense monstrous shadows. Heidi gulps, tension rising in her throat as the large shadows grow horns, sprout tails and develop deadly claws. A group of smaller shadows transform into terrifying goblin silhouettes that hunch at the waist, their long pincer like arms dragging on the ground as they cackle and hiss with malicious excitement.

'They're just shadows, right? Heidi gulps as the shadows skulk along the walls in their direction. 'I mean, they're just meant to scare us, right?'

Roxanne screams as one of the large shadows unexpectedly reaches its lengthy arm from the wall and grabs her Ankle tightly. Heidi and Faith hastily grasp Roxanne's hands as she falls to her knees.

'Don't let it take me!' Roxanne wails, feeling the strain on her body from the tugging on both ends, like family members pulling a cracker at Christmas, both competing for the reward. A crackling sound emits from behind Roxanne, immediately followed by an intense defeated roar. Roxanne is yanked to her feet by Heidi and Faith as the grip around her ankle dissolves. The girls move in behind Isabelle as they notice her eyes have whitened once again, sparkles of power forming before her.

'I'm so glad she's with us,' Heidi whispers as they cram together, keeping their eyes on the slithering shadows around the room. They observe as bright white lightning bolts shoot from a field of energy that Isabelle generates around them. In turn, the lightning strikes zap the forbidding shadows, vaporizing them instantly upon impact. Heidi places her fingers in her ears as the room becomes filled with booming howls and shrieks of anger and anguish.

The huge eyeball glares furiously at Isabelle as she withdraws her power and her eyes flash back to her normal. The immense eyeball begins to cloud, like a crystal ball filling with black smoke. The girls watch with trepidation as the eyeball becomes a solid pitch-black orb. The dark fog that surrounds the black globe of destructive power begins to swirl, gaining momentum as it whirls faster and faster around the blacked-out eyeball. It takes only a few seconds until the entire ice cave is filled with a rapidly swirling mist.

'We have to end this before things get even more out of control! 'Faith yells, her bright silver hair flailing in the gusting wind, frantically whipping around her head.

'What do we do?' Heidi calls back, moving in closer while holding her long, silver hair in a ponytail to stop it from blowing a frenzy, like Faith's.

'Everyone, concentrate on the dagger,' Isabelle bellows as she and Roxanne huddle with Heidi and Faith. 'We must strike the central nervous system in order to destroy it. There is no possible way to get close enough, so we must use the power of our minds.'

Without another word spoken, the girls realise what they must do. The four friends stand close together, staring at the glowing, crimson knife that Faith holds on the palm of her hand. Assuring the dagger isn't blown away by the ferocious wind, the companions focus their undivided attention onto the shimmering artefact. With great ease, the dagger lifts from Faith's palm, hovering within the swirling smog. As if the knife has a life all of its own, it shoots like an arrow from a bow, cutting through the dark mist at tremendous speed.

The black globe of immoral power flashes open, revealing the bloodshot eyeball once again as the dagger strikes in the centre of the large pupil. An almighty roar echoes around the icy cavern as the eye begins to vibrate. For a glorious moment, the friends believe they have been victorious, only to realise the contrary as the dagger drops to the ground. The red hue remains, but the dagger is seemingly powerless against the Devil's mighty force. With their only weapon being rendered useless, the friends' minds fall blank. With no backup plan, the girls, including Isabelle, are clueless about how to defeat their ultimate foe.

CHAPTER 100

As Faith, Heidi and Roxanne stand motionless, perplexed by what they have just witnessed, Isabelle opens her hand. The dagger soars across the ground before springing into her palm.

'What's wrong? Faith asks, noticing the look of confusion on Isabelle's captivating face.

'I was afraid that this might happen,' the dazzling girl replies, the three friends closing in so they can hear her words over the gushing wind.

'Afraid what might happen?' Heidi asks nervously.

Isabelle looks down at the crimson artefact in her hand. 'The energy was insufficient,' she says, seemingly evaluating the situation at hand.

'So, all this... everything we did... was for nothing?' Faith yells, despair overtaking her trembling body.

'Watch out!' Isabelle cries, her attention diverting as a gigantic black bat swoops towards them from within the mist.

'Heidi!' Roxanne shrieks, the immense winged mammal catching them by surprise. Before the group has time to avoid the attack, the creature grips onto Heidi's shoulder, sinking its long fangs into her exposed neck. As Heidi screams in pain, Isabelle speedily places the palm of her hand onto the bloodsucking beast, shocking it with a pulse of powerful white light. Heidi clasps her bleeding neck as the bat drops, sizzling as it impacts the icy ground with a thud.

Isabelle is soon preoccupied as a swarm of the bats swoops from the whirling fog. Faith, Heidi and Roxanne turn away, the constant flashes of bright light invading their vision as Isabelle eliminates the flying enemies, one by one.

'I feel woozy,' Heidi complains, her eyes beginning to look dim and her neck bubbling with a deep purple ooze.

'You have been poisoned,' Isabelle informs Heidi, moving in to take a closer look at the wound. Gently holding Heidi by the shoulders, Isabelle places her ruby lips over the seeping indentations on the young girl's neck. Roxanne and Faith stand back, feeling rather nauseous themselves at the sight. Heidi's neck begins to glow with a pearly white shimmer. After a moment, Isabelle releases her kiss. Heidi's neck has completely healed and no trace of the infected lacerations exists.

'Thanks,' Heidi says, feeling herself drifting back to reality.

'You can thank me later, if my plan works that is,' Isabelle responds, gathering her new friends together for one final time.

As Isabelle divulges her hopeful plan of attack, the dark wind ceases, retreating into the ever seeing eyeball. A squelching sound makes the friends glance around as Isabelle continues to explain her plan. The eyeball has begun to change shape. It begins to pulsate, expanding like plasticine being stretched by the hands of an unseen child. The shape begins to take form. Long female legs emerge, clad in black jeans and black boots. The black fleeced torso next appears and lastly the pretty head with flowing bright blue hair. The girls gaze in horror as an enormous version of Faith now looms above them, her eyes flashing with immense blue power. The huge representation of Faith

369

removes a red glowing dagger from within her fleece pocket, holding it high into the air is it crackles with crimson sparks. The friends watch, open mouthed, as dark storm clouds materialize across the icy ceiling.

'Oh no!' Isabelle exclaims. 'Satan is preparing to banish us from this place,' she warns as cerise strikes of lighting flash within the forming clouds.

'This is what happened last time,' Heidi says, wincing with each crackle of crimson lightening and booming of thunder.

Isabelle refocuses her attention on her friends. 'We must do this now,' she orders, holding the dagger before her. 'If this ultimate essence of evil succeeds to banish us from this place, it is highly unlikely that we will ever return.'

'But we'll lose our powers,' Roxanne retorts, anxious about being left even more vulnerable than they already are. 'And now it looks like Faith, what if... what if it kills the real Faith too?'

'We have no choice, we have to try' Faith says, looking reassuringly at her frightened, young companions. Heidi and Roxanne exchange uneasy glances before nodding in final agreement.

In turn, the four silver haired friends place their dominant hands onto the red glowing dagger which lies on Isabelle's palm. The powerful foursome close their eyes and concentrate, blocking their minds from the activities of evil taking place around them. The ancient artefact begins to heat like a comforting hot water bottle as it absorbs waves of brilliant white light which pour from the friends' fingertips. Faith's evil doppelganger glares menacingly, becoming distracted from its brewing magic. It growls furiously, witnessing the intense silver shimmer draining from the girls' hair, revealing their natural colouring once more as their powers combine within the tremendously potent dagger.

The four friends drop heavily to their knees as the dagger absorbs the final particles of their powers. Heidi and Roxanne cover their heads as intense scarlet lightning bolts, emitted from the ever growing storm clouds, scorch the icily cold ground.

'We have to use it now,' Isabelle pants wearily, glancing above her to see the luminescent dagger hovering mid-air, radiating with a bright white sheen.

'But... how?' Roxanne asks, flinching as another sizzling of lightning strikes the ground in close proximity.

Faith heaves herself to her feet. 'This is my mission,' she says decidedly, taking hold of the floating artefact. 'I should be the one to finish this. Finish this by facing myself!'

Now as powerless as her new companions, Isabelle huddles with Heidi and Roxanne. They gaze up at their friend who stands strong, staring sternly into the snarling face of her devilish lookalike.

'You lose!' Faith shouts authoritatively, raising the tightly grasped dagger. She disregards her overwhelming sense of fear and commences to dash through the ice cavern, the flashes of lightening unable to disconcert her focus. She yells triumphantly, raising the dagger high above her head as she reaches her evil twin who glares down at her with every evil and hostile thought that it has ever held.

'Die!' Faith screams with hatred as she plunges the gleaming blade deep into Satan's thigh. She quickly releases the handle, the realisation of what she has just accomplished suddenly sinking in as the leg seeps mass amounts of thick, black gunge. She steps backwards, avoiding the spilling gore as it pours around her feet. The vision of Faith flashes, instantly transforming into a thin brown creature. Its spindly hoofed leg gushes the black gore as its frail, bony wings flap pathetically, its withered goats head screaming in torment.

'Faith!' Heidi and Roxanne call in unison, waving for her to return. Before she retreats, Faith reaches to retrieve the dagger, but before she can take hold of the handle, the powerful weapon dissolves into Satan's dishevelled body.

Satan roars in defeat as Faith sprints to re-join her friends. As Faith dashes across the cavern, foggy black shadows, in the shape of every terrifying demon imaginable, rapidly expel from the shrieking demon before evaporating into the chilly air.

Upon Faith's return, the powerless friends huddle together on the cold ground, arm in arm as the entire glaciated cavern begins to quake violently.

'What do we do, what do we do?' Heidi trembles as immense sheets of ice dislodge from the frozen walls, shattering around them. As if her questioning has been answered from a higher power, the shrieking king of the underworld abruptly explodes, like the most powerful bomb in existence, flooding the entire cave with a brilliant white light that envelops everything within.

As the intense light fades, the conjoined friends feel themselves gently falling. Blackness now saturates the group as they drift through a seemingly endless ocean of darkness. Colourful and vivid apparitions begin to appear before them. The friends witness moments from each level of the underworld. The girls watch as, in turn, every level smoulders in a brilliant silvery white fire, finally becoming annihilated as they collapse. They witness their false home town up in the dazzling flames, burning to the ground. Through the fire comes the representations from their nightmares; the grotesque man who stalked Faith; the unnerving clown who craved Heidi's blood and the vicious serpent woman who attempted to beat Roxanne to death. The demons howl, screaming as the flames consume and destroy their contorted bodies.

The bizarre beast from the labyrinth on level four; the hoard of sand scorpions from level three; the bloodthirsty giants who occupy level two and the gloomy castle from the very first level of the Abyss, all wither and disintegrate in a mass of scorching pearly flames.

The friends' final vision is a much more pleasing one. The monks who guided them on their long and gruelling journey stand before them. In unity the monks retract their heavy woven hoods, revealing their human faces. They smile contentedly; truly grateful for all the hard work Faith and her companions has given to the great mission. The vision soon fades and the four floating friends fall into unconsciousness.

CHAPTER 101

M y tummy feels all topsy turvey,' Heidi mumbles groggily, her head pounding as she slowly opens her bleary eyes. She gazes around as her vision begins to focus. She lies on a dusty wooden floor, her friends and brother lying in close proximity.

'We're here!' she exclaims quietly to herself, suddenly realising where she is. 'Wake up!' she yells, scrambling excitedly to her feet. 'Everyone, wake up!'

One by one, Roxanne, Faith, Isabelle and Kyle stir from their deep slumbers, Heidi's bellowing filtering through their ears.

Kyle sits bolt upright as he recognises where he is. 'Heidi!' he exclaims, jumping to his feet as his sister greets him with open arms. 'What happened?' He asks, 'is this the fake town or are we really home this time?'

'We're back. We're really back,' she tells him, feeling the truth in her bones as she hugs her brother tightly, not wanting to let go.

The friends find themselves in the living room of the old dilapidated house on Wiltmore Street. Bright sunshine filters through the large grimy window, illuminating the mass of dust and cobwebs which clutter the room. The remains of the ritual remain untouched in the centre of the spacious lounge. The friends look fresh, their appearances clear from any signs of their time in the underworld.

'Where are we?' Isabelle asks, sitting upright and brushing her long, mousey brown hair from across her eyes with her fingertips.

'This is where I performed the ritual,' Faith informs her as she heaves herself to a standing position, before helping Isabelle to her feet.

'So, this is the place where you live?' Isabelle asks, gazing out of the filthy window.

'We all live in this town,' Roxanne says, moving beside Isabelle.

'But not in this house... thankfully,' Heidi adds, joining the others, hand in hand with her brother.

'So... we did it,' Faith ponders, her head finally ceasing to spin and everything starting to sink in. 'We actually did it.'

'How long do you think we've been gone for?' Heidi asks as the friends group together, gawping at the burnt black candles and the blood drained bat.

'I have no idea,' Faith replies, attempting to recall the day that she performed the ritual. 'It feels like we have been away for weeks.'

'Well, all I know is that I'm starving,' Kyle announces, his stomach beginning to rumble. 'Can we please go and get something to eat?'

The warm and welcoming sunshine beats down upon the friends' faces as they open the creaky front door and step outside. A light breeze wafts through the trees and the chirpy chorus of birdsong can be heard in surround sound.

'Do you think it worked?' Roxanne asks Faith as the four companions walk down the street together, leaving the spooky, old house far in the distance.

'I really hope so,' Faith replies with an exasperated sigh. 'But it all feels like one, long, tiring dream.'

'Nightmare you mean,' Heidi chips in. 'But yeah, it better have worked. That was bloody hard work!'

'Mum, are you home?' Heidi yells, flinging open the front door to her house and stepping onto the welcome mat.

'I'm guessing she's around somewhere, seeing as the door was unlocked,' Roxanne says as the friends enter the house before closing the door behind them.

As the group walks into the kitchen, they hear footsteps charging down the carpeted stairs.

'Where have you two been?' Heidi's mum shrieks with a stern, yet relieved tone to her voice as she hurriedly enters the kitchen. 'Your father and I have been worried sick all night. We phoned all of your friends, your school, but no one had heard anything from either of you. We've even had the police out looking for you. Your dad is out there right now!' Heidi and Kyle stand open mouthed, completely lost for words.

'Mum!' Kyle exclaims, gawping in bewilderment.

'You're... you're walking,' Heidi states as her mum looms upon them, red in the face with emotion.

'What are you talking about?' her mum responds in a frustrated manner. 'You haven't answered my question young lady,' she says, placing her hands on her hips while turning to face her speechless daughter. 'Where have the two of you been all night?'

Roxanne decides to step into the conversation before Heidi can say anything crazy. 'We... erm... spent the night at Faith's house,' Roxanne hastily answers.

'You're Faith?' Heidi's mum asks, gazing at Isabelle disapprovingly.

'I'm Faith,' Faith informs her shyly, feeling like a naughty school child and not quite knowing what to say.

'And what were you doing there all night?' Heidi's mum quizzes, refocusing her attention on her confounded children.

'We... we went to study on that big history test that you and dad were helping me on,' Heidi says as a convincing fib filters into her mind. 'You see, Faith works at the library where we study after school and she said that she would help us. Kyle followed us to her house, so we decided to let him stay. I did text you, telling you where we were. Did you not get it?'

'No, Heidi I didn't,' her mum snaps back. 'Why didn't you call me when I didn't reply?'

'Well...' Heidi continues, trying to elaborate on her white lie. 'We all fell asleep in the front room and we didn't wake up until just now. Revising is exhausting work.'

'We're really sorry,' Kyle adds apologetically, looking solemnly at the ground while scuffing his trainers on the carpet.

'It's okay,' their mum finally says, beginning to calm. 'I know you didn't mean to scare us like that, but in future please be a bit more considerate and let me know where you are.' She hugs her children, sighing with relief. 'At least you're both okay, and that's the main thing. Just don't make a habit of doing things like that, okay?'

'Okay, mum, we promise,' Heidi says as her mum retrieves her mobile phone from her jeans pocket and dials her husband's number while heading into the kitchen.

'How come Mum can walk now?' Kyle whispers as his mum's footsteps fade away and she can be heard explaining the situation to Kyle and Heidi's father. The friends stand in silence for a few moments before Heidi suddenly rushes into the living room. The others follow as they hear the television being switched on in the adjacent room.

The five friends gather around the TV as Heidi flicks through the programmes until she reaches the news channel. The group watches attentively as the cheerful female newsreader, Lisa Lapel, announces the top stories. Each and every story is about something positive. No criminal behaviours or tragic stories are mentioned, which is certainly different from the recent daily new coverage on the coronavirus pandemic and the Russian invasion on Ukraine.

'Mum!' Heidi yells up the stairs, leaping to her feet and darting into the hallway. 'What's the latest on the Russian war on Ukraine?'

'War?' her mum answers, sounding confused as she peers over the balcony. 'Are you being serious? You know there are no such things as wars in real life. What has got into you, Heidi?'

'Oh my gosh!' Faith exclaims, not quite believing what she hears.

'Erm... it doesn't matter, Mum' Heidi replies. 'It's... it's a TV programme that I thought you were watching... never mind.'

'I think we did it,' Heidi says in bewilderment, re-entering the living room in an astonished daze.

'I can't believe that I've... I mean... that we've actually done it,' Faith says in joyful disbelief, still not fully appreciating the sudden and immense world changes.

'Does this mean that when I go back to school, I won't get picked on anymore for being short?' Kyle asks, sounding hopeful.

'Yes,' Heidi laughs, placing her arm around her younger brother's shoulder, 'of course it does.' Roxanne, Faith and Isabelle get to their feet and join Kyle and Heidi in a group hug.

'Everything's going to be so much different now,' Faith says, sensing the prospect of an entirely new world opening up before her very eyes.

'No more wars or hunger. No more crimes or illness or bullying,' Roxanne says ecstatically, smiling as she realises that all their hard and gruelling work has paid off, just the way that they hoped it would.

'Thank you,' Faith says, a single tear dripping from her lower eyelashes and rolling down her soft cheek. 'You have all been amazing,' she says, gazing warmly at her friends. 'If you hadn't followed me to that old house, I don't think I would have coped by myself, let alone succeeded. So, thank you. I don't know what else I can say.' She turns to Isabelle. 'Thank you for your help, Isabelle. Without you we wouldn't have made it, that's for sure.'

'You are very welcome,' Isabelle says with a graceful smile, her blue eyes twinkling as the warm sunshine that filters through the windowpane shines upon the group.

'What are you going to do now, Isabelle?' Heidi asks.

'I do not know,' Isabelle responds, seeming a little troubled about the prospect of living in this new and uncertain world that she has helped to create.

'You can live with me,' Faith offers, taking Isabelle's hand comfortingly.

Isabelle gazes at Faith, taken by surprise. 'Are you sure about this, Faith?' she asks.

Faith rubs her hand affectionately. 'I've always wanted a sister,' Faith tells her with a soothing smile.

The five friends hug tightly as they bask in the calm and peaceful ambience of the fresh and improved world.

'Everything in this world is going to be so much better now,' Faith says blissfully. 'Good has finally conquered the most powerful and true evil, once and for all... forever.'

Printed in Great Britain
by Amazon